Praise for M
The Suns[

"A breathtaking story of an extraordinary friendship and the transcendent power of a mother's love. Molly Fader has penned an unforgettable novel that is sure to be one of the year's best."

—Kristy Woodson Harvey, *New York Times* bestselling author of *The Wedding Veil*

"*The Sunshine Girls* takes the reader on a ride brimming with secrets and surprises around every turn. A heartfelt, soulful book that examines how little we sometimes know about the people we think we know best."

—Susie Orman Schnall, author of *We Came Here to Shine* and *The Subway Girls*

"*The Sunshine Girls* delivers in its tender and nuanced depiction of friendship, sisterhood, and self-realization. A worthwhile and rewarding read!"

—Amanda Skenandore, author of *The Second Life of Mirielle West*

The Bitter and Sweet of Cherry Season

"A stunning story about family and hope that unfolds unexpectedly but beautifully, like a Michigan summer sunset over an orchard."

—Viola Shipman, *USA TODAY* bestselling author of *The Clover Girls*

"This page-turning story about family secrets and finding strength will have fans of Jill Shalvis and Jane Green delighted to have another author to watch."

—*Booklist* (starred review)

The McAvoy Sisters Book of Secrets

"Filled with sisters, secrets, surprises, and genuine, heartfelt sentiment. The talented Molly Fader will keep you turning the pages right down to the oh-so-satisfying final twist."

—Susan Wiggs, *New York Times* bestselling author

"The perfect read for a summer day."

—Jill Shalvis, *New York Times* bestselling author

Also by Molly Fader

The McAvoy Sisters Book of Secrets
The Bitter and Sweet of Cherry Season

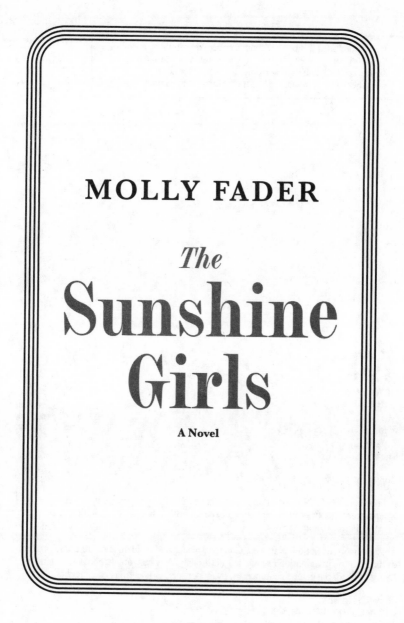

MOLLY FADER

The

Sunshine Girls

A Novel

GRAYDON
HOUSE

GRAYDON
HOUSE®

Recycling programs
for this product may
not exist in your area.

ISBN-13: 978-1-335-45348-8

The Sunshine Girls

Graydon House
22 Adelaide St. West, 41st Floor
Toronto, Ontario M5H 4E3, Canada
www.GraydonHouseBooks.com
www.BookClubbish.com

Printed in U.S.A.

For my mom

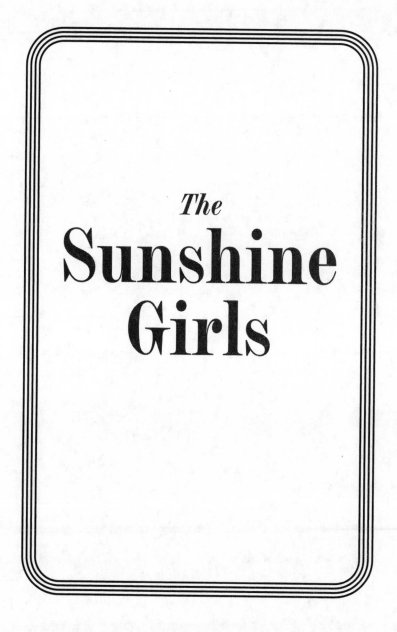

The

Sunshine
Girls

Part
One

1

CLARA

Greensboro, Iowa
2019

THERE WERE TOO many lilies. Clara wasn't an authority on flowers or funerals. But, it was like a flower shop—that only sold lilies—had exploded in the Blue Room of Horner's Funeral Home.

This was what happened when everyone adored you. They buried you under a mountain of your favorite flower—in this case, stargazers with their erotic pink hearts and sinus-piercing pollen—before they actually buried you.

And it was just a cosmic kick in the pants that Clara Beecher was allergic to her mother's favorite flowers.

"Clara!" Mrs. Place, her eighth-grade language arts teacher, clasped Clara's hands in her bony grip. Mrs. Place had not changed at all. She was the kind of woman who seemed middle-aged at seventeen and just waited for time to catch up. "Your mother was so proud of you. You and your sister, you were her pride and joy."

"That's nice of you to say," Clara said, keenly aware of her sister, Abbie, across the room doing the sorts of things that would make a mother proud.

"At book club, she'd go on and on about you and the important work you were doing in the city and, well, most of it went right over my head," Mrs. Place said. There was nothing complicated about Clara's work; Mom just lied about it so, as a former hippie, she didn't have to say the words *my daughter is a corporate shill*. "But you could tell she was just so proud."

Clara pulled her hand free in time to grab a tissue from one of the many boxes scattered around the room and held it to her allergy-induced dripping nose. "Thank you," she said through the tissue.

"Everyone is going to miss Betts," Mrs. Place said. "So much. There's not a part of this town that she wasn't involved in. Church, the library. Park board. Community gardens."

Like an invasive species. Invite her to something and she'd soon be running the show.

Grief is making you sharp. That was something her mother would say. If she wasn't dead.

The Blue Room of Horner's Funeral Home was hot and wall-to-lily packed with people coming to pay their respects to one of Greensboro's favorite citizens.

BettyKay Beecher had lived her whole adult life in this tiny town, and the town had shown up bearing casseroles and no-bake cheesecakes for the reception after the burial, wearing their Sunday best, armed with their favorite BettyKay stories.

She sat with my dad when he was dying.

She helped us figure out the insurance paperwork when our son was in his accident.

They were all mourning. The whole room and the hallway outside and the people still sitting in their cars in the parking lot. People were crying real tears, huddling, sobbing—actually sobbing—in corners. And all Clara could think was:

Did they know?

Had Mom, in true fashion, told the entire town the secret she'd kept from her own daughters for nearly forty years? The bombshell, life-rearranging, ugly secret she'd blurted, exasperated and furious with Clara in their last phone call?

Would they be mourning so hard if they knew?

Clara sneezed.

"Oh, bless you, honey," Mrs. Place said.

"It's just allergies." Clara folded up the tissues before putting them in the pocket of her new black Marco Zanini suit with the sash tie and the sky blue silk lining. She'd thought the lining might be a bit much for a funeral, but that was before she knew about the lilies.

And don't get her started on all the men wearing camouflage. To a funeral. Were they *all* going hunting after this?

"She's with your father now. I hope you find comfort in that."

"I do, thank you." It was, as it always had been in Greensboro, Iowa, easier to lie.

Another person came up with another story about Betty-Kay Beecher. "Is that your sister?" She pointed across the room after sharing an anecdote about their time together in the Army Nurse Corps. "Abbie?"

Abbie was surrounded by her friends from childhood—who used to be Clara's friends from childhood, not that it mattered—who kept bringing her mugs that were not filled with coffee. Abbie's cheeks were flushed and her eyes were bright and she was half-drunk, crying and hugging and not at all bothered by the lilies.

"Yep. That's my sister," Clara said, ushering the woman toward Abbie and not even feeling bad about it. "She'd love to hear your story."

Three years ago, they'd stood in this exact same room, mourning their father, Willis Beecher. It was hard to be home and not see him in the corners of rooms. She couldn't drink rum or Constant Comment tea and not miss him. The smell of patchouli could bring her to tears. A sob rose up in her throat like a fist, and her knees were suddenly loose. She put a hand against the table so she didn't crumple onto the floor.

I'm an orphan. Me and Abbie—orphans.

She was a full-grown adult. A corporate lawyer (about to make junior partner, fingers crossed) who billed at $700 an hour. She had a condo on Lakeshore and a good woman who loved her. Abbie had two kids of her own, a husband of twenty-five years and kept slices of homemade lemon loaf in the freezer that she could pop in a toaster in case someone stopped by for coffee. They were far from *orphans*.

But she couldn't shake the thought.

Clara found the side door and stepped out.

The wind was icy, blowing across the farmland to the west, picking up the smell of fries and burgers from The Starlite Room, only to press her flat against the yellow brick. She felt the cotton-silk blend of her suit snag on the brick.

The first few days of March were cold, too cold to be out here without a jacket, but the freshness woke her up. Spring hadn't committed to Iowa yet and the cornfields were still brown, lying in wait, like everything else in Greensboro, for the last blizzard to come hammering down from the Dakotas.

Her phone buzzed. She left it in her pocket.

Horner's Funeral Home was on the other side of town from the Greensboro University, and St. Luke's School of Nursing's white clock tower was just visible over the trees. The university had all the flags lowered to half-mast for the week. It was a nice touch. Mom had been a student there and then a teacher and for the last twenty years, an administrator.

She closed her eyes, letting the wind do its work.

"Hey."

Clara felt her sister lean back against the wall next to her, smelling of vanilla and Pinot Grigio.

"Hey," she said, eyes still closed.

"The lilies—"

"Yeah."

"You okay?"

Clara hummed in her throat, a sound that wasn't yes or no. That was, in fact, the exact sound of the exhausted limbo the last few days had put her in.

"Me neither," Abbie said. "It just… I feel like I'm missing something, you know? Like I'm walking around all wrong."

Clara felt the same. Being BettyKay Beecher's daughter was a part of her identity she didn't always carry comfortably, but it was there.

"Where's Vickie?" Abbie asked, and Clara caught herself from flinching at the sound of her girlfriend's name.

"She wishes she could be here but she has a case in front of the Illinois Supreme Court."

She felt Abbie's doubt, the way she wanted to probe and pick.

"Did you have to blow up that picture so damn big?" Clara asked, before Abbie could get to her follow-up questions.

All around the funeral home were pictures of the Beecher family. And—God knows why—Abbie had decided to blow up, to an obscene size, the picture of their mother that was on the back of her book: *Pray for Me: The Diary of an Army Nurse in Vietnam.* In it BettyKay was a fresh-faced twenty-two-year-old, with a helmet-shaped brunette bob, wearing an olive green United States Army Nurse Corps uniform.

"Darn."

"What?"

"Fiona's turning into a little parrot, so we don't swear anymore. We say 'effing' and 'darn' and 'poop.'"

"That's effing nonsense."

"Probably." Clara could hear the smile in her sister's voice. "And yes, I did. I love that picture of Mom. She looks so brave."

Clara thought she looked terrified.

"Max and Fiona don't understand what's happening," Abbie said. "They keep asking why Gran is lying down."

Clara's laugh was wet with the lingering allergic reaction to the flowers. "That's awful."

"Denise from the hospital keeps trying to get the kids to touch Mom's hand. So they can feel how cold she is and then they'll understand."

"What will it make them understand?"

"That she's dead."

"That's morbid even for Denise." They were both laughing, which felt alien but sweet.

"She says it will give them closure."

Abbie reached out and grabbed her hand. Clara started to pull away, but Abbie didn't let go.

I should tell her. Part of her even wanted to. To share the burden of information like they were kids again. And Abbie, who liked the view from the perch her reputation as a Beecher in this town gave her, would tell Clara it wasn't true. Couldn't possibly be. That Mom had been wrong. Angry. Something.

Some excuse to keep everything the way it was.

That was why Clara couldn't tell her. Because Abbie had

to live in this town side by side with the memory of Mom. Bringing Abbie into it would make her sister's life harder.

"Abbie, don't get upset but I am going to leave after the reception at the church." There. Done. Band-Aid-style.

"And go where?" Abbie asked.

"Back home."

And here comes the look. "Chicago? You're kidding."

"We have a new client—"

"You're *leaving*?" Accidentally Clara caught Abbie's furious gaze and wished she hadn't. She could see her sister's rage and her grief and it felt worse than her own.

"I'll be back," Clara lied.

"Bullshit." So much for not swearing.

"Abbie—"

"You know. I should have expected this. You show up last-minute in your car and your ugly suit—"

"Hey!"

"With your nose in the air—"

"I'll pay to have the house boxed up."

Abbie sucked in so much air Clara went light-headed from the lack of oxygen around her.

"Can we *please* not make this a big deal?" she asked.

"What did I ever do to you, Clara? To make it so easy for you to leave me behind?"

The wind caught the side door as it opened, banging against the brick with a sound that made Clara and Abbie jump like they'd been caught smoking.

Ben, Abbie's husband, stuck his head out and Abbie stepped forward. Ben was a good-looking guy in a gentle giant kind of way. Constantly rumpled, but usually smiling. He reminded Clara of a very good Labrador retriever.

She wanted to pat his head and give him a treat. And then yell at him for tracking mud across the rug.

"There you are," he said.

"I was just getting some air," Abbie said, with surprising defensiveness. "Is everything okay?"

"There's..." Ben glanced over his shoulder and made a face, bewildered and somehow joyful in a way that made Clara and Abbie push off the wall. It was his mother-in-law's funeral after all. Joy was a strange sentiment.

"What?" Clara asked.

"Well, I think you should come in and see for yourself."

Ben held the door while Abbie and Clara walked back into the packed room. Everyone was silent now, pressed to the walls and corners in little clumps, whispering in that painfully familiar way out of the corners of their mouths and behind their hands. There was a path down the center of the room right to Mom's casket, where she lay with her arms crossed, wearing her favorite green dress and way too much blush.

Standing at the casket, was a woman. A stranger.

Everything about her screamed *not from around here*. She wore an elegant long black skirt and a pair of boots with low heels of rich black leather. A gray sweater (Ralph Lauren Collection cashmere or Clara would eat her own boots) with a black belt around her trim waist. Her hair was long and silvery blond, the kind that appeared natural but Clara would put money on the fact that it cost a lot and took a lot of time to keep that way.

She kind of...glittered.

"Who is that?"

"You don't recognize her?" Ben whispered between Abbie and Clara's shoulders, his breath smelling of coffee and cough drops.

Something about the woman did seem familiar, polished.

"Is she from the publishing company?" she asked Abbie.

"I don't think so. They sent a cheesecake."

"That morning show Mom did sometimes, in Des Moines? Ramona?"

"Ramona Rodriguez died, like, ten years ago."

Clara should know this woman. But her mother's funeral was throwing her off.

"Are you kidding me? You really don't recognize her?" Ben asked. "It's Kitty Devereaux."

2

CLARA

KITTY DEVEREAUX WAS a legendary star of stage and screen. A Bond girl. A model, known for her blue eyes and withering stare. She'd won two Emmys and had been nominated for an Oscar. She'd dated Marlon Brando and Rex Daniels. The prince of Sweden and director Hugh Bonnet.

Married only once, divorced almost immediately.

Kitty Devereaux.

Just saying the name conjured '70s bohemian beauty and sexy counterculture cool.

And now she was causing a scene at BettyKay Beecher's funeral.

"Is this a joke?" Clara asked.

Abbie shook her head, her mouth still hanging open.

"Why in the world would Kitty Devereaux be at your mother's funeral?" Ben asked. People turned to stare at them because Ben whispered at shout volume. "She's...freaking

Kitty Devereaux." Like there weren't any words big enough
to describe her. Her name had in fact become a way to describe other women.

The next Kitty Devereaux.

She's no Kitty Devereaux.

"It's probably just a mistake," Abbie finally said.

"Oh, she just happened to show up at the wrong funeral.
In Greensboro, Iowa?" Ben whisper-shouted.

The room was so quiet you could hear a pin drop. Clara
caught the eye of Mr. Reynolds from the feed store in town
(wearing a camouflage tie) and smiled like everything was
fine. Totally fine.

"Maybe she knew Mom and Dad," Abbie said. "From the
anti-war stuff in the '70s."

"And your parents never talked about her?" Ben asked,
making a rare good point.

Abbie turned toward Clara. "Clara?"

"What?"

"Go..." Abbie flapped a hand toward her. "Do something."

"Me?"

"You." Abbie shot her a hard look that reminded Clara that
Abbie had up to this point managed all the logistics for the
funeral. *The least you could do*, her expression said, *is handle the
surprise celebrity standing at Mom's casket.*

Which, fair enough.

She patted down the jacket of her suit, quickly handed her
sister the wadded-up Kleenex from her pocket because they
ruined the lines of said suit, and walked down the flowered
rug toward the casket. No one was even pretending not to
stare.

The woman turned when Clara stepped onto the dais, smiling as if welcoming Clara to her mother's casket-side party
for two.

Holy shit. That's Kitty Devereaux.

The fashion magazines called her luminous and they weren't wrong. Kitty absolutely glowed in the large parlor of Horner's Funeral Home.

"Can I help you?" Clara whispered.

Kitty looked her up and down with her famous blue eyes, and Clara felt exposed, like the movie star could see what she wore beneath her suit. What she ate for breakfast. The color of her kitchen.

Kitty looked at Clara like she could see it all.

"Well, now," Kitty finally said, her voice touched with Southern charm. "You are most certainly Clara."

"That's me. And you're Kitty. I mean... Ms. Devereaux. Kitty Devereaux."

Kitty's smile was regal and indulgent like she was allowing Clara to keep her head after a criminal offense. "Kitty'll do."

Oh my God, that voice.

Kitty had played a single mom in a television show in the 1990s—a comeback for her after her wild '70s and quiet '80s—and she'd had this signature line: *It can't be a party every night.* The whole world had said it for a decade, in their best husky-voiced, slightly Southern Kitty Devereaux impression.

It can't be a party every night.

"What are you doing here?" Clara asked. If Abbie was within earshot she'd be furious at Clara's tone, but send a lawyer, get a lawyer.

"Payin' my respects." Kitty leaned forward like they were about to share secrets, and she even smelled beautiful. "I know you don't believe it right now, but your mother was very proud of you. She felt just awful about that fight."

Clara stepped back, suddenly dizzy again from the lilies.

"How do you know that?"

"She told me."

"So you knew my mom?"

"I did."

"BettyKay Beecher?"

Kitty smiled. "The one and only. Though I met her when she was BettyKay Allen." Kitty glanced down at the casket. Clara did, too, and wished she hadn't.

That's my mom.

Her short-cropped silver hair. Lips pressed into a thin line. Diminutive without the spirit that made her larger-than-life.

"That blush is too much," Kitty said. "Your mother would hate it."

She would. She really would.

"She would hate all of this," Kitty said, full of what seemed like legitimate grief and affection.

"Clara," Abbie whispered, joining them on the dais. "People are taking out their phones. Mom's funeral is going to be on the internet in about three seconds."

"Ms. Devereaux?" Clara said. "Can we maybe talk someplace else?"

What do you do with a movie star like Kitty Devereaux at your mother's funeral? Where do you *put* her?

"Oh, honey, please call me Kitty. Ms. Devereaux is a figment of my imagination."

Kitty pulled something from her purse, then opened her palm, revealing four pink buttons.

Abbie gasped—again—and grabbed Clara's hand. This time Clara grabbed right back.

Because *those were the buttons.*

They were ugly. Mom always said they were the ugliest buttons she could find in Greensboro, Iowa, in 1968. Big and round narrowing concentric circles on top of each other. Like obscene cartoon nipples.

They were faded now, the edges of some of the circles worn

off, revealing the plastic they were made of. Those buttons had been baked in bread and sewn onto bras. They'd been hung on trees and pickled with eggs. Traded back and forth in countless practical jokes between their mother and an old friend. That's what Mom called her every time they sent something off in the mail, or some package was delivered to them. *An old friend from nursing school.*

"You?" Clara asked.

"Me." Kitty rolled the buttons in her long fingers, shifting them with her thumb, like they were gems in the light. "There used to be five. Before either of you were born."

"Mom told us. She lost one."

Kitty's million-watt smile wobbled at the corners. "She didn't lose it. I threw them at her in the hallway of the Chateau Marmont."

"The hotel? In Hollywood?" Clara blinked.

"You threw them at her?" Abbie asked.

What is happening?

"I was just so mad at her. But when I cooled off, I went back to grab 'em, and I could only find four in the shag carpet," Kitty said.

Kitty slipped the four buttons into the casket, hidden by the cream silk, and then leaned down, kissed BettyKay's cheek and whispered something in her ear.

When she stood and faced them, Clara felt again the sheer heat of her star power. Even the crap lighting of the funeral home couldn't diminish her.

"How?" Clara whispered.

"Yeah. How?" Abbie seconded.

How did BettyKay Beecher, from a farm in the middle of a cornfield in Iowa, and Bond girl Kitty Devereaux even meet?

Much less become the kinds of friends who traded buttons as practical jokes? For decades.

"That," Kitty said. "Is a very long story. Is this one of those dry funerals, or can a girl get a drink?"

3

BETTYKAY

St. Luke's School of Nursing
Greensboro, Iowa
1967

> *September 8, 1967*
> *Tomorrow my whole dang life is gonna change. My mom hasn't*
> *spoken to me in a week and Dad promised to take me to the bus*
> *stop tomorrow morning after chores, but he's broken that kind of*
> *promise before. Todd says I can ring him, even at 6 a.m., and*
> *he'll give me a ride. Even though he and his dad are starting*
> *harvest, too. What a guy. I don't think I'll sleep but I better try.*

GREENSBORO, IOWA, WAS the most beautiful place I'd
ever seen in real life. Granted, I'd only seen Bluffs, Iowa,
population 700, the farm on Wolff Road and once, with my
grandmother, the dog races in Cedar Rapids.

But Greensboro was lush with bright green manicured lawns and grand brick houses along Main Street. The gardens were showing off with red geraniums and purple asters. Black-eyed Susans and end-of-season roses all bobbing in the breeze. There were people everywhere, all seemingly getting in or out of cars.

And the sun was shining on every inch of it.

St. Luke's white clock tower and the wide marble steps beneath it gleamed. The three-story redbrick building spread out like it had wings on both sides. The windows were white and thrown open. It was the biggest, grandest building I'd ever seen.

Behind the dormitory was St. Luke's Hospital. According to the school brochure, the two buildings were connected by a tunnel. An actual tunnel.

A warm September wind kicked up and teased the hem of my new pink boucle coat with the matching headband I'd made for this very day. Mom had taken one look at the Vogue Pattern and told me I was putting on airs.

The headband, I could see in this moment, was a little showy. A lot of the other girls were playing it cool. Some were even in clamdiggers, their hair long and straight from a center part.

I pulled off the headband and shoved it in my pocket, patting down the flyaway hairs.

You can do this. You will not foul this up.

The wooden handle of the suitcase had rubbed raw spots on my palm as I carried it across campus from the bus station, past all those big houses and cars. But I wrapped my hand around it, ignored the sting and carried all my earthly possessions up those marble stairs.

The open foyer was a beehive of activity, the first-year class moving in with suitcases and parents in tow. The marble and wood of the walls and floors and ceiling echoed with the chatter of voices.

Clucking hens, my father would have said, and I shook the thought away.

Women stood with clipboards giving instructions, checking admissions letters. I had to dodge a girl staring at her feet as she was led up the split staircase by her mother.

My own parents didn't come to move-in day. It was early September and it had been a dry summer so the harvest was early. As excuses went, it wasn't half-bad. I had nodded and agreed, and inside I'd been happy to have this day all to myself.

They didn't need to see me so happy to leave the farm behind.

I approached one of the clipboard ladies who wore a nurse's uniform with the white cap and the blue cape, modeled after the one Florence Nightingale wore. Every inch of it was righteous and I longed for one of those capes with every breath in my body.

"I'm BettyKay Allen," I said. "From Bluffs, Iowa." I took out the letter I got from the school, months ago, just in case they didn't believe me. Or thought I didn't look like I belonged with my homemade coat.

"Welcome to St. Luke's," the woman said, her smile revealing dimples in her round cheeks. "You seem pretty keen, BettyKay Allen."

"I am. I really am." My mother would hate this, allergic as she was to enthusiasm.

"Excuse me." A man wearing a fedora and a madras shirt straining around his neck stepped right up to the nurse, as if I wasn't there. I stepped back to give him room. "My daughter is Susan Cundiff. Where am I supposed to take her?"

"Yes, Mr. Cundiff. Susan is in room 202. Right staircase."

He left, a tall girl with stooped shoulders trailing in his wake.

Reflexively, I straightened my own.

"Where are your parents?" the nurse asked, once the man was gone.

"Busy. Harvest."

"Iowa in September," she said with a shrug. "My sister got married last weekend, half our cousins didn't make it to the ceremony."

"But they showed up for the reception?"

"Yeah, you can't keep those boys away from Schlitz and cake. You're up the left staircase. Room 212."

"Has my roommate checked in?" I asked.

The woman nodded. "Katherine Simon. She's already here."

"Thank you!" I called over my shoulder, already heading up the steps on the left.

My beige hard case Samsonite had been a wedding present for my parents. Some relative who didn't know them very well thought they might actually travel. When Mom set it on my bed a few weeks ago, it had been used only once, for their honeymoon in Clear Lake.

Now that I was close, and it was really happening, my feet were sore and the bag, light all day, was heavy. Everything I'd tried not to bring with me sat in the pit of my stomach, my father's voice ringing in my ears.

You think you're better than us? You think you're better than this farm?

I switched hands on my suitcase and pressed on.

Because they were smaller than the foyer, the hallways seemed even more packed. Parents and siblings lingered around doorways. There were trunks outside rooms, bursting with clothes, first-year nursing students standing over them crying, "There's not enough room! Why are the closets so small?"

St. Luke's had opened in 1868, the first class of students the sisters and daughters and wives of men who fought in the Civil

War. That history came with the registration package along with recommendations for what to pack and clear warnings about the size of the closets.

I hugged the honey-color wainscoting, reading the brass numbers over the doors.

A record player was already being put to use, a Joan Baez song I didn't recognize floating into the hallway.

"Sorry," I said, having bumped into a girl with glasses and carrying a black and plaid soft side suitcase. St. Luke's had been integrated for five years but she was the only Black student in a sea of white faces.

"It's jammed here," the girl said.

"It really is," I agreed. "I didn't expect all this." Truth was, I didn't have the imagination to expect all this. Any of it, really.

"Good luck," she yelled over her shoulder.

"You, too!" I said as we were carried on separate streams down opposite sides of the hallway.

Room 212 was at the far end of the hallway closest to the wide bay window, the door ajar. The music was coming from this room. My room.

I had only ever lived in my parents' house, my bedroom tucked under the eaves with the window that didn't shut all the way and the lilac wallpaper I picked out for my twelfth birthday. I hadn't even gone to sleepovers at friends' houses until I was sixteen—an embarrassing age to reveal I'd never spent a night away from home. I just liked my bed, and my home and the sense that my parents were downstairs. But I could admit it, standing here at the doorway to my new home, I'd been scared. Scared of other places. Other people. I was scared the way my parents were. The way they made me.

An only child, I had all the usual dreams of having a sister. Or even a brother. And I wasn't square enough to think that this roommate would be like a sister. But…a friend. Yes.

Yes. I was square enough to think that.

Please let her like me.

"Hello?" I said as I stepped around the corner into the room.

A girl was lying on one of the beds, reading *Movie Life* magazine with Frank Sinatra and Mia Farrow on the cover. She was—there was no other way to put it—a total fox. Blue eyes and skin so fair and fine it was like she'd never seen the sun. She had striking dark eyebrows that gave up the goods on her white-blond hair. Her shoes were kicked off and her black skirt was hiked up revealing the edge of her stocking, the clip of her garter. I turned, giving her privacy to adjust her clothes.

"I'm BettyKay," I said to the record player on top of a dark wooden dresser. The dresser sat next to the room's only desk, which had a new Singer Touch and Sew sewing machine on top. Much nicer and smaller than the one Mom had at home.

"BettyKay?" she asked. "The farmer's daughter."

"Yes. That's…" I laughed, awkwardly. "That's me."

"That's a lot of name."

"I was… I mean, I'm named after my grandmothers."

"Betty and Kay?"

"Right."

"You have a nickname or something?"

My parents called me BettyKay and so did my friends at school, the only one who ever called me anything different was Todd. "Betts," I said. "Some people call me Betts."

"Well, Betts, you waitin' on an engraved invitation?" Katherine asked with a thick Southern accent.

I turned back around to face her. She hadn't adjusted her clothing, or gotten off the bed, or it seemed, looked up from the gossip about Mia Farrow and Frank Sinatra.

Instead she just twirled her hand over the edge of the magazine. *"Entrez-vous,"* she said.

"You speak French?"

"No," Katherine said and turned the page of her magazine. Well, she was a real gas.

"You're from here, aren't you?" Katherine asked. "I-o-w-a." She said every single letter of the word, making it four syllables long.

"My…ah…family has a farm about sixty miles west of here." Far enough away that they wouldn't visit, but not so far away that Todd couldn't. I put my suitcase on the bed on the other side of the room and popped the locks. "You're from?"

"Atlanta," Katherine said.

"There are real good nursing schools out east," I said. "Why come all the way to Iowa?"

"Because it's a long way from Atlanta."

I laughed and glanced back over my shoulder, but Katherine wasn't laughing. I coughed and took out my diary and slid it under my pillow. Next I shook out my good blue dress and hung it up in the closet. My favorite serge skirt and the yellow flowered polyester ship 'n' shore blouse I bought special at Spurgeon's before I left. I had sweaters and another skirt. Blue jeans. A black turtleneck. My winter coat, hat and mitts.

I picked up my underwear and brassieres, my long line and my new Warners with the stretch that my mom had been so skeptical of, the soft form girdle and my own stockings, and hid them against my chest before quickly tucking them in the top drawer of my dresser.

"Honey, did you make that coat?" Katherine asked, and the bed squeaked as she got up. I felt her tug at the back of my coat.

"Yes. I made it." I turned, pulling my coat from her hands. Katherine grabbed onto the wide flat pink button I'd picked out at the Ben Franklin. There were three on the coat.

"That's a whole lotta pink."

"I like pink."

"It's too big for you."

I stepped aside. "I like the way it fits."

"You're swimming in it, girl." Katherine bunched up the back of the coat in her hands. "There," she said. "You're ten pounds slimmer."

I gawked at this stranger from Atlanta with the peroxide hair. "Thanks, Katherine," I said, not at all sure I meant it.

Katherine shrugged and let go of my coat. "Call me Kitty," she said.

The hallways had gotten quiet, all the parents and boyfriends having said their goodbyes, leaving the sixty-eight girls to themselves on the second floor of St. Luke's.

Before dinner, everyone met in front of the wooden door to the formal sitting room at the end of the hall. At exactly five o'clock, Mrs. Margaret Hayes, the floor mother, crossed the hallway and unlocked the door with a key from a chain around her neck.

Mrs. Margaret Hayes, a tall thin woman with steel gray hair set in a stylish wave, flipped on the overhead lights and stood smiling as we filed in past her. She wore a smart blue dress and red belt that matched the cherries on the collar. A touch of frivolous that looked a little wrong on her.

"It looks like she's wearing someone else's dress," Kitty whispered as she walked by.

It was a pretty room with lots of windows and a giant grandfather clock. All the furniture was feminine, narrow delicate legs on the chairs and couches, everything upholstered in robin's-egg blue wool. Mom would love this, I thought. How pretty everything was.

Nothing was pretty at the farm.

There was a formal tea table in the corner, a tea set on a hutch next to it, waiting for some occasion special enough to be put to use.

I sat on the edge of a couch.

"You don't mind, do you?" Kitty said, taking the far end.

"Suit yourself." Oh, there was something about this girl that made me sharp and I was never sharp.

The murmur of the room went silent, so fast it was alarming, and I turned to see what was wrong. It was the Black girl with the serious glasses, standing just inside the door. She walked past every empty spot, but girls were putting their purses on chair cushions and looking away, not letting her sit beside them.

Kitty stood. "Over here. I saved you a spot," she said to the girl, who pushed her glasses up on her nose and came over to sit between Kitty and me on the couch.

"Thank you," the girl said. "I'm Jenny Hopkins."

"Kitty Simon."

"I'm BettyKay Allen."

"You can call her Betts," Kitty said, and I tried not to be annoyed with the familiarity.

Jenny flashed me a smile. Around us girls went back to chatting.

"Where you from?" Kitty asked.

"Grand Rapids," Jenny said, and she and Kitty fell into a conversation about what they were going to miss most about their cities.

I had nothing to add, having lived my entire life on Wolff Road, where a trip into town took twenty minutes. Most of the girls I'd talked to today were from small Iowa towns like me, which I found a little comforting. The girl sitting on the chair closest to me released a sound like a sob, and I turned to find her with red-rimmed eyes, biting her fingernails.

"Hi." I held out my hand. This was Todd's trick not to be nervous, just introduce myself to everyone I met. The rest would take care of itself. The first step, he said, was always the hardest, but once you did it, it was done. But that was Todd for you, he got on with everyone and never met a stranger. "I'm BettyKay. BettyKay Allen."

"Gwen." Tears trembled on her eyelashes as she took a deep breath. "I feel like I've made a big mistake. Nursing school seemed so exciting, but now I just miss my family. My cat."

"I suppose it's normal to be homesick," I said, though I didn't feel any of that myself.

"I've never been away from home before."

"Me neither."

"You're not scared?"

"I was this morning," I said. "But not so much anymore."

The girl's face held so still for a second and then crumpled. "I really miss my cat!"

"Oh no, no, it's—" I tried to stem the waterworks, but Gwen stood and ran for the bathrooms.

"You were a real comfort to poor Gwen," Kitty said, examining her nail beds.

"She lives across the hall from me," Jenny said, one eyebrow raised over the edge of her glasses, giving the impression she did not have time for that nonsense. "She's been crying since she got here."

"You're not scared, either, I take it?" I asked her.

"I'm here through the Army ROTC. This is the easy part."

I gaped before I caught myself. Even Kitty leaned forward, her attention caught. "You joined the Army Nurse Corps?"

"I did."

Kitty whistled.

"But aren't you scared you'll be sent to Vietnam?" I asked. "My dad says they're sending loads of boys over there and where the boys go, nurses follow."

Jenny looked at me with serious eyes. "That's why I joined."

For the second time today I was speechless.

"That's really brave of you," Kitty said.

Getting on the bus at six this morning was the bravest thing I'd ever done.

"If I didn't enlist my brother would be sent over," Jenny said. "They don't send siblings into war zones. It's a rule."

"You're going instead of him?"

"Nurses have a better chance of surviving than soldiers. I take it you don't have siblings?"

I shook my head.

"I have a brother," Kitty said. "But I wouldn't go to war to save him."

"Well, I would," Jenny said, pressing the hem of her skirt flat. "I would do anything to save mine."

"Are you the girl who got into medical school and declined your spot?" Kitty asked.

I had not heard that bit of gossip. Remarkable that Kitty had, since she'd spent most of the day on her bed, reading that movie mag. Getting up only to change the record while I made an effort to meet some of our neighbors.

"I wouldn't have been able to go over as a doctor," Jenny said. "They might send our boys over there to stop the Communists, but Black girls don't get to go and patch them up. Not as doctors. So, I'm going as a nurse."

"I'm sorry," Kitty said.

Jenny smiled. "Thanks for that. Wish my family agreed with you."

"They don't like what you're doing?" I asked, and Jenny shook her head.

"Giving up medical school to go to Vietnam? As a woman? No, they're not happy with me. I think my mom is relieved that I'll keep my brother out of combat, but my dad is real upset. He's got rules about what women should or shouldn't do and I'm breaking every one of them."

"Ladies," Mrs. Margaret Hayes said, and when the room didn't quiet down fast enough she cleared her throat with force then smiled. "Good evening, girls. I trust you've all settled in all right?"

There was a low chorus of "Yes ma'am."

"I'm Mrs. Margaret Hayes. You can call me Mrs. Hayes. My room is the first room at the top of the stairs. My door is always open. If you have trouble with school. Roommates. Other students. Doctors—"

"Oh, the doctors can give me trouble," said a girl in the back, causing a waterfall of giggles.

Mrs. Margaret Hayes's gaze cut off the laughter like a knife. "There are rules. Very clear. Very defined. About nursing students fraternizing with doctors. And every year nursing students break those rules and, ladies, it is you who pays for a flirtation with a doctor. It is you who will be suspended from school. It is your dreams, your career that suffers. The doctor will carry on, he'll find another sweet young nursing student to fawn over him. He'll be just fine and you'll be back at home."

Next to me Kitty shuddered.

"There are a thousand boys on this campus. Boys your own age. Bat your eyes at them. Or—" Mrs. Margaret Hayes gave us this information like it might some day save our lives. I wondered if I should take notes. "—better yet, bat your eyes at none of them. Focus on your studies and take this time. This brief three years you have away from your parents' home and before you begin to make a home of your own and see what you can do." She briefly smiled, and for a moment I saw beneath the posture and the stern visage, something hopeful. For the girls on the floor. She was truly rooting for us. More than anyone I'd met yet in my life. "See what *you* are capable of."

"Oh, bless your heart," Kitty whispered, looking at me

out of the corner of her eye. "You bought that hook, line and sinker."

"You aren't nurses yet," Mrs. Margaret Hayes said. "I like to think of you first-year students as sunshine girls. You are nothing but possibility and your job is to learn and shine as bright as you can."

Kitty rolled her eyes so hard I could hear it.

Mrs. Margaret Hayes passed out class schedules and a sheet with everyone's names and room numbers, so the floor had a chance to get to know each other.

"Whole lot of Susans on this list," Kitty said. "Five Susans. That's got to be a record. I suppose we could call them Susan number one and Susan—"

"Will you stop!" I hissed.

"Both of you stop!" Jenny whispered and shot us an annoyed look.

"Ladies?" Mrs. Margaret Hayes said. "Is there a problem?"

"No, ma'am," I said and crossed my legs away from my roommate, embarrassed by my outburst.

Mrs. Hayes launched into rules for the use of the phone—an extensive sign-up sheet. The sitting room—only for special occasions, with no further information about what kind of occasion that might be. The tea set there was apparently only for show. Visiting hours—from five to six on weeknights, before supper, and afternoons on Saturday and Sunday.

"Absolutely and without exception no boys in dormitory rooms. I don't care if it's your brother. Your cousin. Your father. No boys. Ever. Also, these are the single nurses' dormitories. If you are married, you cannot live here. If you get engaged, you cannot live here. And if you find yourself in a delicate situation—" she gave everyone a long look over the top of her glasses, so no one missed her meaning "—you'll be asked to leave St. Luke's. Am I clear?"

"I can see the women's lib movement hasn't made it to St. Luke's," Kitty muttered.

Jenny made a sound in her throat like affirmation.

The ring on the chain around my neck was suddenly hot, and I forced myself not to put my hand to my chest. The chain was long enough the ring was hidden under my shirt.

There were rules for the showers and lights out and noise and smoking, and on the surface it seemed like I'd traded one strict home for another one. But St. Luke's could have all the rules in the world, and it wouldn't be as bad as the old farmhouse on Wolff Road.

There was light here. And excitement. And hope and learning. I was someone else here, I could feel it happening already.

Sunshine girls.

After orientation, Mrs. Margaret Hayes locked up the sitting room and the group split in half. Half ran for the phone, the other half headed down to the cafeteria.

The big September moon shone through the tall windows of the hallways and across the bright green grass of Long's Meadow between St. Luke's School of Nursing and Fulham Hall of Greensboro College.

Kitty came up alongside me, so silent and sudden I jumped in surprise.

"It looks like we're in anatomy together. I was wondering, if I could use your notes."

"We haven't even gotten to class yet."

"I know. But I know my strengths and note-taking ain't one of them."

"You're really from Atlanta?" She sounded as country as me.

"Close enough."

"Katherine—"

"Kitty."

"Fine. Kitty." I stopped in the hall, the stream of women heading to the cafeteria rushing by. "I'm not cheating."

"Sharing notes is hardly cheating. I just—"

"No," I said and shook my head for emphasis. It was close enough to cheating in my book. "No way."

Kitty shrugged and walked on, swept up by the other girls.

In the kitchen, groups of second- and third-year students were reuniting over coffee while we first-years lined up for food.

"Chemistry?" A pretty redhead in line behind me was studying her class schedule. "My mom told me I would never need it."

"You weren't planning on nursing school?" I asked.

"No. I was planning on marrying Tommy Taylor!"

Jenny, in front of me, picked up a plate and handed it back.

Dinner was a pork tenderloin sandwich, with a cup of three bean salad and a piece of watermelon.

Shakey's Tavern, located between here and the farm, was known for their pork tenderloins. Big as your head, they advertised. Pounded thin and fried up crispy, their tenderloin sandwich was my favorite meal. Todd and I went out to Shakey's after school dances, and my parents took me there for my birthday. I went by myself to celebrate the day the acceptance letter from St. Luke's came in.

"Betts?" Jenny asked.

"I'm not very hungry," I said and turned around and left.

4

BETTYKAY

MOST OF OUR first-year nursing classes were taught in the science department of Greensboro College. Chemistry, biology, sociology, and Anatomy and Physiology. Only Fundamentals in Nursing was taught at the hospital. The classes were small, twenty girls each.

Mr. Kessler's Anatomy and Physiology classroom was full of posters detailing the parts of the eye and big plastic and wooden models of the heart and the respiratory system. There were locked cabinets and dark wooden shelves full of jars with mouse skeletons and what could have been eyeballs floating in liquid.

Jenny slipped into the desk beside mine in the front row, and some of the girls around us glared. One of the Susans went so far as to get up and move.

"Have you seen him?" Jenny asked, opening her notebook

and taking number two pencils from her case like she hadn't even noticed the Susan.

"Mr. Kessler?" I shook my head.

"I've heard he's a character."

"What does that mean?"

"Nothing good, probably."

The door behind the desk opened and out walked a barrel-chested man with a shock of white hair. He slurped loudly from his coffee as he walked toward the desk, some sloshing over the lip and splashing on the floor. He swore under his breath and then took a wide step over it.

"Ladies," he said, not even looking at us. "Welcome to Anatomy and Physiology."

Two clean-cut college boys followed him in navy blue warm-up suits with Greensboro Wrestling in gold embroidery across the front. All the girls in the classroom sat up a little straighter. Next to me Gwen checked the bobby pins over her ears.

"Now," Mr. Kessler belched into his fist. "Some of you passed Anatomy and Physiology in high school. Some of you didn't. Some of you and you know who you are," he said, scanning the room over the top of his glasses, "didn't take it at all. You might be sitting there, having…what do you kids call it? A freak-out?" He straightened his back, moaned a little as if it hurt. "Even those of you who took this class in high school might be a little scared. And that's fair. This isn't high school. It's Greensboro College and for years I have been asking St. Luke's and Greensboro to create a minimum requirement for this class, and for years, they've ignored me. So, you all being a little scared is what we've got. And it's what we're going with." He paused, distracted by cigarette ash down the front of his mustard yellow sweater. He brushed it off.

I wondered briefly what the minimum requirement was for faculty hygiene.

"We're going to have an assessment test," he said. "Today."

An audible gasp rippled through the room.

"Ungraded," he said, and the shoulders that had just hit earlobes lowered. Barely.

He opened a wooden drawer below his belly and pulled out two big markers with black caps. "Here's how it will work. We're going to start with bones. I will name a bone and if you know where that bone is on the human body, you come and write it down."

"Where?" The suspicious question came from the corner of the room. Kitty, in a black turtleneck and the bell-bottoms I had only ever seen in magazines and on television.

As if cued, the two wrestlers, smirking, took off their sweatshirts and stepped out of their warm-up pants.

They were young and fit and wearing wrestling singlets, which meant they were mostly naked. Todd was a wrestler, even went to state championships, so I had some familiarity with the uniform. I would guess some of these Iowa girls knew more than a wrestler or two.

The first-year nursing students blushed. Some laughed. Jenny sighed hard.

"You're going to write the name of the bones on Kip Phillips, my 177 pounder. And we'll be writing muscles on Brian Cater, my 123 pounder. So." He picked up a piece of paper. "We'll start with the distal phalanx."

The room was silent. Not just quiet but hear-a-pin-drop silent.

"You're going to be nurses," he said. "This is the job, ladies. Bodies are the job. These might be the last two healthy ones you see in the course of your education. And if you are too scared or embarrassed or... I don't know, *demure*..." He said it like it was a curse, like we hadn't spent nearly every moment of our lives having demureness hammered into our heads. We needed a minute to get used to new expectations. New rules. "…then you need to rethink nursing school."

But he was right. Bodies were the job.

I stood up. "I'll do it."

The tension went out of the room like a popped balloon. Todd was right, everything got a little easier after someone went first.

Mr. Kessler held out the marker and I took it from him and approached the 177 pounder.

"Don't be shy, sweetheart," he said with a leer.

"What did I say, Kip?" Mr. Kessler asked, and the smirk vanished from Kip's face.

"No talking."

"That's right. No talking. You're running stairs after practice."

Kip blew out a breath and shot me a look like it was my fault. I untwisted the black top from the thick marker, the scent immediately making my eyes water.

"Go on now…?" Mr. Kessler flipped through papers on his desk, like he'd misplaced the class list. "What's your name?"

"BettyKay Allen."

"All right, BettyKay, just do the best you can."

Maybe it was the smirk on Kip's face or the ash on Mr. Kessler's ratty old sweater. Or maybe it was just that this was my very first class on my very first day and I meant to get off to a good start.

"Which phalanx?" I asked.

"Distal."

"Yes. But which one?" I picked up Kip's hand, ignoring how warm it was, the blisters on the base of each finger, and marked a little x on the tips of his fingers. "Thumb, pointer, middle, index or pinky?"

The girls in desks stared at me with open mouths, except Jenny who was all smiles. And Kitty, who looked like she'd eaten a lemon.

"Your name again?" Mr. Kessler asked.

"BettyKay Allen."

As I walked by his desk and back to my seat, I saw him mark something down next to my name on the class list.

It was nine o'clock at night by the time I made it back to my room. Dinner had been meatloaf and Jell-O salad, mashed potatoes that I had to admit were better than my mother's. I'd limited myself to half the scoop I'd been given and felt virtuous.

Though hungry.

Jenny and I sat together and I apologized for running out on her last night.

"I didn't think I was homesick," I said.

"I woke up this morning and missed the sound of my mom and brother talking over coffee in the kitchen." Jenny shrugged. "I suppose it's gotta happen to all of us at some point."

Curfew was at ten so all of us had an hour of free time. To my amazement, some of the girls were rushing back out the door with fresh powder on their noses to see what was on offer at the student union. The actual student union was under renovation, so a temporary one had been established near the Greensboro cafeteria. They called it the TUB.

"We're just going to go get a milkshake," Gwen said as they rushed by. "We've heard they're the best."

The adrenaline of the day had worn off like lipstick at the end of a date, and I was tired down to my bones. All I wanted was the peace and quiet of my room. I didn't care how good the milkshakes were.

The second-floor hallway smelled, just a little, of cigarette smoke, and I wondered who had been brave enough to defy Mrs. Hayes so soon. The smell got stronger as I walked down the hallway, until it became painfully obvious who was brave enough.

"You're going to get us in trouble," I said, opening the door to find Kitty sitting on the windowsill.

She blew a long plume of smoke over her shoulder in the vague direction of the open window behind her and shrugged. "You'll be fine, I'm sure. I'm the one with the cigarette in my hand. Unless..." She offered the pack of Kents and I shook my head.

"The rules were clear."

"Yes, they were." Kitty exhaled a perfect smoke ring with the air of a person who'd long grown bored of breaking the rules.

I projected as much disapproval as I could without saying anything more and set my books down on the bed. I kicked off my shoes and then, because it had been a long day and really what was the point of modesty in this room of flagrant rule-breaking, I unhooked my new Playtex stretch lace bra (that didn't have a whole lot of stretch) and fished it out through the sleeve of my shirt.

I actually gasped with relief.

Behind me Kitty laughed. She had been gone when I woke up this morning, her bed made like she'd never been there, and I was plenty curious to know what got her up and out so early. But I wasn't about to ask.

"I thought you might be going to the TUB with the other girls," I said instead.

"Not really my scene." *What a drag*, her face said.

She took one last pull and then put the cigarette in a glass Coke bottle and placed it down by her bare feet, her toenails painted bright crimson. She left the window open, the September evening creeping in and cooling down the room. The radiators were up too high and keeping the windows open was the only way to stop the rooms from turning into saunas.

"You're doing homework already?" she asked as I sat down on my bed and opened my diary. "You really ate up that sunshine girl business, didn't you?"

"Just writing down what happened today."

"Like a diary?" She made it sound like I had taken a doll from beneath my pillow.

"I want to remember what happened and exactly how it made me feel. There's nothing childish about that." Once I'd asked my mother how she'd felt on her wedding day and she had answered, *It was just another day, I guess.* And that had seemed wrong. I wanted big days with big feelings and I wanted to remember them all.

And yes, so I did like the sunshine girl business.

Kitty crossed her arms over her knees and stared sideways out the window. In her turtleneck and bell-bottoms she looked like a New York beatnik.

"Something was really bugging me today, all day," she said.

"Yeah?"

"They want us to fail."

I glanced up. "How do you figure?"

"Mr. Kessler with that little skin show—"

"It was effective," I said. I'd gone up no less than twenty times, and each time Kip and Brian had been reduced a little bit more to the muscle or bone I'd been writing on their skin.

They were, in the end, just bodies.

Kitty scoffed. "I kept waiting for him to say scrotum just to see who would pass out."

I looked down at my diary and felt my cheeks blaze.

"I don't think they want us to quit," I said. "They just want us to be prepared."

"You know how many first-year nursing students there are at St. Luke's? How many sunshine girls?"

"No."

"Sixty-eight. You know how many graduated last year?"

I did and the numbers were in our favor but barely. "It's a hard program. Did you think it would be easy?"

"Less than forty. Twenty-five girls are going to quit in the next three years."

"That's a lot," I agreed.

"It won't be you, though, will it?" Kitty asked with a smile that had an edge to it, like she was trying to call me square without saying the word.

"No," I said, unwilling to be shamed. "It won't be me."

Kitty stood and went to the desk. She pulled the chain on the lamp and a golden pool of light surrounded her Touch and Sew.

"A nurse, a teacher or a wife, that's it. Those are our choices," she said, and I could feel her frustration from across the room. It was the same frustration I had, even if I never put it in those words. I thought of Jenny, who'd dreamed of being a doctor and still the world conspired to make her a nurse. "And what if we don't like those choices? Or if we're shit at all of them? What happens to us then?"

"It's been one day," I said.

"I can't go back to Atlanta," Kitty said and took another cigarette from her pack. "I just can't."

5

BETTYKAY

I WALKED DOWN the tunnel that connected the dorm to the hospital in my pretty green-and-yellow jiffy dress with the hem I'd redone twice but was still crooked.

"What do you suppose this is for?" Kitty asked. When I awoke this morning, I'd nearly had a heart attack at the sight of her, hair in curlers, notebook open on her bed, scribbling away like a woman possessed.

"The tunnel?"

"Yeah. Blizzards? Bomb shelter?"

"Bomb shelter?"

"My uncle had one, built it in case the Communists bombed Atlanta, but we all knew he was making hooch."

"I don't think anyone is bombing Greensboro, Iowa."

"So? What's it for?"

"I don't know."

But I did. It was in the school brochure, which clearly Kitty had not read. It was because the hospital and the dormitory shared the kitchen. It made it easier for staff to wheel food back and forth. Nurses used it all the time. The boys studying medicine over at Greensboro had to walk from their dorms in the snow. And rain.

It was one perk the nurses got.

"I do something to piss you off?" Kitty asked, and I made sure not to react to her language.

She just wants to be shocking. So don't be shocked.

"No."

"Is it against your religion or something to tell the truth?"

"I'm trying not to be rude. Clearly something you don't know much about."

"Ah, a sense of humor at least. I was beginning to think you were just textbooks and brassieres over the foot of your bed."

I stopped and glared at her, and Kitty smiled in return.

"I don't like you," I said, surprising myself. "And I don't think you like me and I think that's probably fine."

"Probably?"

"I'm taking school very seriously, Kitty."

"I can see that."

"And I don't want to be distracted."

"Heaven forbid."

"All we have to do is be roommates. That's it. I don't think we have to be friends."

Kitty ran a hand down the front of the turquoise sweater she'd paired with trim gray jax pants and bright red flats. Her nails were white. Mod white. The kind of color I never dreamed of wearing. Or if by some chance I did pick it up at the Revlon counter I immediately came to my senses and put it down again. Kitty looked like she could have stepped right off the pages of *Seventeen* magazine. And not at all like she belonged in Greensboro, Iowa.

No. We were not meant to be friends. Friends offered something to each other, filled in gaps and holes where the other was missing something. Todd was my best friend. Had been before we were dating. We grew up together and I knew him down to my toes, the same way he knew me. And when my girlfriends asked if that was boring, I didn't know what to say. What could be better than feeling known and safe and happy with another person?

Wasn't that what everyone wanted?

"Okay, then," Kitty said. "You are very serious and I am not. I guess that's that."

Immediately I felt bad. It wasn't in me to be mean...or even blunt. "I'm—"

But before I could finish the apology, Kitty walked off, the overhead lights above her like spotlights on a stage.

"You coming?" Jenny asked, striding past me. "We're going to be late."

I hurried to catch up, and we pushed open the swinging green doors with the word *hospital* on the fogged glass and stepped into the basement of St. Luke's Hospital.

Laundry. Janitorial. Orderlies in white pants and shirts with black belts and shoes. Nurses wearing pressed white uniforms and caps pinned on their heads. It was loud and hot, the smell of starch and bleach was strong enough to make my eyes water.

A nurse ran by, covered in a spray of red blood. "I swear," she cried, "it got in my mouth."

Jenny grinned at me, like she couldn't wait to have blood sprayed all over her. I grinned back because a little bit, I felt the same way. Not about getting blood in my mouth, but about being in a situation so real.

A sign on the wall with a black arrow pointed down a long white tiled hallway. Classrooms.

"I heard our Fundamentals teacher was in the army," I said.

"Nurse Corps," Jenny said. "She was in France in '45."

"You know her?" I asked.

"Of her," Jenny said and didn't elaborate.

Room 4, in the basement of the hospital, was twenty degrees hotter than outside, and there were no windows. I felt sweat drip down my spine, into my underwear.

There were no desks, only long wooden tables with two chairs at each. Jenny and I, as we'd grown used to over the past week, sat together.

Nurse Bouchet, whose hair was as white as her uniform, stepped into the room and shut the door. As a unit we all groaned.

"You get used to the heat," she said, placing a hand on the brown-paper-wrapped packages stacked in a pyramid on her desk.

"Your uniforms," Nurse Bouchet said, looking at us through thick cat-eye glasses. "You are not permitted on the floor without one. You'll change in the changerooms down the hall and after every shift you'll leave them in the laundry. They'll be returned to you the following Monday so you can wear them again on Tuesday."

She called the class up one at a time, and when I had mine, I peeled back the paper and ran my thumb over the neat starched edge of the collar, the pin tucks on the bright white breast.

"Your role in this hospital," she said in a sharp voice that bounced off the tiled walls, "in any hospital, is to be a good soldier. You act quickly and you follow orders. Anticipate need, but do not anticipate orders. St. Luke's Hospital has seventy beds. We are a surgical hospital and the majority of our beds are in the surgical and ICU wards. We have seven wards, including emergency, labor and delivery, pediatrics, and psych. Next year you'll get accustomed to all of them. But this year you will only have access to the patients in Ward 3, psych. And Ward 1. Long-term care."

"They figure we can't kill the ones who are already dying."

Nurse Bouchet's eyes, like arrows, flew straight to Gwen, who'd made the joke. Yes, you could tell she'd been in the army. You could tell she was someone who did not suffer fools and didn't have time to hold anyone's hand. Jenny sat up even straighter, while half the girls wilted in their seats. *Good solider, indeed.*

"What will we be doing for the patients in long-term care?" Nurse Bouchet asked Gwen, who, bright red, shook her head. "No smart answers?"

"Sorry, ma'am."

"Nurse Bouchet, please," she said and then turned her hard gaze out at the rest of the class. "Anyone have any idea what we'll be doing for the patients in long-term care?"

"Bathing them," Jenny said.

"Correct. Anyone else?"

"Feeding," I said when the silence got to be too much.

"Yes. What else?"

I thought she was asking me, so I said, "Administering medicine."

Nurse Bouchet sighed. "You're very smart, Miss Allen, no need to rub it in everyone's face. But yes, administering medicine. We will be charting. Taking temperature. Monitoring heart rate and other bodily functions and…" She glanced around, white eyebrows raised. "No one. No guesses, even? We'll be wiping bottoms, girls. We'll be wiping a lot of dirty bottoms.

"Some of you applied for and were accepted into this nursing program perhaps understanding that reality. But not *really* understanding that reality, and outside of Advanced Chemistry and the psych ward, nothing, and I mean nothing, gets girls to quit the program like being faced with all the dirty bottoms we deal with on a daily basis."

"Is she joking?" Gwen whispered to Susan #1. "This seems like a joke."

October 2, 1967
Gwen left Intro to Chemistry today. That's the third class she's left in tears. I don't think the teachers want us to fail, like Kitty does. I think they want to weed out the girls who are not cut out for this job. They are not fooling around. Jenny found out the third-year girls have a TV on their floor and we snuck up to watch Mike Wallace on CBS. All the pictures and news make it seem like the situation in Vietnam is getting worse, not better. I wouldn't go over there. Not for a million dollars. But I didn't say any of that to Jenny.

I climbed the stairs after a particularly awful chemistry study session in the cafeteria. All this stuff seemed to come naturally to Jenny and I was struggling. The faint smell of cigarette smoke filled the hallway and my books suddenly felt heavy.

Kitty. Again.

Wednesday night Mrs. Margaret Hayes had opened her door and yelled, "Ladies! I smell cigarette smoke!" And Kitty hadn't even flinched. She'd just taken another drag off her cigarette and all but dared me to do something about it.

But as I entered the room now, Kitty, to my surprise, wasn't sitting in the windowsill smoking. She was at her sewing machine. The record player on her dresser played Stevie Wonder's "I Was Made to Love Her" at a level she could hear over the whir of pedal.

As I walked by, I turned Stevie down. Kitty treated this room like it was her country and I was only visiting.

"Hey—oh." Kitty straightened her spine. "Study hour is over?"

"Yeah. I didn't see you at dinner."

"I've been working."

"Working?"

I put my chemistry textbook down on the bed and, as I'd been doing every night, kicked off my shoes and took off my brassiere.

"Yep," Kitty said.

"Doing what?"

"Alterations. Jenny's skirts are too big, and when I told her she asked if I could fix them."

"You told her her clothes didn't fit?"

"I told you, too," she said over her shoulder, her eyebrow arched in a way that made me feel like I was walking around in a clown suit. "I'd be happy to fix it for you."

"What's she paying you?"

"Fifty cents and her anatomy notes."

I whistled, impressed.

Mrs. Hayes stepped into the doorway, her rigid posture a condemnation of every time I'd slouched in my whole life. Thank heavens Kitty wasn't smoking, for once.

"BettyKay," she said. "You have a call."

"Me?"

"A boy."

That made Kitty turn around to face me, eyes alight. "Well, well," she said. "Look who's keeping secrets."

"I'm not…it's not a secret." It was very much a secret.

"You have ten minutes." Mrs. Hayes glanced at her watch. "Starting now."

I jumped off my bed, scattering my notes on the floor, most sliding under the bed. I stooped to grab them.

"Go!" Kitty cried. "The clock is ticking."

I beat feet in my socks down the hallway, slipping on the polished wood floors, my arms over my chest so my breasts wouldn't bounce everywhere.

The phone sat in a little alcove in the wall, the receiver off the hook. Beside it was a clipboard so students could sign up to use the phone at a particular time. On another clipboard were the names of the people who'd called so girls could see if they'd missed their parents or a boyfriend while in class.

A line of students waited. Bethany from room 206 stood at the front, her arms crossed. She was on the phone every day, talking to a boyfriend who was studying at Coe College.

"You've got—" she looked down at her watch "—nine minutes."

"You going to stand there the whole time?" I asked, picking up the receiver. Bethany didn't budge. "Some privacy, please," I said, and finally Bethany stepped back a few feet and sank down against the wall to sit on the floor.

I took a deep breath, tried, with all my might, to contain the giddy, happy sound that rose up.

"This wasn't the plan," I said into the receiver, attempting a stern voice but failing. "A phone call on Friday and a visit on Sunday."

Because of the harvest, Todd hadn't been able to come yesterday or the last few Sundays, and our Friday night phone calls, which I stood in line for so no one had to come find me, had been brief because we were both so tired. So I was really looking forward to seeing his face this Sunday.

"I couldn't wait until Sunday," Todd said. "I couldn't even wait until Friday. You sore?"

"No," I said, resting my forehead against the wall. I closed my eyes and soaked in his voice. With my eyes closed I could almost pretend he was here in person. "I miss you." The words caught in my throat.

This was why I hadn't talked about Todd with the other girls. Because even thinking about him hurt, and talking about him would draw into painful relief how I'd gone from seeing him every day to not seeing him at all. And if thinking about him turned into missing him, I didn't know what missing him might turn into. The way it might turn me away from everything I wanted to accomplish at St. Luke's.

"Betts," he said. "Tell me everything. Everything you're doing this week."

"Working hard mostly. The classes are getting tougher."

"But you're acing them."

His faith was a buoy, but I couldn't lie. "I'm trying."

"Things getting better with your roommate?"

"Not better but not worse. I don't think she'll make it, that's for sure. But what about you? How is everything at home?"

Todd graduated last year, and even though he had good grades and University of Iowa and Iowa State came knocking with wrestling scholarships, he went right to work for his father on their farm. Once, when he was a little drunk on warm beer out at Shakey's, he told me he wished he could do what I was doing. Go off to school. Learn how to be a veterinarian.

I don't mind living my whole life here, he'd said. *But I'd like to see someplace else. Just for a little bit. Learn something besides farming, just to see if I could do it. You know?*

But he was his father's only son, his job in life cast at his younger sister's birth.

And perhaps it had been doubly cast when he and I started dating. Our fathers, longtime friends who'd served together in World War II, had been thrilled by the idea of all their land being handed down to their children. Kept in the family for another generation. Allen and Ackerman Farms.

It had a nice ring to it.

"We're still bringing the harvest in. Working around the

clock. The harvester is on its last legs and I'm doing every-thing I can to keep it running."

"You told him to get a new one last year."

"Yeah. It didn't do me any good, but I think he's hearing me now. Harvest is taking too long and we might lose the last fields."

"Oh no."

"It's all right, it just means…"

"What?" I sensed bad news.

"Dad said I can't take the day on Sunday. Again. We're not even going to church."

"No, Todd…" I pressed my head against the wainscoting. I'd been trying so hard, so hard to not be homesick.

"Hey." It was Bethany, tapping her watch. "Time's up."

"Todd, I gotta go."

"Okay. I'm real sorry about Sunday."

"It's okay, it'll give me more time to study, I suppose."

"That's my sunshine girl." I'd told him about the first-year nickname and he'd grabbed onto it with both hands.

I closed my eyes again so I could pretend, just a little longer, that he was near enough to touch. If I concentrated I could smell him, my favorite spot on his body—his neck just where it dipped into his shoulder. Right there he smelled of grass and sunshine, sweat and Iowa.

"Todd, I miss you."

"I love you so much, BettyKay."

There was nothing more I could say. My heart was his. I didn't play around with waiting to see who would hang up first. I just handed the receiver, hot from my hand, right to Bethany, and walked with heavy feet to my room.

Kitty turned when I entered, all lit up like we were going to have a roommate moment over that phone call, put aside our differences and talk about kissing boys. All the papers that had slid under my bed were stacked neatly on the bedside table.

One look at my face and Kitty's dark eyebrows dropped right back down. Her smile vanished. I climbed into my bed, pulled the quilt up over my head and put my face in my pillow. I drew the chain out from under my shirt and held it hard in my palm, until the small stone and the gold prongs hurt.

"BettyKay? You okay?" Kitty's voice was different. Softer. I pushed the blanket down.

She smiled tentatively, so unlike the smirk that seemed to live in the corner of her lips all the time. The slightly arched eyebrow that made me wonder, every time I saw it, if I forgot to put on my Right Guard.

All of that was gone, and it was just another eighteen-year-old nursing student really far from home.

I knew Kitty wasn't going to squeal. She was already breaking enough rules for the both of us. And I suddenly needed more than anything to roll some of this weight off my chest.

I opened my hand, the quarter carat diamond Todd bought with the money he'd saved from last harvest gleamed in the lamp light. I should have put the ring in my drawer, but I just couldn't. And if Kitty saw it before now, she didn't say boo about it.

"You're engaged," Kitty whispered and it wasn't a question. I nodded.

"Is he...okay?"

I nodded again, the compassion in that question surprising me and bringing the lump back to my throat. "I just miss him." Tears I didn't want to cry welled up, and I shifted back over and flipped the covers over my head.

Kitty turned on her record player to "The Sound of Silence," loud enough to give me some privacy. It seemed like the nicest thing anyone other than Todd had done for me in a long time.

6

ABBIE

Greensboro, Iowa
2019

IF YOU'D TOLD Abbie this morning that there would be a point, standing at her mother's graveside, when it would be hard not to smile, she'd have called you a liar. But here she was, shivering in her good coat in the cemetery by the Del Monte plant where all the Methodists in town were buried, biting her lip just to keep herself in line.

It was just such an *excellent* funeral.

If Mom were here, she'd be the first one to agree.

You did good, Abs, she would say. *You did real good.*

Abbie'd planned this funeral. Her sister, who'd claimed she had to tie up loose ends at work before coming home, had shown up just in time for the visitation, not the night before, not even the morning of. She'd driven her red sports car right to the visitation like she wasn't BettyKay Beecher's old-est daughter and didn't have some responsibilities. Abbie did it all on her own, and it had turned out better than she could have dreamed. The flowers were beautiful. Ben was playing his part. She'd been the right kind of white-wine drunk, and then Kitty Devereaux showed up like some surprise guest.

It was *amazing*.

Ben and the kids stood behind her and Clara, and behind them was an absolute sea of people. To their left, at a distance, was Kitty Devereaux in sunglasses and a dark trench coat that made her look like a woman in one of the black-and-white spy movies Ben loved. It was so deliciously dramatic.

"Sure seems like more people are here than there were at the visitation," Abbie said.

"They're here because of Kitty Devereaux." Clara turned and looked directly at Kitty, while everyone else was trying to play it cool and glimpse the movie star from the corner of their eyes.

"I suppose. I mean… Kitty Devereaux, can you believe it? And stop staring," Abbie said.

"Everyone is staring, Abbie. Angie Blake is trying to take a picture of her. You know, I googled her in the car. There's no mention of her going to nursing school. Or college in Iowa at all. She's from Atlanta," she said as if no one from Atlanta stepped foot in Iowa.

Abbie gaped at her sister. How sharp had her cynical edges gotten? "You think Kitty's lying?"

"I'm just saying it's suspicious is all."

It was hard to remember sometimes, the way they used to walk home from May Elementary School, hand in hand. When Mom tried to send them to different summer camps so they could get a break from each other, they'd refused to be separated. In high school, they did each other's makeup for school pictures and dances, slept in the backyard hammock in the summer, their sweaty legs stuck to one another.

They were the Beecher sisters against the world. And then Clara went to college in Chicago and Abbie stayed in Greensboro, got married, had kids, and whatever they'd had in common was reduced to loving their parents.

And now their parents were both gone, and Clara was returning to Chicago tonight.

This is going to be the end of us. The thought took the knees right out from under her.

If things between them were different, she might have leaned against Clara for a little comfort. But they weren't those people anymore. No matter how many birthday parties and T-ball games Abbie invited her sister to.

Abbie understood that Clara was *busy.* And *important.* Abbie was just a mom and a wife who planned and organized the lives of four human souls. But would it kill her sister to show up for some *effing* birthday cake? Clara always sent elaborate presents that the kids without fail liked best of all. It was infuriating.

"Mom was an open book, Abbie," Clara said, shaking Abbie from her thoughts. "Literally an open book. Why wouldn't she tell us she was friends with Kitty Devereaux?"

Abbie's only answer was that everyone had secrets, and a woman, even a mom, *especially* a mom, deserved a few secrets.

After Reverend Matthews's eulogy, Mom's old friend from St. Luke's and the Army Nurse Corps, Jenny, went up to give the Nightingale Tribute. So much of funerals was long and quiet, events of endurance, of listening to other people's grief, giving the same answers to the same questions and assuring everyone that if the family needed something, yes, they would ask.

But some parts of funerals were like fists coming out of nowhere to squeeze the breath right out of you. The Nightingale Tribute was just that. Mom had done this same reading and placed the white rose on countless caskets over the years, and that it was suddenly her turn was devastating.

Abbie fished through her pocket for more tissues.

Jenny, seventy-two years old, was a retired army major and wore her Army Nurse Corps uniform with the chest full of medals. She needed no assistance getting to the small podium, and when she caught sight of Clara and Abbie, she gave them a sad smile.

Abbie tried to return it.

"It's never a good day to bury a nurse who was still so active in her community," Jenny finally said. "Still serving the needs of the sick. It's never a good day to bury a friend. Or mother. Clara and Abbie, I am deeply sorry for your loss.

"From the minute I met BettyKay in the nurses' dorm at St. Luke's I knew she was one of those rare people for whom nursing was more than a job. It was a calling. Our floor mother dubbed first-year nursing students 'sunshine girls,' because we were nothing but possibility, like a new day. And that was my friend Betts."

Jenny smiled and scanned the crowd and then, all at once, her face froze. Abbie followed her gaze, but all she saw was the slim figure of Kitty Devereaux, standing at a distance.

"She was a born nurse," Jenny went on, her voice bringing Abbie's attention back. "Practical, unshakable, deeply, deeply empathetic. She set a high bar for herself, her classmates and her students. After school, she went on to make a name for herself with the publication of her Vietnam diaries, displaying the finest ideals of our profession—compassion, bravery and respect."

Abbie felt the hiccuping sob she'd been trying to swallow rise up in her throat. She turned to find her kids, swinging

Fiona up into her arms and pulling Max as close as she could. Fiona's weight, the hard clench of arms around Abbie's neck, and Max's little body against the curve of her hip were like a ballast.

She pressed her face into their warm bodies until she felt the scales shift, until she was more mother than daughter, and she could control her grief again.

Max, who Abbie thought had kept it together pretty well, finally had *enough* and was trying to climb one of the trees. The bare limbs stood out sharply against the gray sky and the red of his coat.

"Max," she whisper-yelled, looking over her shoulder at Kitty and Jenny, who seemed to be having an animated conversation near Kitty's black car. What were *they* talking about? And Clara was heading over to them like a heat-seeking missile. "Please, come down."

"But watch."

"I am, but…" He leaped from one branch to the other like a mini Spider-Man. "That's pretty cool. But you can't climb trees in a graveyard." That was a rule. Right? Lord. Where was Ben? He'd promised to help.

"Mom, it's boring."

"I know, buddy, but it's Gran's funeral."

"Abbie." Clara now had Jenny by the elbow and they were walking toward her. Of course. With her kid in a tree over the McNeills' plot. She could *feel* her sister's judgment.

"Max!" she said, and he got the hint and jumped down and ran off.

"Jenny has to go," Clara said.

Abbie hugged Jenny tight. "Thank you, for the ceremony."

"Of course," Jenny said. "She would have done the same for me."

"Are you coming back to the church?" Abbie asked. "There will be egg salad sandwiches."

"You know I'd love to, but Elroy's gotta get home."

Since a cataract surgery, Jenny didn't drive more than an hour outside of town, so Elroy, her youngest, had driven her from Iowa City. Elroy was a surgeon at the VA hospital where Jenny had finished her career.

"Oh no," Abbie said. "I was excited to catch up."

"I know, me, too. Joshua and Matthew send their love," she said. Jenny's older boys had followed their parents' footsteps and joined the army. They were stationed in Germany and Iraq.

"Give them ours," Clara said. "Tell Matthew he owes me ten bucks on that Federer match."

"That boy can't resist a long shot," Jenny laughed.

"You saw our surprise guest?" Abbie asked. "Kitty Devereaux walked in and I swear the entire place just about had a heart attack."

"Oh, I saw," Jenny said, her smile dropping from her face in a kind of alarming way. "We had a chat."

"About what?" Clara asked.

"She's going back to the church to help the women's auxiliary lay out pie. She said she didn't want to cause a scene. Which…" Jenny shook her head. "That woman was born making a scene."

Between egg salad sandwiches and Kitty Devereaux, the Methodist church basement was going to be the most exciting place for a hundred square miles.

"So, you knew her? Back in nursing school?" Clara asked, like she was gathering hostile witness testimony.

"Once upon a time the three of us, her, me and your mom, we loved each other like sisters."

"Sisters? What happened?" Clara asked.

"Well, I suppose you could say Kitty Devereaux happened."

"Are you not coming back to the church because of her?" Clara demanded.

"Jenny," Abbie said, trying to get a word in edgewise during Clara's cross-examination. "Why didn't we know about her? All those years? The buttons?"

"That's something Kitty's going to have to tell you," Jenny said. She put a hand to the gold cross around her neck, an expression that could only be called worried crossed her face. "When I called her to tell her about your mom, I told her not to do this. Not to show up with all this crap from so long ago. But Kitty was always going to do what Kitty was going to do. You couldn't change her mind no matter what."

Jenny grabbed Abbie's elbow and Clara's hands. "Don't listen to her."

"To Kitty?" Abbie asked.

"She's got her own agenda, she always did. You knew your mother, you knew the kind of woman she was. Don't let Kitty take her away from you."

Beside her, Clara was nodding, her suspicions supported.

Jenny hugged them each again, in the tight comfortable way of mothers, before getting in her car with her son and leaving seven million questions behind.

"I'm going to the church," Clara said and took off like Nancy Drew, leaving Abbie behind to take care of everything else. Again.

Well, will you look at that?

Kitty Devereaux *was* in the kitchen of the Methodist church, wearing a loaner apron and scooping generic brand coffee into the old percolator. Clara stood next to her, counting the scoops, eyeing her up like she might steal something.

Clara just couldn't seem to help herself.

Though after Jenny's warning at the graveside, Abbie couldn't really blame her.

Don't let her take your mother away from you.

The whole of the Methodist Women's Auxiliary was crowded into the old kitchen, finding whatever job needed doing, or might need doing, or could be faked for a while. Abbie watched from the doorway.

"I liked that husband of yours," Mrs. Ritchie said.

"Drew?" Kitty said. "Oh, he was a real sweetheart, broke my heart taking half his money."

The Auxiliary loved that, cackled with true delight, and it was obvious Kitty had been holding court for a while.

"And you were pretty hot and heavy with Rex Daniels. They don't make men like him anymore." There was a chorus of agreement.

"You know the tabloids never could get that right. Rex was a handsome devil, but he and I were just friends."

"Wish I had a friend like that," Mrs. Monroe, the choir director, hooted. Kitty seemed to take it in stride that her life was fair game for people to gobble up and vomit out right in front of her.

"What about that director you were married to? Made all those gangster films?" Mrs. Murphy, who'd been married to the mayor for years, asked.

"I never much cared for them shoot-'em-up movies," Mrs. Ritchie said as she cut through her famous jelly roll.

"To tell you the truth, me neither," Kitty said. "And Hugh and I never married. That was far too permanent an entanglement for Hugh."

"Living in sin?" Mrs. Ritchie wiped the knife on the front of her apron, leaving behind a smear of raspberry jam. "You and BettyKay had that in common, you sure did."

"Mrs. Ritchie," Clara said. "You are the only person left

in the world who is bothered by my parents not getting married until Abbie was one and I was two. Let it go, would you please."

Mrs. Ritchie gasped like Clara had insulted her jelly roll.

Good Lord, Clara, I can't leave you alone for ten minutes.

"Hi, everyone," Abbie said as bright and cheerful a decoy as she could be. "Thank you for all your help, these pies look delicious." She walked in, the cloth bag over her shoulder with two good bottles of snow day wine she'd picked up from home. Kitty Devereaux wasn't going to drink regular day wine. Not on Abbie's watch.

"Beautiful service," Mrs. Ritchie said.

"It was, wasn't it? I think Mom would have approved," Abbie said to a chorus of agreement.

Over in the corner, Clara plugged in the percolator and Kitty set down the mugs. They were two-of-a-kind, both too glamorous for this church kitchen.

As a girl, Clara had had curly hair that went blond in the summer, green if she spent a lot of time at the pool. She'd shove it all through the hole in the back of her favorite Chicago Cubs baseball hat. Now it was stick straight down to her chin and dyed a rich expensive brown with lowlights and highlights. It had real "I need to speak to a manager" vibes.

Abbie dyed her hair with whatever box was on sale at Walmart and only if she had a coupon.

"Greensboro will be talking about this one forever," Mrs. Ritchie said.

"I imagine so." Kitty smiled. "I'm sorry, if it's made a bad day worse."

"Are you kidding me?" Abbie said as she placed the bottles of wine on the counter. She found it hard to look straight at Kitty, she was just so pretty. And famous. Abbie kept wanting to bow. Which she knew was ridiculous, but the urge was there all the same. "It's amazing you're here. And you know, so many things are starting to make sense." Abbie turned to Clara, who was watching Kitty like she expected the movie star to pull a knife.

Clara was always good at killing a mood.

Well, this is an easy problem to solve.

Even though the quality of the snow day wine was wasted on this crowd, and being Methodist she might just scandalize half of them, she opened a bottle and took down a bunch of coffee mugs, stained brown from their years of coffee-hour service. Several of the ladies tutted. "Remember Mom always watched that terrible Christmas movie Kitty was in? No offense," she said to Kitty, handing her a wine-filled mug. "You weren't terrible, the movie was."

"No offense taken," Kitty said with that deflective charm.

"You were snowed in on a train trying to get back to New York City and there was the jazz band and a guy in a gorilla costume? It was a musical? You wore that silver sequined dress."

Abbie gave her sister a mug of wine and Clara gave her a wide-eyed look, clearly disapproving of her making nice with Kitty.

It can't be an interrogation every night. Abbie smiled at her own private joke.

"*Christmas A Go-Go,*" Kitty said.

"*Christmas A Go-Go,* who forgets a title like that?" Abbie cried, passing out mugs to the members of the Auxiliary who approved. She wanted to bring Ben in to show him that funeral drinking was actually a thing people did, not just her. Predictably, Mrs. Ritchie waved her off. "We watched it every Christmas and we could never figure out why."

"It was my first big role. She was…very proud."

"She showed us the picture of you at the premiere," Abbie said, waggling her eyebrows.

"The body paint?"

"Very cool," Abbie said. Kitty had gone to the premiere of that movie naked from the waist up, covered in painted-on vines and flowers. It was so 1969.

"I was a real nobody at the time and broke as could be. But I wanted to make a splash. My roommate Alexander was a makeup artist for one of the studios and he convinced me to do it."

"Oh, you made a splash all right," Mrs. Ritchie said.

"BettyKay was there, you know," Kitty said.

"Where?" Clara piped up.

"At the premiere."

"I'm sorry, what?" Clara said.

"She came out for the premiere. Jenny would have come, too, but she was on her way to Vietnam. I sewed the buttons on the silver sequin go-go dress I wore in the movie and your mom wore it to the premiere."

"BettyKay Beecher?" Clara said. "In a go-go dress? At a movie premiere?"

Kitty shrugged, her eyes glittering over the edge of her mug. "What can I say? Your mom had a wild side."

Abbie didn't have to look at Clara to know they were thinking the same thing. The whole of the Women's Auxiliary was thinking it: *Not that we ever saw.*

"Kitty?" Mrs. Ritchie asked. "Where you staying, if you don't mind me asking?"

"Oh, I hadn't really thought about it," Kitty said.

"I imagine you have important things to get back to," Clara said.

"Not at all. I'll just get a room in a hotel out by the highway."

"No," Abbie said with real horror. "Absolutely not." She

couldn't envision anything worse than Kitty Devereaux in a Motel 6 when her parents' home, with all of its comfort, was sitting there empty.

"Abbie," Clara said in her "let's not get carried away" voice.

"Mom would roll over in her grave, Clara," Abbie said, and the room went painfully quiet.

Okay. Too soon.

She barreled on in the way she'd learned from her mother, who *would* be rolling in her grave even if no one wanted to admit it.

And yes, Jenny said not to trust Kitty, but there was a go-go-boot-wearing side of their mother they were only just now hearing about. And Abbie wanted to hear every story.

She wanted her mother back and this wasn't the next best thing. It wasn't even close. But it was *something.*

"Hey, Janice," Mr. Ritchie said at the door. "You planning on serving that pie today?"

Mrs. Ritchie shooed him out of the doorway, and the Women's Auxiliary started walking the pie out to the serving tables in the dining room giving Abbie, Clara and Kitty some privacy.

"You'll stay at our parents' house," Abbie said. "I won't hear any arguments about it."

"What about Clara?" Kitty asked. "Perhaps she would like a say?"

Abbie arched her eyebrow at her sister. *Go ahead, Clara, tell her how you're too important to stay the night after your mom's funeral.*

Clara scowled but kept her mouth shut, and Abbie relished the rare victory.

"There's plenty of room for both of you," Abbie said, delighted by this turn of events. "I'll come, too!"

Take that, Miss I Have To Get Back To The City.

Kitty glanced between Clara and Abbie, and Abbie wondered if she could sense the fissures and cracks between them, the way Abbie was trying to wrap her arms around her sister and Clara was fighting it.

"Sounds lovely," Kitty said.

"Lovely," Clara parroted.

And just like that Abbie and Clara were having a sleepover with Kitty Devereaux.

Such a good funeral.

7

BETTYKAY

Greensboro, Iowa
1967

December 28, 1967
Christmas with Mom and Dad isn't going well.

Dad gets set off by the news and storms around shouting and then vanishes into the barn for half the day. I tried to talk to Mom about getting him help, a prescription for that new drug Valium at the very least, but she wouldn't hear of it. I told her it would make her life better and she got so mad she slammed the cupboard door and broke a water glass. Which she blamed me for. How do you help someone who doesn't want to be helped? Am I a terrible daughter for wanting to leave?

Two of the guys Todd wrestled with in high school enlisted. I just want to get back to school.

THE SNOW WAS just starting when Todd parked in front of the St. Luke's dorms. In the headlights of his truck it seemed harmless, like fluffy cotton bunting raining down. But I could feel Todd's worry. The weather reports the whole way to Greensboro had been dire, filling the inside of the car with a heaviness no amount of chatter could lighten. And I'd tried. Never in my life had I asked him more questions about harvester repairs.

Storm of the century, they were calling it.

Classes didn't start for another three days, but I'd made up a reason for why I needed to come back early, having had enough of my dark house and my darker-minded parents. Todd had volunteered to drive me.

"I don't want to say goodbye yet," I said. The yellow light of the car bathed his bright blue eyes and the golden mustache and beard he grew every winter. I reached out and ran my hand over the silky pelt and, without missing a beat, he pushed his lips into my hand. "I'm three days early, no one is around. I can sneak you in. Girls do it all the time."

"Well, hell is clearly freezing over if BettyKay Allen is suggesting we break a rule."

"I just...want you to be here for a little bit."

My fingers trailed from his beard to the warm skin of his neck, and I felt him swallow under my palms. I felt the beat of his heart. The car heater had done its job, and beneath the collar of his flannel shirt his skin was toasty. I imagined he'd be toasty everywhere.

"If I didn't know you better I'd think you were trying to get me in trouble." He kissed my lips. Soft. Soft. Soft. I pulled him closer, sensing the heaviness of his body and wanting it against mine. "Sweet girl, the snow is coming. I gotta go now if I'm going to outrun the storm."

I leaned back and let go. "Thank you for driving me. It's such a long day for you."

"Long day with you in the car, trust me, BettyKay. There's no place I'd rather be. And—" he looked back out the window "—I'm really happy to see this place. It's as beautiful as you said it was."

This is why I loved him. Because he got it. He understood.

"That's the Greensboro campus." I pointed out my window to the buildings on the other side of Long's Meadow. "Medical school and engineering—"

"Veterinary science?"

"Those big buildings back there," I said, turning this time to point out the rear window. The barns and stockyards were nearly impossible to make out in the dark and the snow. I guessed, because we only talked about it that one time he got a little drunk, that he was looking at those buildings and thinking about what might have been.

"Hey," he said, and I realized I was staring at him. "Where's that TUB place with the milkshakes?"

"Other side of those buildings, you can't see it. And they're not as good as Shakey's."

"Nothing is."

We smiled at each other, warm from the heater and love, and I couldn't help but kiss him again. Soon enough my coat was unbuttoned and his hair was a mess.

"Go," he whispered. "Please. If you don't go now…"

"I'm going." I jumped out, grabbed my suitcase from the back and slammed the door all before he could get out and help me.

The cold slipped in under my coat, clearing my mind, as I lifted my hand in farewell and he honked and turned out of the driveway, his brake lights glowing red and then disappearing.

Inside, the radiators were on full blast, and it smelled of the floor polish and disinfectant from the hospital. I'd been surprised to unpack my suitcase in my old room at the farm and realize all my clothes smelled that way. Like I'd brought some of St. Luke's home with me.

Mrs. Margaret Hayes had her door open and I poked my head in.

"Hi, Mrs. Hayes, I just wanted to let you know I'm back," I said, smiling because I didn't know how to stop.

"You're three days early," she said and looked up from the crossword puzzle on her lap. Her feet were up on her embroidered ottoman, the lamp beside her casting shadows across her face.

Second- and third-year nurses, who didn't go home for the holidays, were in and out of the dorms depending on their schedules at the hospital, so being back shouldn't be any kind of problem.

"I thought I'd get settled before the first day of school."

Mrs. Hayes smiled. "Well, it's good thinking on your part. We're supposed to get a big storm tonight. Dick Fletcher on the TV is saying two feet or more."

"That's all they were talking about on the radio."

In front of my room, I stopped. The door was shut and there was no smell of smoke or sound of Joan Baez or light seeping out beneath the door.

Things had thawed a bit between me and Kitty after I'd told her about Todd. I was giving her my anatomy notes, leaving my notebook on the edge of her bed every Monday night. Every Tuesday night the notebook was returned to my side of the room. I couldn't say we were friends but we were... friendly enough.

Quietly, I pushed open the door.

"Hello, roomie," Kitty said. She was sitting on the hard floor between the beds, the thin brown paper of a skirt pattern spread out in front of her. The gooseneck lamp was positioned so it glowed down directly over her shoulder.

"Hi," I said and set down my suitcase, shrugging out of my winter coat.

"Careful." Kitty flipped the paper up and out of the way of the snow slipping off my coat.

"Sorry." I stepped back and took off my red knit hat, shaking off the pom-pom in the hallway. Once you got those patterns wet, they were a real drag.

"You're back early," Kitty said.

"Looks like you've been back a while," I said. The room had been taken over. A dress was on my bed. Three pairs of Kitty's shoes in front of my closet.

"I didn't leave," Kitty said. She was pinning the paper to the heavy red satin underneath, sliding straight pins with bright yellow heads along the black dotted lines.

"What?" I moved the shoes that weren't mine to Kitty's closet, dropping them with a thud. Kitty didn't even notice. "You didn't leave?"

"Nope. Mrs. Hayes signed some special paperwork for me."

"What did you do for Christmas?"

"I," Kitty said, grinning, "had a great Christmas with the cafeteria staff. They were open for the hospital. Walter made a turkey with all the sides."

"Walter?"

"The chef. You've probably never met him. He's in the back most of the time. And the nurses all brought dessert and there was wine. Some of the doctors came. There was fraternization, if you know what I mean?" She waggled her eyebrows.

"It's like you want to get kicked out."

"All the third-year nurses do it. Trust me. It's not the crime Mrs. Hayes made it out to be. And really, all we did was share some half-decent Chianti and danced. Nothing too scandalous."

Predictably I was scandalized.

"How was your break?" Kitty asked, her attention back on her pins and the thin red fabric.

It wasn't a tough question. Shouldn't have been. But it felt that way, the answer stuck and buried beneath so many other feelings. "Fine," was all I said.

"Hmm," Kitty said. "Sounds it."

"It just…doesn't feel like home anymore." I hadn't admitted it out loud yet. Truthfully, I hadn't really been aware that was what I was feeling. But walking into this room with all its mess and none of it mine—I realized it had become more home than the bedroom under the eaves on Wolff Road. Having spent the last few weeks being judged by my parents no matter what I did, it was a relief to be in Kitty's company. The only thing she judged about me was my clothes. I could dance the hula naked down the hallway and she wouldn't bat an eye. "And I don't know if I feel sad about that, or happy."

"I think that's a good thing," Kitty said. "Makes you free to find the home you're supposed to have."

St. Luke's felt like home. The wainscoting and the marble floors. Jenny. Nurse Bouchet and Mrs. Hayes. The tunnel. The TUB. Even Kitty.

But Todd felt like home, too.

"What are you making?" The pattern was for a skirt, but her bed was covered with another ream of cloth, a gold velvet and other patterns.

"Winter formal dresses for a few sorority girls over at Greensboro."

"You're joking."

"Nope. Picking up a little work over the break."

Between the uniform alterations she'd done in the fall and now the dressmaking, Kitty had a pretty good side business going. And I could admit it, she was good. Really good. Her dresses looked like something Jean Shrimpton would wear in *Vogue*. "What are you going to do with all that money?" I asked.

"Find a place to call home," she said, head bent, fingers working.

The knock came like a roll of thunder. Caught half in and half out of a dream, I was lost for a second, thinking maybe I was still at the farm. Wishing I wasn't.

"Girls?" Mrs. Hayes called through the heavy wood.

I sat up. The light coming through the window was gray and hazy.

School, I realized with real relief. I'm at school.

"What time is it?" Kitty asked. She'd slept with her hair in rollers and the shadow of her head against the wall was huge.

"I don't know."

"Ladies?" More knocking, louder this time, and I pushed the blankets off.

"Oh my goodness," I breathed, shocked by the cold. My feet tried to find my slippers in the darkness beside my bed. I wasn't even touching the floor and I could feel its chill.

"Ladies!" The knock this time was so intense I abandoned the slippers and ran barefoot to the door.

"Sorry," Mrs. Hayes said. The hallway was full of what seemed like a thick blue light, and I rubbed my eyes, but the strangeness did not dissipate.

"What's...what's wrong?" I asked. The bay windows seemed like they were hidden by blankets, but it was snow and ice covering the whole of the second floor.

"There's an emergency at the hospital, girls," Mrs. Hayes said. "Your help is needed."

"Our help?" Kitty asked from the bed.

"The snowstorm," Mrs. Hayes said. "There's been an accident on the highway and half the staff can't get to work. They need you at the hospital."

"Us?" Kitty said, with what sounded like dread.

"We'll be ready as soon as we can," I promised, which was the answer Mrs. Hayes wanted. Her blue robe nearly melted into the muted light of the hall as she left.

"This has to be a mistake," Kitty said, leaning over to turn on the lamp. She'd worked last night until I'd finally begged her to turn it off at nearly 1 a.m.

My watch now said it was six in the morning. Adrenaline cleared the cobwebs, and I grabbed my uniform, hose and toiletry bag and ran to get dressed and scrub my teeth.

We walked together through the tunnel.

"What do you think we'll do?" I asked, unable to hide my excitement.

"Chart," Kitty said.

"How bad do you think it will be?" I asked. "The injuries from the car accident?"

"Bad enough they're bringing us in," she said. "You want one of these?"

Kitty opened her palm and revealed three thick blue pills.

"What are those?"

"Dr. Fischer gave them to me. Dexedrine. All the third-years take them. It just helps keep you awake. Clears the fog, you know. Like coffee, but...much better."

"I'm all right," I said. My mind was clear as a bell, my heart pounding against my chest. I had enough adrenaline to keep myself awake for days.

"Suit yourself," she said and swallowed one of the blue pills dry.

"Have you been taking a lot of them?" I asked.

"No. Joel just gave them to me at Christmas. Just so I could stay awake a little longer to get the dresses done."

"Joel?"

"Dr. Fischer," she said, like it was no big deal.

We pushed through the doors on the other side of the tunnel and stepped into the usual chaos of the St. Luke's Hospital basement. Nurse Bouchet was waiting for us in her cap and uniform and carrying a clipboard.

"Excellent, ladies, I'm glad you're here. Follow me and listen carefully."

We took the stairs up from the basement. The first floor was the emergency room and ICU. We stopped at the doors, and through the frosted glass I could hear the mayhem on the other side. Truthfully, I could *feel* it.

"There's been an accident on I-80. Seven cars. One tractor trailer." Well, that was no wonder, there was always an accident on I-80. "They are bringing patients here. Because of the storm and the holiday, the hospital is running on a skeleton staff. Listen to me, this is very important that you understand. You will be making rounds to patients in the emergency room who have been assessed and admitted. All you are doing is checking heart rate, pupils, breathing and change in status. If there is any change in status—"

"Like what?" Kitty asked. She was white as a ghost.

"Unconscious. Unresponsive. Confusion. Vomiting. Bleeding. Elevated heart rate, dilated pupils." These were basic fundamentals of nursing.

"Of course," Kitty said, licking her lips. "I just…double-checking."

"You will be fine," Nurse Bouchet said, which had to be more hope than truth. "If you have questions, I will be on the floor as well. Be good soldiers and do what the doctors tell you. You stay out of the nurses' way. You read the chart before you do anything and you write everything down before you see the next patient. Remember, your job above all things and no matter what is to keep your head about you. If you panic, your patient will panic."

"Who is going to panic?" Kitty joked.

Nurse Bouchet pursed her lips and pushed open the door into bedlam.

The emergency room was tiny—St. Luke's was a surgical hospital, and the emergency room only saw kids with broken bones and farmers who got into tractor accidents—and it was already at capacity. The ambulance bays were wide-open, letting in cold snowy gusts of air, and doctors were yelling and people on gurneys were crying and the smell of blood was thick.

"Oh my Lord," Kitty whispered. "I'm panicking."

"Girls." The head nurse came over. Her red hair was slipping out of her cap, and she had a smear of blood across the collar of her uniform. "You help the porters. You tell me if anything seems off. You'll be monitoring the nonemergency patients who are waiting for either a referral or discharge."

We nodded and were pointed to the emergency screening rooms. There were six, and we were to simply rotate counter clockwise through them.

We stood outside a curtained-off area, awaiting further instruction, but I quickly realized that was all we were going to get. I took a deep breath and glanced at Kitty, whose pupils were inky and wide.

I didn't know if it was fear or that damn pill.

"Follow me," I said, and we pushed back the curtain to reveal our first patient, a fourteen-year-old boy with a goose egg on his forehead and an arm in a sling.

"Hi," I said and reached for his chart. He didn't pay much

attention to me, but when Kitty walked in behind me, he did a dramatic double take. "Your name is Sam?"

"Sam Shickney."

"Nice to meet you. I'm BettyKay and this is Kitty and we're going to be checking up on you."

"Sure."

"What happened to you?" Kitty said, smiling for the kid, who grinned right back. He was in that awkward place between boy and man. His skin was spotty and his voice cracked when he talked, but he filled the bed up top to bottom. A skinny but long string bean.

"I was in the middle car in that pileup," he said. "Me and my mom."

Kitty winced sympathetically. "Car crash sandwich, huh?"

He smiled. "I guess you could say that."

Kitty was a natural at getting him to relax. So, I read his chart. He was waiting for an orthopedic referral for the arm, and they were monitoring him for a concussion.

"Any dizziness?" I asked, stepping to the other side of his bed.

"No."

"Nausea?"

"I'm real hungry. Someone was going to bring me some Jell-O a little while ago but they must have forgot."

"I can check on that for you," Kitty said.

"I know everyone's real busy. That was some pileup."

I checked his heart rate with my fingers, my eyes on the second hand of my watch. "Pulse is good." I uncoiled the blood pressure cuff from its metal hook, wrapped it around his good arm and started to inflate the bladder. "Pressure is 110 over 70, which is what you had an hour ago."

I checked the swelling and reflexes of his fingers, which

all indicated good blood flow and no nerve damage. His pupils were responsive.

"Hey," he said. "Could you find out where they took my mom?"

"Sure," Kitty said. "What's her name?"

"Gladys. Gladys Shickney."

"We'll find out what we can," Kitty promised. "And I'm going to get you some Jell-O."

We stepped out in the small hallway between the curtained rooms, and I let out a long slow breath, aware that Kitty was staring at me.

"What?"

"You are a goddamn nurse, BettyKay Allen," Kitty said.

The next few hours fell into a pattern. Quiet and calm followed by intense moments of adrenaline-fueled effort. We helped lift patients from gurneys onto beds, beds onto gurneys. We got pushed aside when one of the men we'd been watching went into cardiac arrest. We'd stood, backs pressed to the wall, watching the doctors perform CPR until the doctor in charge leaned back, sweaty and exhausted, and called time of death.

We charted and charted. Distributed lime Jell-O and then thin soup. We charted some more.

There were other accidents on other highways. A couple people brought in for frostbite.

Kitty, I noticed, took another one of those pills.

"You want one?" she offered.

I, unused to the roller coaster of the day, almost took it. Almost.

In what seemed like five minutes and five hours at the same time, Nurse Bouchet appeared. "Girls," she said, her own cap and uniform rumpled and sweaty. "You're done."

"Done?" Kitty and I were helping the porters sweep up one of the emergency surgical areas. Gauze pads and a man's work pants that had been cut off to treat a bleeding stomach wound. We had stood back and watched a nurse administer ether at the same time a very young doctor had cut into the man's belly to save his life.

"That's Joel," Kitty had whispered about the man performing the surgery.

Joel had not at all acknowledged or seemed to even notice us, and I felt something about his competence and cool head and the way he ignored us, but I couldn't say what.

"I'll walk you back down to the tunnel," Nurse Bouchet said. "The cafeteria's open. You can get something to eat."

And just like that, the exhaustion set in deep, and I could barely finish signing my name at the bottom of the chart I was finishing up for Sam, who'd been taken to Orthopedics an hour ago. The rule of charting was to never put it aside to do it later, never think you'll remember, because chances were you wouldn't and the continuity of care would be compromised. But there'd been so many codes, so many emergencies and needs pulling me and Kitty back and forth from curtained room to curtained room. We'd been down to the basement and back up a dozen times. I had blisters and paper cuts and my feet hurt like the dickens.

I couldn't wait to tell Jenny.

The storm had moved east, causing havoc all along its path.

The sun had come out and melted the ice that had covered the windows, allowing, as the day went on, the appearance of sunshine into the squinted eyes of the staff who'd long since lost track of time.

As we walked like zombies out of the emergency section, Dr. Joel Fischer stepped out of an office and leaned against the doorway, smiling as we passed.

"Ladies," he said. "Thanks for all the work you did today."

Kitty still had enough energy to give Dr. Fischer a wink, and he, under Nurse Bouchet's nose, reached out and squeezed Kitty's shoulder.

"Hey," Kitty asked as we made our way back down the steps toward the basement. "Sam's mom…what was her name again?"

"Gladys." Pulled in twenty directions, we'd forgotten to ask about his mom.

"Nurse Bouchet, do you know what happened to Gladys Shickney?"

"Hip fracture. Internal bleeding. She died on arrival."

Kitty stopped on the stairs, wavering like she might fall over. Her mouth open like there was something she wanted to say but didn't know what. Or how.

"Hey." I stepped up and grabbed her hands. "Hey."

Kitty turned her hand, gripping my fingers as hard as she could. And because we'd survived something together, walked through and now, on the other side, were different, I squeezed right back.

8

BETTYKAY

February 2, 1968

The teachers at Greensboro had a teach-in today, including Mr. Kessler and Ms. Monroe, our English teacher. Kitty, Jenny and I went to the auditorium where they were all gathering to protest the war. It was packed with people talking about the Tet Offensive and how the government wasn't telling us the truth. At the doors there were boys signing people up for SDS, and another group of men and women from Good Park in Des Moines were signing up the dozen black students who went to Greensboro for the Black Panthers. Kitty took a pamphlet from both. We stayed to hear Mr. Simmons, the head of the anthropology department, talk about how the draft was unfairly skewed toward black men and poor men because white men with money were always able to get to college or pay for a doctor to write a phony medical record. I'd never thought about this before and

Jenny was nodding the whole time. Then a kid ran in and said the police were coming. Mr. Simmons tried to keep everyone calm, but we were the last to arrive and closest to the door, and Jenny grabbed me and Kitty and we beat feet right out of there. Police arrested twenty-five people, including all the Black Panthers, even though they weren't doing anything but handing out pamphlets.

"DID YOU HAVE a good day?" Kitty asked, walking up the sidewalk to where I stood watching Todd's car drive away. She wore a yellow wool trench coat that wouldn't keep out a summer breeze, much less the winter winds, but she didn't appear cold. She looked stunning. Of course.

I had to admit, I'd been all wrong about Kitty. She was a good egg.

"We did," I said. We'd gone out to Shakey's for lunch and then spent the afternoon talking in Todd's car.

"You look it," Kitty said with her grin. "Your lipstick's been all chewed off."

I put my mittened hands to my mouth, still tingling from kissing Todd.

"You were up early again," I said. At least a couple times a week I woke up alone in our room and I still didn't know where she was going. "One of these days I'm going to wake up and catch you."

"Girl, you sleep like the dead. I could ring bells by your head and you wouldn't wake up."

"Do you have a job?" I asked as we fell into step and headed back to the dorms.

"You guessed that already."

"Are you bird-watching?"

"What?" She shook her head. "No. Who has time to watch birds."

"Are you a cat burglar?"

"I wish."

"I'll be right one of these days."

"Not if you think I'm the kind of gal who watches birds."

"You went into town?" I pointed at the paper bag in Kitty's hand.

"Ben Franklin. I needed some buttons."

Kitty spent more time at Ben Franklin than she did in the cafeteria. She had a jar full of buttons in her dresser drawer that were just never the right ones.

"You want to study for that Fundamentals test?" I asked.

"That's a week away, Betts."

"Well," I said, linking my arm through hers. "I'm not sure if you understand how studying works. But a little bit every day…"

"Oh Lord, stop. I'll study, I'll study."

"After dinner."

"You really know how to live it up, BettyKay."

"I'm just trying to keep you from failing out, Kitty."

We stopped by the mailboxes and I pulled out two envelopes, a letter from my mother and, surprisingly, a letter for Kitty.

"Hey," I said, jogging to catch up with her. "There's a letter for you."

Kitty stopped, turned and glanced down at the letter and then back up at my face. "For me?"

"Katherine Simon." I handed it to her. All I could read of the return address was Jesse Simon and Georgia.

Kitty snapped the letter right out of my hand and shoved it in her pocket.

"You're not going to read it?" I asked as I hurried up the stairs behind her.

"No point."

"Is it from your father?"

"My brother."

"What if it says—"

"I know what it says."

She knocked on Jenny's door as we walked by. Jenny popped her head out, pushing her glasses higher up on her nose.

"Your dress is done. Come try it on."

Jenny grinned real wide and actually clapped her hands. "I'll be two shakes."

Over the last couple of months, I had even become used to our room and the division of space. Kitty got two-thirds of the room and I got the rest, and it wasn't fair but Kitty fixed all my hems and mended all the holes in the elbows of my sweaters. She played my favorite songs on her record player and bummed me cigarettes at the end of the day, and we sat side by side in the windowsill, blowing smoke over our shoulders.

It was the kind of fair that couldn't be measured. On Friday night a few weeks ago, Kitty snuck in a bottle of Chianti and we drank it in coffee mugs smuggled up from the cafeteria. It was a different kind of friendship than any I'd had before. It blew through windows and knocked down walls and made my world a little bigger.

Inside our room, we shrugged out of our coats, and Kitty put the letter in the top drawer of her dresser, where she kept the money the girls paid for her seamstress work.

"It's just...you never mention family," I said, unable to resist.

"They're not worth mentioning," Kitty said. From her closet, she pulled a new dress of Jenny's that she'd altered so it wasn't so baggy at the waist and laid it down on her bed.

"Kitty?"

"You're not gonna give it a rest?"

"No."

"They're the kind of family who eat their young. Your family is bad, I get it, but at least they want you safe. That's a leg up on mine. And now, honestly, I'm done talking about them."

I had a million more questions, but Jenny knocked on the door.

"Come on in," Kitty said.

I sat down on my bed to make space for three people in the little room.

"I still can't believe you got this done so fast," Jenny said.

"Well, I know your measurements, and pulling in the waist is a cinch." Kitty handed the green chiffon to Jenny. "Try it on so we can see if I need to do anything else to it."

Jenny turned to face the wall, taking off her housedress and tugging the dress down over the slip she wore.

There was another knock at the door, and one of the girls from down the hall shouted through the door, "Kitty, there's a call for you!"

I picked up my diary and wrote, pretending nonchalance.

"This won't take long," she said over her shoulder and walked out.

I caught Jenny's eye.

"It's rude to pry," Jenny said.

"If she wanted to tell us, she'd tell us," I agreed.

We looked at each other for the beat of a heart and then I was off the bed and Jenny had the door cracked open enough so we could peek out and watch the swish of Kitty's skirt as she headed to the phone.

The old tan receiver was lying on the ground. Kitty grabbed it and, without hesitation, hung it up. Hard.

"Goodness, Kitty, you'll break it," said one of the Susans waiting in line.

I could tell Kitty wanted to pick that phone back up and slam it back down again. Maybe break it over her knee. It was all in the set of her shoulders.

"It's all yours," Kitty said to Susan.

Jenny and I darted back into the room, falling onto the bed and trying to act natural.

Kitty swept back in like a black cloud, which really wasn't Kitty's bag. But her face was set in angry lines and she was even prettier with all the electricity around her.

"You want to talk about it?" Jenny asked, braver than me.

"Do I look like I want to talk about it?" Kitty snapped back. We didn't talk about it. Not ever.

March 15, 1968
Marg got pinned to her fella at the Sigma Nu house this week-end. She invited all of us to the ceremony. Half the girls went in their best dresses hoping to get their own Sigma Nu guy, be-cause they are the catches on campus. Jenny didn't go. She had to study. She's trying to get her three years done in two, which means all she does is study and sleep. Kitty didn't go because she said it was an archaic custom. Of course a guy should care more about his girl than his stupid fraternity. I went because it's been nothing but schoolwork and more schoolwork, lately. And they had a rum cake. It was nice to witness people in love. Watch-ing Marg and her guy made me feel closer to Todd. Everything is so upside down right now. It's nice to see something still go on the way it always has.

Thanks to me waking up earlier than usual, I finally found out where she went in the mornings.

"Jogging?" I asked, watching as Kitty put her foot up on the edge of the desk and stretched. She wore a pair of what had to be kid's Chuck Taylors. Her gray sweatshirt was sweaty around the neck despite the cold and said in faded letters Track and Field across the chest. "Where?"

"Around." She shrugged. "It's better than constantly reducing."

"But you don't eat anything anyway!"

Kitty laughed. "Now you know my secrets."

Kitty didn't look like any other girl at school. Or like any other girl I'd ever met. She was sharp and bright. Magnetic, even when she wasn't doing anything. Her hair was no longer white blond but had been changed to a deep red. It didn't suit her any more or less than the blond. She would look good any which way.

But jogging around Greensboro College seemed odd, even for Kitty.

"What are you doing up so early?" Kitty asked. It wasn't even 8 a.m. yet. And on a Sunday, too, our one day to sleep in. I usually took advantage, lying around until lunch at the least. But I'd had a bad dream, and woke up cold and shaking when Kitty had snuck back in breathing hard from all her secret exercise.

Jenny, as became routine no matter what time of day it was, opened the door without knocking and stuck her head in, still wearing the silky headscarf she'd slept in. It was deep purple and made her look like a queen. "Some fool down on the lawn is throwing pebbles at my window."

"What?" Kitty went to our window. "Oh my Lord, I see him. Now, he's throwing rocks at Gwen's old room."

Ten girls hadn't returned from Christmas break. Gwen was one of them. Mrs. Margaret Hayes said that was high for the first cull, but that she wasn't surprised.

I was, though. All those girls giving up and going back to what? Gwen, I'd heard, got hired at the glove counter at Armstrong's in Cedar Rapids.

I pushed off the blankets and crowded in next to Kitty in the windowsill.

"Oh my gosh," I breathed.

"You know him?" Jenny asked, coming in on the other side of Kitty.

"It's Todd," I said. "My Todd."

"Well, your Todd is going to get us all in trouble," Jenny said.

"What's he doing here?" Kitty asked.

"I don't know. Maybe something happened at the farm or—"

Kitty nodded. She opened the window as far as it would go and leaned out. With two fingers in her mouth she split the dawn with a sharp whistle that made Todd's head snap around.

Kitty pushed me half out the window. Todd caught sight of me in my nightgown, my hair in curlers, and with his long loping stride, he ran over to stand right under our window.

"Todd," I cried, trying to keep my voice low. "What are you doing here?"

"I need to see you. I've got some news," he said, seriously, but then smiled so big. "You look beautiful."

"I look a mess. Just…stop throwing stones, I'll be there in a second."

I ducked back into the room and closed the window behind me. "I need to—"

Kitty and Jenny were already in my closet, pulling out clothes.

"It's like my mother's clothes got put in this closet by mistake," Jenny said.

"It's a lost cause," Kitty said and turned to her own closet.

"This one will fit her." She was holding a dress Kitty had made from the scraps of a caftan-style dress she'd sewn for a graduating nurse. The fabric was wild—pink, white and black geometric shapes on a thin polyester. So thin it would be like wearing nothing.

"It's too cold for that," Jenny said.

I ignored their arguing, tore the curlers from my hair and tossed them on the bed, opting for blue jeans and a red sweater. I didn't even bother with a bra. My winter coat went on over all of it.

"Hold on," Kitty said and grabbed the red pom-pom hat my mother had made me and shoved it on my messy head. "You're a total fox," she said, and I didn't get the sense that she was joking. It was strangely sweet.

I practically flew out of the building to find Todd waiting for me by the steps. His cheeks and nose were pink, the tips of his ears red from the cold. "Oh, my girl," he said, tugging me into his arms. "You are a sight for sore eyes."

"What are you doing here?" I asked, putting my hands over his ears, pushing my warm cheeks against his cold ones to thaw him out.

"I need to talk to you," he said. "Is there a place we can go out of the godforsaken wind?"

"The TUB is closed until lunchtime and I can't bring you into my dorm."

"All right. Let's go sit in the car. We'll be warm at least."

He grabbed my hand and started to lead me toward the parking lot, where I saw his dad's old Ford truck sitting like a blast from the past.

"Todd," I said, yanking on his hand, making him stop. "You're scaring me."

"I know," he said.

"Just tell me. Is it my parents? Or your parents? Your sister—"

He stopped and held my hands in his. "Betts, I've enlisted. I'm going to Vietnam."

9

BETTYKAY

HE WAS EXCITED. That's all I kept thinking. My heart was breaking and he was *excited*.

"You're freezing, babe." He turned on the car, directing the vents toward me. "It's an adventure," he said with his big happy smile, like if he just smiled hard enough I'd see things his way.

"It's war."

"It might be all over before I'm out of basic training. That's what the recruiter said. Johnson is clearing things up. And the Viet Cong don't stand a chance against all the boys being sent over there now."

I was trying not to cry. Risking his life was an adventure? Going all the way around the world to shoot at people who'd never done a thing to him was *exciting*?

"You never said anything about even *wanting* to go."

"I know. But I've been thinking about it. Really thinking about it for a while and—"

"You didn't think to talk to me about it? We're engaged, Todd."

That puppy dog excitement drained from his face. "I didn't want you to talk me out of it, BettyKay. I didn't tell my parents, either, because—"

"You knew we'd all try and talk you out of it."

"I'm 1A, Betts. Sooner or later I'm gonna get drafted."

"But Pete Collins, he's a farmer and he got deferred." As soon as I said it I knew he wouldn't defer.

"If I enlist before I'm drafted, this just gives me opportunities."

The draft was sucking up men by the thousands. Kitty and Jenny had shown me pictures in the newspaper of boys burning their draft cards in protest, and now Todd, a *farmer* for God's sake, was enlisting?

"Honey?" he said. "Are you okay?"

No!

"Where will you go for basic training?" I managed to ask.

"Fort Knox, can you believe it? Maybe I'll get a look at all that gold they got stashed there."

He was laughing and grinning like this was all so much fun and my heart was getting squeezed up in a fist.

"Hey," he said, touching my cheek, tugging on my earlobe the way he did when he wanted my attention. "Don't be sore. I supported you wanting to do something different. Wanting to make something of yourself."

My dream won't get me killed. Won't take me halfway around the world to some place we've never even heard of. To shoot at people who never did anything wrong to us.

But I didn't say that. I remembered him in that back booth at Shakey's, wishing he could have a different life, a chance to see who he'd be.

It didn't seem like I had any choice but to support him. It

was too late to stop him, he'd made sure of that. All I could do was dry my eyes and try to smile.

"I'm just scared is all," I said. "I love you, Todd."

"Baby, I love you, too. And you'll see, I'll be fine. I got sixteen weeks before I'm sent anywhere."

Sixteen weeks was a long time. A lot could happen in sixteen weeks. But could a war end?

"When do you go?"

He kissed me instead of answering, and desperate for the comfort, I almost let him get away with it. But I wasn't going to be a fool. "Todd," I whispered, leaning back.

"I gotta report first thing tomorrow morning. I'm on my way there now."

"What?" I jerked away.

"Shhh." He drew me closer, as close as he could, and it still wasn't close enough. "I'll be back after basic. I promise. I promise, honey. I will be back and we'll have a real goodbye."

Real goodbye? I thought. What did that look like? Getting married at city hall? Renting some cheap hotel room by the highway? How was I supposed to say goodbye to my fiancé and let him go off to war?

"Hey," he said against my ear. "Everything will be okay."

My parents and I had established a routine from the get-go. I called them on Saturday nights. Mom talked first about the neighbors and how stubborn my father was and how upsetting the news was. Hippies! War protests! Drugs!

And then when she asked about school, she wasn't resentful, really. But she wasn't excited, either. So I learned right away to keep the answers neutral. Then Mom would ask, *Do you want to talk to your father?* And I'd say, *Sure*, and there would be two minutes of grunting about the weather from my father.

But with Todd going to basic training and the world upside down, I missed my mother.

Jenny and Kitty had hugged me and let me cry and be angry and cry again. But when it was all said and done, I longed for something familiar, the sense, perhaps, of not being so terribly grown-up.

So I called the next night.

"Are you all right?" Mom asked.

"I'm fine, Mom. I'm just…" I turned my head away from the girls wandering from room to room and pressed my forehead to the wainscoting, closing my eyes to block it all out, all this life going on as usual. "I suppose you heard about Todd?"

"He enlisted."

"He did."

"Did you even try and talk him out of it?"

"I didn't know he was doing it—"

"Well, honey, don't you think you should have known? Why wouldn't he tell you?"

"Maybe because he didn't want to be talked out of it." I raised my voice, which wasn't a thing that was done at our house. It made me feel out of control, like there was nothing I could rely on to stay the same. Not even myself.

This wasn't why I had called. This wasn't comforting.

"He always had his head in the clouds, that boy."

"Head in the clouds? He's going off to war—"

"That's what I mean. Why does he need to go all the way around the world when his family needs him here?"

"Mom, he was going to be sent anyway."

"You don't know that."

I'm choosing to believe it.

"Mom, I'm not calling to argue about Todd. I'm just…well, I guess I'm just lonely."

"Well, what did you expect moving all the way to Greensboro where you don't know anyone? You know, Todd would never have thought about leaving his family if you hadn't done it first. You and nursing school put ideas in his head—"

"Okay, I gotta go."

"Do you want to talk to your father?"

"Next time."

I went back to my room, where Kitty was painting her toenails a bright pink, and fell face-first onto my bed.

"Heavens," Kitty said, jabbing the brush back in the bottle. "What happened now?"

"I made the mistake of calling my mom."

"Oh, honey," she said with sympathy.

"I'm just homesick for a home I don't even want to be in anymore. I'm just…" I sucked in a breath and tried not to cry, because there'd been enough of that, too. "Sad."

"I get it. I come from a nest of vipers. Every member of my family worse than the last, and my Meemaw was the queen snake, but when I feel real bad, what I want more than anything is my Meemaw's spoon bread."

"I don't know what that is."

"Of course, you don't. But it's the food that makes me happy, that reminds me of an easier time. Not *better*, because it wasn't." She laughed a little, the secret of her family still secret. "It was just simpler, and sometimes that's enough. Now, what's that for you?"

"Food that makes me happy?"

"Instead of people who make you unhappy."

"Tenderloin sandwich out at Shakey's Tavern."

"Sounds like a dream." I could never tell when Kitty was being sarcastic. "Where is it?"

"By the river. Between here and Bluffs."

And then, like a miracle, Kitty reached into her purse and pulled out a set of car keys. "Let's go."

"You have a car!"

"Shhhh. Stop screeching it to the world, would you?"

"You have a car?" I whispered.

"It's not mine," Kitty said and raised one perfectly plucked eyebrow. "And before you ask—you don't want to know whose it is."

Kitty was still dating the doctor. How in the world did she find the time?

"What about curfew?" I asked.

"I think it's safe to say the girls on this floor treat curfew like a suggestion rather than a rule, wouldn't you agree?"

I didn't, actually. But tonight I was ready to bend the rules. Break them if it was required. Because I could taste that sandwich in my mouth and hear The Ronettes on the jukebox. I could feel the cool breeze through the cattails by the river. I pushed my feet into my Keds and grabbed my purse.

"It's about an hour away."

"Good." Kitty handed me the keys. "You can drive. I need a nap."

We stopped by the phones, where Jenny was just finishing a call.

"I know, Mom," she said. "No, of course I want to talk to him but...please stop. You're making it harder. Okay. Yes. I love you, too."

She hung up with a heavy sigh and I jiggled the keys. "Field trip?"

The only person who cared more about curfew than me was Jenny, and it wasn't only because she was trying to graduate early. We'd seen how the rules were different for her because of the color of her skin.

But the call with her parents must have been real bad, because she turned toward us with a big grin. "Where are we going?"

* * *

The car was a white Cadillac Fleetwood with cream leather interior, the nicest car I had ever seen much less driven. I paused by the driver's side door, suddenly full of nerves.

"Kitty. I don't know—"

"It's a car," Kitty said. "She ain't gonna hurt you."

"But what if I hurt it?" I was used to driving tractors and lawn mowers, Ford trucks with crappy suspensions.

"She's tough," Kitty said. "I doubt you'd be able to."

Kitty's confidence was so powerful, she just rolled over all my doubts. So I let go of them.

The car handled like a dream, and I kept looking down at the speedometer only to be shocked by how fast we were going. Kitty, true to her word, told Jenny to turn on KSTT out of Davenport, slipped her sunglasses down over her eyes and went right to sleep in the back seat.

"Your dad still isn't talking to you?" I asked Jenny, who sat in the passenger seat.

"No one does the silent treatment like Roy Hopkins."

"Does he think he's going to change your mind?" I asked. Jenny didn't change her mind, she didn't get sidetracked. On the rare nights we drank Chianti out of mugs in our room, she would join us. But she didn't look at fellas or go down to the TUB in fresh lipstick. She studied and she went to class and she watched the news out of Vietnam.

"I don't know what he thinks outside of he's right and I'm wrong."

"He'll come around," I said.

"You don't know Roy Hopkins. He's got a brother he hasn't spoken to in thirty years. If he wants to send me off to Vietnam without a word, he's just stubborn enough to do it."

"He's just scared for you."

Jenny made the loudest, juiciest raspberry noise with her mouth, and it was so startling I laughed.

"The worst part—" she held up a finger "—is he's put my mom right in the middle. He thinks he's teaching me a lesson or some nonsense. But really, he's punishing her. She loves us. She just wants us to be a family, and he's got to make it so difficult. Is that what marriage is? Taking care of a grown man's feelings?"

It certainly was in BettyKay's parents' house.

"My brother moved out over it."

"What? Jenny, you never said."

"Mom just told me. He's living over a laundromat. Me going into the Nurse Corps was supposed to keep my family together. Now look at us."

"If you quit would it make it better?"

"I'm not quitting."

"I know you're not. But if you did, would that fix anything?"

She took a deep breath and let it out. "Maybe. But the rock's been lifted, you know. I've seen all the bugs underneath."

"That must hurt," I said. It had to, even though she was good at pretending it didn't.

She'd put a scarf on over her hair and put her hand out in the breeze. She looked so sad. But then she gave herself a shake. "Listen, I don't want to bring all that mess into this stolen car."

"It's not stolen!" I shrieked.

She shook her head, her eyes twinkling. "I don't think we know that for sure. Come on. No more upsetting talk."

She turned the radio up and "Reflections" by The Supremes blasted through the car, so loud it pushed out all our worries. Jenny tipped her head back and sang along.

I unrolled the window and the cornfields went by in a blur. The road was long and the sky was endless and soon the aching I was feeling, that strange desire to see my mom and be taken care of, to be a child again with childish worries, it blew away, revealing the hard rock of my fear. I needed to learn how to live with it. How to breathe and go to school and walk around terrified the man I loved was going to be shot and killed halfway across the world.

This, I thought, the Iowa sunlight on my face, *is being an adult.*

Shakey's was a timber shack situated in a picture-perfect bend in the Cedar River. The building had a big plank porch dotted in picnic tables and bird poop, and there was a dock where people could fish or go swimming when it was hot.

"What a dive," Kitty said, genuine excitement in her voice.

"It's even better inside." I pushed open the screen door.

It took a second for our eyes to adjust to the gloom. Shakey himself was behind the bar and he waved. "Heard about your boy," he said. "That's a brave thing, he's doing. Signing himself up before that lottery gets a hold of him."

"I'm real proud of him," I said, which wasn't a lie. But it was far from the whole truth.

"You want the usual?" he asked.

"Three," I said. "Extra crispy. One order of onion rings and three Cokes."

Shakey nodded and yelled at his wife in the kitchen to drop in three tenderloins.

Jenny took a napkin and wiped at the sticky wooden table in the far back booth.

"Don't bother," I told her. "The sticky doesn't come off."

The smell of fried food, cigarettes and old beer had soaked into the wood walls and the beamed ceiling. Underneath it all was the fresh muddy smell of the river outside the open windows, snaking through the tall grass. There were old concert bills on the walls, bands who traveled through on their way to bigger and better things.

"We saw Martha and the Vandellas out here," I said.

"No fooling?" Kitty said.

"Todd loves them. Sang every word right in my ear. Shouted, really. My ears rang for a day after."

Our icy cold bottles of Coke arrived. I slipped a straw into the top of each, took a sip of mine.

"Are you really proud of him?" Jenny asked.

"Sure."

"Come on," she said. "You can shoot straight with us."

"I'm angry," I said, the words popping out. "That he did it without talking to me, without even telling me he was thinking about it. When I wanted to go to nursing school, I asked him. He'd proposed and I knew it changed our plans, but I asked if I could and he said yes, that I should go to school."

"What would you have done if he said no?" Jenny asked.

"What choice would I have?"

"There's always a choice," Kitty said.

"Break up with him? So I could be a nurse?"

Kitty shrugged. "Does that seem so ridiculous?"

"Not anymore," I realized. Seven months at school and I'd changed so completely. "But back then, if he said no, I wouldn't have gone. Thank heavens he said yes." Though I'd known he would say yes. It was part of the reason I loved him.

"Plenty of guys would have said no," Kitty said.

"I know, and still, I worried about his feelings. I worried about my parents and his parents. I worried about how they would feel and what they would think. And when he told me he'd enlisted without talking about it with me or his parents, all I could think was, how nice that must be. To make a decision about my life and not have to worry about anyone else. Much less ask permission." I laughed. "I mean, can you imagine?"

"I made a decision about my life and my dad's still not talking to me," Jenny said with a shrug.

Kitty hummed and lit a cigarette with a match she blew out and tossed in the ashtray.

"I wish we could volunteer to go fight," Kitty said, propping her elbow on the table.

"What? Kitty!" Jenny shook her head in pure disbelief.

"I'm serious. Why should the boys get all the adventure? All the training and uniforms? I can shoot a gun."

"You can?" I asked.

"Sure," she said in the way of a person who had no practical experience but figured it couldn't be very hard. "Can't you?"

I nodded. "I can shoot a gun and skin a deer and make a pretty good squirrel stew."

Kitty curled up her nose. "Eww, Betts. Eww."

"You want adventure and uniforms you should sign up for the Nurse Corps," Jenny said.

"No way," Kitty said. "I'm not that brave."

"Yeah," Jenny said with a smile. "You're all talk."

"And lipstick," Kitty laughed. "I'm all talk and lipstick."

Our tenderloins arrived, crispy and hanging over the sides of the soft-as-butter potato bun. The onion rings, freshly dipped and fried, were piled high on wax paper in a red plastic basket between us.

"Brace yourself," I said. "Nothing will be the same after one of Shakey's sandwiches."

I took a bite and the familiar flavors exploded in my mouth. The crunchy batter, the tender juicy meat. Kitty took a bite, too, and moaned.

"Can I tell you something?" Kitty asked, putting down her sandwich.

"Sure, Kitty. You can tell us anything." I reached for an onion ring and took a bite even though they were still too hot to eat. The Vidalia onion slipped out and nearly burned my chin.

Jenny handled her onion ring with a bit more grace.

"I've almost saved enough money to buy a bus ticket."

"To where?" Jenny asked.

"Hollywood."

I blinked. Blinked again.

"You think I'm stupid," Kitty said into our silence.

"No. No. Not at all. I think… I think that sounds about right for you. You could be an actress or a model—"

"I want to be a seamstress," she said. "Make the fancy costumes like Elizabeth Taylor's in *Cleopatra*. Or Audrey Hepburn—can you imagine? Making dresses for Audrey Hepburn. Or suits for Rex Daniels, or I don't know, cloths for a table in the corner of the screen. Anything. I'll do anything, you know? But I think out there, Hollywood, Los Angeles, I think that's where I belong."

Kitty was animated like I had never seen her, like a light bulb was glowing inside her head.

"I think," Jenny said, "it's the perfect thing for you. You'd be swell at it."

"Yeah?" Kitty said, sitting taller.

Then I recognized something in Kitty that I knew to be true about myself. No one told her she could do whatever she wanted, in this world. Lots of girls set up their entire lives within the boundaries of what other people said they were capable of, and they were just happy with what they had and never asked for more.

Kitty wanted more.

Work she loved and was good at. Something to feel passionate about.

I wanted that, too.

"Yeah," I said. "I agree. I think it's a great idea."

"Well, don't start moving me out yet," she said. "I need money for the ticket and then a few months' rent when I get out there. But hopefully by summer."

It occurred to me that I would miss her, this strange roommate who expanded my boundaries and forced me out of where I was comfortable.

I took another bite of my sandwich.

"Feel better?" Kitty asked.

"Yes. Yes. I do."

"We're going to need more onion rings," Jenny said.

10

BETTYKAY

May 15, 1968
Today I started in Ward 3. We don't take breaks during the
summer, so I'll be in the psych ward until September. It's real
quiet in there. No news. No radios. In Ward 3 it's like MLK
hasn't been assassinated. There's no war. No cops beating stu-
dents. No election. There are three patients right now. Mrs.
Bastille is my favorite. She carries a baby doll around and asks
for hot dogs. Two patients are drugged heavily. I wheel them
over to the windows where the robins have built a nest in the
cherry tree. I wipe their chins as their eyes follow those birds.

KITTY AND JENNY found me in the cafeteria, where I was
picking at my rice pudding and trying to finish my chemistry homework.

Intestinal components with a pH measuring 8.5 is...
"Your Todd is back," Kitty said.

It didn't register.

"You remember Todd, that fiancé of yours?" Jenny said. "He's outside the school with a crew cut and freshly pressed uniform asking everyone he sees if they know you."

Levels of pH forgotten, I stood up. "He didn't say he was coming." His last letter had made no mention of it, of being done with basic training.

The war wasn't over. It was only getting worse.

I pressed a hand to my stomach but it did nothing to make me feel better. "He's going," I whispered, feeling the tears burning up in my eyes. "He's going to Vietnam. He's going—" I half sobbed, half laughed. This couldn't be real.

Jenny nodded once. "Girl, get it together. You need to smile and tell him he'll be fine. And that you love him and you'll stay true, and you'll write. That's what you need to do. No crying."

"No crying," I repeated, though the tears were streaming down my face.

"Hey." To my surprise Kitty came up and touched my cheeks with rough hands, pushing the tears away. "Stop. Betts. Stop."

My breath shuddered and I felt myself shaking, but I stopped.

"What do I do?" I asked.

Jenny handed me a thick, long winter jacket belonging to Marg Davies—the six-foot-tall nurse from Northern Minnesota—and my own red pom-pom hat.

"I am going to go have an emergency that only Mrs. Hayes can help me with," Kitty said. "I'll shut the door. You put that coat and the hat on Todd and tell him to look down and the two of you calmly and coolly make your way back to our room."

"That's never going to work."

"You'd be surprised. Margaret's jacket has gotten plenty of fellas onto the second floor. I'll bunk in with Jenny for the night but you have to get him out before Mrs. Hayes wakes up. Before first bell."

Jenny nodded in agreement with the plan.

He'd spend the night and I'd get him out before dawn and then he'd go to war.

"Betts," Jenny said. "Don't think about what happens next. Think about what happens now."

"You'll be okay," Kitty said. "You're one of the toughest, smartest girls I've ever met."

I wanted that to be true. Standing with my two best friends, facing down the possibility of losing Todd, I wanted to be smart and tough.

"There is no way this is going to work," Todd said once I found him outside.

He was so different with his short hair. His face was different too, rough-hewed and drawn. I'd never seen him with such cheekbones before. He was a stranger in that uniform.

A very handsome stranger. I was scared and worried but also...

"Keep your head down," I whispered. "And stop talking."

We walked arm in arm up the staircase, and at the entrance to our hallway, I saw Mrs. Hayes's door closed.

Well done, Kitty.

Girls were coming in and out of their rooms like they always were, records playing and the faint whiff of tobacco, which for the first time ever I was sure wasn't coming from my own room, and together we practically sprinted down the hallway to room 212.

I locked the door behind us and allowed myself a breath before turning back around.

No crying. Only smiles. Only confidence.

"I could have gotten us a hotel room, BettyKay," he said, removing the coat and taking off the hat.

"I don't know," I said, hoping my smile was right. "It's kind of fun breaking a few rules, isn't it?"

"Where's BettyKay Allen and what have you done with her?"

"It's me," I said, feeling bolder because there were no rules for me to follow anymore. The world as I knew it was gone. We were in uncharted territory.

I stepped up to him, so close when I breathed my stomach pressed against his, our clothes between us. We did it again, each inhaling at the same time, and I felt our love like it was solid. The ground beneath my feet. The bed behind him.

"I want to marry you," he said.

I smiled and put my hand against his chest. He'd always been strong. Fit. A wrestler and a farmer. But now the body beneath his jacket was hard. A soldier's.

"I want to marry you," I said.

"Then let's go right now to city hall." He grabbed my hands, leading me toward the door.

"How much time do we have?"

"I've got to be back tomorrow morning."

It wasn't enough time, and we both knew it. There were special licenses to secure. Appointments to make.

"I feel married to you," I said. "In my heart."

"I feel the same way. I have since homecoming last year, months before I gave you that ring."

I smiled at him, breathed in. Breathed out. "Let's skip to the honeymoon."

"BettyKay," he said, like he wasn't sure he could believe me. He wanted to. I could feel that now, between our bodies. "You don't have to."

He'd never once pushed. That night after homecoming in

his dad's truck, when we'd been so close, when saying no had been harder than usual and my body under his calloused hand had felt foreign and wild, I'd sat back and didn't even have to say the word. He knew. He'd opened the driver's side door and stepped out onto the dirt road where we'd parked out by Kyte Creek, put his hands on his hips and tilted his head back while I fixed my dress and my stockings, feeling shaky and hot.

My friends told me he was different. Their boyfriends and winter formal dates all pushed and pushed. Mitsy Berkshire had to smack her boyfriend when she told him no twice and he kept trying to get his hand up her skirt.

Not Todd. He'd been kind and patient, and now he was going to war and waiting, or saving myself for our marriage night, seemed childish.

"I love you," I said, drawing my sweater over my head.

Todd sucked in a breath, and I was glad I was wearing the Playtex. It was a pretty bra.

"BettyKay, you don't have to—"

"I know. I want to." He still seemed to want to protect me and I loved him more than I ever had before. "This is how I want to say goodbye, Todd."

He kissed me as sweetly as he always did, and when he touched me, I tried to stay in my body and feel how good he was trying to make me feel. But my brain was cataloging all that I was saying goodbye to.

Goodbye to the back of your neck. And the way you smile. And the taste of your mouth. Goodbye to how you touch me like I'm a sandcastle that might collapse. Goodbye to the weight of your body on mine and the smooth warmth of your skin.

"Are you okay?" he asked, braced over me in my single bed. The moonlight came in through the window, the curtains still open, our skin silver in the darkness. "Are you ready?"

He was, I imagined in this moment, as if I could see the

whole of my life in front of me, the sweetest man I would ever know. The kindest.

"I love you," I said again, and it was the permission he needed to enter me. It hurt. A stinging pull and stretch between my legs and in my heart.

There. I'm yours. And you're mine and whatever happens next, this happened first.

Following Kitty and Jenny's instructions, Todd and I slipped down the hallway before dawn. I walked him to the truck, promised to write, promised to stay true. Promised not to worry. The last promise was a lie, and we both knew it.

"Go," I said, "before I kidnap you and take you to Canada."

"You hate the cold," he said, calling my bluff, like I wouldn't suffer any kind of winter to keep him safe.

He hugged me close and I whispered a prayer against the stiff collar of his uniform. *Keep him safe. Bring him home. Don't, please don't let him be scared.*

Finally, he drove away, and numb, I made my way back up to the second floor. I headed toward my room, the sheets that needed to be dealt with, but all of the sudden knew that I couldn't. I couldn't walk into the room that still smelled of him, with sheets still warm from his body. Instead I knocked as quietly as I could on Jenny's door, and as if they were waiting for me, Jenny and Kitty opened it.

"You okay?" Kitty asked.

Jenny just pulled me into her arms and every tear I held back and every sob I swallowed gushed out.

This, I thought, *this is as bad as it gets.* The worst that can happen. There can't be a pain or a fear larger than this one.

Two weeks later I missed my first period.

11

BETTYKAY

June 10, 1968

My first letter from Todd is full of swear words. The guy wouldn't say "damn it" if he dropped a hammer on his toe and now he's all kinds of blue. He likes his lieutenant, doesn't like the food. And he says it's hot. Actually, he says it's so fucking hot. I kind of like the swearing. Todd says the nurses he's met over there remind him of me. Smart, sweet girls who run the show. I told him to stay away from those smart, sweet girls. I asked if he heard about Robert Kennedy? I told him I was scared. Scared of so many things. Then I erased it. What was my fear compared to his? Instead I told him that we followed our patients around for a day, writing down everything they did, and Nurse Bouchet said my charting was so good, I could be a writer. Can you imagine? My birthday came and went. Jenny and Kitty got me a cake and a brand-new diary. It was real sweet of them, but I think they saw my heart wasn't in it.

"I NEED YOU to try this on," Kitty said, holding up the furry, polyester minidress she'd made. The sleeves were sheer lavender gathered in a silk cuff at the wrist, kept together with four tiny iridescent buttons.

"I'm busy," I said, flipping the page of my anatomy book. The final was tomorrow and I was having trouble focusing.

"Real quick," Kitty said and reached down to pull me to my feet. "You're the same build as Cheryl and I want to make sure I got the length right."

"When you say build, what are you talking about?"

"You're both chesty."

I scowled at her. "You know, I think you should be giving me some of what people are paying you for the amount of time I spend modeling these dresses."

"Do you?" Kitty said, eyes on the dress's zipper.

"I do." I threw off my loosest, baggiest turtleneck, keeping my body turned away from Kitty, even though modesty and privacy between us had long gone out the window. "Gimme the dress," I said, thrusting my hand out behind me. My other arm went across the breasts that had grown a cup size what felt like overnight.

Chesty. I'll show you chesty.

"You okay?" Kitty asked as I hauled the dress over my head. Kitty zipped me up and I unzipped the only skirt that fit me these days and let it fall to the floor. The dress was tight around my breasts. Everything was tight around my breasts.

It had been seven weeks since that night.

"BettyKay," Kitty said, her voice serious.

"Maybe I need to go jogging with you in the morning," I said, trying to laugh.

"How could you when you spend most mornings throwing up in the bathroom?"

"Don't," I whispered, looking at the little red record player on the dresser. *Don't say it out loud. Don't make it real. If I never talk about it, it's not happening.*

"You're pregnant, BettyKay."

"I'm just…" I ran through all the excuses I'd been telling myself since I'd missed my first period. And now my second was late. "Eating too much at dinner. And stressed, about finals and Todd."

"That's some bullshit, and you know it."

I drew the dress up over my head, crumpled it into a ball and tossed it onto Kitty's bed, which she usually hated. She treated the clothes she made and altered like precious treasure, but now she ignored it. Instead she just stood beside me while I got dressed in my own clothes, my body suddenly so unfamiliar. "Can I have some privacy?" I asked, when I nearly hit Kitty as I put on my turtleneck.

"No. Because you hide behind privacy and you can't hide anymore."

"I'm not hiding." I couldn't hide. My boobs were the biggest thing in this room. I was retaining water everywhere and I was throwing up every morning. I grabbed my books and sat back on my bed.

Kitty put her hands on her hips. "BettyKay."

"I can't be," I insisted.

"Did you use a rubber?"

"He didn't have one. So he…pulled out." But did he? It had been dark and it wasn't like I *knew*.

"That's not always effective, honey."

"But it was our first time," I said.

"Oh my God, you're a nurse, Betts. You know how this works."

I blew out a long breath and felt the ever-present nausea rise up in my throat. This wasn't how things were supposed to work *for me*. I was a good girl. Engaged. We had waited. We had a plan.

"I can't be pregnant," I whispered. "I'll lose everything."

I knew the church I grew up in would say it was a sin to think that way, to not think of this baby as a blessing. Oh, Todd would. Todd would be so happy about this baby and we'd get married and I'd drop out of school and the family I thought we would start in a year or two after nursing school would happen right now.

I would be a mom and a wife.

And never a nurse. But that would be okay because I would have Todd.

Right?

There was a knock on the door and I dried my eyes. Kitty waited to open the door until I nodded. On the other side, Mrs. Margaret Hayes, the stalwart woman, seemed ill at ease.

"What's wrong?" Kitty asked.

"BettyKay," Mrs. Hayes said, wrapping her blue cardigan tighter around her waist if that was even possible. "Your parents are here. I've put them in the sitting room."

The sitting room? My parents? The sentence hardly made sense. What in the world would my parents be doing here?

The words fell into place in my brain like doors slamming shut.

"No," I breathed.

"She'll be right there," Kitty said. "We just need a minute."

Mrs. Hayes and Kitty shared a look, some terrible sympathetic look, and I couldn't stand it. "No," I said louder. Definitively.

"Come on," Kitty said, her hands under my elbows, lifting me from her bed. "We need to go talk to your parents."

"It's not Todd," I said. "I just got a letter from him. It's not him."

"Probably not," Kitty said.

"He's fine."

"I know. But let's just go see what your parents have to say."

Hysteria was rising up in me and I kept trying to swallow it down. It was how I felt every morning, hoping I could just vomit this feeling out.

And then I could get up and get on with my life the way it was supposed to be.

"My parents don't ever have anything good to say."

Kitty hummed and agreed as she walked me into the hall. I could feel the girls standing in their doorways watching me with fear and pity in their eyes.

"Hey!" Kitty finally snapped at a Susan as we walked past. "Have some fucking respect."

At the sound of Kitty's voice, Jenny stepped into the hall-way and then ran toward us. She took my other hand, and together the three of us continued moving forward.

I stopped just outside the door to the sitting room and turned to my friends, the fog I'd been living in clearing for just a second. "They can't know," I whispered.

Kitty nodded. "Okay."

"Don't let them take me home."

"Okay," Jenny said.

"They'll want to take me home and… I'll die there."

"We won't let them take you home."

"It's not Todd," I repeated. "I would know. I would feel it."

"Okay," Kitty said, like she believed me, and for that, for the rest of my life, I'd be grateful.

I stepped into the doorway and saw my parents, so out of place in their dark clothes. Mom wore her best dress and it still looked shabby next to the pretty blue wool of the chairs. They were so small against the tall windows of the sitting room. They only loomed large on the small scale of the farm. In the small scale of my life before nursing school.

"BettyKay," Mother said, and I braced for impact. "It's Todd."

The pain went right through me, through my entire life. Changing everything.

There was everything before this moment and then there was nothing.

He was killed in Trung Luong Valley with three other men. A mortar. I didn't know what that was. Dad tried to explain it to me and I let him. Todd and the other men who were killed were involved in a mission with a name that made it seem important. But it wasn't. Nothing was important.

"You'll want to come home," Mom said, putting an arm over my shoulder.

Maybe it was the grief. Or the shock. The fear. But it felt almost as if she was happy that this had happened, that the world had revealed its cruelty in such a way that I could no longer deny it.

"I can't," I said.

"Course you can," Dad said. "We brought the truck." As if it were a matter of logistics.

"You can tell the school you quit," Mom added. "They will understand."

"I'm not quitting school," I said. "Todd would want me to stay and finish."

"That's crap," Dad said, his face getting red either from the unreliable heat in the sitting room or anger. "He let you have your fun, try this nursing thing on for size, but now you're needed at home."

"For what? Todd is dead."

"Listen here, BettyKay. Your place is at home. Ruth will need you. Your mother will need you." Dad was yelling. He was yelling in the pretty blue room, in this women's dormitory where men's voices were rarely heard. He was yelling like this space was his.

But this place. This life. It was *mine.*

I looked at these two crows, dour and dressed in black, and my life in their home stretched out before me, every dream or wish I ever had ground under their heels.

"We can talk about it in the car," Mom said, again with the arm over my shoulder. Again with the smile in her eyes.

"No," I said. "There's nothing to talk about. I'm staying here."

Dad started up again, and then suddenly there was Jenny, Kitty and Mrs. Hayes chatting away, talking so much and so fast that Mom and Dad couldn't get a word in edgewise.

It was all over their faces, their dumbfoundedness.

Jenny and Kitty took me one way and Mrs. Hayes took my parents the other, going on about finals and visiting hours and how she would take good care of me and they didn't need to worry.

"The girls on this floor are like family," she said.

I called Todd's family. Ruth could barely speak and I felt numb to her condolences, resistant to the way she wanted to share our grief, like it might make it easier. I was hoarding mine, curling up with it at night. It was all I ate. All I drank.

"Was he scared?" I asked Ruth.

"What?"

"Was he scared?" It was the most exquisite of all my tortures, imagining him hurt in the mud, scared and alone, and I couldn't go on anymore not knowing. It seemed, in the middle of the night, if I just knew the answer to this question, I could move on in some way.

"No, BettyKay," Ruth said, like she, too, had spent long hours wondering the same. "They told me he died immediately."

12

BETTYKAY

June 15, 1968

*The funeral was today. There wasn't a body to bury, but they
had a casket and everything. Kitty and Jenny drove me back to
Bluffs and they didn't leave me alone, not even for a minute.
There was a color guard and Ruth took the flag from the soldier's hands and they shot the guns twenty-one times. I felt like
it was a funeral for someone else. Not Todd. Not my Todd. We
had the reception at the VFW and all the talk of the war and
the thick shroud of smoke from the men in the corner, well, it
was so different from any funeral I'd been to. My parents tried
again to keep me home, but I told them I had finals and patients who needed me. Dad followed us out to the car, yelling
the whole way that if I left I shouldn't think about ever coming
back. We got in the car and Jenny peeled away from the curb
like a race car driver. Kitty turned and asked if I was all right.
I was relieved. Never having to go back there? A relief. And*

then…we were gone. And Todd was buried. And nothing is
what I thought it would be.

THE DAY AFTER the funeral, Kitty and Jenny walked into
our room and locked the door behind them.

"Hey," Kitty said. "You've got to deal with some things."

"Go away," I said, pushing the blankets up over my head.

Jenny, of all people, snapped them away, scowling down at
me. I closed my eyes to block her out. "Kitty says you might
be pregnant. We're going to find out for sure," Jenny said.

That made my eyes open. "How? You got rabbits lying
around somewhere? I can't go to the doctor at the hospital.
I'll be kicked out of school."

"Good thing I grabbed this while you were here not washing your hair." Kitty pulled from the pocket of her uniform a
stoppered test tube, filled with a red liquid in a stand, a mirror attached to the bottom of it.

"You stole a pregnancy test?" I asked.

Kitty shrugged like it was the least of what she'd stolen
and that this tragedy unfolding in my bed was the least of the
tragedies she'd seen.

It was, admittedly, a comfort.

"Come on now. You go pee in this thing." Kitty handed me
a small plastic trough as Jenny pulled me out of the bed. "Take
a shower while you're at it, and in two hours we'll know."

I didn't need the red rings in the bottom of the test tubes,
reflected in that little mirror, to know the truth. I was pregnant. Eight weeks. But Jenny and Kitty saw those red rings
and swore.

Ah, sorry to burst your bubble, girls, I thought, sitting on my
bed in my robe, my wet hair dripping down my neck. While

I'd been washing my hair, Kitty and Jenny had stripped the bed and put on fresh sheets.

"I'm sorry you are dealing with this on top of losing Todd," Jenny said. "I am sorry. It's more than anyone should have to bear, but you're here now and you need to figure out what you're going to do."

"What can I do?" I asked the question that had been floating around the edges of my grief.

"The way I see it," Jenny said, taking a seat next to me, "you can leave school. Go home, have the baby and come back, finish your degree."

"I can't bring a baby back here. How would that work? Classes and a baby? Besides, my parents won't let me come back. I'd lose the tuition we've paid for this year and if I go home and have a baby..." The door would close behind me and I'd be locked at that farm forever.

"Even if you give it up?" Jenny asked.

There would be no giving it up. If Todd's parents knew I was pregnant, that their son lived on in me... I curled forward over my knees, the pain too much, again.

"An abortion," Kitty said.

"What?" Jenny cried. "Are you out of your mind?"

"BettyKay, look at me." Kitty got down on her knees in front of me. "What do you want?"

Todd, I thought, but that wasn't an answer. It was an impossible wish.

"You want to give up nursing, have this baby and go back to that farm with your parents?"

"No."

I recalled the way this place felt like home to me, how Kitty had said *you're a goddamn nurse* and the way I had sensed that in my bones. There was a life of my own I could have as a nurse.

But not if I had a baby. An unmarried nineteen-year-old

girl with a baby in Bluffs, Iowa? My parents would punish me. The baby would isolate me. That would be who I was for the rest of my life, until some man who wasn't Todd came along and legitimized me all over again.

"You can stay here," Jenny said. "An apartment in town. We'll help. Me and Kitty. They do it in the city all the time."

"This isn't the city. And you're leaving Greensboro after school. Both of you," I said. Vietnam and California. Their futures were bright. Mine was shrinking every second. "And it's not your job to help me. You've both already done so much."

"We can figure it out if you want an abortion."

"Kitty," Jenny said. "It's illegal."

"Not in Canada."

"We're in Iowa and we could all be kicked out of school for even talking like this."

"Then go," Kitty said to Jenny. "I'm serious, go. If you don't know what's happening, you can't get in trouble."

Jenny looked like she wanted to leave, but she was a loyal friend. "You know it's harder for me, a Black woman at this school," she said, talking about the thing that never got talked about. "You know I gotta work twice as hard and we get caught, my punishment will be—"

Kitty stood face-to-face with Jenny. "Jenny," she said, "I can't imagine the things you've had to deal with just to be here. And I don't want to jeopardize any of that. I'm telling you to leave. We know you're a good friend. And if the world was fair in any way, you'd be here."

"None of this is fair," Jenny said. She kissed me on the forehead. "I'll pray for you," she whispered and walked out the door.

"You could get in trouble, too," I reminded Kitty.

"Nah," she said.

I didn't know if Kitty didn't care because she was planning to leave school, or that the idea of trouble never bothered her.

"Hey," Kitty said. "What do you want to do? It's your life. Your body. Your decision. You know me and Jenny will support you however we can."

In the end it was the hardest and easiest decision I ever made. "I want the abortion."

Kitty sat down next to me, her arm around me.

"I don't even know how to do this," I said. "How do we find a doctor who will do this?"

"We work in a hospital, Betts, I think we can figure it out."

Kitty did not fool around, and by the next day, while I was still struggling to keep my breakfast down, she already had it all figured out.

"Tonight," she whispered, sitting next to me in our English class. "At eleven."

"Where?" I whispered back, feeling like the world was moving too fast. Was this a decision I'd made? When had I made it?

My relief felt sinful.

"Need-A-Nap, by the highway."

A rent-by-the-hour motel at the intersection of I-80 and Bishop Road.

"How much?" I asked, knowing it couldn't be cheap. Renting the motel. The procedure. I put my hand to my chest, touching the small bump of Todd's ring.

I'm sorry it's so small, he'd said, slipping it on my finger. *I got the best diamond I could with the money I had. That's why the setting is so plain.*

It's simple, I'd said. *Not plain.*

I'd felt that day out by the river with the wine he'd brought and the picnic he'd made of ham sandwiches and his mother's lemon bars, that the ring was a personification of me. Of us. Simple, but dazzling. True.

Kitty shook her head. "Don't worry about it." She went back to her seat.

At 10:45, Kitty and I snuck down the stairs and into the far parking lot, where she unlocked a dark sedan.

"What happened to the Cadillac?"

"A little showy for tonight's mission," Kitty said. Once we were in the car, she handed me two small white pills. "Take them," she said. "Doctor's orders."

"What are they?" I asked, swallowing them dry.

"Does it matter?" Kitty asked.

Guess not.

"We're alone," I said. "You can tell me who we're meeting."

I expected one of the nurses and had the ring and chain in a small blue velvet bag as payment. In my purse was whatever was left of my Christmas money. Not much, but hopefully enough.

"Joel," she said.

"Your boyfriend?"

"*Gentleman caller* might be a better word."

Kitty shot me a smile that was pure Kitty, all the devil-may-care she had in the world.

"How will I ever repay you?" I whispered, my voice breaking.

"Life is long, BettyKay," she said. "I imagine you'll get your chance."

Kitty parked in the shadows away from the doors of the Need-A-Nap and all the closed and curtained windows. The sounds of the highway were muffled by trees and dark. She grabbed a suitcase from the back seat that I hadn't even noticed and we walked, heads down, to door three.

We'd barely knocked before it was opened a crack and Kitty and I slipped in.

Dr. Joel Fischer was different in the shabby sad hotel room. He wore plain clothes and a tight expression. I could *feel* his judgment.

"You brought everything?" he asked Kitty.

She opened the suitcase to reveal sheets she'd managed to steal from the hospital's laundry room. Kitty pulled the ratty coverlet off the bed and I helped her spread the sterilized sheets over the mattress. Three different sheets. The floor was covered in newspapers.

"She's taken the diamorphine?" Joel asked, like I wasn't even there.

Kitty nodded, and the small white pills still burned in my throat.

Joel, at the hospital, was a charmer. He smiled and joked around, treated every patient like they were a distant cousin he was so happy to see again. Now he didn't even meet my gaze. I took off my skirt, folded up my underwear and lay down on the bed in the way he'd instructed, my bottom right at the edge.

As I stared up at the ceiling, its cracks and water stains, hot tears burned at the edges of my eyes. The pills kicked in and the world got hazy.

From Kitty's suitcase, Joel pulled a speculum and I felt the cold brutal invasion. The Pratt dilator he used to open my cervix. Then the curette he'd use to scrape out the inside.

"You'll feel this," Joel said, his hand against my knee, pressing it out further.

Kitty held my hand, and there was a terrible searing pressure and a pinch, and I bit my lip against the pain.

"There was this chicken we had when I was a kid," Kitty said.

"A what?"

"A chicken. Pay attention." I poured all my attention into Kitty, eyes locked on her bright blue ones. "We had a lot of chickens. But this was a big old hen. Like bigger than any other chicken. And she followed me around everywhere I went. I named it Bertha."

"Bertha?"

"That bird was a Bertha all the way through. She'd roost outside my window and make a fuss when anything came close."

"A guard bird?"

"Exactly. She killed a snake once. About took out my brother's eye."

"What happened to her?"

"Well, she died, of course. She was just a bird."

The gush of gratitude I felt for Kitty was more powerful than the grief and pain.

I grabbed Kitty's hand. "I'm scared." The words—the truest I had—whispered out of me. I was scared we would get caught. That Kitty would get in trouble. The doctor. I was scared I would go through with this and get kicked out of school anyway. That I was hurting myself in a way that would make children impossible. I was scared I'd never love a person after Todd. Scared of what my parents would say. Todd's parents. I was scared the shame would overwhelm me. I was scared of regretting this for the rest of my life.

I was scared I wouldn't regret it.

I was scared of my relief.

"Listen to me," Kitty whispered, her voice and her eyes so fierce, so strong. She leaned down so her beautiful face was all I could see. "What you're feeling, everything you're feeling. You feel it and then you let it go. You hold on to it and it'll break you right in half. You can't break, Betts. The world needs you. I need you."

The world was wobbly and scary, fluid around me and inside of me. "Don't leave me."

Kitty shook her head. "I'm not going anywhere."

Twenty minutes later, Kitty was helping me back to the car. The suitcase empty. The sheets in the dumpster. A Kotex pad thick between my legs.

"There will be bleeding," Joel said to Kitty. "If she runs a fever take her to the emergency room, tell Osgoode she tried to use a coat hanger. Do not under any circumstance—"

"Mention your name," Kitty said. "We know."

"Kitty," he said, "this is serious—"

"Stop. You think we need you telling us what this is?" she snapped and pulled me from the room.

We were halfway across town before I realized I hadn't given him the little blue bag to pay him.

"Don't worry about it," Kitty said. "It's been taken care of."

Jenny was in our room when we got there. "Don't say a word. What I don't know, I don't know," she said and helped me into bed. She had set ice-cold Coca-Cola, Jell-O, a big box of Kotex and a thermometer on the table between the beds. She sent Kitty to sleep in her room, and every so often pressed gently on my stomach, making sure it stayed soft.

The next day, shaky and exhausted, two Kotex pads between my legs, I was back in class.

It felt like a dream I'd had. A nightmare. Todd was real. Missing him was real. So was the grief. But the memory of the pregnancy faded over time, until it didn't feel real at all.

Like Kitty said, it had bent me. But thanks to my friends, I was not broken.

13

BETTYKAY

IT TOOK A month to realize that Kitty was showing up to every class and had joined study groups in the cafeteria. Despite my help, she'd been in danger of flunking out of most of her classes. Her plan had been to coast until the end of August, when she planned to leave, doing just enough that she wouldn't get kicked out and lose the roof over her head.

And now, suddenly she was trying.

It was highly suspicious.

One morning, while Kitty was out jogging, I crept out of bed and to her dresser, where she kept the cash she'd earned making dresses and tailoring uniforms in an old jewelry box.

I opened the box, the music played, the ballerina spun.

And it was empty. She'd been saving for a bus ticket and rent and it was all gone. I checked the rest of her drawers, looking for money or a bus ticket. But there were only her clothes and a pack of Kents. No bus tickets. Nothing.

Kitty? What did you do?

The answer when I really thought about it was obvious.

When Kitty returned, sweaty and panting, I didn't say a word. I didn't say a word as I got dressed. Or when Kitty came back to the room, freshly showered, and pulled out the gray suit she was making for Mrs. Margaret Hayes.

"I need to go into town, you need anything?" I asked.

Kitty, looking down at the fabric and the pattern in her hand, said, "Buttons."

"You have a hundred buttons." There was a jar on her desk.

"Different buttons. The ones she's picked are too dull. The gray needs something flashy. Pink, maybe?"

"You want me to pick out flashy buttons?" My lack of style was a constant topic of wonder and vexation for Kitty.

Kitty laughed and bent back over the gray suit. "Lord no. Save me from your taste in buttons."

I walked a mile along Broad Street, taking the long way to Elm because there was a Frank Lloyd Wright house across from the park that I loved, with its long windows and dark wood. It was a special house where I imagined special people living.

Someone like Kitty, if Kitty wasn't going to Hollywood.

The bravest of the first-year students came downtown for the Sunday roast dinner at Paddy's and the cheap wine they bought with fake IDs. There were a few other student bars. Meyer's Furniture. Personality Dress Shop, which must have been feeling the pinch of Kitty's superior dressmaking skills. The Ben Franklin with its double windows. At the far end of the street, right next to the bus depot, was Quinn's Jewellery and Pawn Shop.

I started at the bus station to find out how much the ticket would cost.

"Heading out for the bright lights?" asked the man with the mustache behind the counter.

"Just want to know how much it costs," I said.

"It's a three-day trip," he said. "Stops in Kansas City, transfers in Tulsa and Las Vegas, and the ticket costs..." He flipped through his schedules and routes book, writing down numbers on a pad of paper at his elbow. "Seventy-five dollars."

My Christmas money covered a bus ticket to Los Angeles, leaving at the end of the month, with a little to spare.

But Kitty had been saving up for rent, too.

At Quinn's I took the ring with the chain from the blue velvet bag, and Mrs. Quinn, a gray-haired lady who did not at all seem shocked to see a first-year nursing student hocking an engagement ring, put in her loupe and held it under the light.

"It's a nice stone," she said. "Small. But nice. I'll give you a hundred."

"That's not enough."

Mrs. Quinn laughed with her belly. "You new to negotiating?"

"I need a hundred and twenty-five dollars."

"Well, the ring's not worth that. But you throw in the chain and those earrings you're wearing and we'll call it even."

I lifted my fingers to the small pearl studs my grandmother had given me for my sixteenth birthday. I wore them every day.

It's too much, my mom had said after I'd opened the present, trying to give the earrings back.

A girl deserves something pretty, Grandma had said, *and Lord knows you and Abe won't give it to her.*

Sorry, Grandma, I thought as I took out the earrings and passed them over with the ring and the chain. I had no idea if I was being swindled but it hardly mattered. I had exactly what I needed.

Mrs. Quinn gave me five crisp twenty dollar bills, two tens and a wrinkled five, more money than I'd ever held in my hand.

I walked back through town, nearly giddy from the power of having done something good and true.

A woman exited the Ben Franklin as I passed, and I stopped, considered the little bit of Christmas money I still had in the blue bag and ducked inside.

On the bottom corner of the button rack I found just the thing. There were five of them, plastic concentric circles stacked on top of each other like big pink nipples. *Ugly* didn't really do them justice.

Five of them cost a dime, and I walked out of there smiling.

Back at the dorms, Kitty was where I had grown to expect her: at the sewing machine with the record player up too loud. I was hit with a pang that soon, she'd be gone, how empty this room would feel without her. How empty my *life* would feel.

Anticipating Kitty's reaction, I slipped the buttons on the corner of the desk.

She jumped like a mouse had leaped out of nowhere. "What are those!" she cried.

"You asked for buttons," I said with a straight face. "Flashy."

"Betts," she gasped like she just couldn't believe how terrible my taste was.

I smiled, unable to help myself, and Kitty was suddenly in on the joke.

"Oh," Kitty laughed. "Aren't you a clever one."

"They are literally the ugliest buttons I could find."

"I'd say so."

"I got you something else," I said and slid the bus ticket and extra money for rent onto the desk. "It's good until the end of the month."

"What—" Kitty stopped, sat so still, staring down at that bus ticket. "What did you do?"

"Me?" I said. "You paid for my—"

Kitty lifted her hand. "I couldn't let you hock Todd's engagement ring."

"And I couldn't let you spend your California money on me. It's too much, Kitty, even for—"

Her pretty eyes were swimming in tears. "For what?"

"A friend like you," I whispered.

Kitty reached out and grabbed my hand, but that wasn't enough. She stood and we pulled each other into a hug as fierce as a hug could be.

"You're going to California," I said. "If I have to pack you on that bus myself. And you're going to go have an incredible life because you're an incredible person, Kitty Simon. I don't know what I did to get so lucky to have you as a roommate—"

"Stop," she said. "It's me that's lucky."

"You're getting on that bus?"

"I'm getting on that bus." She leaned back, dried her eyes. "But—" she picked up the buttons "—I am not using these god-awful things."

14

CLARA

Greensboro, Iowa
2019

I'm not coming home tonight, Clara texted Vickie.

Good, came the response, almost immediately. You should be with your sister. You want me to come? I can help box up the house. I'd like to see Abbie. You okay?

Vickie's understanding was excruciating. When Clara didn't answer right away, the phone rang. Clara hit custom message and texted: Sorry. Can't talk. And then added: The funeral has been busy. I'll call you tomorrow morning.

Clara watched the little dots appear and then disappear, appear and then disappear, and she could imagine what Vickie was typing. You have to talk to me sooner or later. You can't pretend like everything is okay. Why are you shutting me out? But the message that finally came through was:

Sure.

Clara waited for the *love you* that usually followed, but it never arrived.

"Y'all right?" Kitty asked, approaching her on the sidewalk in front of her parents' house.

Abbie had talked Kitty out of staying at the Motel 6, and then of course had to go home and take care of her kids. Which left Clara to manage her.

Classic Abbie.

"Fine." Clara put the phone in her pocket. She was about to walk into her childhood home with Kitty Devereaux, after burying her mother. *Fine* wasn't the right word for what she was feeling. But maybe there was no right word.

"Come on. It's been a long day," Clara said, picking up Kitty's Louis Vuitton bag and taking the steps up to the screened-in porch. "You can sleep in Abbie's old room."

"You don't have a bag?" Kitty asked.

"I wasn't planning on staying." She turned away so she didn't have to see Kitty's reaction.

Clara opened the big prairie-style door into the living room. Mom always joked that her house was a Frank Lloyd Wright knockoff, of which there were a surprising number in Iowa. Lots of wood. Lots of thin, high windows. Stained-glass lamps and light sconces. Levels between every room.

After Dad died, Clara tried to get her mom to move, terrified she would trip over the short staircases between the kitchen and the dining room, between the dining room and the living room. To say nothing of the big staircase up to the second floor.

But Abbie had told her she was being ridiculous.

And Mom had flat out refused.

"I need to warn you," Clara said. "This house hasn't changed much since my father died…"

"That doesn't sound ominous at all," Kitty said. The movie star was unexpectedly funny.

"You'll see."

Dad wasn't a hoarder so much as a collector. A tinker-er. An amateur art lover and avid reader. The man couldn't pass a garage sale without stopping. There wasn't a corner of the house that wasn't filled with watches and music boxes he was going to fix. The landscapes on the wall in cockeyed frames. Piles of books everywhere. When he was alive, there was always a cold cup of coffee balanced on top or a half-eaten piece of toast. Some of the books and a few of the music boxes that would never get fixed were gone, but the rest still remained.

"Are you hungry?" Clara asked, turning on lights and flipping the edges of the rugs that had been pushed askew, probably by the EMTs. "I'm sure there's something—"

But Kitty wasn't behind her. Clara retraced her steps only to find the star still standing on the dark porch that was filled with mismatched mittens, terra-cotta pots and Dad's cross-country skis.

"Everything okay?" Clara asked.

In the moonlight, for a tiny second, the movie star, the legendary beauty, was gone. There in her clothes she was just a regular human, grieving.

Oh shit. Clara wished Abbie were here. Abbie was better at this stuff.

"Hey," she said from the doorway, in the kind of quiet voice the vet used on her old cat when he administered shots. "Come on in and have a glass of water."

"Your mama?" Kitty pulled in a breath that sounded like she was crying. "Was she happy here?"

"Yes. Mom…" The image of her mother sitting in a lawn

chair in the backyard, face tilted to the sun, cup of coffee growing cold. *There's no better place on earth*, she'd often say. "Mom was very happy here."

"And you? Were you happy here, too?"

That's complicated, she almost said. But it wasn't, not really. Or maybe it just wasn't in this moment. She'd been very loved. Accepted and safe. They'd had fun, together, her family. There weren't a lot of families who could say all that.

"Yes."

Kitty sniffed and wiped at her eyes. "Good," she said. "I'm glad to hear that."

Clara wondered if she should hug her. Abbie would hug her, but Abbie hugged everyone, and sometimes people didn't want to be hugged.

"I'm okay. I just…need a second. I didn't think being back here would affect me like this."

"Greensboro?"

"This house."

"You were here?"

"A lifetime ago. Sorry," Kitty said, wearing that smile like a Halloween mask she could take off and put on. It was disorienting to watch her go from shattered back to dazzling. They walked through the porch and into the living room. "On second thought I'll take you up on that glass of water."

"Sure. I'll be right back." Clara took the two steps up into the kitchen and turned on the faucet, running the water until it was cold.

With her other hand she got out her phone and texted her sister.

Where are you?

Putting the kids to bed, why?

You said you'd be here. I can't handle this Kitty thing alone.

Kitty thing?

Abbie

Fine. Gimme ten.

She returned her phone to her pocket, relieved the cavalry was coming.

Back in the living room, Kitty was scanning the pictures on the piano.

"Here you go," Clara said, handing her the glass.

Kitty picked up a picture of Abbie and Clara when they were kids.

"The summer we both lost most of our teeth," Clara said, taking the photo from her and immediately setting it back down. "Mom had to take the corn off the cob for us to eat."

In the picture, Abbie had her arm slung around Clara's neck and they were both grinning, wide, practically toothless grins. It was the day they'd spent at the Tulip Festival and had their faces painted. Abbie was a princess and Clara was a cat. She remembered that night they'd refused to wash their faces and Mom let them sleep in the paint. The sheets had been ruined, but they'd been so thrilled.

"Your mother always said whatever you did, Abbie wanted to do it immediately, too. She would have pulled her teeth out to look like you."

As children they'd done everything together. They learned to walk, talk. They rode bikes and learned to swim at the same time.

Now she dodged Abbie's phone calls.

Clara put the picture face down.

"Grief is funny," Kitty said, like she could read Clara's mind. "The day your mother died I was in the garden. I'd planted roses that weren't doing as well as I thought they should, and when Jenny called and told me the news... I swear to God, the next thing I knew I'd pulled up all my roses. Every last one. And I'm standing here right now without the slightest memory of doing it."

Clara didn't know what to say to that. How to say she hadn't cried, that she was still so mad. That in the two weeks since Mom died, Clara had woken up in the dead of night in a cold sweat, not sure of where she was. Or who she was.

"Abbie's on her way over by the way," Clara said, instead. "I hope that's okay."

"Of course. I hope it's okay with you."

"What does that mean?"

Kitty shrugged. "You two just seem...tense."

"She's mad because I was planning to head home after the reception."

"And why are you mad?"

"I'm not mad."

"You were born mad," Kitty laughed.

"You know," Clara said, the hair on the back of her neck standing on end, "I would think you might understand how a confident woman who is unafraid to say what's on her mind can be mislabeled as mad, and would perhaps, not do it."

Kitty blinked at her and then laughed. "Oh, you're mad as a wet hen."

"Fine. I am. I am mad."

"Let 'er rip," Kitty said, waving her hand in a circular motion.

"Why are you showing up with this grand story of secret friendship on today, of all days? Is this a publicity thing? Or is this about Mom's book? You think now that she's dead we'll sell you the film rights—"

"I don't want the film rights to that book," Kitty said, her outrage sharp enough to embarrass Clara.

Clara bent down and picked up a throw pillow from the floor and then another. The blanket Mom liked when she sat on the couch was on the wrong chair.

"We never even heard of you. We called Jenny *Aunt Jenny* because she was at every birthday and we went down to visit her in the summers. Her boys are cousins to us. My dad and Jerome went on fishing trips. She wrote a letter of recommendation for me for Loyola. And she was there for Mom, during that breast cancer scare, and when those internet trolls doxed our house. When Abbie's kids were born, when Dad died—" Her voice cracked, and she shoved the coffee table back into place too hard and it banged into Mom's chair.

"You're right. I wasn't here like Jenny, but I was there for her. In ways you don't know about. And you're not all that angry about me showing up out of the blue."

"I'm not? Please enlighten me, Kitty—"

"This is about the fight you had with your mother."

Dad's old cuckoo clock that never told the right time chimed, and the anger that had sustained Clara since that fight with her mom abandoned her, leaving her exhausted and weirdly nauseous.

Kitty was right.

"I'll take your bag upstairs and change my clothes. You can make yourself at home," Clara said, ending the conversation. She stopped on the first step, her hand on the newel post, worn smooth over the years. "My sister is on her way over here and she doesn't know."

"About what?"

"The fight," she said. "What Mom told me."

If Kitty had a reaction to Clara keeping that kind of secret from her sister, she didn't show it. "And you think I'm going to tell her?"

Clara laughed. "I've known you for four hours and it's been nothing but secrets coming from you. So yeah. I think you're going to tell her."

"Oh, honey." Kitty bent to look at Mom and Dad's wedding picture at city hall. "I've kept much bigger secrets than yours."

15

ABBIE

ABBIE PARKED IN the drive and took a deep breath, shaking off that fight with Ben.

Lord, that man sure knew how to pick his moments. Wanting to tell the kids? Now? Like the day hadn't been awful enough.

"How long do we do this?" he'd asked. She didn't have an answer. On a good day she didn't have an answer. On the day of her mom's funeral she *really* didn't.

She went in through the back door that opened right up into the kitchen. Abbie loved this kitchen. It was *exactly* what a kitchen should be. Soft overhead lighting. Warped oak floors from the time the pipes froze and burst when they were in Florida. Cockeyed cupboards. A fifteen-year-old stove and a three-year-old fridge covered in her children's art and appointment cards for doctor's offices. There was a big window over the sink and all kinds of figurines and dishes and failed sprouting attempts cluttered along the wide windowsill.

"Abbie?"

Around the edge of the fridge she saw Kitty sitting at the kitchen table. By herself. A cup of tea steaming in front of her.

"Hi!" Abbie said, looking for Clara. "Did my sister—"

"In the shower."

Abbie peeled off her coat and hung it with her purse on the hook where she always hung her stuff. "I should have brought over some of the food at my house. We have way too much. I can run back. There's some jelly roll left and pounds of Tater-Tot-and-broccoli casserole. Are you hungry?"

"Abbie, honey, sit. You look after everyone all the time. Just sit. Let me make you a cup of tea."

"Oh gosh, no, you stay where you are," Abbie said. "I can make my own tea. Unless you want something stronger? Mom's usually got some Moscato—"

"I'm fine with tea."

Abbie really wanted that Moscato. But she'd already taken an Adderall a friend had offered from her son's prescription. Only because Abbie was exhausted and rattled by Ben and still had to deal with Clara and Kitty. A little something to get her over the hump. Not a big deal. But a drink on top of the Adderall was probably a bad idea.

She put the kettle back on and puttered, cleaning the dishes in the sink, a cup with an inch of black coffee in the bottom.

After dumping it, she realized it was her mom's coffee cup, from the day she died. All these dishes. The toast crusts and the half-brown apple on the cutting board, all signs of a life stopped mid-living.

"Abbie?" Kitty said softly. "You all right?"

She sucked in a breath, her heart suddenly racing. "How do I box all of this up?" A whole life. Two really. Mom and

Dad, with remnants of Clara and Abbie's childhood. It was too much.

"Clara will help you," Kitty said.

No. She won't.

"Abbie?"

"Clara is going to drift away," Abbie said, stunned to have spoken it out loud. "And never come back."

Abbie's eyes were bone-dry, an effect of the Adderall, but she felt like crying. Like wailing. Forget this tea. She went to the fridge and pulled out the Moscato, splashed what was left in her mug.

"It's always you, isn't it?" Kitty asked from beneath the strange spotlight of the lamp. "Making sure you and your sister still have a relationship."

"It is!" she said, grateful and surprised at the recognition. "Just once…just one time it would be nice if she did the work. If she made the effort."

"Tell her that," Kitty said.

"I don't think she knows how. I don't think she even cares." Clara only saw what suited her. What served her. She made up her mind about something and cherry-picked evidence to support it. "It's been so much worse since our dad died."

Dad had been a magnet, keeping Clara around, and Abbie hadn't realized it until he was gone and Clara went spinning off into the distance.

She sat down in her usual spot at the kitchen table. Kitty, whether she knew it or not, was sitting in Dad's place closest to the door.

"Did you know my dad?"

"Sure. A little."

Abbie didn't expect to be mourning her father so much after her mother's funeral. Or maybe it was because she missed Clara so much and thinking of one always made her think of the other. Or maybe it was *them* she was missing—the Beecher family. The whole they'd been and would never be again. "Wasn't he the best?"

Even Kitty's laugh sounded rich and famous. "He was perfect for your mom. She told me after the war that she couldn't date someone who hadn't gone to Vietnam, but then Willis came along. He was very sweet. Very silly. And he loved your mom so much."

There was a creak on the stairs and Clara arrived, freshly showered, dark hair pushed slick off her face.

"Oh my Lord," Abbie said. "What are you wearing?"

"Only thing I could find in my room," Clara said.

"Your track warm-ups from high school?"

"Still fit," Clara said, running her hands down her trim stomach.

Abbie spent a good part of her teenage years jealous of the way her sister's long and lean body fit her clothes. Abbie adjusted the neckline of her dress. The pin keeping the bottom of the V closed had lost the fight against the power of her boobs. She took after their mom that way, busty and broad-shouldered.

Abbie thought she was over it, but looking at her sister standing there in her old sweatpants and a thin T-shirt with boobs that never caused her a minute of trouble, the injustice of genetics was still excruciating.

"You want some tea?" Abbie asked, hiding the fact that her own mug was full of the last of the wine. "Kettle's hot."

"Actually," Clara said, rummaging in the cupboard where their mom kept the stand-up mixer and big bags of potatoes and onions. "How about this?" She pulled out their dad's special occasion rum.

Grateful it wasn't her who'd suggested it, Abbie drained the last of the Moscato. "Good idea."

Clara filled rocks glasses with ice and gave everyone two fingers of the sweet smooth rum. The rum tasted like icy cold winter days when Dad would take them cross-country skiing out at the Conservation Club. When they got home he would build a big fire and they'd sit in front of it in their long johns. He'd give her and Clara each a tiny bit of rum. *Our secret*, he'd say, because Clara was fifteen and Abbie was fourteen, and Mom would not approve.

"You know what Jenny said to us at the funeral?" Clara asked.

"I can only imagine," Kitty said, completely inscrutable. Abbie noticed she hadn't touched her rum.

"She told us not to let you take our mother away from us."

"That's dramatic even for Jenny," Kitty said, rolling her movie star eyes.

"Jenny hates drama," Clara said.

"And that makes her plenty dramatic. Listen, I can't take your mother away from you. That's impossible and you know that."

Abbie actually wasn't so sure about that, but she kept her mouth shut.

"Why are you here? Now?" Clara asked.

Kitty lifted her mug, one of Dad's old Iowa Hawkeye mugs he'd bought at a garage sale, and shot back the rum. Like she needed the courage. "I need to tell you something. And even though you don't know me very well, I need you to hear me. Really hear me."

Clara stiffened. Abbie longed for her mother.

"Your mom was worried about you. The two of you. She was worried that the distance between you right now will keep growing until you are strangers to each other."

Too late, Abbie thought, sitting next to a stranger in her sister's old track warm-ups.

"You have to get rid of these secrets the two of you are keeping..."

Hold on. Abbie looked over at Clara, only to find her looking back.

"What secret are you keeping?" Clara asked at the same time Abbie said, "I don't have any secrets."

"Wait," Abbie said, "what secret are *you* keeping?"

The darn cuckoo clock in the other room was so loud.

Clara got to her feet and Abbie sat back, aware that this was real. Clara had a secret. A big one.

"This is bullshit," Clara said to Kitty. "You're forcing my hand."

"Well, your mom sent me to make sure you did. You can't keep this on your own, Clara."

Kitty knew the secret?

"What is going on?" Abbie asked, a fluttery panic building along her already overloaded synapses. Maryanne warned her not to mix booze with the Adderall. But she was in it now. "Clara?"

Clara blew out a long breath and then gathered herself. Even in their old kitchen, wearing her old track warm-ups, Clara still managed to look like a lawyer. Calm, cool and distant.

"About a month ago I called Mom and we got in a fight."

"That's not a secret. You fight all the time." Too alike, Mom always said, and Clara would say they weren't and then they'd fight about that.

"This was..." She shook her head. "It was bad, Abbie."

Once, when they were little, riding double on Clara's bike, Abbie on the handlebars, giving directions, they hit a stone in the road and the bike went right out from under them. Abbie skidded across Main Street on her face.

Hey, Clara had said, *it's not that bad.* She'd smiled real big and walked her home, leaving the bike on the sidewalk. Mom took one look at Abbie's face and took her to the hospital. She'd had a rock in her chin and needed ten stitches.

So when Clara said it *was bad*, it was real bad.

"What did you fight about?"

"I don't actually remember." Even as Clara said that Abbie could tell she was lying, but she filed that away for later. "But Mom said that thing about how I pick everything apart. That I'm not happy unless I've ruined something."

Mom did say that about Clara and Abbie always thought it was mean, but it was also a little true.

"And I got on this thing about Dad. I said all these hateful things about how she wasn't a good wife to Dad or mother to me and that our whole life everything was about her and then it… I mean, it just fell apart and I don't even know what we were saying to each other. And I'd take it all back if I could, every single word, but then she said…"

She stopped, her hand over her mouth like she was hoping to keep the words inside. Abbie got to her feet now, too, her body twitching. Electric.

"What did she say?" Abbie whispered.

Clara closed her eyes, pulled in one hiccuping breath and then dropped her hand. "She said Dad wasn't my dad."

"Dad wasn't…wait…what?"

"Willis Beecher is not my biological father."

Abbie's brain was crammed and empty at the same time. A million thoughts. Even more questions. And the only one that came out was:

"Then who is?"

Slowly Abbie and Clara turned to look at Kitty Devereaux, luminous in Mom's old kitchen.

"Sit down, girls. Your mother had some secrets of her own and it's time you heard the story she never told you. From the beginning."

Part
Two

16

BETTYKAY

Greensboro, Iowa
1969

November 17, 1969
The weather finally turned yesterday and the air tastes like winter. Gardens are full of dead plants and the boys don't play football in the meadow like they did last week. Winter is coming and after tomorrow rotations are officially over for me. I have one more shift on at the hospital and then my boards and then... done. Mom isn't even asking if I'll come home for Christmas this year. Denise tried to set me up with one of Carl's friends. Again. I keep telling her to stop and she keeps telling me that if I wait too long on the shelf that's where I'll stay. I couldn't even imagine putting my lips on another man. Todd was the only man I ever kissed. What if I'm kissing weird? Doing it all wrong and I don't even know?

Kitty's gone. Jenny's about to leave. I remember when coming to Greensboro felt so brave, and now I'm too chicken to go on a date. Maybe I'm more like my mom than I thought. Everything seems to be changing. Except me.

DIANA ROSS WAS singing about that mountain as I made my way through our very crowded room to get to the open window. I stepped out onto the roof and crab-walked over to where Jenny was sitting near one of the old chimneys, wearing one of my worst efforts at knitting wrapped tight around her body. Her hair was in a perfect round cloud around her head, and she'd ditched the cat-eye glasses for square gold frames.

"You know that bon voyage party in there is for you," I said, collapsing next to her. From my coat I pulled two cold cans of Coors.

"Where in the world did you get this?" she asked, because Coors was hard to come by outside of Colorado.

"A very grateful trucker brought me some after his surgery last month."

"The hemorrhoid surgery. I'm drinking hemorrhoid beer?"

"We don't need to get into details. Just say thank you." I smiled, trying hard to feel the happiness that I knew her and not the grief that she was leaving.

"Thank you." Jenny popped her can and took a sip. I did the same. "I appreciate the party you all are throwing me. I just appreciate the peace and quiet out here a little bit more."

"Donna brought her chocolate mayonnaise cake."

"Well," Jenny said with a laugh. "That changes things a little."

Chocolate mayonnaise cake was Jenny's idea of a party. Some things never changed.

"I told her to save a piece for you."

"You figure out where you're going after graduation?"

After Todd died, I threw myself into school with so much force that I had all the credits to graduate half a year early with Jenny. She and I were officially done with rotations and everyone else in our class would be done in May.

"I'm taking that apartment on Fern with Denise." Two bedrooms with a furnished living room. Denise wasn't my first choice as a roommate but it wasn't like I had a bunch of options. Jenny had been my roommate since Kitty left, but she was heading off to officer training with the Army Nurse Corps. A couple other girls would be joining her once they graduated in the spring. Kitty was in movies now, actually *in* them, not just dyeing fabric. Susans #3 and #4 were planning to go back to their hometowns to work in family practices.

I felt like the last one standing. Well, me and Denise.

"You don't sound too excited," Jenny said.

"I am," I lied. Because the truth was, I didn't know how to do this without Jenny or Kitty. I didn't want to be roommates with anyone else. I didn't want to be left behind.

"It's not too late you know," Jenny said.

"So you've been saying."

"The war is winding down, boys are being sent home. By the time we get there it might be over."

Todd had said the same thing, but I kept my mouth shut.

"You'd be good at it. That's all I'm saying," Jenny said, then zipped up her mouth and threw away the key.

"You're not scared?" I asked. "I know you're putting on a good front out there, but it's just you and me right now. And I hate to think you're scared and keeping it to yourself, because it's not like I'd judge you or try to talk you out of anything."

"I'm not scared," Jenny said in a quiet voice. She pulled at that ugly sweater with the lopsided arms and the big thick orange wool. I'd knitted that thing while watching *General Hos-*

pital during my break. There was a lot of Lee and Meg in that sweater. "For one thing, I'll be wearing this sweater as armor."

"It's not going to save your life," I laughed.

"I don't know. Not even the moths can get through it."

"If I could knit you an actual sweater of armor I'd do it in a heartbeat."

"I know you would," she said, pushing her shoulder against mine. "Vietnam feels immediate. And necessary. What nursing is, at its foundation, for me. Forget racist Mr. Jenkins in post-op with his in-grown toenails."

"Mr. Jenkins can suck an egg."

"Bedpans and Jell-O and dirty bottoms."

"They have dirty bottoms in Vietnam, too."

"Yeah. I imagine they do," Jenny laughed. "But no. I'm not scared. I'm excited. For the first time since coming to this school, I'm actually excited about nursing."

It was because nursing had always been her second choice. Second choices had a way of being unsatisfying.

"You should have been a doctor," I said.

"Woulda, shoulda, coulda."

I tipped my can so it tapped the edge of Jenny's and we both took a sip.

"My dad called."

I turned, mouth agape. "When? What did he say?"

"This morning." Jenny toyed with the edge of the can. "He said he was proud of me."

"Oh, Jenny."

"He wasted years not talking to me. Awkward Christmases and breaking my mother's heart. And the day before I leave he calls?" She shook her head.

"You're mad at him."

"I'm going to war, Betts. I just wish he didn't waste time being sore he couldn't change my mind."

"I could have told him he didn't stand a chance of that."

"We're so alike. Me and my dad," she whispered. "I'm stubborn like him. Full of pride. Convinced I know best. It scares me sometimes."

"You're not like him, Jenny." I put my hand on her knee. "You're not."

We took sips of our beer. The record inside changed to The Rolling Stones and the volume went up.

"How are you going to resist all those handsome men in uniform?" I asked, trying to lighten the mood, and she laughed, tilting her head up at the stars. "You can't avoid the opposite sex forever."

"Oh, you're one to talk. When are *you* going to stop avoiding the opposite sex?"

"Touché," I said, and we both laughed. I wanted Jenny to be swept off her feet by a good man who understood her ambitions. She deserved that.

"You working tomorrow?" Jenny asked.

"Last day in Labor and Delivery." Last day for everything. After tomorrow I had a month off until my boards. I was standing at the edge of four weeks with nothing to do but study and move in to my new apartment.

Jenny's eyebrows were raised over the edge of her glasses. "And how is it going with Dr. Fischer?"

I shook my head. No change. He was flat-out mean to me. Condescending. He yelled at me in front of other nurses and students. Working with him was an exercise in humiliation.

"You should report him."

"You're one to talk." Whatever harassment I had encountered was garden variety compared to what Jenny had faced over the years. I had urged her to report the worst of the racist doctors, nurses or patients, but she never did.

You think reporting it will change anything? she'd said. *I'll get called a troublemaker and it will only get worse.*

"I am leaving this place behind. You're going to be working with that man. Kitty left and he's been taking it out on you for two years."

"I don't know if that's true," I said. But it certainly did feel personal. I thought it had more to do with how he'd risked his career to help me, but whatever it was, Dr. Joel Fischer was the only doctor in that hospital who made it clear he did not like me.

I was a good nurse, top of the class right behind Jenny. All the other doctors and nurses liked me. There was no reason for Dr. Fischer to treat me like I'd failed first-year Fundamentals of Nursing.

"Besides, I'll be in Emergency," I said.

"Right, and Labor and Delivery never crosses paths with Emergency?"

Having the promise of a job after I passed my boards in my first-choice department at St. Luke's Hospital should have thrilled me. Gainful employment in the prettiest place I'd ever been, and all that. But working in the same building with Dr. Fischer was a dark cloud.

"You should clear the air," Jenny said.

"I should."

Jenny laughed and I had to smile. I wouldn't clear any air and we both knew it. I had a real aversion to rocking the boat.

"How is our movie star doing?" Jenny asked.

"Good. Her premiere is in two weeks."

"That girl," Jenny said with a fond shake of the head.

"She got some part in a new movie with Rex Daniels."

Jenny wrinkled her nose.

"Rex Daniels doesn't do it for you?" Because he seriously did it for me. The life Kitty was living out in California was so thrilling, so different. It made my life look a little gray in comparison.

"Old cowboy types? Gimme Mr. Poitier all day long. So, you going? I know that girl offered to get you there and make you a dress. If I wasn't shipping out to officer's training, I'd be on my way to Hollywood right now."

"She did. And I don't know. I have the boards next month and I should study."

"Girl, you have every opportunity in the world and you're going to stay right here in Iowa." It wasn't a question or even a judgment. It was just a fact.

"I like Iowa."

"I know you do, now, come on, I need to let some other people cry on my neck and say goodbye to me." Jenny finished her beer and crawled back down through the open window toward the sounds of friends and classmates and soon-to-be coworkers having a good time.

I finished my beer and stayed right where I was, watching the clouds float over the moon.

At the end of a long shift, I passed by the Labor and Delivery doctor's lounge and saw, through the cracked door, Dr. Fischer in one of the armchairs, a cigarette in one hand and a pen in the other, working on the Sunday crossword. Before I changed my mind, I knocked lightly on the door.

"Dr. Fischer?"

He glanced up, saw me and glanced back down at his crossword. "Everything all right with Ms. Claiborne and the baby?"

"The baby is feeding every two hours. Ms. Claiborne still hasn't had a bowel movement and I gave her some stool softener."

"Fine."

I didn't move and Dr. Fischer looked back up at me. His gaze was absolutely withering. "Is there something else?"

"I just… I…this is my last day in Labor and Delivery and I wanted to thank you."

"You're welcome," he said, dismissing me.

"But I also wanted to tell you that I will be working in this hospital in the emergency room."

"So I've heard."

"And whatever…" *Oh Lord, what was the right word? Beef? Bad Blood? Resentment?* "…personal problems there might be—"

He smacked the paper down on his leg and I stopped talking, my heart pounding so hard I could feel it in my eyes.

"Do you know what I see when I look at you?" he asked, and for a moment I was struck dumb by the bluntness. "I'm asking you a question."

"Kitty?"

He laughed without any humor. "No. I see what Nurse Bouchet would call a bad soldier." My spine stiffened at the same time my stomach curdled. "You don't listen, Miss Allen. You follow orders only when you agree—"

"That's not true?"

"The Cesarean last year? The twins born in March? And those are only in my rotation. There was the appendix with Dr. Osgoode." He started to tick off his fingers. "Mr. Jenkins's infected toe."

"Those were—"

"All times you decided you knew best."

That was hardly true. I was a student with no power, and he was a doctor with all of it. I couldn't make a decision or administer a drug. I barely *talked* to the doctors. Yet he remembered every time I'd asked the nurses for clarification or reminded the doctors of a drug allergy or, sure, in the case of the twins, waited too long to call the nurse to call the doctor in to administer the scopolamine/morphine cocktail to induce a twilight birth.

"She didn't want to be under for the birth."

"That's not your decision."

"It wasn't. It was hers."

"It's not her decision, either. I am the doctor, Miss Allen. I know best."

I forced myself to keep my mouth shut. You could not argue with a doctor who believed he was God. I knew that. Every nurse working knew that.

"Do you know what is the most important quality in a good nurse?"

My answer to that question was also irrelevant so I didn't respond.

"Trustworthiness. And I don't trust you. So, in my mind, that makes you a bad nurse."

I stepped back and my shoulder hit the doorjamb, his words hitting me where I didn't even know I could be hurt. Did other doctors feel this way about me? Did the women I worked with?

Was I a bad soldier?

The hospital PA system crackled to life. "Paging Dr. Fischer to Emergency. Paging Dr. Fischer to Emergency."

He stubbed out his cigarette and I ducked as far out of his way as I could.

"You're coming with me," he said as he walked past.

"My shift—"

"You're coming with me."

We were met by Head Nurse O'Neill, who spent her shift between all the wards making sure the nurses were doing all right and no wards were shorthanded. But it was midnight and the shift was changing. Some nurses had left and others hadn't arrived yet. It was a scary time for an emergency.

"Mother is thirty-four weeks pregnant with her third child," Nurse O'Neill said, filling Dr. Fischer in as we raced through the ward, our white shoes squeaking on the floor. "Husband says she went into labor last night. He brought her in twenty minutes ago after she lost consciousness between contractions and started to convulse. She lost consciousness and did not revive in the car on the drive here."

"How long has she been unconscious?" he asked, washing his hands at the scrub sink. When he stepped aside, I did the same.

"Most of the drive. Two hours."

"Jesus," he muttered. "The husband?"

"Waiting room."

"Keep him there."

We walked to the last curtained bed. There were panicked hushed voices, and beneath the edge of the curtain was a small puddle of blood, a shoe print from one of the nurses tracked through it. I stopped, a sense of dread in my stomach. Whatever was on the other side of that curtain wasn't good.

"Don't get squeamish now," Dr. Fischer muttered and pushed aside the curtain.

Dr. Billingly, the emergency room doctor on duty, had the mother in stirrups, his hand inside of her.

"Thank Christ, Joel," he said. "I can't tell if this baby is breech. I can't feel a foot or a head." He shifted away from the mother. More blood spilled onto the floor. "There's a lot of blood."

"I see that." Dr. Fischer stepped between the mother's legs and probed her abdomen, his face giving away nothing. "Prep for surgery. Emergency Cesarean section."

Within seconds, the gurney, the mother, Dr. Fischer and

three nurses, including me, were in surgical suite four, robed, masked and prepped with blankets, gauze and a scalpel.

"Scopolamine?" Nurse Rose asked.

"No time. She's out."

The mother's heartbeat was steady, if weak, but a Cesarean section without morphine or scopolamine would be a nightmare if she woke up. But that weak heart rate might not recover under heavy narcotic. Dr. Fischer was walking a tightrope.

"Scalpel," he said, and one was placed in his hand. There was a bright slash, a waterfall of blood. The mother made a sound and went into convulsions. One of the other nurses held her down and Dr. Fischer, from inside her womb, pulled out a purpled baby.

The silence was eerie.

"My God," Dr. Fischer breathed, and for a moment, the baby resting on the mother's legs, he just stood there, frozen.

Nurse O'Neill, at the mother's head, made a quick sign of the cross. I was holding the blankets to receive the child. Normally Dr. Fischer would clear the baby's mouth, smack its bottom, forcing the baby to pull in its first breath and let out a startled and affronted cry. I had seen it a dozen times. But Dr. Fischer handed the baby to me without doing any of those things.

I wrapped the tiny person in warm blankets and rushed over to the baby station. I could feel beneath the blanket the baby's heart beating and the struggle of its body against the cold and foreign sensation of the blanket.

Not stillborn.

"Hello, hello," I cooed and set the baby down on the cushioned scale, unwrapping the blankets to start the examination. "Hello, baby. It's okay. It's..." The words died in my throat.

The baby had catastrophic birth anomalies. More than I

could process. The legs were fused and ended without a foot. The skull had not fully formed in utero.

And somehow, by some miracle, the baby was still breathing. Her heart was beating.

A baby girl. By route, a product of my training, I weighed her.

Four pounds. Four ounces.

Measured her.

Thirteen inches.

Small, but I'd seen smaller.

I've never seen anything like this.

I began the Apgar test but couldn't figure out how.

And still the baby didn't cry.

Dr. Fischer stepped in to examine the baby, his hands and demeanor brusque as he examined eye sockets that had no eyes.

He stepped back, yanking off his gloves to drop them on the floor.

"What do we do?" I asked.

"Nothing."

"She's alive," I said.

"Not for long. Wrap her up, keep her comfortable, but under no circumstances should you resuscitate. That baby is going to die and any efforts to prevent it will only prolong her suffering. Do you understand me, Miss Allen?"

"Yes. Of course." Do not resuscitate. It only made sense.

The mother was stitched up and taken to Recovery, and in the mayhem of that violent birth I was left alone in the surgical suite with the dying baby. She didn't cry. Her hands lifted, like she was reaching for something, but she didn't cry.

"Hey, baby," I whispered over and over again, and the world shrunk to us.

I cleaned off the blood and wrapped her in a warm blanket, put a hat over her head and set her in a bassinet. And still she breathed. And her heart beat.

Nurse O'Neill came back into the surgical suite. "Everything okay?"

"She's still alive."

"My God," she said and again made the sign of the cross. "You need help?"

"I'm just taking her to the nursery now." I started to wheel her out the door toward the nursery when suddenly, the baby went into distress. She stopped breathing and her face turned blue, her body twisted, arms lifting. Out of pure instinct, I grabbed the blue infant Ambu bag from the infant resuscitation kit on the shelf beneath this bassinet, placed it over her mouth and began squeezing the bag, putting air into her body, making her lungs work.

"What are you doing?" Nurse O'Neill asked, appalled.

"I don't know," I said hysterically.

She shook her head at me and I didn't know what I expected her to do, but she took the bassinet and walked slowly down the hallway to the nursery while I worked the Ambu bag.

The nursery was empty and Nurse O'Neill pushed the bassinet into the corner.

"What should I do?" I asked.

"I'll get Dr. Fischer."

I wanted to tell her to stop, that nothing good would come of Dr. Fischer walking in, that surely she and I, a nurse and a student, could figure this out. But I was just a student who'd done something wrong. And she reported to the doctors.

A minute later Dr. Fischer was there, furious and still blood splattered from the operation.

"What did I say, Miss Allen?"

"Not to resuscitate. I know." Tears, embarrassed and angry and so sad for this tiny little soul, burned behind my eyes.

"She's young. A student," Nurse O'Neill said at Dr. Fischer's elbow, urging sympathy.

"I'll expect you to write up a disciplinary letter for her file," he told Nurse O'Neill, who seemed like she might argue but then only nodded. He stepped right up to me, so close he jabbed me in the chest with his finger. "This is what I was talking about, Miss Allen. This is why I don't trust you."

"Just tell me what to do," I said, proud that my voice was strong.

"You'll stay there, with that Ambu bag, until the baby's heart stops. You started it. You finish it." With that, he turned and left.

Nurse O'Neill looked at me with all her years of experience.

"I'm sorry," I whispered, and now that he was gone, I couldn't stop the tears. They dripped off my chin and I wiped them away as best I could with my shoulder.

"I know." Nurse O'Neill gave me a small tight smile. "I'll finish your charts. You're a good nurse, BettyKay. One of the best students we've had in years. Don't let Dr. Fischer rattle you."

It was past midnight after a long shift, and normally I would be feeling every inch of my body. Tired feet and sore back. The headache behind the eyes from not enough water and too much coffee. But I didn't feel my body at all, except for my breath.

In, I breathed and squeezed the bag. Out, and I released the bag. The baby's tiny chest lifted and fell. All the time I could see her heart pounding low in her belly, where it shouldn't be.

I forced air into lungs that were not formed enough to breathe on their own, forcing life into a body that couldn't hold on to it.

Breathe in, squeeze, I'm sorry.

Breathe out, release, I'm so sorry.

Breathe in, squeeze, Dr. Fischer is right.
Breathe out, release, my parents were right.
Breathe in, squeeze, I'm not cut out for this job.
Breathe out, release, it's all been a terrible mistake.

I thought of my dad yelling and how the wallpaper in my room didn't change the sound of his voice. Todd dying alone in some place without anyone to hold his hand. I was crushed under every mistake I'd ever made. And everything I'd ever done felt like a mistake. Every decision. Every moment I thought I knew what I was doing.

It took twenty minutes for the heart to stop.

Finally, I wrapped the baby back up and called Nurse O'Neill, who in turn called Dr. Fischer. I stood to the side while the doctor examined the baby, called time of death and left the nurses and the porters to clean up.

"There's no chart," I whispered.

"No," Nurse O'Neill said with compassion. I turned my head just enough that I couldn't see her face.

"The father?" I asked.

"He was told the baby didn't make it."

"His wife?"

"Stable. But still unconscious."

Who was I supposed to tell about that baby's last breaths? The twenty minutes of her heart still beating against all those odds? Surely there was someone who should know. Someone I should tell.

"Go, honey." Nurse O'Neill patted my shoulder. "Go on home. I'll handle this."

I left the nursery, aware as I walked of people watching me. It was a small hospital, and the story of what I'd done, how I'd disobeyed the doctor, would make its way to everyone by the next shift change.

I pushed open the double doors that led to the tunnel between the dorm and the hospital, and when the door closed behind me, the shock and the adrenaline vanished. My knees trembled, but I didn't stop. I didn't slow down. I had done all the thinking I intended to do in those twenty minutes with the baby and the blue Ambu bag. I was, if I could manage it, not going to think again for a long, long time.

I walked right to the phone on the third floor and made a long-distance collect call to Kitty.

"You're going to come?" Kitty cried.

"I wouldn't miss your first real premiere," I said, my voice shaking.

"I can't tell you what that means, Betts," Kitty said. "I've missed you."

"I've missed you, too," I said, covering the phone with my hand so she couldn't hear a sob escape.

"BettyKay, are you all right?"

"Fine. Totally fine."

"I'll wire you money for the ticket," Kitty said. "First class and don't you dare cheap out."

17

ABBIE

Greensboro, Iowa
2019

"WHAT ARE YOU DOING?" Clara predictably hissed as Abbie crawled into the empty side of her double bed.

Kitty Devereaux was sleeping in Abbie's bed under the girl power gaze of a Spice Girls poster. Abbie put clean sheets on the bed and swapped out the old pillows. It didn't seem at all like enough, but it was what they had.

Which could suddenly be applied to so *much* of her life.

"I'm not sleeping in Mom's bed."

"You have a bed in a house five minutes away."

"And miss whatever you and Kitty talk about over coffee? No way. Shove over."

Clara made a big production of moving over and Abbie curled up on her side, facing her sister's profile.

"Clara?"

"I knew you were going to want to talk."

"Why didn't you tell me about the fight?"

Clara pulled her old cat quilt up to her chest. "Because it was awful, Abbie. Because it's this big ugly thing that's kind of ruining my life right now and I didn't want it to ruin yours. After Mom said that thing about Dad I told her to fuck off and I hung up. That was the very last thing I said to her."

Abbie got up on her elbow to look at her sister, who was staring up at the ceiling. Clara hated eye contact.

"I kept waiting for her to call and apologize. Or at least explain. And then I was going to call and apologize and then," Clara shrugged. "She had the stroke."

"You didn't talk to her for two weeks?"

Clara shook her head. Abbie talked to her mom almost every day. Two weeks was unfathomable.

"We weren't tight like you were. But we talked at least once a week."

Why didn't I know any of this? The fight? Clara's dad? Kitty Devereaux? If Mom and I were so tight, why were there so many secrets?

Abbie was embarrassed by this sense of betrayal. BettyKay didn't owe her children her whole life, every part of her past. Abbie even understood why she would keep Clara's father a secret—Abbie would have done the same to keep her family together. To keep the *idea* of them together.

But there was just *so much*, all of a sudden. She felt unmoored.

"I showed up at this funeral so mad at her," Clara said.

"Mom would have forgiven you."

"I know. That makes it worse, somehow."

"Are you still mad?"

"I'm just sad. I miss them. And I miss who I thought our family was."

"*We're* still the Beechers." Abbie had been trying to make this clear since their dad died. "*We're* still that family. *We* are family."

Clara finally turned to her, eyes luminous. "I'm sorry I was going to leave after the funeral. That was awful of me."

"It really was." Abbie lay back down. "But, I understand."

Clara smiled with all the knowledge her sister had of her, of childhood loyalties and teenage dramas, and Abbie felt beneath the grief and the confusion—relief.

She'd *missed* her sister, she missed being known by someone the way her sister knew her. Ben tried, but he was a man. And…well, there were secrets there, too.

"At the visitation I kept looking at all those men we'd known our whole life and wondering if they were my father."

"Oh my God, like who?"

"Mr. Beck?"

"The band teacher?"

"Mom always said she admired his mustache. Mr. Dennis."

"From the park board?"

"He was just such a flirt."

"You should have just stood up and asked."

"Right," Clara laughed. *"Excuse me, show of hands? Who here slept with my mother in the fall of '84?"*

They laughed, and the springs in Clara's ancient mattress chimed in.

"So…this means she must have cheated on Dad," Abbie said, putting words to the thing she did not want to put words to. BettyKay and Willis had been together years before Clara and Abbie came along. They were—to use one of Mom's old phrases—peas and carrots.

"Maybe they were on a break?"

"Maybe she was…" Abbie couldn't say it. "Hurt?"

"I don't want to think about that, Abbie."

"No. I don't, either." Abbie paused. "Do you want to know? I mean… Willis Beecher was your dad in the only ways that mattered. If Kitty has information to the contrary you can tell her to keep it."

That would be Abbie's vote. She liked the status quo. Worked hard keeping it.

"I could do that."

Yeah, she wasn't going to do that, Abbie knew. If Kitty hadn't begged exhaustion tonight, Clara would still be grilling her, trying to get to the part of the story about Clara's biological father.

"Willis Beecher *was* my father in the only way that mattered. But, this isn't just about who my dad is." Clara rolled over to face her. "It's about who our mom was? Think of everything we've learned just today. My dad. Kitty. California? Quitting nursing? What else didn't she tell us, Abbie? And *why*? Aren't you curious?"

Abbie couldn't tell her sister she was scared. That she liked everything the way it was. She didn't mind a few secrets if it kept everyone happy. But Clara wouldn't and had never understood that.

The room got soft and quiet again, but Abbie was wide-awake from the Adderall. She tried to remember the last time she and Clara had been in this house together. Last summer. Mom's birthday? She and Vickie had come for the night.

"Hey, Clara? Why isn't Vickie here?"

"I told you—"

"Clara, I'm your sister. I know when you're lying."

Clara plucked at the edge of the quilt Mom had made when Clara was deep in a cat phase. "She wanted to be. I told her to stay home."

"Why?"

Clara flopped over on her back. "She wants to get married. Have a baby."

"What? Clara, that's…isn't that great?"

"Can you imagine me as a mom?" Clara craned her neck to look at Abbie.

"Of course I can. You'd be so good at it." A mom lion. Fierce with love.

"That's exactly what Mom said, but I work too much."

"So stop."

"Mom said that, too."

"Did the fight with Mom start because of Vickie?" Clara always put so much weight on what their mom thought, and when Mom's opinion didn't agree with Clara's, the arguments started. She could imagine Clara going to Mom expecting her to say, *But your job is so important to you.* Or, *Not every woman needs a child to be happy.* And being angry when the opposite had happened.

"Yeah," Clara said.

Abbie didn't know if being a good sister meant validating Clara's feelings or changing her mind. But Mom was right, Clara would be a good mom.

The house groaned in that familiar way, comforting almost. Clara yawned so big her jaw made a sound, and Abbie resigned herself to lying awake staring at the ceiling.

"Mom loved you," Abbie said.

"I know. And I loved her. It just hurts that I can't tell her how much I loved her. And how sorry I am."

Abbie turned off the light and curled up on her side, facing her sister, and Clara did the same, facing her.

"I'm glad you're here," Clara said.

Abbie forced herself not to react. To play it cool.

"Me, too."

CLARA

Clara's internal clock was set to sunrise and so, despite the late night and the emotional hangover, she was up early and coaxing coffee out of her mom's ancient Mr. Coffee. Outside the window her dad's bird feeder was doing brisk work feeding the squirrels who had learned how to distribute their weight on the long windmill arms to access the dried corn without sending the whole thing twirling.

It was, as it had been since Betts got it for him for Christmas twenty years ago, hilarious. Willis named the squirrels and bought them big bags of dried corn from the Farm and Fleet on Main Street. He sent Clara videos, the sound of his laughter always a welcome soundtrack.

Missing him was a fist around her chest, and she turned away from the squirrels as the coffee maker hissed and then beeped. She should call Vickie. She'd be coming back from her workout, sitting down to one of her neon green breakfast smoothies.

Your father is still your father, she'd said after that fight with Mom. *Blood is irrelevant.*

But lies aren't, Clara had said, outraged and reeling. She was still reeling, but the outrage was long gone, hollowing out a path through her on its exit.

Now she just wanted to know. Who was her dad?

And really? Who was BettyKay Beecher?

Clara's parents shared the wood-paneled office, nestled in a dormer at the back of the house. An old computer sat on a wide desk cluttered, as ever, with bills and notices and letters and newsletters for food co-ops and Fair Fight and Planned Parenthood and a dozen other organizations. Dad's original Woodstock poster was framed on the wall, along with his Marine Corps and POW/MIA flags that had hung outside their house for decades. In the corner, by the window and next to a lamp, was a leather chair with a good ottoman in front of it and a basket of yarn, full and unused for quite some time, to its side. Mom was a terrible knitter but very dedicated to it.

It was an office for two aging hippies. Mom would sit in her chair. Dad would sit at the desk. And their world spun round.

On the low wooden shelf that ran the length of the wall between the chair and the door were dozens of Mom's diaries. Hardback, wire bound. Fancy leather portfolios. Cheap composition notebooks from Walmart.

Growing up they'd been commonplace, not a single thing mysterious about them, and because they were so ubiquitous, they were uninteresting. Because they were Mom's, they were boring. Because moms were boring, weren't they?

Did Clara ever tell BettyKay she was a good mom? She'd like to think she did. Before the fight. She liked to think that she'd told her mom in a million different ways how thankful she was that BettyKay Beecher had been her mother. How loved and safe she felt growing up in this house.

She wiped her nose on the collar of her T-shirt and sat down in front of the diaries.

The diaries weren't off-limits growing up. There'd been no rules that they couldn't read them. But there'd been no invitation, either. And digging into them now, after Mom was gone, in an effort to find out what else she'd been keeping from them…well, it didn't feel great.

Should I wait for Abbie? she wondered. And then recognized her own stalling tactic.

So? Where to start? She pulled out the first one. A diary with a sleeping cat on it, kept shut with a snap. She opened it.

Dear Diary. I got you for my birthday from Judy VanVlack. What do people usually write in diaries? I'm in grade 5. My best friend is Judy VanVlack because we are peas and carrots. John Bisk is in my class. He's awful.

Clara smiled and slid it back into its spot. She slid out the last one.

December 12, 2018
Another Christmas without Willis. Jenny said we should plan a trip somewhere. Two old widows. When Jerome had that heart attack in 2009 I'd offered her the same thing. A trip away from all her grief, but she'd just wanted to be alone in the home they'd made.

And I didn't understand that at the time because Willis was alive. But I understand now. I told her we'd go someplace in the spring. I got her to consider going out to California to see Kitty. Which is a small miracle and the idea of it made me feel something besides grief.

Oh, the girls are trying so hard. Abbie in particular. She's baked and decorated and brings the kids over for hot chocolate and I want to tell her to stop. I want to tell the whole dang world to stop. I'm tired. Clara came home and offered to help clean up some of Willis's "treasures." I didn't have the heart to tell her I'd tried and tried to throw some of that junk away and I can't. She started and she couldn't, either. Sat down on the living room carpet and tried not to cry. That girl. She worries me sometimes. They both do, in their own ways. Abbie thinks she's got the world fooled. And Clara thinks she's got the world licked. That's the two of them and it's been the two of them since they were born. I wish they could see how much they need each other.

I wish my husband was here.

Clara closed the diary and pressed it to her forehead. Her sharp sob came out as a laugh.

She'd spent years of her life thinking her mother didn't really understand her. And in this moment she couldn't remember why. Because they were so different? Because she liked money and fancy cars? Because of a thousand superficial things?

No one knew her like her mom. Except maybe Vickie. Which only made the way she was pushing her away worse.

Looking through these diaries wasn't supposed to hurt like this. But now that her anger was gone all she had was her grief, regret. God, she'd wasted a month holding a grudge against her mom, and years before that believing she was too busy for her family.

Too important.

Looking at all these diaries, she was choked with embarrassment and sorrow.

She could stop. Go get Abbie, ask her to go through the diaries because she was so much better with this stuff, feelings.

If Vickie were here Clara would say to her: *You really want to have kids with me? Look at how I run away from emotion. From pain.*

But then she thought of the story Kitty just told them about Mom and the newborn and the blue Ambu bag. How scared she must have been, how brave. This moment, sitting in front of a stack of diaries, was nothing like that moment.

She was a Beecher. It was time to act like one.

She took out a notebook from the middle of the row.

September 8, 1967
Tomorrow my whole dang life is gonna change. My mom hasn't spoken to me in a week and Dad promised to take me to the bus stop tomorrow morning after chores, but he's broken that kind of promise before. Todd says I can ring him, even at 6 a.m., and he'll give me a ride. What a guy. I don't think I'll sleep but I better try.

Mom's first year in nursing school. Clara flipped through the rest of the book, picking up on Kitty's name used liberally throughout. How strange to realize that Kitty was right there, hiding in plain sight. Which only made it stranger that her parents kept her a secret. Had that been Mom's doing? Or Dad's?

Kitty had said Mom left nursing school before her boards to live with her in Hollywood, so Clara ran her finger to the diary right before Vietnam and removed a hardback with a sun embroidered on the cover, the pages yellowed with age. She turned to the very last entry.

November 19, 1969
Jenny left. Snuck out at dawn so there wouldn't be a big scene. I knew that was the way she'd choose to go, so I was at the bus station to meet her with a thermos of coffee and a bacon and apricot jam bun from the cafeteria. She thanked me. I hugged her as hard as I could and just like Todd, I promised to write. I smiled and waved as the bus pulled away and then sat down and cried my eyes out. I've never felt so alone.

Clara next drew out the infamous Vietnam diary, a blue wire-bound notebook BettyKay had bought at an airport.

July 4, 1970
I've learned how to march in officer's training. Isn't that ridiculous? What will marching do for me in Vietnam? For any of us? The girls I've met are interesting. Some are fun. Some are intense. And all of us are here for different reasons. Patriotism. To get nursing school paid for. To do good work where good work is needed. Barbara says she's going for adventure and I believe her. I've passed around Jenny's advice and we're all bringing heating pads to dry out our beds so the mildew doesn't get in our sheets, loads of tampons and perfume. I'm scared, I can admit that here, in these pages. I'm scared I've made a mistake. I'm afraid Kitty is right. I'm afraid instead of forgetting the man I'm

doing all of this to forget, I will only miss him more. I'm scared
I'm not the person I wish I was and Vietnam will break me
apart. I've started to pray and I imagine that would make my
mother happy, when nothing I've done has. I'm praying for the
end of this war. I'm praying for Jenny and all these other nurses
who are going where so few people would choose to go. I hope
someone will be praying for me when it's my turn.

There were nine months missing before Vietnam. Clara
put that diary back and went searching for November 1969–
July 1970.

Nowhere. Not in any of the journals.

And what man was she trying to forget? Todd? Going to
Vietnam to forget a man who'd died there seemed like bad
logic.

"Clara?"

It was Abbie walking down the hallway.

"In here," Clara called, not bothering to keep her voice
down so she didn't wake the actress in the bedroom directly
above. The sooner Kitty was awake, the sooner they could
get some answers.

"Hey," Abbie said, her hair a wild mess. She had mascara
around her eyes and was wearing a Garfield sleep shirt, and
Clara felt a giddy stab of affection for her sister. Abbie was
Abbie, a person could count on that, and that wasn't something you could say about everyone.

Abbie's face fell when she saw the stacks of diaries. "What
are you doing?"

"Looking for a few answers," she said.

"About your father?"

"About our mother. There are nine months missing. Jenny
goes to Vietnam and then nine months later Mom's in officer training."

"Isn't that the time Kitty says she was in Hollywood, with her?"

"Mom has kept a diary her whole damn life, Abbie. Why would she stop? Or," Clara said, "if she did keep a diary, where is it? Did she destroy it? And why would she? And in the Vietnam diary she said she went to Vietnam to forget a man. Who? Why was that taken out of the book? What is she hiding?" BettyKay had published the Vietnam diary five years after the war ended, but all the names in that version had been changed except for Mom's. Clara never considered who her mom might be protecting.

"It's too early for you to be in full lawyer mode."

"Is Kitty awake?" Clara asked.

"Her bedroom door was open when I woke up and I knocked to see if she was awake." Abbie shook her head and handed Clara a piece of paper. "She left sometime this morning. Before we were up."

One of the great benefits of her law degree and years of practice fighting on behalf of people who didn't need all that much help was that Clara was able to compartmentalize her emotional reaction to just about anything. So, while part of her was dreading the contents of this note, it did not slow her down one bit.

Girls, the note read.

I am so sorry but I've been called back to Los Angeles for an early meeting. I called a car and left so I would not disturb you. I know you must have more questions and I have answers that I would love to share with you, but Greensboro, Iowa, is not the place for these stories. There were a lot of ghosts in your mother's house last night and I think I brought them in with me. You have an open invitation to my home in Los Angeles.

Call the number below and a flight will be arranged for you. For your families. Everyone is welcome and all your questions will be answered.

"Is it really...worth all this?" Abbie asked, and Clara's mouth fell open.

"How can you think that?"

"Because I'm sad, Clara," she whispered. "Because we buried our mom yesterday and I'm...scared."

"Of what?"

"Of finding out things that are going to change us."

"We're not going to change." Clara picked up that last diary again and handed the entry she'd read to Abbie. *Abbie thinks she's got the world fooled. And Clara thinks she's got the world licked.* "We're BettyKay Beecher's girls and I'd like to know her half as well as she knew us."

Abbie sighed then blew a giant raspberry and Clara hid her smile.

"Okay, but it's going to be tricky to get away," Abbie said, handing back the diary.

"Bring your family." Clara slipped the diary back in the slot and got up off the scratchy rug.

"I don't...want to?" Abbie grimaced. "Does that make me terrible?"

"Other moms and wives get away from their families for weekends. All the time," Clara said gently.

"How nice for them."

"Abbie," Clara said. "I'm just saying it's not that big a deal. Mom used to do it, remember?" Every few months Mom would go on a trip to some place they didn't much care about, and Dad and Abbie and Clara would stand on the stone steps of the porch and wave her off. The second the car was out of sight Dad would turn to them, eyes alight and say, *Girls, what kind of trouble should we get into?*

There would be trips to Family Video and the rental of all the R-rated movies she never let them watch. They'd order in pizza and camp out in the living room in the sleeping bags with popcorn and ice cream. Bedtime was abolished and doughnuts for breakfast were required.

"It will be a big deal to Ben."

"Why?"

"Because…" Abbie flattened the hem of her Garfield night-shirt over and over again. "It's not like a *thing* or whatever. But we're fighting a lot, too."

"About what?"

Abbie pulled in a big breath and Clara felt braced some-where internal. She and Ben were high school sweethearts. They were bedrock. And as much as Clara might not like Ben, Abbie loved him and had since the spring play her junior year.

"Nothing," Abbie said, with a shake of her head. "Every-thing. You know how it is."

"Are you okay, though?" Clara asked. Abbie wasn't the only Beecher girl who knew when her sister was not telling her the whole truth. Not by a mile. "I know you were drink-ing at the funeral."

"Everyone drinks at funerals, Clara!"

"Methodists don't."

Abbie gave her a sour look. "Don't you start, too. You aren't around enough to judge me."

"Okay," Clara said, putting her hands up. "Well, I'm going to Los Angeles. I know I have let you down as a sister, and particularly since Mom died I've been selfish. But I want you to come with me."

"You do?" Abbie asked like she didn't believe her, and Clara realized how the distance she'd kept between herself and Greensboro had affected her sister. In so many ways her sister *was* Greensboro.

"I do." When she and Mom had that fight, she'd been locked inside her own little world and working hard to shove everyone who might try and help her out of it.

Abbie's easy way with emotions had always been a joke to Clara. Something to roll her eyes over. But when Dad died and Abbie had been able to carry her grief, and Mom's, and tried to help Clara with hers—she'd recoiled. But she could see now how helpful it would have been to lean on Abbie. And how, in the days to come, she might need that kind of support.

"I don't think I can do this by myself," Clara said with all the honesty she had in her.

Abbie's eyes went wide at the admission. "So, what you're saying is you need me?"

Clara laughed. "I need you, Abbie. I really do."

"Well," Abbie said. "I can't let you go to Kitty Devereaux's house all by yourself."

Abbie put her arms around her, and Clara let herself be hugged, even managed to relax into it.

"Thank you, Abbie."

"No problem, Clara. I'm your sister."

18

CLARA

"IT'S SO…RUSTIC," Abbie said, looking out the window as they made their way through eucalyptus-lined hill roads.

She'd been talking nonstop since they stepped on the private jet on the Des Moines Airport tarmac at dawn—Abbie's nervous tick. Clara tried not to be annoyed by it, but she was foggy from lack of sleep and nervous herself.

"I just wasn't expecting it to be so rustic," Abbie repeated.

The driver was silent as she maneuvered the tiny confusing streets.

Out her own window and through the tall pine and privacy bushes, Clara caught glimpses of the city stretched out to the ocean. There were mansions on the other side of all those bushes and gates, but not one of them seemed rustic to Clara. It seemed very rich. Very enviable.

"I heard Jennifer Aniston lives around here," Abbie said. "Does Jennifer Aniston live around here?" she asked the driver, who shook her head. "Right. Sure. Privacy and all that. Sorry. Well, if I were Jennifer Aniston, I would want to live up here. It's so rustic."

Vickie would love this, Clara thought, guilt-ridden about how she'd mismanaged everything with her girlfriend. *I'll make it up to her. A weekend at a resort in Mexico. We'll wear bikinis all day and nap in a cabana…*

"We're here," the driver said, turning toward a large gate that slid open to reveal a home that was half log cabin, half modern glass box, all of it surrounded by a beautiful garden.

They'd been invited, they were welcome and invited, but still, she felt so presumptuous showing up like this. Wearing a Des Moines Marathon T-shirt from 2002, running tights and beat-up sneakers—the only clothes she'd left at her mom's house. Abbie was in jeans and a purple sweater that looked nice on her but was all wrong for the California weather.

As they pulled into the parking area surrounded by potted orange and red bougainvillea, a woman about their age came out the door of the glass box.

"Here we go," Abbie said. "You ready?"

"No?"

Abbie laughed. "Too late."

She threw open the door and said hello to the stranger.

God, Clara thought, watching her sister at work. Abbie was so much like their mom, just catapulting herself into the fray. For years that made Clara roll her eyes, but at this moment she saw the strength in it, the kindness. She was paving a way for Clara to follow.

"Hello," the stranger said cheerfully once Clara got out of the limo. She had black bangs and her hair came to a sharp edge that ended right at her chin. She wore a white eyelet top and sleek black pants. Her shoes were bright red espadrilles. Clara had never felt so rumpled in her life. "Abbie and Clara, it's so nice to meet you. I'm Sophia Kim, Kitty's assistant," she said. "You'll be staying in the guest suite." She gestured to the old cabin part of the building.

"Where's Kitty?" Abbie asked.

"Resting." She smiled. "The flights aren't as easy for her as they once were and she needs an extra day to recover. She wanted me to get you settled and let you know that she would see you at dinner."

"I think maybe…Abbie and I should go stay at a hotel," Clara said. They could shower, she could find a Macy's and get better clothes, meet in the morning when everything felt arranged and set up.

"Don't listen to my sister, she's an outdoor cat," Abbie said. "The guest suite sounds lovely."

That was Mom's old joke and it stung coming from her sister's mouth the same way it always stung coming from Mom's.

Clara wanted to dig in her heels, but Abbie and Sophia were already chatting away like good friends. She pulled out her phone.

We're here, she texted Vickie. The house is stunning.

Cool

You're mad.

I told you I wasn't

It all happened so fast, babe

Clara, maybe you need to examine why you feel so guilty right now?

Clara had let Vickie know about the change of plans, and Vickie was adamant that she wasn't upset about the kind of plans that involved an indefinite extension of time away and a private jet to a movie star's house.

Because I would be mad at me, she wrote back. That was the problem with all of this—she would be furious if Vickie was treating her this way. Like an afterthought. So why the hell am I doing it?

Call me later, Vickie texted.

"Clara?" Abbie stuck her head out the cabin door, her eyes wide with wonder. "You have got to see this."

Inside, the cabin was dark from all the wood, but one wall had a big sliding glass door overlooking a stunning garden and beyond that the rolling greens of one of the canyons, the city and then the ocean. All laid out like a scenic carpet before them.

She could not for the life of her imagine BettyKay Beecher looking down at that same view.

"It's beautiful," Clara said.

To the right was a dining room with a low-sloped wooden beam ceiling that held two old chandeliers, and a giant table with benches down either side. There must have been a million dinner parties there, a thousand glasses of wine spilled. Laughs and tears and good stories circled the room like ghosts.

Clara walked through to the kitchen, shelves full of spices and flours and herbs and seeds in jars with handwritten labels. The fridge and sink were pure 1950s. The countertop pattern seemed to be gray and yellow boomerangs on a cream Formica background.

"Kitty tried to keep this building as original as she could," Sophia explained. "She had the walls rechinked and the windows replaced, the foundation rebuilt, but everything else is exactly as it was when she first started renting a room in the house in 1968."

"Clara!" Abbie yelled, and Clara made her way back into the main room with the couches arranged around the fireplace.

On a funky teak shelf was a record player and hundreds of records, beside it a glass bar cart right out of *Mad Men*. Clara glanced over to see if Abbie had gotten into the booze yet, and then felt guilty for thinking it.

"Look at this," Abbie said, standing at a wall of framed pictures hanging from the log walls.

Photos of people gathered around the dinner table. On couches different from the ones in the living room now, but positioned in the exact same spots. Sunbathers on the front lawn and campfires. Kitty was in some, often with a slight man in impeccable clothes and tasteful eye makeup. Rex Daniels appeared in a few looking grizzled and gorgeous, posing with Hugh Bonnet, the English director Kitty had been in a relationship with for years.

"But look," Abbie said, now a foot away, in front of a different section of pictures. "All these photos of Mom."

There were dozens, and not just of Mom as a young woman, but with that perm she'd had in the '90s, when she'd lost all that weight on Jenny Craig, and even as recent as two years ago.

"Oh my God," Clara said. "Mom's been out here. A lot."

"Jenny, too."

There were pictures of Jenny, pregnant on the chaise lounge. Standing with her arms around Jerome, the two of them so young and in love. She and Mom in fits of giggles while Kitty acted the clown.

"This one," Abbie said.

There, at the center of all the pictures, was a shot of Kitty, breathtakingly young and beautiful in tight, hip-hugging bell-bottoms with stars all over them. The top of her body was painted in flowers and vines.

"It must be from the premiere of that Christmas movie."

Next to her was their mother, who wore a silver sequined minidress with long-belled sleeves and, along the neck, sewn at perfect intervals, the pink buttons that matched her pink suede boots.

The buttons.

Her hair was long and wavy, and she had perfect cat-eye eyeliner. Clara had never seen her mother in eyeliner before. Much less a perfect cat's eye.

"Mom looks so glamorous," Abbie said.

"Mom looks so happy," Clara said.

"Oh my God, Clara, look at this one."

In a black-and-white Polaroid that had no business being framed, Rex Daniels sat at the edge of one of the benches in the dining room. A woman in a gingham shirt tied at the waist was in his lap, arms around his neck, lips pressed passionately to his.

And that picture, more than anything else, seemed like irrevocable proof that they didn't know their mother at all.

19

BETTYKAY

Los Angeles, California
1969

FANS OUTSIDE THE theater smacked on the windows and trunk of the limo as it peeled away from the curb. We could hear their muffled screams from inside the car. There were flashes and pops of cameras in every window.

"Kitty! Kitty Devereaux!"

"Oh my God," I said, looking out the back as we barreled through the yellow traffic lights of Hollywood Boulevard, leaving behind Grauman's Chinese Theatre. "I think you're a movie star, Kitty Devereaux."

As if she couldn't believe it herself, Kitty shook her head, the neon lights turning her hair pink and then green. Her eyes sparkled and went dark. It had been more than a year since I'd seen her, and looking at her, she was familiar—Katherine

Simon in room 212. But she was also Kitty Devereaux, famous actress waving to an audience on its feet.

It was like watching a butterfly splitting open a cocoon, coming out damp-winged and brand-new.

The car left behind the lights of the city and headed up into the dark mountains and twisty tree-lined roads to the house Kitty and Alexander shared, called affectionately The Birdhouse because of the hummingbirds and nightjars that lived in the trees on the hills surrounding it.

I grabbed Kitty's hand, which was a little limp and sweaty. She'd been running on adrenaline and whatever pills she and her friend Alexander took when she thought no one was looking. I wondered if it was still Dexedrine, or if she'd graduated to something else. But Kitty was in a new world now, with new rules, and I kept my worry to myself.

"You were astounding," I told her. "The movie was fantastic."

"It wasn't as bad as I thought it would be," she said with the same Kitty honesty I loved and missed so much. "The gorilla suit was a little much, wasn't it?"

"No." I shook my head. "The gorilla suit was amazing. That music was amazing. You were amazing. *Christmas A Go-Go* is my new favorite movie."

"What was your old favorite movie?"

I screwed up my face trying to think of a movie, any movie.

"That's what I thought," Kitty said, and I smiled at her, my heart in my throat with excitement. She grabbed my hand on the seat between us. "I'm so glad you're here. So glad you came. I can't tell you how much I appreciated having a real friend here for tonight."

"You had a lot of friends at the premiere."

"They're not friends. They're just...people."

Yes. People. People were around constantly. The Birdhouse

was filled with them all the time. Someone told me when I first arrived that the cabin had been a hidey-hole for Katharine Hepburn and Spencer Tracy. I didn't know if that was true, but it was fun thinking it might be.

When I went to bed, the house was full of people. I woke up, and they were all still there, sleeping on the living room floor. They brought food and liquor, cigar boxes full of joints and points of view I'd never heard before.

"Don't you get it?" Alexander had said the night before. "Don't you see how the government has us fighting each other, man? So we won't fight them? They're the enemy. Not the GIs coming back, strung out on dope. Not the Vietnamese being killed by the thousands."

Kitty had nodded. I remembered her at Shakey's saying she wished she could go fight. Go have an adventure. I wondered when her opinion had changed.

"A couple people are coming up to the house," Kitty said, reclining back against the headrest in the limo. The body makeup was smudged now, revealing the pale skin beneath.

"You sure? You look like you could use a good night's sleep." I slipped my hand from hers to find the pulse on her wrist. Still fast.

"For a woman who doesn't seem like she's in any hurry to get back to her job as a nurse you sure are acting like one," Kitty said, watching me with a sideways grin.

"Old habits." I tucked my hands back in my lap.

"You're honestly going to sit there and try to make me believe you aren't going back to Greensboro? What happened, Betts?"

I'd made the mistake, the first night I'd arrived, drunk on one Harvey Wallbanger, of telling Kitty that I wasn't sure I was going back to Greensboro. That perhaps, nursing wasn't for me.

"Kitty," I said. "The whole time we've been friends you've been seeing me out of trouble. Can we just spend some time on you for a change? You just had the biggest night of your life. Hugh Bonnet brought you all those flowers!" I pointed at the flowers on the other seat, a sharp modern bouquet with birds of paradise and some other plant that looked like a purple fungus under a microscope. It wasn't pretty as much as it was striking. And possibly dangerous.

"I never thought I'd feel this way." Kitty giggled, actually giggled. A girlish silly sound from the least silly woman I knew. She clapped her hand over her mouth and I pulled it down. She shouldn't be embarrassed when all her dreams were coming true.

"What way?"

"Like I could do anything."

The limo stopped at the sand-and-gravel driveway of The Birdhouse and Kitty and I hopped out. The driver carried the bouquet and the case of champagne the studio had given Kitty into the house.

"Look at you, Betts," Kitty said as we stood in a pool of bright moonlight. The silver sequins in my dress picked up the light, casting prisms on the pine trees and eucalyptus bushes. "You look like one of those disco balls."

"I feel like a dancing girl." In my high-heel pink suede boots that matched those damn buttons sewn onto the collar of my dress, I did a little mashed potato and Kitty did the swim. Then we both started the twist, and then Kitty grabbed me and we were doing a wild laughing polka on the dirt.

"You're a goddamn movie star, Kitty!" I cried.

A red pickup truck pulled into the parking area, its headlights illuminating our impromptu polka, and we stopped to shade our eyes.

"Don't stop on my account," said a deep Texas drawl as a

man got out. He was tall and lean in a pair of jeans and a work shirt with the sleeves rolled up. I caught the silver of a bracelet and a couple of rings on his fingers.

And the white glint of his teeth beneath a thick mustache. For a whole second I could not breathe.

"Rex!" Kitty cried and ran over to hug the man.

Holy shit. That's Rex Daniels.

"I brought tequila and some limes from my tree," he said, holding a bottle in one hand and three limes in the other. He tossed the three limes to Kitty.

"Betts, this is Rex, he's in the new movie we start shooting in the New Year. Rex, this is my dear friend BettyKay."

"Nice to meet you, BettyKay," he said, shifting the bottle under his arm to shake my hand.

I slipped my palm against his and felt an electric current zip up to my brain and down to my toes, settling in my chest, where it felt like it set my whole body aglow. "Call me Betts," I said.

He had beautiful eyes, blue with green and gold on the farthest outside edge, eyes that I'd only seen on movie theater screens and on TV.

"Call me Rex." To my surprise, he tossed Kitty the bottle of tequila, bowed over my hand and whisked me into a waltz.

After the premiere we lost track of days. Or maybe the days lost track of us. We were marooned on rafts of sunlight and boilermakers, night-blooming jasmine and Lambrusco, and my goal to not think, to not remember the blue Ambu bag, was easy to achieve. If the memory came back, a chill along my spine, I asked for a cigarette and another gimlet. A double.

We spent our days lying on green chaise lounges with yellow cushions, getting pink from the sun.

"Now," Kitty said one time, closing her eyes beneath the big white sunglasses she wore. "Now we're sunshine girls."

Alexander left for work at 20th Century-Fox before we were awake and was back just as we were having our morning coffee. He'd collapse on the couch and tell us all about what was happening on the set of *Escape from the Planet of the Apes*, before his boyfriend would roll in with a few dancers from the rehearsals of the new Fosse film.

At some point, the roommate who lived in the third bedroom was cast in the touring company of *Promises, Promises* and I moved in to his room between the fireplace and the bathroom.

Rex always stopped by with Cuba libres and doughnuts, icy cold beers and hard-boiled eggs. When he walked in the back door we all cheered like he was a hero home from war.

The date of my boards we drank clam diggers out on the chaise lounges.

Rex wore a pair of aviator sunglasses and his shirt was unbuttoned over his furry chest. He leaned back against the cushions, the yellow electric behind his dark hair. His clam digger, heavy on the vodka, held loosely in one hand.

"So, Betts, what do you do when you're not hanging out with degenerates?"

"Are you the degenerate in this situation?" I asked.

"In most situations, actually." His grin was pure charm. I found it hard to look at him directly unless I was a little drunk. He was the handsomest man I'd ever seen in real life, and I didn't even feel disloyal to Todd thinking that. Todd would agree. But my attraction to him felt foolish, conspicuous and probably, to a man like Rex Daniels, unwelcome.

"What makes you think I'm not a degenerate?"

He laughed. "You couldn't be a degenerate if you tried."

"She's a nurse," Kitty said from the lounge next to mine. "Betts is a nurse. Right? Betts?"

Kitty hadn't been applying direct pressure on what I was doing in California and how long I was planning to stay, but there'd been subtle questions as these long sun-drunk days became a week and then a month.

"I was in nursing school," I said.

"You graduated."

"I did," I said.

"You had a job lined up at the hospital. In the emergency room."

"An emergency room nurse?" Rex asked into the loaded silence of the backyard. "That's a special kind of nurse."

"Betts *is* a special kind of nurse." Kitty's words had hard edges like she was daring me to correct her. "She was second in her class, one spot behind our friend Jenny who has gone to Vietnam."

"Shit," Rex said and whistled through his teeth. "Pretty and smart."

"Kitty!" Alexander yelled from the screen door. "Phone for you."

"Twenty bucks says that's Hugh Bonnet," Rex said, and I shook my head.

"No way I'm taking that bet." The writer/director of Kitty and Rex's next film called almost daily, and only wanted to talk to Kitty. If this were the regular world, I'd guess he was keen on her. But maybe this was just how Hollywood worked. Daily phone calls at all hours.

"You should just invite Hugh over," Rex said, eyes closed behind his sunglasses. "He's gagging for an invite."

Kitty tightened the sash on her satin robe and went back inside, leaving me and Rex and the bluebirds, the purple and orange lupine at the edge of the garden.

"You think she minds so much that Hugh is calling?" Rex asked and I laughed. Kitty lit up like a sparkler every time the phone rang. She pretended to be irritated but it wasn't hard to see the truth.

"So, what is it you're not telling her?" Rex asked.

"Nothing," I lied, startled by the question.

"Ah, honey. I can't tell if you think you're a good liar and that's why you're hanging on the way you are. But let me clear something up for you. You're a terrible liar."

I made the mistake of looking at him. He'd taken off his sunglasses, revealing his beautiful eyes. He was laughing at me in such a good-natured way I couldn't take offense.

"I don't think you know me well enough to tell if I'm a bad liar," I said with a smile. Fueled by the clam diggers, I was flirting with Rex.

"Well, here's what I know," he said, crossing his feet and linking his fingers over his bare belly.

I had seen a lot of bare bellies. A lot of men in general over my three years of school. Injured men. Healthy men. Even handsome men. But looking at Rex's ringed fingers on his own skin sent something hot through me.

"You're a practical woman," he said, counting my attributes on his fingers. "You're unflappable. Not a bigot or a snob. You've got a beautiful smile, and I don't know that I've ever met someone as sincere as you."

"Come off it," I said, blushing so hard I thought I might burst. "Maybe you've been in Hollywood too long."

"Maybe I have. But I know the real deal when I see it. And you're a terrible liar, so you might as well spill it, kid."

"I missed my boards," I said, the answer loosened out of me by the flirtation, the very strong clam diggers sweating in the grass. "The test I have to take to be an RN."

"That's what you're not telling Kitty?"

"Part of it."

"And let me guess, no job unless you've taken them?"

"No job."

"Any particular reason you stopped so close to the finish line?"

I wanted to tell someone. I wanted to tell *him*. And that night at the hospital, the Ambu bag, the baby, Dr. Fischer—it all came pouring out of me.

"My God, honey," he said. He'd sat up and turned to face me.

"I got into nursing because it was a way out of my home. Because it was a job I felt like I could do. Really do. I knew it wouldn't be easy, but I had no idea it would be *that* hard. And, I never once wondered if I was the right kind of person for it," I said.

"You don't think you are?" Rex asked.

"Those twenty minutes with the baby…it showed me I'm not who I thought I was."

He didn't try to tell me I was wrong, and I appreciated that because Kitty would have. She would try to bury my doubt with a thousand reasons why she thought I was a nurse, without once understanding that what she thought was irrelevant.

I didn't think so anymore.

It was why I wasn't telling her.

"My whole life," he said, "I wanted to be a pilot. I wanted nothing to do with cattle or shit tractors that always broke down. I wanted speed, excitement. I wanted a hundred-mile view of the world, not my folks' thousand acres of dirt."

"Did you get it?" I asked, sitting up to face him.

He nodded. "Joined the air force and I flew Sabres in Korea. It was everything I thought it would be. It asked more of me every day than what I thought I had to give."

"Is this your way of telling me I should go back to nursing?"

"Hell no. I don't know you even a little bit, BettyKay Allen. Maybe you're a terrible nurse."

"Thanks for the shot of confidence," I laughed.

"You're welcome," he said with a smile.

"Did you like being a fighter pilot?"

"I don't know if it's something you like or not. All I know is that when I had to walk away from it, a lot of who I thought I was did not come with me."

A cloud moved over the sun and changed the landscape.

"Do you like being an actor?"

He laughed. "I smile and point fake guns and sometimes I get to ride a horse and sometimes I get to kiss a pretty woman. And the world out there—" He waved his hand out at the city past the garden and down the hill. "It tells me who I am. And that suits me fine right now."

"That sounds sad," I said.

"Does it?" he asked and picked up his half-full, sweating collins glass from the grass between us. "Have another drink."

"Good Lord!" Kitty cried, the screen door slamming shut behind her. "That man can talk."

"Hugh?" Rex asked with a lazy, knowing smile.

"Yes, Hugh. It's a good thing he's got something to say or I'd think he just liked the sound of his own voice. He's almost done with the new script." Kitty sat down on her chaise. "Your friend is here, Rex," she said.

"If you'll excuse me, ladies," he said and took himself and his glass inside.

"So?" Kitty wagged her eyebrows at me. "What'd I miss?"

Christmas A Go-Go had had a great opening week at the box office, and the studio sent Kitty a box of oranges and a bright red Fiat Dino. So on Christmas Day Kitty and I drove down to Zuma Beach to eat oranges and watch the surfers. We sat around a bonfire wrapped in a blanket, throwing orange peels into the flames.

"We got a letter from Jenny," I said, pulling the frail light blue airmail from my back pocket.

"What did she say?" Kitty asked, knowing I would have read it immediately.

"That she likes that we're together—"

"Because she only has to write once?" Kitty laughed. "How is she?"

"She says she's lonely. Most of the white nurses don't talk to her and all the Black soldiers are enlisted and there's no fraternization between enlisted men and officers."

"And she's what...a lieutenant?"

I nodded. Nurses went to officer's training and came out with a higher rank than the enlisted men. "She's stationed at some place called Cu Chi. She sleeps under her bed at night because of all the air raids."

"I thought nurses weren't being sent into combat?"

"She says there aren't any front lines. It's just...the war is everywhere."

"Another government lie." Kitty's feelings about the war had grown dark and jaded, but I didn't always agree with her. She thought everyone who went over there was a government tool, being used by Nixon to murder innocent people. "I don't understand why she'd sign up to be a part of Nixon's killing machine."

"Well, she didn't sign up to do that," I said, tired of the way everyone lumped all the soldiers and nurses together with Nixon and called them immoral. "And remember out at Shakey's you said you'd go. You didn't understand why all the boys had the adventure."

"That was before I woke up and realized Vietnam wasn't any kind of adventure."

"And before you went to Hollywood."

"What do you mean?"

"I mean, you were meant to be an actress, Kitty. It's given you purpose. And sometimes people want something different. To be useful. Fulfilled. That's why Jenny went. To save her brother and to have purpose."

Kitty watched me a long time.

"What?" I said, wiping the side of my face. "Is there something on my—"

"Would you go?" Kitty asked.

"I'm not a nurse."

Kitty rubbed her face with the blanket like she'd just had enough of me. And I realized the fear that had kept me in Greensboro, contemplating a two-bedroom apartment with Denise and working in a hospital with a doctor who hated me, was gone. I could look at that plan and see how wrong that life would have been for me. I didn't know what was next, but it certainly wasn't that.

But I still wanted to be *useful*.

"Yeah. Maybe," I said, surprised even as I said it.

"Well, thank God you're not a nurse."

I laughed because Kitty could shift on a dime. Endlessly constantly pragmatic. That was my Kitty. I picked up another orange and sunk my thumbnail into the skin, releasing a mist of juice that perfumed the air and made my hands sticky. I tossed the peel into the fire where it hissed and curled in the flame.

Early the next morning Kitty shook me awake.

"What are you doing?" I cried, rolling away from her to the middle of the bed. My head still pounded from last night's brandy Alexanders, and my stomach wasn't real happy, either.

"I told Hugh and the costume department I have a twenty-inch waist, I need to go jogging."

"Then go, why are you bothering me?"

"Come with me."

"Kitty."

"Betts. You're awake. You might as well come."

Somehow ten minutes later, in a pair of her old Chuck Taylors and sweatpants, I found myself on a rocky trail leading down into the canyon in front of The Birdhouse.

"Isn't there an easier way to lose weight, Kitty?" I panted, struggling to keep up with her. "Drink some of those shakes or whatever."

"I like exercise," Kitty said.

I did not. I really did not. But the sun came up over the rocky hilltop behind us and the light hit the distant water and made it sparkle. The sky went pink and then blue and the air shimmered.

"Not bad, huh?" Kitty asked as I stopped to catch my breath. "Prettier than Iowa."

It wasn't prettier. It was just different.

Forty minutes later, sweating and blistered, Kitty took pity on me and we walked up the last part of the trail and onto the road, toward the dirt and gravel driveway of The Birdhouse.

"Honestly, Kitty. I am not doing this with you again. If you need a jogging friend, you're going to have to find someone else. I'll drink that buttermilk with you and eat grapefruit ten times a day, but I'm never doing that—"

There was a pickup truck in The Birdhouse's drive. Not Rex's immaculate Chevy, but a beat-up rust bucket with Georgia plates.

"Hey, Kitty, you expecting…?"

Kitty wasn't beside me; she'd stopped by the mailbox. Her face, just a second ago flushed from all the exercise, was pale as a ghost.

"What's wrong?" I asked, reaching toward her.

"Katherine?" a voice asked from our front step, hidden by the truck.

The hair on the back of my neck stood up.

"Is that you?" A man stepped out from behind the truck. He was clearly Kitty's family, they had the same face. His hair was carrot red, though, and he was deeply freckled from the sun. He wore a plaid shirt with the sleeves torn off and a dirty ball cap. "Holy shit, Katherine, I barely recognize you."

"Jesse," Kitty said. "What are you doing here?"

"Visiting my big-shot sister," he said with a smile that was not at all friendly. My skin crawled and tightened. He stepped toward Kitty, his dusty work boots kicking gravel that went pinging off the truck. Instinctively, I stepped sideways. My body between him and Kitty.

"Well now," he said, his blue eyes, colder than Kitty's, followed me. "Who is your friend?"

"Who are you?" I asked.

"Jesse," he said, like I should know that name. When it was obvious I didn't, he looked over my shoulder at Kitty. "It's like that, is it?"

"How'd you find me?" she asked, her voice shaking.

"There are folks down there who sell maps to movie stars' homes," he said, jerking his thumb behind him to the whole of Los Angeles. "You're not big enough to be on the map, but for a buck a guy told me where you live. I was expecting something fancier, sis."

He drew closer and I didn't budge. This guy had bad news written all over him. But someone needed to be brave, and Lord knows, Kitty had been brave enough for me on more than one occasion.

"I saw your movie," Jesse said. "Dad didn't go, but I went. Twice. It was silly but I liked the gorilla."

"It wasn't real," Kitty said. "It was a guy in a costume."

"I know that," he snarled. "You think I don't know that." He stepped forward again.

"Stop," I said. I even put my hand up, like I stood a chance against this guy. He was a little scrawny but he could still wallop me if he wanted.

"This is between me and my sister." Jesse was near enough now that his spittle hit my face.

"Say your piece," I said. This wasn't all that different than working the emergency room on a Friday night. A stubborn man thinking he was better than me because he had a belly full of beer and a penis. And Lord, I was sick of that nonsense. Right now, in this moment, I was sick to death of it. "But say it from there."

"This is how you're going to treat your brother?" Jesse asked Kitty, but he did indeed stop.

"What do you want, Jesse?" Kitty asked like she was tired down to her feet.

"You took the car when you left."

"That car didn't make it out of Georgia," Kitty said.

Jesse shrugged. "It was the only one we had. And you took it."

"You're here for money?" I said. "For a couple hundred bucks?"

"Who asked you?"

"I've got your money," Kitty said. "Just give me a second." Kitty stepped around me toward the front of the house and Jesse reached out, quick as a snake, and grabbed her by the arm. He shook her hard enough that her head snapped back.

"You always thought you were so special. You ain't special. You're just like me."

When I shoved him, I surprised him enough that he staggered back, his hat falling into the dirt.

"This some kind of sex thing?" he asked, picking up his hat. "That's what you are now, Kitty. Some kind of—"

I shoved him again. My hands weren't even my own. I was floating in anger.

"You're lucky I was raised not to hit women," Jesse said. "Or you'd be—"

"Sorry? You're the one who's sorry. Bullying your sister, begging for money."

"Here!" Kitty cried. She'd gone in to get her purse. "Here's the money. Two thousand dollars. Take it. You won't get more."

Kitty tore off the check and held it out to her brother. It trembled in the sunshine.

Jesse snagged it and shoved it in the front pocket of his shirt.

"Dad's dead. That's what I came out here to tell you. He's dead and it's just me out on that farm now."

Behind me Kitty was silent.

"You told her," I said. "You can go on, now."

"You left," he spat. "You took the damn car, but you left me."

Before Kitty could say anything else, Jesse shoved me backward and I fell into her.

And then he was in his truck and gone, dust and stones kicked up as he drove away.

"Kitty," I said, hugging her trembling body. "I'm…so sorry about your dad."

"I'm not."

"Are you all right?"

"Me? You're the one picking fights." She tried to smile but instead sagged against me, her head on my shoulder. In all our years together, I'd never seen her so vulnerable. "Thank you," she breathed.

"I didn't do anything."

"You were here. That's more than anyone's ever done."

20

BETTYKAY

"HOT OFF THE PRESS!" Hugh Bonnet said, standing in the doorway like he'd never been in a room he didn't immediately command. He lifted two stacks of paper, kept together by big binder clips.

It was a few days after Jesse's visit. We didn't talk about it, but Kitty didn't go running alone in the mornings anymore. Instead we ate grapefruit and did sit-ups at night.

Kitty jumped up off the couch and tried to grab one of the scripts. Hugh held it up just out of reach, grinning at her until she scowled and smacked his chest.

"It's about time," Rex said, unfolding himself from the couch to take the other copy.

"Piss off, you wanker," Hugh said good-naturedly. He was a lean man, in plaid pants and a bright yellow short-sleeve sweater, his blond hair shaggy, his grin absolutely full of the devil.

"We can go in my room," Kitty said, looking between Rex and Hugh. "To read them?"

Hugh gestured with his arm as if to say *after you*, and the three of them filed into Kitty's room, leaving a void behind them.

In the kitchen I found Alexander opening a jar one of the dancers had brought.

"Is it strange," I asked, "that he's just finished the script and they're about to film in two weeks?"

"He's an auteur," Alexander said. "Writer-directors have different rules."

"Like what?"

"Like they have no rules."

He got the lid off the jar and then, suspicious, sniffed it and motioned for me to sniff.

"What is it?"

"Hummus."

"What do you do with it?"

Alexander handed me a saltine and we dipped it into the jar, scooping up a glob of the beige dip. "Oh," I said. "That's good." Lemony and garlicy and something else I'd never tasted before.

"It's all yours," Alexander said. He opened the old fridge and pulled out a bottle of Coke, set the top against the edge of the counter and slapped his hand on it, sending it somersaulting to the ground. "How long are you staying?" he asked. "Because I can get fifty bucks a month for that room."

"I can pay you fifty bucks a month."

"Can you?" His eyebrows arched over his sparkling eyes.

"Well, I can pay it this month," I said.

"Okay," he said with a nod, and just like that I had a bedroom in California in addition to the one I'd put down first and last for in Iowa. I'd called Denise weeks ago to tell her she could sublet my room, that I wasn't sure when I'd be back.

The air changed in the kitchen, which meant one of the

bedroom doors had opened. The whole place was like a wind tunnel when all the doors were open. There was a chorus of cheers and Alexander and I went out into the living room to see what the commotion was about.

"Drinks!" Hugh cried, his arms around Kitty and Rex. A Polaroid camera hung from a strap around his neck. There was no reason for me not to like him. He was extremely likable. Handsome. Gregarious. Charming. And still... "We need to celebrate."

Rex clapped his hands together and stepped into the dining room, where the table had become our impromptu bar. I followed him.

"I take it you like the script?" I asked Rex, who had a kinetic energy about him.

"We're going to win Oscars," Rex said. "Or we'll never work again."

"Well, I guess both options would change your life, wouldn't they?"

He laughed. "I suppose so." He poured three shots of tequila and took them back out to Kitty and Hugh in the living room, who had his arm slung over Kitty's shoulder, right along her neck in a part hug, part headlock.

"To us," Hugh said. "And this brilliant fucking movie we're going to make."

"To you," Kitty amended, and he pulled her in close.

"Let's change the world," he said, and the three of them shot down the tequila.

I hung back, watching. In all our time as friends, Kitty's relationships with men were simply stories she told me, or alluded to. But here she was with her hand in Hugh's back pocket.

"Who's the sourpuss?" Hugh asked as he and Kitty came up to me, smiling like it might take the sting out of his words. He reminded me of Dr. Joel Fischer.

"This is my friend BettyKay," Kitty said. "And you'll be nice or I'll skin you."

"I'm nice," Hugh said, acting affronted. "I'm always nice. Not sure what you heard about me, Sourpuss, but I ain't all bad."

"It's nice to meet you," I said, holding out my hand.

"Come on, now." He wrapped me in a hug, thumped me—too hard—on the back. "Any friend of Kitty's is a friend of mine."

"Rex?" Alexander said, coming to stand in the doorway. Behind him was a square man in a black cowboy hat and a matching mustache. "Your friend is here. Said you needed to see him."

"That I do." Rex stood up. "If you'll excuse me."

"Can I come with?" Alexander asked.

After a moment, Rex nodded yes, and I opened my mouth to ask if I could, too, but Hugh, of all people, placed a hand on my shoulder.

"You don't want to go there," he said in a low voice.

"Why? What are they doing?"

"You don't ask," Hugh said. "You don't ever ask."

Hours and many more drinks later, Rex was sitting alone at the dining room table, rolling a joint, his hair burnished red and gold in the candlelight. He was relaxed, his eyes soft. He'd vanished for a while. Kitty said he was taking a nap.

He caught my eye, licking the paper and rolling it smooth. "You want some grass?"

"I…um… I've actually never smoked before."

"A resident of The Birdhouse living the straight and narrow? Say it ain't so. Want to try it?"

"Does it burn? Your throat, I mean?" It seemed like every time someone smoked in the living room they ended up coughing like they might bring up a lung.

"Come here," he said and turned sideways on the bench, his

long legs in tan denim. "Sit." He patted his knee and I narrowed my eyes at him. "You're going to inhale what I blow out," he said and lit the joint. "It's a lot smoother that way. No coughing. Usually. But you do have to get close."

I leaned forward, my hands braced on the table in front of him. "This is close enough," I told him, aware of everyone in the other room.

"Sure," he said, then leaned forward and his lips, an inch from mine, blew out a long stream of smoke, right into my pursed ones.

I sucked in, the smoke tasting earthy and hot. I pulled away almost immediately.

"You all right?" he asked.

"Fine. It's just…hot."

"Well, it is smoke."

He was teasing me in a very kind way, and I realized all at once how childish I was being. How square. It was 1970 in Los Angeles, California, and Rex Daniels was offering to get me high. What was the point of walking away from my life if I wasn't going to try a different one?

I got up, walked around the table and sat on Rex Daniels's knee.

"Well, hello," he said.

"Let's try it again."

He took another long pull from the joint and put his free hand against my cheek, as if drawing me close and holding me still all at the same time. I wanted to tell him not to bother because I wasn't going anywhere.

He felt different from Todd. His touch, his body and his smell. His lips, literally a breath from mine. He blew out and I sucked in, and then I tilted forward and kissed him.

Bold as can be, I kissed Rex Daniels. Me. BettyKay Allen.

His hand, so careful against the side of my face, slid into

my hair, holding the back of my head as he deepened the kiss. Rex Daniels tasted like marijuana and limes from his garden, a flavor I'd never had before. I liked it.

Quite a bit, I liked it.

There was the overload snap and whir of Hugh's Polaroid, and we jumped apart to find Hugh and Kitty standing in the doorway. Hugh was waving the Polaroid dry and Kitty was watching us with arched eyebrows.

I jumped off Rex's lap, and he grabbed my hand, not letting me go as far as my panicked first reaction wanted me to. He squeezed my hand.

"I don't hate this," Kitty said, sauntering slowly to the table. "But I'm not sure I like it, either."

"I like it. A lot," I said, Rex's warm palm in mine giving me confidence.

"So do I," Rex said, sliding his arm around my waist and pulling me just a little back against his body.

"The camera loves it," Hugh said and flipped the picture on the table between us. I was stunned to see the Polaroid actually took a clear picture. Proof that I'd kissed Rex Daniels.

I felt light and buzzy, and Kitty's expression was so serious I had to laugh. I clapped my hand over my mouth because maybe it wasn't funny. But then it was absolutely funny.

Quick like a snake, Kitty leaned right into Rex's face. "Don't hurt her," she said.

That shouldn't have been funny.

But we howled.

I woke up to the sound of a slammed door.

"You're being unreasonable," Hugh said, his voice a whisper.

"I'm not. I'm being totally reasonable and you just want what you want," Kitty hissed back.

"You're going to tell me you don't want it?"

"I don't want to fuck the director of my next film."

"Well, sweetheart, you've done everything but—"

"And clearly that was a mistake." Kitty was yelling now, and I pulled myself out of my bed, surprised to see I was still in my clothes. My head was full of cotton. "Please, Hugh. Go." There was rustling, a man's low grunt. "I said go!"

Unintentionally, I banged open my bedroom door, sending it crashing against the wall. "Oops," I said, and in the shadowy main room, Kitty pushed Hugh away and he stepped back.

"Betts," Kitty said, and I wondered if I was imagining the relief in her voice.

"Hey, Sourpuss." Hugh's charming smile flashed in the light. "Sorry if we woke you."

"You didn't," I lied into the charged air. "I was just…getting some water."

"I was just leaving," Hugh said. "Kitty, I'll see you next week."

"Sure," she said.

His Porsche roaring away broke the silence of The Birdhouse. Kitty worried the sash of the robe.

"You want to come sleep with me?" I offered, only because she looked so alone.

"No," she said. "Go to sleep, Betts. I'm sorry we woke you."

I changed out of my shorts and tank top and slipped into my nightgown, the cotton so cool against my skin, I shivered. I wasn't back in bed ten minutes before Kitty was crawling in next to me.

"He's just…a really passionate man," Kitty said.

"Hugh?"

"Yeah. I mean…what he loves, *he loves*. You get that?"

"Of course," I said because that was what she so clearly wanted me to say, and I was still high and so unmoored from myself that it was too easy to lie.

21

BETTYKAY

JANUARY 8, A car came for Kitty at five in the morning to take her down to Studio City, where production was starting for *The Petticoat Kid*. An awful name if you asked me. No one did.

Kitty played Jo, a young woman brought out West as a child by her father who is murdered by a wealthy prospector after finding gold. She disguises herself as a man and has plans to steal the gold from the man who killed her father so she can try to get back to what's left of her family in Philadelphia. Rex played Father McDermott, a priest, beaten and left for dead by a band of outlaws who Jo nurses back to health. They share a complex and intense connection that is consummated under the stars.

Father McDermott, tormented with guilt for betraying his vows, but powerless against his attraction to Jo, helps her steal the gold, but when the wealthy prospector catches them red-handed, he sacrifices himself so Jo can take the gold and run.

It was dramatic and uncomfortably sexy and thrilling, all at the same time.

Rex was right—they were going to win Oscars or never work again.

Alexander and I cleaned the house that first morning Kitty spent away. We picked Cara Cara oranges and tiny sweet little mandarins from the fruit trees on the hill below the house. I found a recipe for marmalade in a two-year-old *Good House-keeping* magazine in the bathroom rack and tried my hand at making it. Not a success.

It felt strange to be in this house without Kitty, reminded me how without purpose I was. And how I didn't like it.

Thank God, Alexander put on Simon & Garfunkel and rolled a joint. We lay on the couches, stretched out in the sunlight and passed the joint until it was gone. It certainly didn't make me feel any more useful, but it made me stop caring so much.

"I have to ask," he said after, entering the living room from my bedroom, which I hadn't even seen him go into, with the dress I'd worn to the *Christmas A Go-Go* premiere a few months back.

"Hey," I said. "You shouldn't be going through my room."

Alexander ignored me. "Why did she put these hideous buttons on this dress?"

"That's been bothering you?" I asked, pulling my languid and limp body up onto the macramé pillow I'd been reclining against.

"Like a hair shirt."

I explained the buttons, how I'd bought them. She'd put them on my nursing uniform, I'd mailed them baked inside a chocolate mayonnaise birthday cake that Walter in the cafeteria made for the occasion.

"I remember that cake," Alexander said. "She insisted it was all right to eat it." He made a face.

"She cleaned them up and sewed them on the dress," I said with a shrug.

"And you wore it."

"I thought it looked all right."

"Only because no one was actually looking at you." I laughed because it was true, and I was too high to take offense. "Now it's your turn? To give her the buttons?"

"It's my turn."

"How long are you two going to do this?"

"I don't know. As long as we have ideas, I suppose."

"What will you do next?"

"I haven't come up with anything."

The stereo sat on a wide dresser, and from one of the drawers he pulled a lethal-looking pair of scissors and snipped each of those buttons off the neck of the dress.

"Hey!" I said, sitting up to pick the buttons from the floor.

"We're going to think of something," he said. "Something great. When you go back to Iowa you'll leave her with something she'll never forget."

I took the buttons and the dress back into my bedroom, slipped the buttons into the silk pocket in the suitcase I kept under the bed.

Iowa, I thought, remembering the way snow smelled, the strange burn of ice caught between a mitt and the tender skin of a wrist.

Kitty came home at nine that night and we sat down at the table to eat the very first meatloaf I'd ever made.

"That's awful," Kitty said, having choked down one bite.

"It really is."

"You don't have to cook, you know."

"I just wanted to be useful," I said.

"Oh my God, wanting to be useful is going to be the end of you. Come with me tomorrow," she said, pushing away the plate.

"And do what?"

"Anything but cook. We start on location, it will be fun. Rex is asking about you."

"Really?"

Kitty laughed. "A car will be here at 5 a.m."

It was a different world on the other side of the Santa Monica Mountains. Forty miles from The Birdhouse and our orange trees, the world sun-scorched and thirsty. The colors were yellow and sage green. The pine trees grew out of rocks, and the car had to swerve around snakes sunning themselves on the asphalt.

We pulled off the state highway 118 onto a smaller road and then a smaller road until we were bouncing along dirt to the Simi Valley Movie Ranch. Within moments, it was like we had gone back in time. There was an Old West main street with clapboard buildings, an adobe house and a barn with horses in a corral. There were cameras and crew and a giant crane. Sprinkled amongst them were men and women in costume, bonnets and gun belts. In the middle of the road, Rex stood in his black jacket, the white collar of a priest, talking to Hugh.

It had been days since that kiss. I'd tried to be grown-up about it, blasé, even. But by trying not to think about it, I ended up thinking about it all the time.

Kitty got out of the car and was met almost immediately

by a crowd of people with clipboards and walkie-talkies. She was whisked off to a trailer near what appeared to be a saloon.

When she came back out an hour later, she was utterly transformed, in leather pants and a leather vest and a cream linen shirt that was made to look dirty. She wore a big wide hat with a string under her chin, and all of her hair was tucked up into it.

If I didn't know her, I'd think she was a young boy.

"Wow," I said.

"I know. They do a good job. Come on. We're shooting up in the canyon."

The canyon was far enough away from the town setup that it looked like pure wilderness, a canyon and a cliff with a cave set way back in the rocks. Camera, light and sound were ready for a shot that involved Rex falling off a horse and onto the rocks, only to be discovered by Kitty.

Kitty, Rex and Hugh and two other men were in a tight huddle at the top of the cliff, a wrangler with two identical horses nearby. One of the men was dressed in the same dusty beat-up black jacket and white priest collar as Rex.

"Hey there, BettyKay, right?" An older man built like a fire hydrant came to stand next to me. He had the bulbous nose and broken blood vessels of a guy who liked a nightcap or twenty, and wore dark green pants and a wide straw hat to protect his face from the sun.

"Yeah. Who are you?"

"Dan. I'm Rex's medic."

"Medic?"

"Yeah. Rex likes doing his own stunts. I'm around to patch him up and get him back in the saddle."

He pulled a long licorice whip from the pocket of his shirt and offered it to me.

"No thanks," I said.

He bit the top off and chewed, open-mouthed. "In *Run with the Devil* he broke three ribs and two fingers in a car explosion."

"Did he go to the hospital?"

"What would they tell him at a hospital?"

"To rest."

"Yeah, that wasn't going to work for Bob Matthews. Bob was the director and the man knew how to use a whip if you know what I mean."

"So he went back to work with broken ribs and fingers?"

"And maybe a concussion. But didn't cost a day shooting, which is the important thing," Dan said proudly. "Today is a simple stunt. He's just got to fall off that horse."

"Who are all those people up there?" I lifted my hand to shade my eyes from the unrelenting glare.

"Well, the guy dressed like Rex is Buddy Howe, he's the stunt coordinator and Rex's double."

"You just said Rex did all his own stunts."

"Well, the other guy up there all stressed out is Gary, production coordinator. He's trying to convince Hugh and Rex to use Buddy in the shot."

"Why don't they?"

"Hugh likes that he can get a face shot of Rex falling off that horse. Makes it more authentic. And Rex, well." He shrugged. "Rex's the star. The star gets what he wants. Anywho, Kitty told me to introduce myself. She said you were a nurse."

"I didn't pass my boards."

Dan smiled. "She said you would say that, too. But that you would be good if there was any kind of problem."

"Oh, well, I suppose I'm happy to help."

He nodded and offered me another licorice whip. This time I took it.

"How do you know Rex?" I asked.

"We served in Korea together."

"Were you a medic?"

He shook his head. "Mechanic."

"Do you have medical training?"

"I got this." He tapped his toe to a beaten-up green metal box the size of my suitcase with a red cross on the front of it. A first aid kit. "And now I've got you."

"Great," I said sarcastically. "Looks like we're all set."

In the end, Rex and Hugh won, and the production manager, poor guy, left shaking his head.

"Don't be like that, Gary," Hugh yelled after him. "I'll make it up to you at the box office."

Gary scrambled down over the rocks and flipped Hugh the bird.

Rex wasn't just falling off a horse. He was falling off a horse at full gallop, landing on a mattress hidden in the rocks, and then tumbling down over the rocks (without any mattress) to land at Kitty's feet.

"Don't worry," Dan said to me. "Rex knows what he's doing."

Hugh yelled action and Rex started at a gallop and immediately slipped down over the horse's neck, looking convincingly semiconscious. The horse, trained for this kind of thing, Dan assured me, stretched out, while Rex slipped further and further down toward the hard earth.

And then, at just the right moment, Rex dropped from the horse in a heavy heap and threw himself over the stones and boulders of the cliff.

"They'll put it together in editing," Dan whispered, and I couldn't breathe.

Rex landed at Kitty's feet, Kitty made a face of surprise and Hugh yelled cut.

Rex jumped up, seemingly none the worse for wear. "Did you get it?" he asked.

Hugh shook his head.

"What happened?" I asked Dan.

"Rex must have missed the mark. Fell out of frame."

And then they were setting up the shot again.

"Are you going to check on him?"

"Check what?"

"His pupils or reflexes. His skull or check for obvious injuries that Rex might not feel because of adrenaline?"

"Nah," he said. "Someone would tell me if he was hurt."

This seemed like a terrible process. But I was just a guest who didn't pass her RN boards. What did I know?

They did it three more times, and each time something else went wrong. He was too late. Too soon. The horse changed course by a few inches. After the fifth fall, Hugh yelled cut, and as Kitty crouched down, the hair on the back of my neck went up.

"Dan," I said. "I think there might be a problem."

Kitty stood up. "Betts!" she yelled, and I grabbed that first aid kit and flew up those rocks.

Rex was still on the ground, white-faced and sweating under the makeup and dust. He was cradling his arm. I opened the first aid kit only to find it mostly full of amber pill bottles, glass bottles of morphine and cortisone. Not a sling or glove or penlight to be found.

Hugh ran up, sending rocks like shrapnel across all of us. "Everyone all right?" he asked.

"Did you get the shot?" Rex asked through his teeth.

"We got it," Hugh said and then crouched beside Rex. "Can you sit up?"

"Don't move him," I said.

"I'm sorry?" Hugh asked, his eyebrows raised.

"Don't move him until we know what's wrong with him."

"Well, hello, Sourpuss," he said with a smile. "Good to see you on my set staying true to form."

"Rex?" I said, ignoring Hugh's subtle dig as I got onto my knees beside him. "Where does it hurt?"

"Hello, Betts," he said and managed to grin, the dumb charmer. "Did you see me?"

"I saw you fall off a horse and down a mountain five times," I said, running my hands over his skull, feeling for soft spots and goose eggs. Sure enough, he had a doozy at the back of his head.

"This hurt?" I asked, pressing on the skin an inch away from it.

He winced and I took that as a yes. "Pretty impressive right?"

"This goose egg of yours? I've seen worse."

"The stunt."

"Looked pretty wild from down there. Can you move your arm?"

He moved his right arm just fine.

"The other arm?"

"I'd rather not."

I reached under his beat-up coat and felt right away the dislocated shoulder, the ball of the humerus just below the socket.

"Dislocated," he said, like he was all too familiar with the term.

"Yeah. You hurt anywhere else?" I patted down his chest and around to his back, then his hips and down his legs.

"You should ask me out to dinner if you're gonna get fresh."

I shot him my best Head Nurse Bouchet look, which only made him laugh.

"It's just my shoulder and the bump on the head," he said.

"I think so, too. You need help sitting up?"

He gave me his good hand and Kitty stepped over, helping me get Rex to his feet. "He needs to get to a hospital to get that shoulder put back in place and a doctor should look at that—"

"Can you do it?" Rex asked. His blue eyes were focused right on me, and I felt the weight of his attention.

"Do what?"

"Put my shoulder back."

"You're kidding?"

"Nearest hospital is a half hour away. And, Betts, I don't need to tell you, it hurts like a bitch right now. Can you?"

"We'll pay you," Hugh said. "A medic's day rate."

Well, that would come in handy with the rent check I needed to write for Alexander.

"Please," Rex said like no one else was around.

Anything I might have used to protest was all dried up in my mouth.

"Sit down," I told him, and he sat down on a stone.

And that's how I ended up taking off Rex Daniels's clothes for the first time. I peeled off that white collar and dropped it at my feet, each button slipping free to reveal more and more skin. The dark brown hair of his chest. The muscles of his stomach. There was a hematoma forming on his right side over his second and third rib. As gently as I could I felt for something broken.

"Take a deep breath," I said.

"Do I have to?" he asked.

"Yes."

His breath was slow and steady, and I didn't feel anything broken, just badly bruised.

"When did you do that?" I asked.

"The first fall."

"Rex!"

"Shhh," he said. "Don't say anything or you'll ruin my tough guy reputation."

A flirty guy in the emergency room on a Saturday night was a fairly common occurrence, some frat boy who had too much to drink and did something stupid to impress a girl. I could handle a flirty frat boy.

A flirty Rex Daniels was another thing altogether.

I tugged the shirt off his shoulder, and Hugh made a gagging noise at the sight of the visible dislocation. It was already bruising, which was bad news.

"Do you have tingling?" I asked.

"Sometimes," Rex said. "When I look at you."

I felt a blush roar over my skin. "In your fingers. Numbness? Tingling? Can you—"

He wiggled his fingers at me.

"Okay," I said. "Let's get you on the ground."

The spot where he landed was wide enough to accommodate Rex on his back and me beside him. "This is going to hurt. A lot."

Holding on to him by the wrist I slowly moved his arm out from his body at a forty-five degree angle and then I began pulling on the arm with slow and steady pressure, waiting to feel the ball of the bone slip past the lip of the socket and settle back into place. Rex swore a blue streak, and I pulled and pulled, and when my body weight wasn't enough, I put my foot in his armpit for more leverage.

Finally the head popped back into place.

"You okay?" I asked.

"You're something else, BettyKay Allen," he said, reaching up and tugging on the end of my ponytail.

When we got him back to his feet, Hugh, the production coordinator and Buddy were talking about the next shot.

"We need to get him to the hospital," I said.

Rex hissed as I slid his shirt up over his arm.

"Rex," Hugh said, boxing me out. "All we have left is your close-up on the ground and the scene between you and Kitty when she helps you into the cave."

"We're already two days behind schedule because of the Teamsters," the production coordinator joined the guilt trip.

"Sure," Rex said, despite his obvious pain and exhaustion from throwing himself off a horse and down a mountain five times. "No problem."

"No," I said because someone had to be reasonable. "He's got a probable concussion, a deeply bruised, if not broken, rib, and there could be nerve damage in that arm."

"You can use that," Hugh said, like this was just a gift from God. "As Father McDermott. You can use that pain."

This was the biggest load of bullshit I'd ever heard, and I was about to say so when I caught Kitty's eye. She shook her head at me, and I swallowed back my words, remembering that I was here because she'd invited me. I didn't want to cause her any trouble.

"Dan!" Rex shouted, and Dan made his huffing and puffing way to where we were standing.

At his arrival, Hugh, the production coordinator and even Kitty stepped away to give Rex privacy. I was left standing there, not realizing what was happening.

"What do you need, Rex?" Dan asked.

"Just a painkiller," he said, and out came one of the amber bottles. Rex swallowed two pills.

Dan closed up the case and headed back down the hill, and

I was left staring at Rex. My worry and my helpless attraction to him and my nurse's sense of responsibility all coalesced into something unpredictable.

"You should take better care of yourself," I said. "Because they clearly aren't."

"You are."

"Clear set!" Hugh yelled.

"That's you," Rex said, and I scrambled my way back down to Dan.

"Good thing you were here," Dan said. "We would have lost half a day of filming."

"You can't fix a dislocated shoulder?" I asked, wondering how he got the title medic without even that basic training.

"Hell no. Like I said, good thing you were here."

Filming went on for another two hours, and Rex was fading fast. If I'd had any power, I would have yanked him out of there, but the entire system seemed designed to use him up until he was nothing.

Finally Kitty said, "Hugh? I think we need to call it."

I watched Hugh and Kitty. If there was something between them after that week at The Birdhouse and the fight they'd had that night, they did not reveal it. He was businesslike, she was deferential. It was a Kitty I'd never seen. A Kitty, not with her light and power turned off, just…focused.

"That's a wrap!" Hugh yelled, and a swarm of people seemed to arrive to take down cameras and sound equipment.

I ran up the rocks to help bring Rex down, but the stunt coordinator was already there, arm around Rex's waist.

"You're not driving," Buddy was saying.

"My guy will drive," Rex said.

"You need a hospital," I said.

"I need to go to bed." Rex gave me an exhausted smile.

"Are you alone at home? You absolutely shouldn't be alone. Someone needs to wake you up every two hours."

"Sounds like a job for a nurse," Rex said, looking right at me in a way that said *Come home with me.*

BettyKay Allen was not a person who made big decisions at the drop of a pin. But maybe it wasn't that big. And maybe this wasn't so sudden. Maybe this had been brewing since he'd swept me up in that waltz in the dust and moonlight the first time we'd met.

"Kitty," I said. "I'm going home with Rex. To keep an eye on him."

If Kitty had an opinion about that, she didn't let on. "Sure," she said. "Smart idea."

22

===

BETTYKAY

THE GUY WHO drove Rex home in his powder blue, brand-new Ford Bronco was his friend in the cowboy hat who sometimes came by our house. Rex introduced him as Rick, his "body man," and I nodded like I knew what that meant.

Rex lived in Point Dume in Malibu, about an hour from The Birdhouse and an hour from the film set. We pulled off the PCH onto a smaller paved road and then a gravel road that traveled past green fields behind wooden fences.

"Are those horses?" I asked, twisting in my seat to get a better view of a chestnut horse racing along the fence line with the truck.

"I got a couple. Old stunt horses past their prime mostly. A few retired studs and a quarter horse champion who went blind."

I was delighted that everything I wanted to be true about him was true. "You run a retirement home for horses."

He laughed and then winced, his hand at his head. "I guess so."

The dirt road ended at the roofline of a house built into the cliff below us. It was nondescript and tiny in every way. I hid my surprise.

No wonder he liked to spend all his time at our house.

Rick helped him out of the car and then told Rex he was going to check on the horses.

"Does he live here with you?" I asked, wondering if this was another Birdhouse arrangement.

"He's in the guesthouse on the other side of the stables. Come on," he said, holding open the door for me.

I walked past him into a dark and shadowy hallway, following the sunlight to a sunken living room with an expansive view of the ocean.

"Oh my goodness," I cried.

"Yeah, it doesn't look like much from the driveway, but it's got a great view. I just had it remodeled," Rex said, pressing the light switches with his good shoulder.

The living room was orange, from the shag rug to the low couches along the wall. The dividing wall was made up of heavy glass sconces with candles to be lit. The kitchen had yellow countertops and a gleaming gas stove.

"It's cheerful," I said.

"It's ugly."

Rex untied the knot keeping his coat in a sling and dropped it on the floor. "You hungry?"

"Rex," I said. "I'm not a guest. You don't have to worry about me. How about we get you in the shower and I'll make some dinner."

"I won't turn any of that down, Betts."

"I hope not. Now...do you need help in the shower?"

He gave me a long look and a slow smile that I'd seen on

the big screen a time or two, and I shook my head at him. "Don't even try it."

"I can handle the shower. I have a gal who leaves some food in my fridge a few times a week. There's something in there you can probably put in the oven for us."

He headed down another dark hallway. In the fridge I found a dozen casserole dishes, each carefully marked with contents and cooking times and temperatures. I set the oven to 375 and slid in the chicken cordon bleu.

From the back of the house there was a thump and I stuck my head out into the hallway.

"Rex?" I called.

"Damn it!" he yelled.

I ran down to his bedroom. He had a king-size bed with rumpled blankets. On one side was a table stacked high with books and on top of the stack was a pair of reading glasses. "You all right?"

"Fine," he grumbled. "I'm just trying to get some ointment on these cuts."

"Can I...do you want some help?"

"That would be swell."

"Are you decent?"

"I've got a towel where it counts."

I trusted Rex not to trick me or make me uncomfortable on purpose. The bathroom off his bedroom was full of steamy mirrors and dark brown tiles. On the counter was a hexagonal jar of yellow cream.

"Whoa," I said, blinking my suddenly watery eyes. "What is that smell?"

"Tiger Balm. Buddy got me onto it."

He turned to show me his back and side, the bruise of his ribs spreading almost to his spine.

"Oh, Rex," I said. "Nothing that comes from tigers is going to help that."

He laughed and then winced. "It's got menthol and camphor in it. It's nothing to do with tigers. But could you?" He glanced at me over his shoulder and I nodded.

The nurse in me couldn't lie, the woman in me was pretty interested in all that skin. The big white fluffy towel was wrapped low on his waist, every muscle, bruise and scar on full display. But he was hurt, so I pushed that reaction aside as I scooped up some yellow ointment with my fingers and applied it to the top red edge of the bruise near his spine, where it was swollen and warm.

He sucked in a breath and I stopped. "Does this hurt?"

"No."

I glanced over in the mirror and caught his eye. He was watching us, or perhaps just me. Not knowing what to wear to a movie set, I'd erred on the side of dressed up and had worn a yellow dress with a belt at the hips and pleats that fell to the knees. I was tan and freckled from all the sun, my dark hair pulled back in a ponytail.

Rex, a few inches away, his chest and back and shoulders a series of curves and dips…

We look good. The two of us. Together.

I scooped up more of the ointment and rubbed it in. There was a scar, old and flat, that cut a terrible path on his side. It wasn't surgical. Or if it was, it wasn't a good surgery.

"What happened?"

"MiG Alley," he said. "Got in a dogfight and my Sabre was torn to shreds. The canopy came clear off. I didn't realize I was hit until I ejected into the Yellow Sea and the sharks got interested."

"It's a bullet wound?"

"And then some. But I got a nice vacation in Japan out of it."

He had a terrible scrape on his elbow and another on his shoulder blade. I covered all of them with the ointment and then stepped back.

"I think that should do it."

He turned and presented his palms, both ravaged by scrapes. I smoothed ointment there, too, and found myself resisting the urge to lift those battered palms to my lips to kiss away the pain.

"Anywhere else?" I asked.

He lifted his chin to show me a scab forming there, and I applied the yellow cream, terribly and wonderfully aware of the pulse in his throat, his breath brushing the side of my face as he exhaled.

"Thank you," he whispered.

"You're welcome."

"Betts," he said. "I'm pretty beaten up but I'd have to be dead not to want to kiss you right now."

"Are you asking if you can kiss me?"

"Can I?"

I laughed at the sheer ridiculousness of Rex Daniels asking me for a kiss, and then got up on my tiptoes and kissed him.

He opened his mouth and I jumped at the touch of his tongue.

"Is this all right?" he whispered against my mouth, and I had full body chills so powerful I could only nod. Yes. It was all right. Everything was all right.

He kissed me again, and this time I was ready when his tongue touched mine.

It felt good and strange and powerful. My heart was pounding in my chest, and I wrapped my arms around his neck trying to get closer to him, as close as I could get.

He hissed in pain and I pulled my hands away. "I'm sorry."

"No, honey, I'm sorry. Trust me. No man has ever been

sorrier than me right now but, I have to confess… I don't have the starch to finish what we started."

"No. Of course. Right. Sure." I was like a top spinning between the sink and his body, turning to put the lid on the cream and then turning back. "Let's just…let's get you in bed."

He let me help him to the bed. I straightened up the covers and held them back, looking anywhere but him, as he pulled off his towel and slipped into the sheets.

"I think this might be one of the most humiliating moments of my life, being put to bed by a woman I'd like to take to bed."

"Stop," I said. "I'm a nurse. There's nothing to be embarrassed about."

In the kitchen the timer on the stove went off. "Oh my Lord, dinner. Let me go see if it's burnt."

I ran back to the kitchen and found dinner not at all burnt but looking pretty delicious. I spooned a chicken breast with cheese dripping out of it onto a plate, grabbed a big glass of water and took it back to Rex's bedroom, where I found him with his eyes shut.

Figuring he needed sleep more than food, I stepped backward to take the plates to the kitchen.

"Betts," he said, his voice rough with sleep.

"Yeah."

"Stay."

"Stay here?"

"Yeah. Eat something and crawl in here. Bed's as big as a raft and you know I'm no threat. Well, at least I hope you know that."

I did.

"You gotta check on me every two hours, right? Go get one of my shirts out of the closet. I figure it's big enough to cover you from head to toe."

"Okay," I said. "Go to bed. I'll… I'll be back."

I went back to the kitchen and sat down at the table facing the ocean. It was black out there, no moon or stars. An airplane blinked and flashed its way north. Planes never went over the farm on Wolff Road. Or Greensboro. There were only the highway and freight trains full of pigs.

Back in Rex's room, I opened his closet and pulled out a chambray work shirt I recognized from the first time I'd met him. I changed in his bathroom, put some Colgate on my finger and brushed my teeth.

And then I just…crawled into bed beside Rex Daniels.

I set my fingers against his wrist. His pulse was good. So was his temperature. His breathing was even.

"Rex," I said and shook him awake.

"Hi."

"Hi. Can you tell me where you are?"

"My bedroom with the cutest nurse I've ever known."

"What year is it?"

"Seventy."

"Go back to sleep," I said. Then I rolled over on my side and somehow managed to do the same.

Hours later I woke up to check on him again, only to find his side of the bed empty.

"Rex?" I said, knocking lightly on the bathroom door. But he wasn't there.

Rex's living room was silver and blue. The clouds had cleared and the moon hung up in the sky.

"Rex?"

"He's here." I recognized Rick. Or rather his hat. He sat on the couch, Rex on the other side in sweatpants and nothing else.

"Is everything all right? Is he—"

Rick held up his hand, stopping me from running into the sunken living room. "He's fine. I gave him some medicine. He'll be in in a few minutes."

"What kind of medicine?"

"The kind he always takes," Rick said in a flat tone. "The kind that's private."

I opened my mouth to argue and saw on the low table in front of him a small brown case unzipped. There was a syringe. A length of rubber tubing.

"Go on back to bed," Rick said.

I would have liked to be stronger, tougher. Go right on up to Rick and toss him out, like I had been with Kitty's brother. Take that syringe full of garbage and throw it away. But I didn't do any of those things.

I turned around and went right back to Rex's bed.

23

CLARA

Los Angeles, California
2019

"BETTYKAY BEECHER? You're talking about our mom, right? Not someone else?" Abbie asked for maybe the millionth time.

Their food was growing cold in front of them. But eating during that story Kitty just told was impossible. It was almost impossible to breathe.

"I can't get over Rex Daniels," Clara whispered.

"I can't get over Mom smoking weed!" Abbie cried.

"It was the '70s," Kitty said, taking a sip of sparkling water. She was good at telling this story. Drawing it out for effect. The woman knew how to work an audience. "Come on, now. You hardly touched your dinners and I pay my cook a ton of money to make fancy food."

On the ivory china was fish in a creamy sauce with a salad of nuts and berries.

Clara picked up her fork and bravely dug in. Her phone buzzed.

"Sorry," Clara said, silencing it in her pocket.

"If you need to take a call—" Kitty said.

"It's my girlfriend," Clara said. "I'll call her back."

"Vickie?" Kitty asked. "Your mom really liked her."

"She did?"

"She liked that she made you happy."

"They're fighting," Abbie said.

"We're not fighting," Clara said. "We're just not agreeing."

"Oh!" Kitty laughed. "Those are some fine hairs you're splitting. How long have you two been together?"

"Seven months," Clara said.

"You should invite her out here. A lover's trip. Jenny and Jerome came out here for their honeymoon."

"We're fine," Clara lied. "Really."

"Suit yourself, I suppose. But a trip to California always fixed your mother right up."

Something about that statement struck Clara all wrong. All these allusions to a version of her mother that she didn't know. That had been kept secret. She ate another miniscule bite of fish and tried to let it go.

The dining room table was roughly seven miles long, and she and her sister were sitting opposite each other and halfway down the table from Kitty, who was at the head in a throne-like chair. Or, Kitty just made it look like a throne. The table and chairs were the only furniture in the dining room, which was decorated in ivory, gray, light blue and brown, and had a wall of windows overlooking the dark garden and the city below it. Opposite the window was a painting of a nude woman, about six feet long, face averted, lying in a field of flowers.

Clara really hoped it wasn't Kitty in that painting. Call her a prude, but eating dinner under her host's naked body was just too much.

"It really is delicious," Abbie agreed, but she, too, seemed to be struggling. Clara nodded, trying not to actually taste the fish.

"You two are lying out both sides of your mouth," Kitty laughed.

"We only had fish if it was fried," Clara said.

"And came in stick form," Abbie added.

"Your mother wasn't much of a cook," Kitty said. "That meatloaf set a low bar she wasn't interested in jumping."

"She was busy," Clara said in defense. "And Dad made most of the meals."

"Yeah." Abbie put down her knife. "He might be to blame for the fish sticks."

"How about we skip to the cheese course?" Kitty said, and the woman who'd been refilling their water glasses all night rushed forward to take their plates. "Are you two settling in all right?" Kitty asked.

"The cabin is amazing," Abbie said, topping up her wine-glass. Clara had tried not to count, tried to give her sister the benefit of the doubt. But this was her fifth glass and that seemed like a lot. But two was a lot for Clara so maybe she wasn't the best judge.

"All those trips she took with friends, it was just her coming out here?"

"A few times a year. Yes."

"Our father knew?" Clara asked.

"Your mom and dad were not the type to keep secrets from each other."

"No, they just kept secrets from us," Abbie said, setting down her glass in the wrong spot. It wobbled against her plate, and she made a big show of catching it, only to slosh more onto the lovely white tablecloth.

"I had hoped you'd bring your family, Abbie," Kitty said.

"Oh," Abbie said. "I don't know. The kids are wild animals. They'd break all your pretty stuff."

"I doubt that."

"No. It's true," Abbie said. "But really, what would be *most* amazing is if you finished the story about Mom and Rex."

Clara stood up, like her legs were springs. This wasn't logical, she knew that. It wasn't like the timelines worked out. This romance was years before Clara was conceived in 1984, but something about not knowing who her father was made anyone her father.

"I'm going to make a quick phone call," she said and walked down a small hallway to a book-filled study. She pulled the phone out and finally called Vickie.

"Hey," Vickie said, and Clara slouched at the relief of hearing her voice. "How is everything going?"

"Rex Daniels might be my father."

"Really?"

"Probably not."

"Are you all right?" Vickie finally asked.

Yes. No? She wasn't sure anymore. Every story Kitty told eroded something she thought was immutable. It was one thing to learn about her father, but this slow strange reveal of their mother? It felt like a dream. She'd think it a lie if it weren't for all the pictures.

She studied the books in the bookshelves and the lovely couch, leather with fancy nails in it. There was a blue velvet armchair with a table beside it, the Sunday *Times* crossword puzzle half-finished, folded up under a lamp.

Her mother did the same, and she wondered if Betts Beecher and Kitty Devereaux talked to each other about that crossword, like they apparently talked about Clara and Abbie. How had they been so close and still able to keep it hidden?

Were they lovers? Was that why Kitty had been kept a secret?

The why of it all was starting to bother her.

"I wish you would let me be there for you," Vickie said.

"What do you mean? You have," Clara whispered.

Vickie laughed but it wasn't joyful. "You know what's wild? I think you mean that. I think you believe a couple of phone calls and text messages from your girlfriend during your mother's funeral is me being there. But, Clara, that's what coworkers do. I *love* you."

"I love you, too."

"Oh, Clara." Vickie's breath hitched. "I'm beginning to think we have really different definitions for that word."

From the other room there was a thump and the shattering of glass.

"Clara!" Kitty cried, her voice tinged with panic.

"Vickie, I have to go."

Clara rushed from the den down the dark hallway to the beautiful dining room where Kitty was helping Abbie to her feet. Kitty was strong, but Abbie was way off-balance, and the two of them were in danger of going down. Clara grabbed her sister, giving Kitty a chance to step away.

"I'm okay," Abbie said, her words slurred. She pushed her hair off her face "That's embarrassing."

"What happened?" Clara asked.

"Nothing. I'm fine. It's a-okay," Abbie said.

"She fell over," Kitty said. "About took the table with her."

The tablecloth and the light Persian rug beneath it were splashed with red wine.

"Oh no," Clara said. "We'll clean that—"

"It's fine," Kitty said. "It will be taken care of."

"It's just jet lag," Abbie said. "Everything is totally cool." She turned toward Kitty and knocked over the glass again. It hit the chair and broke. "Oh shit," Abbie said. She crouched to pick it up and knocked into the chair.

"How about we get you to bed."

"I don't want to go to bed," Abbie said. "I want to hear more about Rex and Mom."

"I'll tell you more tomorrow," Kitty said, magnanimous to a fault.

"No, it's fine. Don't listen to Clara, she's a buzzkill. Has been her whole life," Abbie said.

Clara let go of Abbie and she lost her balance, bouncing against the table, shaking everything on it. Kitty grabbed the wine bottle so it wouldn't spill.

"Come on," Clara said into Abbie's ear. "Before you make a bigger mess." The fight went out of Abbie's shoulders and Clara led her sister away. "Thank you, Kitty. For everything."

Kitty reached out and touched Clara's shoulder, squeezed it.

"You know when your mom came out to stay with me, I tried to get her to tell me what had happened. Why she'd walked away from being a nurse," Kitty said. "But…after a while I stopped asking. Stopped pushing her for an answer. Because I got caught up in my own thing. My own drama. And I was just happy she was there. With me. And your mom was always so strong. I didn't realize how she was spiraling out of control."

"The fight with your brother?" That part of the story had stood out because she'd never known her mom to be confrontational, much less violent. Picking a fight, no matter how much an asshole deserved it, was not BettyKay Beecher's style.

Kitty nodded. "The drinking and weed. That wasn't Betts.

Even Rex, to some extent. She was dealing with something big and I was too selfish to help her."

"Clara," Abbie breathed. "I'm gonna throw up."

Clara, supporting her sister, practically ran out of the beautiful glass box to the cottage and the bathroom with the old-fashioned black and white tiles and the toilet flushed by tugging a cord.

Abbie retched into the toilet and Clara did the good work of holding her hair out of the way, stroking her back the way her mom would when she was home sick with the stomach flu.

"This is embarrassing," Abbie said.

Clara ran a washcloth under the faucet before putting it on the back of her sister's neck.

"What is going on, Abbie? It's just you and me sitting here," Clara said. "You can talk to me."

"I'm just tired," Abbie said, slumped between the wall and the toilet. Her face was different without the smile she always wore. She did look tired.

"Of what?"

"Everything." She lifted her hand and it flopped back down onto her lap. "Making dinner, pretending, missing you, missing our parents. My boobs." She grabbed her boobs, cupping them in her hands. "So tired of my boobs."

Clara tried not to laugh. It was serious. But...come on.

"You're laughing."

"I'm not. I swear."

"You're laughing at me."

"Because you're funny. And you're my sister. And your boobs are magnificent."

Abbie put the washcloth over her face, but Clara pulled it away only to see her smile. She won't be laughing tomorrow, she thought.

"Come on," Clara said. "Let's get you in bed. Things will be better in the morning."

"That's such a Mom thing to say," Abbie said, leaning against Clara as the room undoubtedly spun. "I miss her."

"Me, too."

"Can you believe Mom had sex with Rex Daniels? Oh my God, Clara—" She turned red eyes on Clara.

"He's not my dad."

"You don't know that. Not until Kitty finishes the story."

Clara got Abbie down onto the bed and tugged the blankets out from under her, took off her shoes and her socks because she knew her sister hated to sleep in socks.

"Sleep with me," Abbie said, shuffling sideways to make room for Clara. "Come on. I'm lonely. Hearing all that stuff about Mom makes me sad."

"You know what Mom used to say to me?" Clara kicked off her old sneakers and climbed into Abbie's bed. "She told me that some people were meant to bend and some people were meant to break, and that I was a bender. And you—" she pushed damp hair off Abbie's face "—were a breaker. And that I had to bend so you wouldn't break."

"Mom told me the same thing," Abbie whispered. "Except I needed to bend so you wouldn't break. It was her way of telling us to look out for each other."

"I haven't done a very good job of that lately," Clara said.

"It's all right," Abbie said because she was hardwired to say those kinds of things.

"No. It's not," Clara said. "And that's going to change."

24

BETTYKAY

Los Angeles, California
1970

I WAS DREAMING about the psych ward. Mrs. Bastille lost the baby doll and we were all searching for it while she cried. I woke up with a start, nearly headbutting poor Rex.

"Honey," I said, patting his cheek as he kissed my shoulder. His face was smooth and his hair was damp. "What time is it?"

"Still early." I hadn't meant to sleep in. I sat up, but he pushed me gently back down on the bed. "Shhh, stop, darling. You sleep."

"But the car—"

"We're doing all the interior shots in the bar. No stunts. No need for a nurse."

"Kitty—"

"Has the day off. Hugh wants there to be nothing but

masculine energy on set for these scenes." That sounded like something Hugh would say. Rex smiled like he knew how obnoxious that was. "You and Kitty have a lunch reservation at the Beverly Hills Hotel and then massages, and then, I don't know, whatever else you gals cook up."

"Rex," I whispered. "You planned all that?"

"Just a little thank-you for how hard you and Kitty are working on the set."

"That's so sweet."

"I'm a sweet guy." He kissed me once and then again. There was a honk outside and I knew it was Rick in the blue Bronco. I flinched, and Rex felt it, too, but we didn't talk about it.

It had been five weeks since that first night and I'd all but officially moved in with Rex. I was going with Rex to set every single day. Hugh gave me a job—assistant medic, which paid more than nursing ever would. Rex was still doing his own stunts and I tried to make things safer for him, but I learned quick, no one listened to the assistant medic.

A half hour after Rex left, there was a knock on the door. Too early to be the driver to take me to the Beverly Hills Hotel, but Rex was always having things delivered. A few days ago, there'd been a dozen roses and a first aid kit. A week ago, he'd paid someone to gather all the information they could about the RN certification in California.

I threw open the door to find Kitty, windblown and beautiful, a scarf tied over her hair that had been dyed dirty blond for the movie and big sunglasses covering her eyes.

"What are you doing here?" I cried, hugging her. "We're supposed to meet at the hotel."

"I can't have one other person touching me today, Betts," she said with the exhaustion that came from all the days in hair and makeup. "Let's go to Canter's and have a gigantic breakfast and walk it off on the beach."

"But Rex..."

"Is working. And for the first time in five weeks I am not. Unless you want some stranger touching your naked body?"

I didn't. Of course, I didn't. And she knew that because she was my best friend.

We sat in a booth in the back by the stairwell. Kitty ordered frankfurter and eggs with tomatoes on the side, and I got the hard salami omelet and black coffee.

Kitty took off the glasses but not the scarf.

"How is it possible I miss you when I see you on set almost every day?" I asked her.

"Beats me but I'm with you." Kitty held up a small silver flask. "Irish?"

I shook my head. I'd stopped drinking, since I got hired, and I only smoked the occasional bit of grass when Rex was asleep and I found myself too worked up to lie beside him.

Kitty tucked the flask away without pouring any into her coffee, either.

"How is Alexander?" I asked. I missed my old roommate.

"Fine. He's working on the new Robert Redford movie. He's got a new boyfriend."

"Did you get someone to take my bedroom?"

She shook her head.

"Are you keeping it open for me?"

"Maybe?" Kitty said and held out her hands. "Don't be sore. It's an insurance policy. On-set romances burn hot and heavy, but when filming is over they can fizzle out."

"Rex and I are not fizzling out," I said, blushing so hard I had to press my cool hands to my face.

Kitty laughed. "Happy to hear things are good in the sack, Betts."

"I'm just…" I leaned forward. Kitty did the same. "No one ever told me."

"About the big O?" she whispered, and I nodded. "They don't want us to know what we're missing. How are things otherwise?"

I sat back, fiddling with my coffee cup. She was my best friend, had helped me through the darkest part of my life, but I didn't know how to talk about *this*.

"Answer one question and we don't have to talk about it again," Kitty said.

"Okay."

"Are you using heroin, too?"

I sucked in a deep breath, light-headed, like I'd been underwater for ages and had just come up for air. No one ever said that word, but it screamed in the silences. The silence around Rick. Around the nights I woke up alone in the bed. The way Rex's hands shook on the way home after a long day on set and he yelled at me that he was fine. How after he took his "medicine" he would apologize and stare out at the ocean like he wasn't seeing anything.

Heroin. Rex was using heroin.

I'd known that. *Guessed* it, maybe was the better word. Whenever I brought it up with Rex, he pushed me off topic, or started kissing me and taking off my clothes. I was so happy, so impossibly happy, I'd let it go. Because in my head, I knew that string could unravel everything. So I left it unpulled.

"I'm not," I said.

"Good." Kitty was fierce. "Don't. Ever."

"Does everyone know?" I asked.

Kitty shrugged. "It's not the secret Rex thinks it is."

Kitty removed something from her purse. A pale blue airmail letter from Jenny.

"You already read it?" I asked when I found it open.

"It's addressed to both of us. She thinks you're still at The Birdhouse."

"Is she all right?"

"She's gotten a promotion to captain and been transferred to Da Nang. And she's got a thing for a helicopter pilot." Kitty and I smiled at each other.

"Is she still lonely?"

"I think the helicopter pilot is taking care of that. And she says she works with a doctor who lets her assist in surgeries."

"Really?" We sat back as our food was delivered, the smell making my mouth water. I asked for more coffee. "What kind of surgeries?"

"Everything." Kitty covered her eggs with pepper. "She said she removed shrapnel from some guy's eye and is tying off blood vessels on the regular."

Actual surgery? Surgical nurses handed over tools, helped prep and clean. They didn't tie off blood vessels, much less remove shrapnel from an eye. They couldn't even press a scalpel to skin!

What would it be like to be so involved? So important? I wasn't sure what I was these days, taping Rex together so he could get another shot, ignoring the poison he was putting in his veins, but it felt like the opposite of useful. I was spoiled rotten by Rex, by his gifts and orgasms. But inside I was a blank space, waiting for something to come along and fill me up.

As Kitty tapped a little puddle of ketchup on the side of her eggs, all these things that were wrong with my life, and even some that were more right than I could even put into words—they twisted inside of me.

"It was my last night in Labor and Delivery," I said, clumsy with the story. I hadn't had practice telling it, save for that one time I told Rex and then buried it down deep where it never saw light again. "With Dr. Fischer."

"That's a name I haven't thought of in ages." Kitty rolled her eyes at me and then stilled. She put down the ketchup. "Betts?"

"He told me I was a bad nurse. A bad soldier is what he said. I always thought he didn't like me because I reminded him of you but he said he didn't trust me."

"That man was an ass."

The rest spilled out of me like I'd been turned upside down like that ketchup. And whatever horror I'd expected from Kitty, or full-throated support of my leaving nursing behind, I should have known better.

She pushed aside our plates and grabbed my hands. Her nails were clipped short and kept ragged by the movie makeup team. "You expect me to agree that story makes you a bad nurse?"

"I broke the rules—"

"You were with her all that time, and all that time she would have been alone. And cold. You talked to her and you kept her warm and you tried to make better what you could. That's what nursing is, Betts. I could take a strap to that man for making you feel this way. For taking away what you're so good at."

"I miss nursing," I blurted.

"Of course you do. Because you are a goddamn nurse, BettyKay Allen. And now you can get certified in California." She was all lit up, and Kitty all lit up was a force of nature, impossible to resist. "You can work at County and we'll go on double dates and we'll have breakfast right here every Sunday."

Tears burned in my eyes at the relief that the story was out there. Relief that Kitty had affirmed what I'd wanted to be true, that I was still who I'd thought I was. Who I wanted to be. I laughed and dried my eyes with my napkin.

"Who are you taking on these double dates?"

"Once this movie is over, and he's no longer my director, I'm going to make Hugh a very lucky man," Kitty said.

"I thought you didn't want to sleep with him?"

"I didn't want to sleep with *my director*. Once he's not my director…" Kitty batted her eyelashes at me.

"Hugh reminds me of Dr. Fischer."

"Really?" Kitty made a face.

"A little?"

"They're nothing alike. Dr. Fischer was a Neanderthal. You know he told me once if I quit school he'd marry me? And Hugh is totally with it. Totally cool."

"Really?"

"You read the script, Betts," she said, cutting into her frankfurters. "I am free in the end and Rex is killed. I'm telling you, Hugh is a feminist. He just hides it sometimes. Come on, Betts. Your eggs are getting cold."

25

BETTYKAY

HUGH LIVED IN one of the poolside cottages at the Chateau Marmont, which, frankly, I'd expected to be grander considering Jim Morrison sometimes stayed in the penthouse. A week after shooting on *The Petticoat Kid* wrapped, he had a blowout party, renting out all the available cottages around the pool for cast and crew. He practically bought out the Liquor Locker next door and the booze was free-flowing.

When Rex and I arrived late, Kitty pulled me into the bedroom in Hugh's cottage. "You okay?" she asked.

"Fine." I wasn't sure why I lied. "Why?"

"'Cause I haven't seen you since we wrapped."

"It's been busy. Rex... Rex's been busy."

"Is he all right?" she asked. "I heard he was sick."

"Where'd you hear that?"

"Mimi in makeup."

Mimi and Rick had a sometimes yes, sometimes no thing

going. I wondered if Rex knew that Rick was telling people he'd been sick. He didn't like people talking about him.

"Betts?"

"I think he just caught a bug on set," I said. If I took a minute to think about it, I might have been concerned, but there didn't seem to be time. Everything seemed to be moving so fast. I'd just gotten to Hollywood. Wasn't I just finishing my last night at the hospital? Wasn't I just signing a lease for that apartment with Denise?

And now I was covering for Rex Daniels.

"Yeah," Kitty said carefully. "A bug. That means you can't pick up a phone?"

"You know men when they get sick," I said and pulled her into my arms.

"You look beautiful," I said, which wasn't a lie. She wore a white lace dress with bell sleeves and a short skirt. She'd cut her hair after all the styling products and dirt on set had made a mess of it, and the short Twiggy haircut—of course—looked amazing on her.

"Thank you," she said. "Tonight I'm going to tell Hugh if he wants to go on a date he should ask me."

I laughed. "That should go great," I said. Hugh did not like to be led around, but the two of them had a chemistry that was undeniable. If there was one thing I wasn't worried about right now, it was Kitty taking care of herself.

"You laugh, but just you wait. Hugh Bonnet is going to be eating out of the palm of my hand."

"Speaking of eating," I said. "I'm starved. Is there anything around here?"

"Hugh ordered in some food. It's set up by the pool."

I hooked my arm through hers and started to walk away, but she stood, rooted. "If something was going on, you'd tell me. Right?"

"Kitty," I laughed, and it sounded fake to my own ears. "What would be going on?"

For fourteen bucks, I'd booked Rex and me a room in the hotel, hoping that a change of scenery might help us reconnect after what had happened last Saturday.

And it would keep Rick away.

The room was in my name, the tasseled key in the pocket of my double-breasted purple polyester suit.

Hugh was holding court on the blue-tiled pool deck, tiki torches lit up around him. He wore jeans and a linen shirt. His pale skin had burned red during filming, and his nose was peeling.

"I'm telling you," he was saying, drink in one hand and a cigarette in the other. "If this movie doesn't make Kitty Devereaux a star and Rex Daniels a god, I don't know what will."

"I don't need to be a god, Hugh," Rex said, stretched out on a chaise nearby.

"Well I wouldn't mind it," Hugh joked.

I walked up to Rex's side and he reached up for my hand. I took it, pressed my fingers to his wrist.

Checking his pulse. Fast.

He pulled his hand free and gave me a glare. Kitty noticed and I smiled as wide as I could.

"You want something to eat?" I asked him.

"I'm fine," he said, cold as ice.

I got a plate and lined up at the small buffet for food I wasn't going to eat.

"A toast!" Hugh said, and around me people lifted their champagne and highball glasses. "To Rex, I don't know if he's brave or foolish doing those stunts of his, but he's one in a million."

"Hear! Hear!" people cried and lifted their glasses higher.

Stop, I wanted to yell, *don't praise him for his recklessness. Don't make that his value, it's making a mess of him.*

"And to Kitty." Hugh paused and shook his head, looking at Kitty in the golden California end-of-day sunlight. She positively glowed pink and cream, sexy and innocent, and if I didn't know her already I'd wish I did.

That was the power of Kitty Devereaux.

"Beautiful, fierce, sexy Kitty. I've never seen a woman so beloved by a camera. Now. Will you put me out of my misery and let me take you to dinner?"

Everyone laughed and clapped, and for a second Kitty pouted as if her thunder had been stolen. "I suppose," she said. "But you should know right now, I have expensive tastes."

Which wasn't true, but the crowd loved it. Hugh brought her close and kissed her cheek and flash bulbs popped.

This world, I thought with an ache, *was a mirror reflecting all the wrong things.*

I smelled Rex's Aramis cologne next to me, but I didn't turn to face him. I focused on putting deviled eggs on my plate.

"I'm sorry, darling," he said. "Snapping my hand away like that. I'm sorry."

"I know," I said.

"You were taking my pulse and I, well, I guess I'm tired of you taking my pulse."

"I don't know how to stop," I whispered. "I almost lost you."

"It was an accident, sweetheart." He took my plate of eggs, handed it to a waiter and then drew me close and said, for perhaps the hundredth time, "It won't happen again."

"I got us a room here," I said. "I thought it might be nice. A break. You've been working so hard."

"Betts," he said. "Please, look at me."

Finally I turned to face him and his sweet grin and sweeter

eyes didn't flip me inside out the way they used to. All I saw were blown-out pupils and blue lips.

"That's sweet of you," he said, wrapping his arms around me in the way I liked best, so I was right up against him from the top of my head to my knees. I could bury my face in his chest and pretend the world didn't even exist. It was him and it was me, and there was nothing else. "You're the sweetest girl I've ever known, Betts."

I shook my head into his chest, holding him as tight as I could.

"Well now, Sourpuss." Hugh came up, clapped his hands around both of us, ruining the moment. "I need to thank you, too. Without you I don't know that Rex would have made it through that movie in one piece. You've got a job on my set anytime you want."

"No, thank you," I said, surprising them both. "I don't think moviemaking is for me."

"Well, then, you're hanging out with the wrong crowd," Hugh said, scoring a laugh.

An hour later, Rex came up to me, his rough edges smoothed by a few drinks. "Hey, darling," he said. "You got us a room here?"

"Yeah," I said and kissed him because I was eager to fall into that hotel bed with him. "You want to go?"

"Can I have the key?" he asked. "Rick and I are going to go up for just a second."

"No."

"Darling—"

"No. He can't use our room. I rented that room."

"It's just for a second."

"I know what it's for," I said.

"Keep your voice down," he said, leading me into the banana leaf trees that surrounded the cottages.

"You nearly died, Rex. In my arms, you near—"

"If I can't use your room, I'll find another."

I hated him when he was like this, distant and removed, indifferent to everything about me. When he was like this, it was very easy to believe he didn't love me. He just loved having a woman like me around. One who wanted to have sex and put food in the oven and kept him standing when his job and his drugs would have him flat on his back.

"Don't. Please don't, Rex. Please."

He shook off my hand and walked off into a group of people who would do whatever he wanted. Get him whatever he asked for. Who would cheer and support and aid him until he was dead.

I told myself not to follow, that if he wanted to do this to himself then that was his business, his life. But even as I thought that, I knew it was a lie. I couldn't let him kill himself in one of these rooms. As I raced to follow him, I ran into Kitty.

"Have you seen Rex?"

"Yeah, he went upstairs with Rick. Is everything okay?"

I pulled in a breath that cracked and broke, and Kitty took me by the hand. "Come on. Let's get you some privacy." I fished out the tasseled key ring from my pocket and pressed it into her hand.

The room, however, was unlocked, and when we opened the door, Rex was already sitting on the edge of the bed, rolling up his sleeve. Rick was there, too, and shifted to try to hide the gear.

"This is my room," I said.

"Front desk gave me a key. Give us a minute, would you, honey?" Rex said, coming to his feet.

He was going to gently push me out of this room, and if I

went, I'd lose myself entirely. The person I was and the person I wanted to be would be gone, all so I could be with him. Because, I could see it now, those were the rules. If I wanted him, I had to vanish.

"No," I said, quietly. "It's my room."

"Betts." Rex never yelled, but when he was upset, his voice got hard in a way that hit a button in me, some remnant of my father. It was hard to resist doing what he wanted, if only to keep the peace.

Thank God Kitty was there.

"You should leave, Rex. It's her room," she said.

"Betts," Rex said, ignoring Kitty. "This is between us."

"I think it's between you and Rick," I said.

He took a deep breath and blew it out through his nose.

"Go," I said to Rick, who'd been waiting for Rex to tell him what to do next.

"You're not my boss," Rick said and pointed to Rex. "He is."

"Go on, Rick," Rex said, slapping his old friend on the back. "I'll find you in a few minutes."

Jesus, I thought. *Me and Rick, peas in a pod taking our cues from Rex.*

That was how it worked for guys like Rex, who surrounded themselves with people who would do what they asked without question. Was it loyalty or some kind of empty spot Rex could spot in us, the way we wanted to be useful, close to him? I didn't know.

Kitty touched my hand and I nodded.

"I'll be right outside," Kitty said. "Shout if you need me."

"We aren't going to need you, Kitty," Rex said with his charming aw-shucks accent and smile. "This is a whole lot of fuss for nothing."

"Will you quit?" I asked as soon as the door closed.

He blinked, somehow stunned by the question. "There's nothing to quit—"

I pulled my suitcase out of the closet and opened the dresser drawer, removing the cream silk negligee I'd bought special for tonight, the extra clothes I'd packed hoping Rex and I could hide away for a few days.

"Betts," he said, grabbing my shoulders. "Stop. Talk to me."

I turned and crossed my arms. "We've talked. We've talked and talked, and every time we talk I get turned around inside my head until what you're doing is okay. And it's not, Rex. It's not. You nearly died."

"But I didn't." He smiled at me. All the filming out there in the desert had given him a tan. He was so handsome he took my breath away.

"Because of me," I said. "You're alive right now because of me. You would have died, Rex, with that fucking needle in your arm."

"But I—"

"Stop!" I yelled, my hands to my head. "Stop it. You over-dosed, Rex. You overdosed and Rick couldn't save you." I'd dragged him into the shower, doused him with cold water and gave him CPR until he came back, coughing and limp, but alive.

"Maybe you're right," he said, and for the first time in all our weeks together I saw the fear in his eyes. "That's why I need you to stick around, darling."

I laughed but it caught on a sob. It didn't take a great imag-ination to see how this would go, where it would end. More overdoses. More close calls. He'd ask me to be the one to put the garbage in his veins. *You're a nurse*, he'd say. *You'll be safe*, he'd say. And I'd do it because I was a nurse and I wanted to keep him safe and I loved him.

"I love you," I said.

"I love you, too, you know that." He put that big rough hand of his around my neck, the calluses catching on the fine hair at my nape.

I stepped away. "I need you to fire Rick and quit the drugs and choose me. Choose a life."

"I choose you," he said. "You live in my house. You work with me every day. I give you everything you need."

"Fire Rick and quit the drugs."

"Honey," he laughed, and I realized that was a tactic of his. Laughing. Like nothing was wrong, like I was overreacting. The world around him was burning and he wanted me to sit down and have a drink with him.

Just relax. He said that a lot. Like the problem was me.

"Stop, Rex. Just stop. This is serious. I can't... I can't pretend anymore." My hands still remembered his cool skin, the pulse I couldn't feel in his wrist or neck. I'd pressed my head to his chest knowing what I'd hear.

Nothing.

The smile fell from his face, and this version of him, his eyes clear and resolute—this was the version so rarely seen.

"I need it, honey," he said. "Since Korea. The stunts, the wear and tear on my body, the pain—"

"There are other ways to manage pain."

"I've tried them. And I'm not interested in other ways." There. At least that was the truth. "Some days I've got more control than others and for the days I don't, Rick is there, keeping me on the straight and narrow."

"Rick nearly got you killed."

"No system is perfect, honey." His grin broke my heart.

I shook my head. "I won't be around to save you next time."

"What are you saying, Betts?"

He knew what I was saying. I looked him in the eye until he was forced to look away.

"That's it? You're just leaving?"

There was some part of this dynamic I recognized from the house on Wolff Road. Mother asking for some tiny thing that might give her room to breathe or a sliver of sunlight in that gray house, Father getting mad that she didn't find everything perfect already, thinking something for herself was a condemnation of him. And his anger making her take back whatever she'd asked for.

I felt that instinct to make this moment all right. To kiss Rex and tell him I wasn't going anywhere. But I stood my ground and let the silence be silence.

"I thought you were made of sterner stuff than this, Betty-Kay," he said.

"You have no idea what I'm made of," I told him. He had no idea because I'd never shown him. I'd been hiding here, had hitched my wagon to his star and let him determine who I was the past few months. The same way he did with his fans. We were not so different after all. "Give me the key you got from the front desk and get out of my room."

In some part of my brain, I must have seen this coming. Perhaps I'd even been planning it. I had everything that mattered packed in my suitcase and the only things I'd left at his house were things I could replace.

He slammed the door behind him, and I sat down next to my suitcase, open on the bed. I heard more arguing in the hall, Kitty giving him both barrels, and I smiled through my grief. From the silk pouch of the suitcase I pulled out the pink buttons.

"Jesus," Kitty said, coming in and shutting the door. "I had no idea he could be so mean."

"He's just hurt," I said. "He gets mean when he's hurt."

"That's no excuse. You all right?" Kitty sat down next to me.

"No," I said.

She pressed her shoulder to mine. "You going to give those to me?" she asked, pointing at the buttons.

"I was going to put them in a jar of orange marmalade."

"That's the grossest thing I've ever heard."

"Make them into earrings?"

"That might work."

"He nearly died last week," I said. "After the last night of shooting."

"He overdosed?"

I nodded, remembering Rick's voice waking me up, telling me there was a problem.

"Rick wanted to shoot milk in his veins, can you believe it? And now every time I fall asleep, I'm having nightmares about milk. Like the heroin isn't bad enough."

"Why didn't you tell me?" Kitty whispered.

"Because he said it was private. A secret. He didn't want people talking about him, and I didn't want people talking about him like that." A tear slipped onto my hand and I wiped it off.

"Betts," Kitty breathed. "I'm so sorry."

I bit my lip and nodded. Anger was bleeding into my grief, anger that I couldn't change him. That this place was going to use him up and leave him to die and that no one cared. And it would use me up, too, if I let it. All those wasted days in the sunlight, the false sense of purpose on the movie set.

It was like waking up from a dream.

"I have to go," I said.

"Your room at The Birdhouse is waiting for you."

"I have to leave California," I said, the decision made. I had the money I made as a nurse on set. I could get a plane ticket to Chicago and a train ticket from there to Des Moines and a bus after that to Greensboro. I'd be home by morning.

"Right now?" Kitty asked.

"Yeah," I said, holding back the tears, my mouth and heart twisted in a knot. "If I go to The Birdhouse, he'll be up there tomorrow morning with roses and limes, and he'll pull me right back into this spot."

"I won't let him," Kitty said.

"But I will." I put the buttons in my pocket and started to pack up the suitcase my parents had taken on their honeymoon.

"So, that's it, you're going to run away again?"

"What do you mean 'again'?"

"Your parents' house. The baby and Dr. Fischer. You're just…running away."

I recoiled, shocked she would say something like that. That was certainly what it *looked* like I was doing, but it didn't feel that way. The baby and Dr. Fischer, I'd needed time and distance to process that, and I'd gotten that. But I couldn't *stay* here.

"I don't have another choice."

"Of course you do. You stay. You fight for the life you want."

"I don't want this life!" I cried. "I need to be useful, Kitty. I need to have purpose and work."

"Take your boards and get a job here."

I shook my head.

"He'll forget about you once the movie is done," Kitty said, regretting it immediately. I could see it on her face. I could see everything on her face—her fear, her grief, her love for me. I had to look away.

"You're probably right."

Kitty stroked my shoulder. "I'm sorry," she whispered. "I didn't mean that."

I flipped the locks shut on the suitcase and gripped the wooden handle.

"So, that's it? You're going to go be a nurse in small town Iowa?"

It was hard to imagine going back there with all this emotion seething through me. Even the emergency room would leave so much quiet, so much time to wonder about Rex, whether he was going to kill himself, if he was already dead.

I would miss Kitty so much.

And then I remembered Jenny. Assisting in surgery. Having purpose. So busy she didn't have time to think. And in that moment, that sounded not just appealing but exactly right. But it was just an idea, not even close to a plan. I would, no doubt, come to my senses somewhere over Nebraska.

"Betts?" Kitty stood and clutched my shoulder. Of course she knew what I was thinking. That was how well she knew me. It was the nature of our friendship. "Don't. You're emotional and you're not thinking clearly."

"I'm not thinking anything."

"That war is wrong!"

"I'm not going to Vietnam, Kitty."

"You can fool everyone but me, Betts. I can see where your head is."

"Fine. The war might be wrong, but those boys aren't. Jenny isn't. All the other nurses and doctors over there, they're not wrong."

"You're going to go to bed tonight and you're going to wake up and see this for the terrible idea it is."

"Probably," I said.

"Stay the night," Kitty said. "We'll go back right now. Pop some popcorn, put on that Dolly Parton record you love, and we'll talk."

"I can't," I said and pulled her stiff body into my arms. "You know I can't." Because he would be there in the morning, and

I would let his lies be truth. "I love you, Kitty. Thank you for letting me hide here awhile."

She didn't hug me back. "Don't leave like this," she whispered. "You're scaring me."

I took the buttons from my pocket and held them out to her.

"I don't want them like this," she said.

"This is how I'm giving them to you."

"No. I want them in marmalade. You need to—"

I grabbed her hand and placed the buttons in her palm, curling her fingers around them. "I'll call you when I get home."

"What about me?" Kitty followed me down the hallway. "What am I going to do without you?"

I pivoted and faced her, separated by ten feet of brown shag carpet.

"You won't need me," I said. "You're going to be a star."

"I won't be there to pick you up," she called, her fear making her a little mean. "I won't be there to get you out of trouble. You'll be by yourself."

Maybe that was what I needed.

"Take these fucking things!" she shouted, and one of the buttons ricocheted off the brown patterned wallpaper. Another hit a light sconce, cracking it. The third hit my back.

I turned the corner and strode out of the Chateau. The party by the pool was just warming up, Rex in some empty room risking his life, Kitty Devereaux a star about to ignite.

And I walked away from all of it.

26

ABBIE

Los Angeles, California
2019

KITTY'S OFFICE WAS the most beautiful place Abbie had
ever been. Cream and pink with gold highlights. It was like
the After reveal in those home renovation shows she liked to
watch in the middle of the night when the house was quiet.

Kitty sat on the other side of the desk, looking both like
a million bucks and deeply chagrined, having just confessed
she threw buttons at Mom as she left the Chateau Marmont,
because Mom couldn't stay in California and *pretend to be*
happy there.

Mom couldn't pretend.

Not one more minute.

"I need...a second," Abbie said and stood up from the plush
white chair she'd been sitting in, sweating into the fabric.

"Abbie?" Clara said, all concerned from her own plush white chair where she *wasn't* sweating into the fabric.

They'd been invited over for breakfast, far too early, if you asked Abbie. Clara had eaten a bowl of yogurt and fruit. She'd sipped her coffee and asked Kitty questions about Mom and Rex Daniels while Abbie nursed a cup of coffee and oozed red wine from her pores. Pretending to be fine. Pretending all the time.

"Can I—?"

Abbie shook her head. She didn't want her sister around. She didn't want anyone around after last night. After that story. She tried to open the sliding glass door leading out onto a stone veranda and then the elaborate garden, but her arms felt like jelly.

"You have to—" Kitty said, standing up from her spot behind the desk.

"Let me—" Clara said.

"I got it," Abbie snapped and then regretted it. She regretted everything. She was one big ball of regret.

Abbie unlocked and shoved open the door, getting out into the fresh air before she threw up all over that beautiful room. She made sure she was out of sight before bracing her hands on her knees and pulling in big breaths.

The hangover wasn't the worst she'd ever had. But the embarrassment sure was.

"Abbie?"

Of course. *Of course* her sister followed. She wiped her eyes and stood up. "Three months ago I couldn't get you to answer my phone calls, and now you won't give me a minute of privacy?"

"Are you okay?" Clara asked, pushing her way right through Abbie's anger.

Abbie remembered once, slamming her bedroom door in

Clara's face—she must have been eleven. Clara, who would have been twelve, that werewolf-y place between child and teenager, lay down on the ground outside her bedroom, whispering into the crack between the door and floor, guessing what was wrong.

Is it Maryanne? she'd asked. *Jim down the street? Is it Mrs. Ophangee? Is it Mom? Dad? Oh my God, Abbie, is it me? Are you upset with me?*

Abbie had opened the door to tell Clara it wasn't her, that she didn't *know* what it was so therefore it was everything, and Clara, still on the ground, rolled right into her room. Abbie had laughed and forgotten why she was mad, and they'd gone for a bike ride to the baseball fields.

"Abbie?" Clara stepped toward her, and when Abbie didn't flinch or snarl, Clara came closer.

"Mom was so brave," Abbie said. "Leaving like that. Like she knew she had to do it because she couldn't change him if he didn't want to change. Clean break and on her terms." *And I'm such a chicken shit.*

"She was," Clara agreed.

"I'm hungover."

"Yeah."

"And embarrassed."

Birds were loud in the trees below them. But Clara was quiet, and Abbie appreciated that.

"Ben's leaving me."

There. The words were out.

She waited for the world to end. For the unraveling of her life to begin. She looked at Clara, expecting to see judgment.

But Clara's surprise and hint of outrage was a balm on her wounded pride. "He's leaving *you*?"

Abbie nodded.

"Because of the drinking?"

"No. I'm drinking because he's leaving." Abbie shook her head, the last year a tangle she couldn't keep straight. "Or maybe... I don't... I don't even know."

"This is the secret you were keeping? The one Kitty said Mom was worried about?"

Abbie nodded.

"Have you and Ben tried counseling?"

"Oh God, we've done so much counseling. Hours of *honoring each other's feelings* and *listening with our hearts*." She could see now what a waste that was. How Ben had agreed only for the kids, which was sweet, but he hadn't actually *tried*. He'd checked out ages ago.

"Why is he leaving?"

"Because we got married too young? Because having two kids ten minutes apart isn't as fun as it seems? Because he wants... I don't know, something else."

"Someone else?"

"Maybe? Probably. Who the fuck cares?" God, it felt good to swear. "He doesn't want *me*. Us. Our life." She pressed her hands to her chest and felt her pounding heart, proof she was alive, that this hadn't killed her when there were times she was so sure it would.

"Do you want him? I mean, do you want to fight for him?"

Fight for a man who didn't love her anymore? Fight for a life that didn't make anyone happy? How long had she been pretending?

Way too long.

The joints in her neck protested but she shook her head no. She wasn't happy. Not with Ben. Hadn't been for years.

Admitting it felt like failure and relief all at once.

Carefully, like Abbie was some kind of feral beast, Clara reached out and pulled her into her arms. And Abbie, so good at giving comfort, stood there stiff as a board wondering what the hell was wrong with her.

"Jesus, Abbie," her sister whispered in her ear. "Let go."

One sob broke through. And then another. And then she was in pieces, holding on to Clara's shoulders like the ground beneath her feet was breaking away. Clara held her up through all of it, patting Abbie's back and saying all the right things.

"He's found an apartment in town and wants to move out and I've been telling him no," she said, once she got herself together. "That the time wasn't right because…when is the time right for that? When is the time right to tell the kids Dad's moving out? When is the time right to split up our friends and have people whispering about us in the grocery store and…" She ran out of words.

"Never," Clara said. "There is no right time, Abbie. It's just a shitty thing you have to do. Because you can't go on like this."

The drinking, the special occasion Adderall. *Oh my God, I've been taking a kid's ADHD medicine. When did I decide that was okay?*

"I want my mom."

"I know," Clara whispered back and squeezed Abbie hard. It had been a long time since her sister had hugged her so much. Abbie soaked it up like a neglected garden. "But you're not alone. I'm here. I'm here, Abbie."

Abbie buried her head in her sister's neck, comforted until she got swept up in a wave of embarrassment.

"I ruined that rug," Abbie breathed.

"Yeah."

"I can't pay for it."

"She knows."

"I don't… I don't even know how to do this. How to stop… everything."

"Are you drinking right now?"

"No."

"Keep doing that. And maybe it's time to call Ben."

Abbie thought of him sleeping on the couch for the last six months and knew it was past time.

"What are you going to do?" Abbie asked. "About Vickie."

"We're talking about your messed-up love life, not mine."

Abbie shrugged. "I can multitask."

Clara smiled. "All she wants to do is love me and I keep pushing her away," she confessed.

"I'm familiar with that move," Abbie said.

"Why do I do that?" Clara asked, and Abbie realized that her sister with all the answers, the sister who always had something to say, really didn't know.

It was kind of sweet.

"Because love is hard," Abbie said. "And intimacy is uncomfortable."

"It's like peeling off all my skin," Clara said, shuddering.

"Gross," Abbie said.

"You know what I mean."

"I do. It's hard and uncomfortable but… Clara, it's worth it."

"Abbie!" Clara laughed. "Your marriage is splitting up. I'm not sure you're a reliable witness—"

"Ben and I are a terrible example," Abbie said. "But Mom and Dad? No matter how Kitty's story ends we know what they had was real. Mom and Kitty? That's real. This?" Abbie, her arms still around her sister, gave her a jostle. "Real. And worth it."

Clara looked right at Abbie like they were kids again.

"Do you love Vickie?" Abbie whispered. "Enough to spend your life with her?"

"Yeah," Clara said. "I do. I know you don't know her very

well but she's..." Clara shook her head like she couldn't find the words.

Abbie had never known that feeling when there weren't big enough words to describe how you felt about another person. She and Ben had always been comfortable, completely describable. Utterly *known*. There'd never been a moment of mystery or wonder.

"I've really messed up," Clara said.

"It sounds like we both need to make some phone calls," Abbie said.

"I'm going to go back and talk to Kitty, clarify a few things," Clara said, pointing her thumb back at Kitty's office. "You want to come with me?"

"No," Abbie said, her stomach roiling. "I'm going to call Ben before I run out of courage."

Abbie watched her sister walk around the edge of the building and, once she was gone, stepped back into the darkness of the cottage. She faced the wall of photos and pulled her phone out of her pocket, wondering if this was something she should do in person. Would it be easier this way? Would it be easier *any* way? Or was it just hard no matter what?

In one of the pictures, of the dozens of Mom and Kitty on the wall, Kitty was wearing a big blond wig and Groucho Marx glasses, her foot up on BettyKay's chair. And BettyKay had her head tipped back, wide-mouthed with laughter.

That picture, that woman laughing because her best friend was doing everything she could to make it happen—that was love. Ben never tried to make her that happy. It wasn't his fault, he didn't know how, and if asked, she wouldn't know how to make him that happy, either.

She hit Ben's number and did what should have been done a while ago.

"Abbie?"

"Hi, Ben," she said.

"You all right?"

"I am, I'm fine. How are the kids?"

"Good. Max is asking about you. He said I don't read the bedtime stories right."

"You've got to use a voice when you read the dog parts."

"Oh. Okay."

She swallowed, closed her eyes and tried as best as she could to imagine the moment after this one. The moment after everything changed. The moment that wasn't the end, but the beginning of something new. "Ben?"

"Yeah."

"You can get that apartment and we'll tell the kids when I get back."

CLARA

The Beecher sisters were not having an easy time of it this weekend.

It was hard work letting go.

And Clara had never been very good at it. Something in Kitty's story was really bothering her. Or rather, something Kitty had been leaving out. And maybe if she was a different kind of person she'd let it go.

But her mother was right, she did like to pick things apart.

And she was about to pick some things apart.

Because she needed to know *why* Kitty had been kept a secret. The way Clara saw it there were only two possible reasons:

1. BettyKay and Willis didn't want Kitty in the girls' lives. Which frankly, after all these stories, Clara didn't buy. Mom and Kitty had been close and Dad wasn't the kind of man to try and control his wife's friendships. Which left…

2. Kitty didn't want to be in their lives.

This in her cynic's soul, felt far more likely.

She slid open the glass door to Kitty's office, only to find the movie star looking at her phone through reading glasses. When Clara came in, she put the reading glasses away, like they were a secret she kept.

"Everything all right?" Kitty asked.

"Not at the moment. But I have hope for the future."

Kitty laughed. "That's a good answer."

"Mom used to say it."

Mom? Is dinner ready? Mom? Can you take me to the pool? Mom? Is my track uniform clean?

Not at the moment, but I have hope for the future.

"I am going to try and fix things with my girlfriend," Clara said.

"Attagirl. And Abbie?"

"She's going to end things with her husband."

Kitty sat back. "You've been gone ten minutes."

"We are our mother's daughters," Clara said. "When we make up our minds we act fast."

"Apparently."

"You going to throw buttons at us?"

The morning sunlight did Kitty no favors, but she was somehow more beautiful with everything revealed. She wore a pair of black running tights and a loose gray jacket with what appeared to be an elaborate hood, zipped up to her chin.

Kitty pressed her hands to her stomach and took a deep breath. Clara's comment about the buttons must have hit home.

"I was scared when your mom left," Kitty said. "Everything was changing for me. Not just because of Hugh, but the movie had a lot of energy behind it and I wanted her close to me. To keep me grounded. It was selfish, but I was selfish." She shrugged. "I'd like to think I've grown from my mistakes."

"I'm sorry," Clara said. "I shouldn't have said that."

"Well, it's true. It wasn't kind of me, and I lost a button in the shag carpet."

Clara smiled at the quip, but she was just warming Kitty up, and Kitty was watching her like she knew it. If Abbie were here she'd hate this tension, she'd do everything in her power to make it go away. Which was why she had to do this now, while Kitty and Clara were alone.

"I've been trying to figure out why Mom and Dad kept you a secret."

"That's really bothering you, isn't it?"

Clara nodded, sitting back down in her chair. She'd bought clothes online last night and they'd already been delivered this morning. The navy blue silk shorts with the bow at the waist and the red-and-white linen shirt and red sandals made her feel more in control than the old running stuff she'd worn on the plane.

"Were you lovers?" Clara asked, and Kitty's eyes went wide.

"Your mother and me?" Kitty laughed. "No, honey. Why do I feel like I'm being cross-examined?"

"What about you and my father?"

"Oh, now that's a twist isn't it? Something right out of a movie. But no. Willis loved your mother, he never would have strayed."

Clara nodded. These were answers she'd expected. "Did Mom ever tell you that Dad wanted to foster kids?"

"No. She never mentioned that."

Ah, Clara thought, *something Kitty didn't know.*

"Yeah. When Abbie and I were in high school, I think he was feeling the threat of an empty nest and wanted to try to fill it up a little. Dad always wanted people around. He loved it when we held sleepovers and Girl Scout meetings at our house. When I was in high school, he'd make these huge dinners for the whole track team after meets. Barbecues for Abbie's theater friends."

"He was a very generous man."

"And forgiving. You know? All that work with the VA. Helping vets get back on their feet when they got home from the war. He didn't judge any of them, no matter what they had going on in their lives. He was patient and kind."

Kitty smiled, but her eyes were cold. "What's your question?"

"What did you do that was so bad he didn't want you around us?" Clara asked.

"What makes you think it was him? Deciding that kind of thing?"

"Because the alternative is that you didn't want to be around us?"

And bingo.

Kitty's face went pale and then bright red. She fussed around on her desk, lining up pencils and her phone, the glasses she pretended not to need. Her smile was that of someone who was stalling for time.

"What are you hiding, Kitty?"

"You're so smart," she whispered. "Your mom always said that about you, too smart for your own good, and I never understood how that could be a thing. There have been a million times in my life I wished I'd been smarter. A million times I wished I'd been more like you."

Sophia, in a bright green knee-length romper with a blue batik shirt beneath it, a combination that had no business looking as good as it did, stuck her head into the office.

"Kitty? I know you asked me to hold your calls, but Spencer Davis is on the phone and he is getting rather impatient."

"I can take it," Kitty said, jumping at the chance to end this conversation. She put on her glasses and shifted her chair to face the landline phone on her desk. "Clara, would you mind?" she said without looking up.

27

CLARA

CLARA LOOKED OUT over the garden. It was early, seven in the morning in Chicago, five in the morning here. The sky was still, the moon just beginning to fade. A warm breeze blew down from the mountains behind her.

Her plan was to catch Vickie just as she finished her morning run. She was always relaxed after her run, chatty and a little silly, high on endorphins.

Breath held, Clara called her.

Oh God, she thought as the phone rang. She should have gone to Chicago, made some kind of grand gesture. Met her on the run. Presented her with a smoothie—

"Clara?" Vickie asked. She could hear the wind and Vickie panting.

"You're still running."

"Just finished. What are you doing? It must be six in the morning."

"Five."

"Is everything okay?" She imagined Vickie's black hair slipping out of her clips, her cheeks flushed.

"Yes. I mean, no. But, I wanted to hear your voice. I'm sorry. And I miss you. So much."

"Clara? You're...rambling."

"I know. And I know I've made things hard. And being with me isn't easy and clearly I have some boundary issues."

"In that they are fortress walls."

"Exactly." The bushes rustled in front of her and a fox darted across the grass like she wasn't even there. "My sister and her husband are splitting up."

"Oh no," Vickie said.

"No, it's a good thing."

"Well, it's a lot, even if it is a good thing."

"It is," Clara sighed and squeezed her eyes shut. "It really is."

"Clara?"

"I wish you were here, Vickie. I really just...wish you were here."

"I can be there tonight."

"Vickie, I can't ask—"

"I've been telling you that, Clara. You don't have to ask. I want to be there. If you want me there. I will be there."

"I want you here," Clara said.

"Then I'll see you tonight."

Clara hung up and above her the sky was turning a crystal blue, so bright it felt new.

Abbie came out an hour later, eyes swollen and face red, with two cups of coffee. She sat on the other chaise lounge in the garden.

"You okay?" Clara asked, putting down her phone and the

work emails she'd been scrolling through to take the coffee from Abbie.

"No. You?"

"Vickie's coming."

"Really?" Abbie asked.

Clara nodded and Abbie poked her shoulder.

"I'm happy for you." She took a sip of coffee and exhaled, closing her eyes against the bright sun of a new day.

Clara knew she should tell Abbie about the conversation she'd had with Kitty and how it had ended. But Abbie would not like how brusque she'd been with Kitty. And Abbie looked exhausted. And sad. And she didn't want to give her sister one more thing to be upset about.

In fact, while sitting out here and feeling slightly guilty about the way things had gone yesterday in Kitty's office she'd had a brilliant idea.

"I've been thinking about the house," Clara said, reclining back herself.

"Hmmm."

"I think you should keep it."

Abbie turned her head. "It's worth a stupid amount of money. Greensboro Historical Society keeps wanting to put a plaque on it. Years ago I tried to get Mom to find the deed to the house so we could get it all appraised, but she couldn't find it."

Couldn't find it? That didn't sound like Mom.

"We'll find the deed and you give Ben your house and you move in to Mom and Dad's. Think about it. I hate the idea of someone else living in their house. All that work they did to fix it up?"

"I need your help going through it, Clara," Abbie said. "That's going to be so hard."

"Vickie is a Marie Kondo acolyte. She'll keep us in line."

Behind them, someone cleared their throat, and they shifted up and around to see Sophia holding a bright orange Nike shoebox that could have been a prop from a 1980s movie set.

"Hi," she said with a small wave. "Sorry to bother you."

"You're not bothering us," Clara said.

"Kitty is out for the day," Sophia said, which was absolutely the most blatant lie Clara had ever heard. "But she wanted me to give you this."

She held out an ivory envelope, which Clara took, and then the box, which Abbie took.

"Will she be back tonight?" Abbie asked.

"I'm not sure of her plans."

"Vickie is coming tonight," Clara said. "Is that…okay?"

"Of course." Sophia smiled. "Please shout if you have any questions." She made it three steps before she flipped back. "I'm sorry about your mother. Betts was a special woman."

"You knew her," Abbie said, and Clara noted it wasn't a question.

"I always looked forward to her visits. She and Kitty would sit out here and laugh so hard they'd startle all the birds out of the trees."

Sophia left, and they sat there as the lights flickered on in the city below.

"What do you think is in here?" Abbie asked, giving the box a tiny shake. Over her head two dragonflies twirled and flew for the birdbath near the roses.

"Only one way to find out," Clara said, but she didn't open the envelope and Abbie didn't open the box.

"You'd think after everything that's happened we wouldn't be scared of a little shoebox." Abbie shook her head. "But I am."

Clara understood. There'd been seismic change, a complete overhaul of what they knew to be true about their family.

"I'll go first," Clara said, and she peeled open the large ivory envelope only to find two more envelopes. "Holy shit," Clara said, removing a check from the first one—a bank draft for two hundred and forty thousand dollars. She handed it over to Abbie.

Clara opened the second envelope and found a letter, which she read aloud.

"Clara and Abbie,
You are two beautiful, strong and fascinating women. Your mother was so proud of you and I understand why. She told me, when your father died, not to do this, a sentiment Jenny echoed at every opportunity. But I have always been foolish and shortsighted. Your mother accused me once—at the top of her lungs—of being in the movie business too long. Not everything could be wrapped up in a Hollywood ending. Your mother was right. I should not have started this ball rolling and if I could take it back, I would.

I would have broken the promise your mother and I had about those stupid buttons and not gone to the funeral. I would have mourned her alone. I am sorry for the upheaval I have caused.

With this letter is a box of some things I have kept over the years. I know you, like millions of others, read your mother's Vietnam diary, but I asked her to remove the pages that mentioned me or Rex in any substantive way and she—thank heavens—listened to me. The pages are in the box. As is the deed to your parents' home in Greensboro. I bought it from them when they were struggling with money when you girls were very little and I have tried over the years to sign it over to them, but you know how stubborn your parents could be. The check is the sum of the rent they insisted on paying me over the years. It's yours. As is the house. As is the box. As is every memory you have of your parents. Your father was a good man, noble and

caring with the kind of sense of humor your mother found irre-
sistible. Your mother loved you deeply, and the secrets she kept
from you were not kept out of shame or maliciousness. Some of
them, I believe, were just too painful to talk about and some, I
am so sorry to say, were a favor to me.
Best, Kitty"

Abbie popped the lid off the shoebox, revealing dozens and
dozens of pages from one of Mom's diaries, torn out at the
edge.

28

Pages torn from BettyKay's Vietnam diary

September 30, 1970
I got a letter from Kitty today.

I knew you weren't going to change your mind. That was the first thing she said in the letter and it made me laugh. Pure Kitty. Jenny told me where you were stationed, she wrote. Don't be sore with her. Or me. Please. I can't take it.

She asked for news, for forgiveness. Anything to know I'm alive and I'm all right. I don't know how to do it. Forgiving her is easy. I did that ages ago. But how do I tell her I've only been here a month and already the sounds of the incoming helicopters make me cry? I can't tell her about the hospital mess food, which somehow manages to be gross and delicious at the same time. Or how I saw Jenny last week for the first time and we ran to each other and sobbed in each other's arms. How do I tell her that I spend twelve hours on my feet fighting for a guy's life and then he's evacuated and I don't know what happens to him? Last night I held an eighteen-year-old kid's hand, a poor kid only a few years younger than me, and pretended to be his mom until he died from the burns that covered most of his body.

I don't know how to tell her about the rain. The mud. The smell of pseudomonas.

I don't know how to tell her that I made a mistake coming here, but that mistake is the most important work I've ever done in my life. I can't tell her how much I miss her and how I'd give everything I had for one more night at The Birdhouse. Or room 212. All of it.

My grief and longing. For her. For Rex...oh God. Rex. It's all too much to put in a letter. So, I put it here, and I don't write her. I'll regret it. I know I will. But everyone has their own way of surviving here. This is mine.

November 15, 1970
After a month of The Odd Couple, Jerome finally got his hands on a new movie. Came to us special, he kept saying. He was pretty excited as he set up the projector, and Delores and I hung the sheet we used as a screen. We put the boys who needed it in wheelchairs and carried a few of them in on cots. Ed from mess managed to get his hands on popcorn, which he of course burned. Not that it mattered. Doctors and nurses who'd gotten Mickey's in care packages passed them around, and Jerome shouted at us to keep it quiet and turned down the lights.

The Petticoat Kid. I mean...can you believe it? All the way over here we get not just a current movie but a bona fide hit. When the credits started and there was Rex Daniels in gold block letters, I almost stood up and walked out. But then Jerome snuck up on my side, handed me a box and said it came with the movie and he was supposed to deliver it to me by hand.

One little shake of the box and I knew what was in it. The buttons. I watched that whole movie with tears running down my face, remembering every single day of shooting that movie. I re-membered the weather and the heat and how Hugh had charmed

and bullied Rex and Kitty into working harder. And the prod-
uct on the screen was...breathtaking. Beautiful and painful and
sexy. It was handy that Rex's character was nothing like Rex
or I might have just self-combusted. The music soared and my
heart did with it. When it was over and all the boys were back
in their beds talking about how they'd know Kitty Devereaux
even if she was dressed up like a boy, I went back to my tent
and finally wrote her back. It wasn't a long letter.

I miss you. Thank you. Please keep writing. You were amaz-
ing in that movie and I am so proud of you. I'm sorry.

December 19, 1970
I dreamt about Rex last night. I woke up in a dark hooch, the
sound of Delores rolling over on her cot, and I couldn't shake off
the sensation that something was wrong. Perhaps it's just that
I miss him so much. I would pay good money for one last hug.
But it isn't that. Or it isn't just that. Missing him is something
I'm used to. This feels different.

December 25, 1970
Kitty wrote. Rex overdosed. Rick called the ambulance, but it
was too late.

December 26, 1970
I thought I could do anything for a year. But I can't do this any-
more. If I'd been there, I could have saved him. I know that. I
shouldn't have left. How do I stop feeling this way? Jenny says
I should put my head down and work and she's right. I have to
turn something off so I don't feel anything anymore.

January 27, 1971
I don't even know where to start. The last four days have been
a whirlwind. It's hard looking back at my diary entries from the

last month. I did what Jenny suggested and buried myself in work. I stopped thinking about home. Stopped thinking about Rex, which was a good thing. And Kitty, even though she wrote all the time, I didn't write back anymore. I had to put them out of my mind just to be in this place. Just to survive every day. I guess Kitty must have gotten worried and took matters into her own hands. Let me start from the beginning. I got four days R & R. Four whole days. I asked Jenny if she wanted to meet me in Saigon, but she told me I oughta come visit her. There was a USO tour swinging through Da Nang, and her cowboy helicopter pilot Jerome could get me and return me the next day. Jerome and Jenny were peas and carrots, and that man would do anything for her. I've gotten into the habit of praying in Vietnam, and I prayed for him every night. My relief when I saw his wide smile in mess was profound. But Jerome was an enlisted man and Jenny as a nurse was an officer, so their relationship was against the rules, and under scrutiny by some of the more racist folks Jenny worked with. Forget the fact that those bigots are sleeping with anything that moves, enlisted or officer.

God finds a way, Jenny always says. And I say: so do horny twenty-four-year-olds.

As he was about to start up his baby bird, as he called it, Jerome said Jenny had a surprise for me. Something about an old classmate, he said. And I knew. I told him I forgot something, ran back to my tent and grabbed that box of buttons and the first piece of clothing I could get my hands on. Which was how I ended up sewing the pink buttons onto a bra. If Kitty wasn't the surprise, I was going to be embarrassed.

There was a stage set up between the Quonset huts that comprised the hospital wards. Jenny greeted me with a hug, and Jerome got a wink and a thanks. Then Jenny pulled me through the base toward the stage where a band was playing.

Don't be mad, she said, and I burst into tears.

Kitty came out onstage wearing a miniskirt, white go-go boots and a yellow macramé sweater that was only barely decent. She was so glamorous and so clean. We were all in jungle green, and I hadn't shaved my armpits in I don't know how long, and she looked like she'd just walked out of the cold case at a grocery store. When they saw her, the boys went wild, and she waved and clapped and did a little dance with the band. I was breathless. Just so dang full of relief and pride and happiness.

She looks good, Jenny cried.

I gotta get up front, I yelled, and Jenny made a face but Jerome led the way, his big body moving the crowd in front of us. We got right up to the wooden posts that made the stage and the host, an AFVN radio DJ the boys loved, asked Kitty questions about life stateside. She talked about The Petticoat Kid and the new Bond movie she was going to be in. Someone made a crack about Jane Fonda and the crowd booed.

I took that moment to throw my bra onto the stage.

What the…? the radio DJ said, and Kitty found me in the sea of army green.

I clapped my hands over my mouth, holding back a sudden and strange sob, and she ran right over and picked up the bra, the pink buttons hanging perilously from the cups and the straps. It was ridiculous.

"Shall I put it on?" she asked, and the crowd yelled take it off, which didn't make any sense.

The band started to play something else and MPs came through the crowd to grab me, something I had not anticipated. The GIs could jump up onstage, but one woman throws a bra and they had to call the military police.

We were heading toward backstage, when Hugh Bonnet, who was standing at the stairs leading up to the stage, spotted us. Sourpuss, he cried, and then in his Hugh Bonnet way he convinced the MPs to let me go. I suppose you owe me, he said, drawing me in for a hug.

I asked what he was doing here and he looked at me like I was nuts. I couldn't let my girl come over here by herself, he said.

And then Kitty was there, grabbing me so hard and fast into a hug that we nearly toppled over. I'm sorry, I kept saying, and she kept saying, Me too. I can't believe you did this, I told her. I'd do it a million times to see you.

I leaned back and saw the bruise around her eye. She'd covered it with makeup so you couldn't see it onstage, but up close was a different story. She said she'd gotten hit by luggage when they'd landed in Saigon.

Jenny and Jerome appeared, and we pulled Jenny into our hug.

We'd known each other for only a handful of years, but so much had happened, it had felt like a lifetime.

29

ABBIE

Los Angeles, California
2019

THERE WAS NO sign of Kitty for the rest of the day. Abbie wasn't all that upset by her absence, to be honest. The hangover was fading, but the embarrassment lingered. All she needed was one tiny little glass of wine, to clear the fog and grease the wheels.

And resisting felt like an act of God.

Vickie arrived before dinner wearing Converse and a pretty yellow dress. Abbie had only met Vickie once, last summer when Clara brought her home for Mom's birthday. All she knew was Vickie was funny, ran every morning and liked her coffee with an ungodly amount of sugar.

Her family had fled Honduras when Vickie was an infant,

and she worked as a lawyer at the National Immigrant Justice Center.

And most importantly, when she got out of the Uber, Clara lit up like the sun.

She was happy for her sister, she was, but Abbie started to wonder what the hell she was even still doing here. Her life was falling apart in Iowa and she was a day away in a movie star's glamorous house, feeling like a fifth wheel.

After hugging Vickie, she and Clara gave her a tour of the little house. Abbie tried to go to her room to give them some privacy after, but Clara and Vickie wouldn't have it. Vickie ordered sushi and they sat down around the coffee table.

"You need a plan," Vickie said.

"Yes." Clara nodded.

"A plan for what?" Abbie asked.

"To get Kitty to stop hiding. So you two can hear the rest of the story. So Clara can find out who her father is?"

"Right," Abbie said. *That.* "What I don't understand is why she's gone. She brought us here and was so into telling us that story and now she's just vanished?" *Was it me? Spilling the wine…?*

"I think I might have had something to do with that," Clara said, and Vickie and Abbie turned on her, eyebrows raised. "Well, first I asked if she and Mom were lovers."

"Clara!"

"They weren't. And then I asked if she and Dad were lovers."

Abbie put her head in her hands.

"They weren't."

"God, that never even occurred to me. What else did you accuse her of?"

"*Accusation* is a strong word," Vickie said, popping open

an edamame and Abbie started laughing. *Peas and carrots*, as Mom used to say.

"So then I accused her of hiding something. Namely, why we never knew about her. Why Mom kept her a secret all these years." Clara split her chopsticks and dug into the spicy tuna.

"And you think whatever her reason is, it's bad?" Abbie couldn't take any more *bad*. She was full up on bad.

Clara shrugged and looked at Vickie, who was nodding. "People don't keep good things a secret."

That's what Abbie was afraid of.

After sushi, Abbie and Clara knocked on the door of the glass house.

"I don't like this," Abbie said, which was an understatement. Confrontation? While sober? None of this seemed like a good idea.

"I know," Clara said. "Just don't forget the plan."

"We *just* talked about it. How could I forget?"

"Sophia might not even be here," Clara said.

"We can call the phone number," Abbie said. If they were lucky maybe they could just leave a message.

"You're leaving day after tomorrow," Clara said. "We're running out of time."

Abbie wished she could stay longer, just to stop this pressure, but she'd promised Ben. Her family needed her.

"I'm trying not to be mad," Clara said. "Kitty brought us here with the promise of answering all our questions and then ghosts us? What is going on?"

"What if this is like the movies and she brought us out here and she's like…dying?"

"I don't think she's dying."

Clara knocked again.

The door opened and Sophia stood there in a pair of black jeans and a white T-shirt, a long silver necklace resting against it. "Abbie and Clara? Is everything all right?"

"Fine. Great, really," Abbie said.

"We need Kitty," Clara said, cutting through the small talk.

"Is there something I can do to help?"

"Not unless you know who my father is, and why Kitty showed up at my mother's funeral," Clara said, and Sophia was blank-faced. "Like I said, we need Kitty."

The plan was silence. Ask for what they wanted and then don't say a word. Don't smooth the rough edges, don't crack a joke. Just silence.

Clara said it was one of the most powerful tools in her repertoire.

Abbie *hated* silence. She opened her mouth to make it go away, and Clara smacked her thigh, a not-so-subtle instruction to keep her mouth shut. Minutes ticked by until finally Sophia's helpful smile vanished and she took a deep breath. "I warned her this would happen," she said. "I'll see what I can do. Keep your phones on you."

The next morning Clara and Vickie got back from their run just as Abbie was crawling out of her luxurious bed. They met in the cabin's kitchen for coffee.

"So?" Vickie said, her hair slipping out of the clips she wore. Clara tenderly kept tucking it behind her ears. "What should we do for your last full day?"

"I'd like to go to the beach," Abbie said. She couldn't stay in this house waiting for Kitty to show up and reveal whatever horrible reason she had for staying out of their lives all these years.

"You hate the beach." It was famous family lore that when she was ten years old, they visited their uncle in Mobile, Alabama, and Abbie got burned so badly her skin bubbled up after a day at the beach. She blamed the beach because she'd never been very good at blaming her parents. Clara was able to point to things their parents had done or not done as reasons for something being wrong in her life. Abbie, not so much.

Abbie shrugged. "I'll bring extra sunscreen."

A knock on the screen door sent the room into silence. Abbie crossed the kitchen to push it open to find Kitty in a yellow tunic and white pants.

"Kitty!" Abbie said in surprise, and suddenly Clara was at her side. "You're back."

"I am." Kitty's smile, for the first time in the days and hours they'd known her, seemed unsure. "I didn't mean to interrupt?"

"Kitty, this is my girlfriend, Vickie," Clara said, and Vickie stepped forward to shake Kitty's hand.

"It's so nice to meet you," Vickie said. "I'm a huge fan. My family and I were religious about your show. Our whole family stopped what they were doing every Wednesday night to watch it."

"Well, that's awfully sweet of y'all," Kitty said. "And it's real nice to meet you, too. What do you have planned for the day?"

"We were just talking about going to the beach," Abbie answered.

"Well, then, I'll let you get to it."

She walked away and Abbie stared at her sister, unsure of what to do.

"Kitty," Clara cried, catching up to her in the grass between the cabin and her house. Abbie followed, wishing she was wearing something other than her Garfield shirt. "Did you want to talk?"

"I got the message that *you* did," Kitty said with a strange kind of distance.

"Yes," Clara said. If she noticed Kitty's strangeness, she didn't react. Meanwhile Abbie was sick to her stomach with the awkwardness. "We'd love to talk."

"Well, then," Kitty said. "I suppose we might as well get this over with."

30

BETTYKAY

Greensboro, Iowa
1984

August 15, 1984

It's my Vietnam anniversary. I've been out twelve years and it seems like yesterday and a lifetime ago, all at the same time. The strangest memories come back to me. Drinking in our hooch because the officer's lounge was harassment city. Meeting Jenny in Saigon and sitting in that bath so long she had to come and pull me out. Getting off my Freedom Bird in California and realizing the army was not going to help me get home. Sales of my diary are going up the further we get from the war. I find that interesting. When we all got back, no one wanted to talk about what we were going through. But now people are interested. They're even making movies about it. I don't know how I feel about that. About any of it. Though, I won't lie, making a little money for the diary is nice. It's not a lot but I've put it in a rainy day account. I'm going to call Jenny tonight…

"THE APPENDIX IN room 10 is awake," Denise said as she slid by the PACU nursing station. "He's asking for you."

"He is not," I said. "He's not even my patient." My patient was Colonel Cooper. I swiveled around in my chair to refile his chart.

Cooper was stable and lucid, and we were going to have to send him home, but there would be no question he'd be back soon. He'd had twenty pieces of shrapnel removed from his belly at Long Binh and the scar tissue was causing obstruction. And Colonel Cooper only came in when the pain was acute and the surgery was an emergency. We never had the chance to get him to the VA hospital in Iowa City.

The suck had followed him home.

"I'll trade you. I'll take Cooper, you can have the appendix in room 10."

"Stop trying to set me up with patients, Denise. Honestly."

"Well, there's not much else to do," Denise said.

St. Luke's Hospital was quiet, which I'd wanted. Working there had become routine, another thing I'd wanted. And it was boring. Which I'd thought I'd wanted, but I'd been wrong. Being a nurse stateside was radically different from being a nurse in country. Less responsibility. More rules.

Dr. Fischer was long gone, that was a plus. He'd retired to Arizona, but rumor had it he got the wrong nursing student pregnant, and her father kicked up a mighty fuss.

Nurse Bouchet was retiring soon, and she was encouraging me to get my master's so I could take her place. The idea was an interesting one since it gave me more responsibility.

"Room 10 teaches science at the high school, did you know

that?" Denise waggled her eyebrows at me. "I looked at his vein—"

"Denise!" I snapped.

"No drugs," she whispered. "I'm just saying."

Denise had gotten married two years ago, and her mission in life now was to see me married off, too. She'd always bordered on annoying, but with this she was over the line and into infuriating. Or maybe that was just me.

The suck had followed me home, too.

At the beginning of her mission to get me dating, I made the mistake of telling her that I didn't think I could marry a guy who hadn't served in Vietnam, mostly as a way to shut her up because there weren't a whole lot of GIs in Greensboro, Iowa. But every time one of them showed up, she let me know. Colonel Cooper, the first time he'd been admitted, had sent Denise into absolute delight, but she hadn't had any dealings with the guys experiencing heroin addiction so I had to explain the marks on his arms to her.

Denise was called away, and I stood up to check on the appendix in room 10. It was always nice to chat with a guy who'd seen time in Vietnam.

And Denise was right, there wasn't much else to do.

The room was a double, but he was the only patient. I found him in the bed closest to the window, trying to use his IV pole to open the curtain.

"Hey!" I said as the bags slopped around and nearly fell off the hooks. "What are you doing?"

"Let the sunshine in." He had a happy, doped-up post-op voice.

I smiled and yanked open the curtains, took the IV pole from him and checked the saline and his IVs before setting it down.

"That button right there will bring a nurse if you need help." I pointed at the red button on the right side of the bed.

"Couldn't reach," he said and lifted his right arm, amputated just above the elbow.

"But you could reach the IV bag?"

"When you put it that way..."

Dimples were visible over the edge of his beard. His long hair had curl to it, and it was a mess against the pillow.

"How are you feeling?" I asked and walked around to take his pulse on his left wrist.

"Real good."

"Do you know what day it is?"

"The day of my appendix surgery."

"What's your name?"

"Don't you have that on a chart somewhere?"

"I do. But I'd like to hear it from you."

"Willis Beecher."

His pulse was fine. I touched the US Marine Corps tattoo on his forearm. "You served?"

"Two tours in Vietnam."

"Thank you."

"For what?"

"Your service. Your sacrifice."

Some guys, when they come out of surgery, flying high on the morphine, get real emotional. Willis Beecher's brown eyes filled up with tears.

"No one ever says that to us," he whispered, and I nodded. "I know."

September 30, 1984
Talked to Kitty for an hour tonight. Hugh is back in her life, can you believe it? After all this time she runs into him at a party in London three months ago! She says it's casual. But nothing

is casual with that guy. He's always cranked to a hundred. She dumped him after that trip to Vietnam and I thought for sure it was because of the black eye. She says he's different. Older, wiser. Her picture is ALL over the tabloids. Some of the headlines say she and Hugh were fighting at a club in New York. Another had a picture of them kissing in the back of a car. The Midnight Globe says she's pregnant and doesn't know who the father is. She says the tabloids never get anything right. Jenny and Jerome drove out to Hollywood for vacation and she says Kitty is skinnier than she looks in those pictures. Too skinny.

Kitty's leaving for Georgia next week to film a new movie she sounds really excited about. I went and put flowers on Mom and Dad's grave this morning. Sometimes I think about all the time they wasted being disappointed with me. How even though I tried to make things right with them before I went to Vietnam, they could not let go of their anger. Jenny said they were scared. And she's right, but I sometimes still find myself unable to forgive them for the way they tried to keep me scared, too. The way I sometimes still feel scared. I go to church and pray on it. And I put flowers on their graves. It's not much, but it's all I've got. Willis volunteered to drive Colonel Cooper to Iowa City to get him the help he needs at the VA hospital down there. I don't know what to do with this guy, I've known him for two weeks and he's different. Different from Todd. Really different from Rex. There's just something in him that shines. Really, really shines.

October 1984

"I can't believe you haven't seen this movie," Willis said, passing over a five-dollar bill to the long-haired kid in the ticket booth. "Hey, Mike. Two please."

"Here you go, Mr. Beecher." The kid handed over two tickets and change.

"I can't believe you've seen it ten times," I said to Willis. The movie theater in town had three screens, and one of them was always dedicated to older movies. I wanted to see the new movie *The Natural*, but when Willis found out I hadn't seen the one in theater three, he had a fit.

"You'll understand soon enough," he said.

We stepped into the dark foyer, and he walked right up to the concession booth, manned by another teenager. "Hey, Jennifer. Two popcorns, two sodas." He slid money across the glass counter.

"No," I said, grabbing his money and putting my own five down. "You're not paying for everything. This is not a date."

Willis smiled through his beard and addressed the girl behind the concession stand.

"She's never seen *Star Wars*. Can you believe it?"

"You live in a cave?" Jennifer asked me, which delighted Willis. He laughed as I shook my head and pocketed my change. I picked up my small popcorn and soda.

"You know every teenager in this town," I said.

"It's a small town and I teach freshman earth science." He shrugged.

At the ticket taker he was so smooth, setting down the popcorn with his left hand, reaching into the back pocket of his jeans, handing over the tickets. The soda was balanced between his chest and right arm. *Don't*, he'd said when we went for coffee last week at Mitch's Diner and I tried to help him with the sugar and milk. *If I need help, I'll ask.*

So far he'd never asked.

"I got a real thing about my seats at a movie," he said as we walked into the theater.

"Sure," I said, imagining he didn't want too many people around him. Or he needed to be by the exit. At least on an aisle.

"Middle of the middle row. Best view," he said. "Thick of the action."

Willis was a constant surprise. If I ever wanted to lump him in with my experience of the war, or other GIs' postwar experience, he bucked me. He joined the marines under the GI bill, served two tours doing something he couldn't tell me about.

"If I told you, then I'd have to kill you," he'd told me over coffee like it was a joke, but something told me he wasn't joking. He'd returned with one less arm and went to school to be a teacher. He said he was on medication for anxiety and that he met monthly with a group of marines in Iowa City to talk about their Vietnam experiences. He said it helped.

A few students in the back of the theater called out to him as we made our way to our seats and he smiled, acknowledged them all by name. Told them not to throw popcorn at him.

When we sat, our legs touched, and his shoulder brushed mine and I could smell him, Irish Spring soap and a little patchouli. I didn't hate it.

"You find a place to live?" he asked.

I'd told him during coffee that I hadn't tried to find a new roommate since Denise got married, but couldn't afford rent on my own anymore. I didn't want another roommate and was looking for a new place.

"No," I said. "Not yet." I took a sip of my root beer. "Where do you live?"

"Hey now, we're not even dating."

"I'm making small talk," I said.

"Oh, well in that case, you know that weird-looking house across from the park on Elm?"

"The Frank Lloyd Wright house?"

"Look at you. Beauty, brains and an architecture fan."

"I wouldn't say I'm a fan, I just...like that house."

"Well, it's not a Frank Lloyd Wright. But it's prairie school and it's an absolute shithole inside. I'm fixing it up and the owners are giving me a break on the rent."

"Look at you, brains, beauty and brawn."

"I have been waiting for you to notice."

I ate a piece of popcorn instead of smiling at him.

He put his popcorn between his legs and his soda on the floor in front of him.

"Are the kids weird about your arm?" I asked and then winced. "Sorry. That was rude."

"Most people ignore it or work really hard not to look at my arm. It's kind of refreshing, actually, to talk about it."

"How do the kids react?"

"They don't, really. Someone will ask me about it on the first day and I'll answer and they just move on in the way of teenagers." He leaned forward, dropping his voice. "The parents are actually worse. A few signed a petition to have me removed because I was too upsetting for the kids."

"Wow."

"My principal called them in and tore up the petition right in front of them."

"He's a good guy."

"The best. He served in Korea so he gets it."

I flinched at the mention of Korea, thoughts of Rex and that scar on his side intruding where I did not want them. But Willis didn't notice as the curtain opened and the lights went down.

Star Wars was like nothing I'd ever seen before. It was all breathtaking good fun, until Luke went back to the moisture farm to find his uncle and aunt burnt to cinder, and suddenly the smell of burnt flesh filled my nose. The music, which I'd been loving, now sounded like the air raid siren.

All at once I was in a full cold sweat. A headache exploded behind my eye.

"You okay?" he whispered, grabbing my shaking hand.

"I need to leave," I whispered, embarrassed but dying inside. Willis didn't say anything, just led me past disgruntled moviegoers, out the door and into the fresh air.

"You all right?" he whispered, stroking my back as I sucked in breaths that didn't seem to get all the way into my body.

"Fine. Just…memories, you know?"

He pulled me into his arms.

"I know."

November 1, 1984

Willis is really into Halloween. He wore one of my uniforms and it mostly zipped and I'm going on a diet tomorrow. I dressed up like the scarecrow in The Wizard of Oz *and he did my makeup. We sat on the steps of his house and drank a bottle of wine and handed out candy.*

I told Kitty on the phone that it was one of the best nights of my life and she asked me why I was being so careful with Willis. What are you scared of? she kept asking me. Turning into your parents? The answer to that was a resounding maybe. She assured me that was impossible, but sometimes I feel my mom in me. The way she wanted to keep the peace at all costs. And I finally said that I didn't know if what I felt for him was enough. I thought what I felt for Todd was enough, but we were children and if we had gotten married I wouldn't be this person I am now. And Rex…well, I got lost in his orbit. But without him I wouldn't be this person, either. And I want Willis to be right for the person I am now. And the person I'll be in fifty years. I want him to deserve me. And for me to deserve him. All his kindness and intelligence and bravery. I just wanted it to be right.

Kitty told me to just sleep with him. Then I'd know. She said that was how she knew with Drew, the basketball player she eloped with in Vegas in '79. You were married for all of ten minutes, I reminded her. Which was an exaggeration but not much of one. They eloped, he cheated on her within the year, and she had half his money and a divorce by their first anniversary. Yeah, she said, but they were a fabulous ten minutes.

Classic Kitty. But she's probably right.

November 1984

"This still isn't a date," I said, shrugging out of the top of my uniform while he undid my bra. We were in his double bed on the second floor of the prairie house and I'd woken him up, knocking on his door after my shift.

"Not a date," he said, unclasping my bra and then groaning into my breasts. "Why isn't it a date? Your skin is so soft."

"Because…" He pulled my nipple into his mouth and I saw sparks. He lifted me, rolled me onto my back in his rumpled bed that smelled like him. Patchouli, Irish Spring and sawdust. If there was only one smell I could have for the rest of my life, I'd pick this smell. He yanked the rest of my uniform off and then managed to peel down my nylons.

GD nylons.

"Focus, Betts. Why isn't this a date?"

He kissed the skin of my belly, inching down my body.

"Because," I said.

He laughed against my thigh. "Okay, Betts."

Well, I thought after, sweating and seeing stars. Kitty was right. Sleeping with Willis answered a whole lot of questions.

"Tell me," he said, as we lay in bed after, my head on his chest. "Why you're knocking on my door at…" he looked at his bedside clock "…1 a.m.?"

"Because it was becoming this big deal in my head," I said.

"Sex?"

"Yeah. Sex. And dating you—"

"Oh." He shook his head. "I have it on good authority we are not dating."

I stroked his face, the silk of his beard. His body was wiry and strong. He had to keep covered the Marine Corps tattoo on his forearm when he was at work. His other tattoo, a dragon on his shoulder that he had done while on R & R in Saigon, he claimed he was so drunk that he had no memory of having it done.

He toyed with my hair and I told him about Rex and then about Todd. The abortion. The baby and Dr. Fischer. I told him that in Vietnam the sound of incoming helicopters had made me cry, and sometimes, even now, I dreamt I was trying to tie off blood vessels in a chest wound but I couldn't find them, and the blood rose up out of the patient's chest to cover my hands and drip onto the floor until there was so much blood I woke up gasping for air. I told him how my parents died one week apart two years after I got back and I didn't feel anything about it.

He told me about Sue, his high school sweetheart who sent him a Dear John letter his first tour, about Cambodia and the tunnels and the Bouncing Betty that took his arm, and his best friend.

He said sometimes the hate and the rage were so big, he felt like he was going to get lost in it. He dreamt of POWs in bamboo cages, and his lieutenant who would sing dirty songs in a church choir voice.

I told him about Jenny and Kitty.

"I've had friends. Good friends. But we don't love each other like that."

"They're one of a kind."

"Hey. Don't be mad," he said as the sky turned pink out the window.

I yawned, wondering if I could ever be mad at this guy. "About what?"

"Well, frankly, it's not all my fault. Some of the responsibility is yours."

"For what?" I pushed off his chest to look at his serious face and laughing eyes.

"I love you, BettyKay Allen."

I put my head back down against his chest, the comforting thump of his heart against my ear.

"I know."

December 12, 1984
Kitty and Hugh are all over the tabloids. Again. Hugh showed up in Georgia where she was filming and made this big scene. I told her she should call the police and she laughed at me. I'm worried. Just when she gets away from him, he shows back up. Jenny is ready to fly out to LA and stage an intervention. I almost told both of them my news. But I haven't told Willis yet. And he really should be the first to know.

"You got a box," Willis said, opening the front door between the house and the screened-in porch. He'd been shoveling snow with a new prosthetic that gave him marginal control over the shovel.

"What kind of box?" I asked, picking up the drop cloths from the floors.

The first floor of the prairie house looked pretty good if I did say so myself. I'd moved in the day after we slept together the first time, and when we weren't having sex we'd painted the walls and ceiling a crisp clean white, refinished the wood trim and brought someone else in to do the floors. The whole place gleamed like a new penny. I helped pay for some of it with my rainy day fund and felt pretty great about it.

"An airmail box."

He positioned the box on the wood floor and slid it over to me. He shook off his coat and took off his boots on the porch.

"It's from Kitty," I said, getting a pair of scissors and taking the box to the sofa.

He entered just as I got the box open. I lifted a card out of the tissue paper. "For Your Tree," it said. "I miss you. Kitty."

Beneath the paper were four glass Christmas tree ornaments. And inside each ornament was a pink button.

Honest to God, it looked like they were pregnant and I wondered, my hand over my mouth, if she'd somehow guessed.

"Those are the buttons, huh?" Willis asked, sitting down next to me. "Those ornaments look pregnant. How'd she get them in there?"

"I don't know. Can we go get a tree this afternoon?" I choked out, overcome with awe and affection for my friend. Overcome with Willis. This house. With all the love I was feeling.

"Of course. Hey. Hey, don't cry. We'll get a tree. We'll hang those ornaments up right in front. And then I think we should head on down to city hall and get hitched. A Christmas wedding."

We joked about it just about every other day, running off and getting married. But neither one of us seemed to take it too seriously. We didn't need a piece of paper telling us we belonged with one another. I could feel my mother rolling over in her grave at our arrangement. But frankly my mother was part of the reason why I liked this arrangement. If I never got married, I couldn't have an unhappy marriage, like my parents.

The tears kept coming.

"Oh, come on now. We don't have to get married, honey," he said. "I'm just kidding. We're okay the way we are."

"No, I want to," I said between sniffles. "It's just..."

I couldn't find the words to tell him how happy I was. How beautiful this house was and how excited I was to make it a home, with him and this baby. How unbelievable it was to have found him. How bittersweet it all was. This life and this love. Him. Me. Us.

"Oh, honey," he laughed, pulling me into his arms. "I know."

"You don't," I whispered. "Those ornaments aren't the only thing that's pregnant."

31

CLARA

Los Angeles, California
2019

CLARA LAY WIDE-AWAKE, staring up at the ceiling and very aware that the bed was supercomfortable. She should be sleeping.

But she couldn't.

Her mind was reeling from the day spent with Kitty. The way Kitty so casually peeled back all the things they took for granted about their mother. All the stories they'd heard, the foundation of their whole family. She and Abbie knew about their parents' date to *Star Wars*. About their first Halloween. They even knew about the ornaments with the buttons inside of them. But everything was different coming from Kitty because Abbie and Clara hadn't known about *her*.

Clara would still be in that office, grilling Kitty about why

Mom kept their friendship a secret, but Abbie had pulled her out of there.

Kitty is tired, Abbie had said when Clara had protested. *You need to give her a rest.*

"Clara?" Vickie whispered, rolling onto her side to face Clara. "Are you all right, babe? It's almost midnight."

She almost claimed jet lag, even though she'd been in LA for four days. Putting up that boundary was second nature and she had to actively resist the urge. Vickie deserved better, and frankly, so did she.

"I grew up really thinking my parents were in love and it's nice to know it was real. Comforting."

"But you still don't know who your dad is."

"You know," Clara laughed. "I barely care about that anymore. I feel like I don't know who my mom was. Not really."

"Because she kept Kitty a secret?"

"They were like sisters, Vickie. Why keep that kind of friendship secret?"

Vickie stroked Clara's arm, her unspoken sympathy shoring Clara up. She'd been a fool to keep this woman at arm's length over the last week. A total fool.

"You want to scratch my back?" Vickie asked.

"Yes."

Vickie rolled away from Clara and Clara put her hand up the back of Vickie's tank top, scratching her smooth skin in circles and just along the spine, the way Vickie liked.

"We should have a baby."

Vickie got up on one elbow. "If you're joking it's not funny."

"I'm not joking."

"Clara," Vickie whispered. "We're going to revisit this conversation when we're home. But…that makes me so happy."

Clara didn't argue, just leaned in and kissed Vickie until she softened against the *extremely* comfortable bed.

A knock at the door made Clara sigh and Vickie groan.

"Yeah?" Clara said.

"Clara?" It was Abbie. "You got a sec?"

Clara laughed and sat up in the bed. "Come on in." She flipped on the reading lamp on the bedside table as Abbie pushed open the door in her Garfield pajama shirt and a worried expression.

"What's wrong?" Clara asked.

"It might be nothing," Abbie said in a tone that indicated otherwise. "And maybe, Kitty just remembered the details wrong. Or maybe Dad did. Or maybe me."

"Abbie," Clara said, pushing her sister toward the point.

"The math is all wrong. Mom had to break those ornaments to get the buttons out and she made those new ornaments out of the glass, remember?"

"They were so ugly."

"So ugly. And every year when we decorated the tree, Dad told me about how he found out Mom was pregnant when she got those ornaments in the mail."

"So?"

"Dad always said Mom was pregnant with me."

Something cold and strange rippled over Clara's skin.

"And in the story Kitty just told us—you weren't born, yet."

"What are you saying?" Clara asked, though she knew. Of course she knew. There was a chance she'd known all along.

"If that story is right, forget about who your father is. I don't think BettyKay Allen is your mom."

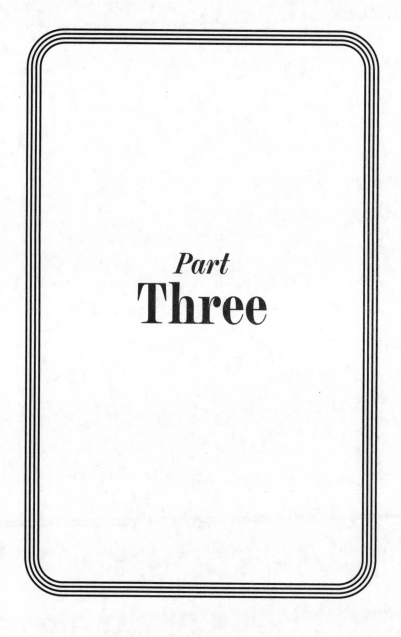

Part
Three

32

KITTY

Los Angeles, California
2019

SUNRISE WAS SO...GAUCHE. So naked with all its wide-eyed optimism.

Kitty hated it. Always had. Entirely overrated. Unless of course she'd managed to stay up to see it. If the night was endless and she could ride it out until the sun came up, well, who could argue with the magic of that?

But it had been years since that magic had visited her.

Morning was when she hid. When she used to run literally and figuratively. It was in that half-light that she did the messy work required of her life.

Her survival.

There'd been hundreds of predawn appointments to plastic surgeons to hide the aging, the sagging and drooping. Tummy tucks. Breast lifts. Colonics. Beauty salons. Private trainers, therapists and, during a very strange time in her life, a psychic. There were lovers and husbands and dozens of dawn exits from bedrooms that weren't hers.

Betts told her once that Kitty's lifestyle required a price that most people would find too high to pay. But she'd been referring to that cabbage soup diet Kitty had been on in the '90s.

Kitty ironically had thought the same of Betts's life. The cost of staying in one place, turning every ounce of her person over to the care of other people, keeping all the secrets she kept from them. The cost of all that, Kitty was too selfish to pay. She wasn't proud of it, but she'd made her peace with it. It was just her nature.

Kitty's sleep had been restless and awful. Dreams of Dr. Fischer and Meemaw and a long terrible drive through the night.

It was Betts of course, meddling in her dreams, calling to her from the grave, furious with Kitty for showing up at her funeral.

This is what you get, she could practically hear Betts saying. *This is the price you pay for breaking our promise. For ruining my legacy. For hurting my family.*

Kitty washed her face and put on the makeup that hid the dark spots and the fine wrinkles around her eyes. The larger wrinkles would be dealt with next month in a very private surgical suite in Santa Barbara. At dawn. She brushed her hair with its extensions that filled in what she'd started to lose.

Betts always laughed at Kitty's vanity. But really, looks were all she'd had. Looks and money.

And Betts.

I'm so sorry, Betts.

But perhaps it was time for honesty. Betts was the one who'd told Clara, *Clara*, of all people, about her father. That hadn't been part of the plan. Was Kitty supposed to leave that poor girl twisting in the wind like that? Identity in turmoil? It was obvious Clara would run herself ragged trying to find answers.

And the case could be made that Kitty was bringing Abbie and Clara back together. Or The Birdhouse was, along with these secret stories about Betts.

That's awfully convenient, Jenny had said at the grave site. *Blaming a dead woman for starting this so you don't have to take responsibility.*

Kitty filled her belly with air and slowly let it out the way the child who taught her yoga told her to do.

Yoga, Betts. I do yoga. In a chair sometimes. It's so pathetic it hurts. I need you here to tell me how to get out of this fix I got myself in. At the least to laugh at me. I don't laugh anymore. And I'm scared maybe I won't again.

Kitty went out into the garden on the side of the glass house away from the cabin. She'd done a number on it the morning she'd heard about Betts's death. The roses were ruined. Kitty had stomped on the herbs. She had been unable to go back in there since, and now the weeds were creeping in. But she could not find the will to do anything about it.

See, she would say to Betts if she were here. *I'm not good at caring for anything.*

Betts would argue with Kitty and had plenty of times in the past, offering herself up as proof that Kitty could take extraordinary care of a person if she chose to. But Kitty's actions the last few days certainly won the argument.

She took another deep breath, tasting this place on her tongue. The eucalyptus, the pine trees, the cool dawn. Years ago, a lifetime ago, she'd told Betts she wanted to find a place that she could call home and she had. She had found herself a family—Betts, Jenny, Alexander, Sophia—and disappointed all of them at one time or another.

"Kitty?" It was Clara. Vickie was with her, walking up from the trails where they'd clearly been running.

"Good morning," Kitty said. "How was your run?" She remembered those days of knee aches and sore heels. She couldn't believe how she missed them. Yoga simply didn't have the same therapeutic pain.

"So good," Vickie said, wiping the sweat off her face with the neck of her shirt. Kitty liked her for Clara. She took no shit. Held her own but was still soft. "I'll take that nice trail over the winds along Lake Michigan any day."

"I'm glad."

Vickie and Clara shared a look. A quick, barely there look, but Kitty saw it. She saw it and she knew.

They'd figured it out. Or part of it. They didn't know the worst of it yet, but they were right there on the edge.

"Kitty," Clara said, stepping closer. Kitty turned away, unable to meet her gaze. A coward to the end. "This has been an amazing gift for us. Getting us here and letting us stay. We can't thank you enough—"

Clara wielded diplomacy like a sword. It was almost elegant. "But you want answers?"

"I do. So does Abbie. She leaves tonight and we're running out of time."

She'd known that even as she went and hid at the Chateau Marmont, hoping the box of money and diary entries would be enough for them. She'd known in her heart only the truth would be enough for Clara. Even if it destroyed everything.

Betts had worried for her oldest daughter over countless phone calls, and Kitty would tell Betts every time that Clara would be all right. That she was a fighter.

Why did I think this time would be different?

"Come join me for coffee," Kitty said. "Just you and Abbie. I'm sorry, Vickie."

"I totally understand," Vickie said. "Family is family."

Indeed.

33

BETTYKAY

Greensboro, Iowa
January 1985

"WHEN CAN WE tell people about the baby?" Willis asked at lunch on Saturday.

All I could keep down was toast, so he'd made toast for both of us. His had a fried egg on top, which I made him eat on the other side of the room so the smell wouldn't send me to the bathroom.

"You tell people about the baby and they're going to ask when the wedding is."

I had made it clear I would not be walking down any aisle when I couldn't go four hours without vomiting or taking a nap. And we were so beautiful just the way we were. I didn't care what people said, or what they thought. We were so happy, and all I wanted was to stay in this bubble.

"You know I don't care about a wedding. I just… I want to tell my friends and colleagues we're having a baby. It's good news, babe. And we could all use some good news."

"Okay," I said. "Soon. When I'm feeling better."

Willis taught with Mr. Schutte in the science department, and if Mrs. Schutte, who was the head of the Junior Women's Club and the uncrowned queen of the high school teacher social scene, knew I was having a baby, she'd want to do a shower and make a whole thing of it. And what was the point of a celebration without Jenny and Kitty? I hadn't even had the energy to tell them yet. Jenny had just had her second baby and Kitty was in Georgia? Or London? Or back in LA? I couldn't keep track.

I was busy with my shifts at the hospital and the house anyway. And trying to keep down my meals.

And I didn't want to tell them over the phone. I wanted to see their faces. I wanted their arms around me. Their laughter and joy in my ears. Phones were amazing, but it wasn't the same. I wanted my friends. My sisters. My sunshine girls.

"You know what I think?" he said. "You should take a little time off while you're feeling so bad and you and Jenny should go out and see Kitty. Soak up some sunshine."

Like he'd read my mind.

Predictably I burst into tears. He really was the sweetest guy. Willis chuckled and kissed my head.

"I'm gonna go see if I can get some of the snow off the roof," he said, shrugging into his big brown coat with the fake fur inside that made him look like a bear walking to school every morning. "They're calling for another storm and I'm worried about the attic."

"You're going on the roof?"

"I'll be careful."

It wasn't twenty minutes later that I heard the brakes of a car squeal down the street and a thump on the roof.

"No," I said, imagining the worst. "No. No." I jammed my feet into my boots, didn't worry about a coat and threw open the front door.

Only to find Willis holding up a woman in an elaborate white fur coat. She had long black hair that hung down over her face. I had no idea who it could be until she lifted her head and revealed a black eye, a split lip and a swollen contusion on her cheekbone.

"Hey, Betts," Kitty said.

And she passed out in Willis's arms.

We got her inside and laid her down on our secondhand brown plaid couch. She was unconscious but her pulse was strong and her eyes, when I lifted the lids, reactive.

"What happened?" I asked Willis.

"I just saw this red car jump the curb in front of our house and the driver side door opened and she fell out."

"Fell out?"

"Shouldn't we get her to the hospital?" Willis asked, standing over my shoulder.

"We will. Let's just see what we're dealing with," I said, calmly running triage in my head. I pushed open the fur coat and found a billowy red satin top and black velvet pants. Her gold heels were apparently somewhere in the yard. I lifted her top to palpate her stomach.

"Oh shit."

"What?" Willis asked.

Her stomach swelled up over the pleated waistband of the pants, held together by a safety pin that had popped open. "She's pregnant."

I pressed on her stomach, near her right hip, and felt the flutter of the baby kicking.

She was too thin for being this pregnant. She was too beaten up to be this pregnant.

"Should we call an ambulance?" Willis asked.

I nodded and braced my hands on the side of the couch to stand, but Kitty roused, turning her head on the pillow. Her eyes opened and she wrapped her palm around my wrist. "Tell Willis to hide my car," she said. "The keys are in it. No hospitals."

"Kitty, you're hurt. And you're pregnant."

"If he finds out where I am, he'll kill me."

"Hugh?" I asked, jumping to the conclusion like it had been waiting for me. "Hugh did this?"

"He can't know where I am. Promise me." Mascara and dark eyeliner bled down her cheeks. It was smeared into her hairline at her temples. She didn't look like herself. My best friend, the most beautiful woman I'd ever known.

"I promise," I said.

I got a bowl of warm water and the softest washcloth I could find and wiped away the mascara and the blood, then the tears that slipped out under her eyelids.

She grabbed my hand and I squeezed it carefully.

"Am I hurting you?" I asked, my whisper cracking despite my efforts to keep my emotions in check.

"No," she said. "I just hurt."

Willis of course hated that we weren't calling the ambulance. Or taking her to the hospital. He only relented when I promised we would if things got worse. And he moved Kitty's car into the garage and went for groceries while I woke her up every two hours, making sure if she had a concussion she didn't go sliding into a coma.

"I don't think we've been properly introduced," Kitty said

when he came back in from the store, bags in his arm. "I'm Kitty."

He smiled, and I could tell he was starstruck despite wanting to play it cool. "It's nice to finally meet you," he said. "I'm—"

"Oh, I know all about you, Willis Beecher. You're a god-damn knight in shining armor."

"Oh," I laughed. "Don't tell him that, he'll get a big head."

"Too late," he said. "And I'll be anything you two ladies want." He kissed my head as he walked through to the kitchen.

"Did you drive here from California?" I asked Kitty later that night.

Willis built a fire for us and the light flickered over her where she still sat on the sofa. The tabloids weren't wrong about how thin she'd become. And maybe it was the black hair, but she was so pale, accentuating the bruises on her face.

"We were in Idaho. A new festival there that Robert Red-ford started. Hugh's trying to re-create himself as some kind of independent director," she said through her split lip.

"What happened, Kitty?"

"Hugh Bonnet happened," she said.

"Is the baby his?" Her good eye narrowed and she looked right down, deep into me, drilling her words into a place where only fundamental truths lived. Where all our secrets and the truth of our friendship resided.

"No," she said. "Not if I want to be alive in ten years. The baby is not his."

"I don't know what that means," Willis said as we sat in the kitchen drinking tea he'd made.

Kitty was now asleep in our bedroom. Willis's idea, of course. Our bed was the only real mattress in the house at the moment. He and I would sleep on the foldout couch in the living room, though we weren't in any hurry to sacrifice our spines to the metal bar in the middle of the bed.

"I think it means the baby is his, but no one can know that if she wants to be free of him."

"Did you know? About this? About Hugh? I mean, he beat the shit out of her, Betts."

I thought of The Birdhouse and the way he stood with his arm around her neck and her black eye in Vietnam. They'd broken up after the Vietnam visit and she'd gone on to marry Drew and date a rock star. But when Hugh showed up in those tabloid pictures this past year and Kitty said it was no big deal and that he'd changed... Jenny said a man like that doesn't change, but I wanted to believe Kitty. And I'd been too pre-occupied with my own life to say anything.

It would have made me feel a lot better to say no. To say I had no idea, that this was all such a surprise. But it wasn't.

I nodded.

"How can we help her?" Willis asked, and it was hard to imagine loving him more.

After Kitty slept a full ten hours, showered and ate soft scram-bled eggs through her sore mouth, we sat in front of another fire and the truth came out. This reunion with Hugh had been stormy and more off again than on again. After they met again at that party, he'd shoved her into a door and she broke it off. They'd had a brief reconciliation seven months ago that had immediately gone sour. She'd left him in London, went back to California and signed on to the first movie her agents sent her way, a campy thriller set in Georgia. Filming was almost over when Hugh showed up, begging for forgiveness and making a scene on set, pushing his weight around with the younger director.

"I used to admire that about him," she whispered, her hair

slicked back off her face. I hadn't seen her without makeup in a long time. She barely had eyebrows. And her cheekbones were so prominent they cast shadows on her face. It was like she'd been cut away, parts of her chiseled off. "The way he'd walk into every situation and bend it toward him. I thought it was proof of how strong he was. But I realize now he just can't bear that there are things in this world that aren't about him."

"How did you end up in Idaho?"

"I can't explain it to you, Betts. He said that I owed him, and he kept saying it and saying it until I believed him. Until I was convinced that my career going well had somehow hurt his career. Any person with any amount of power took away from his perceived power. And my God, if it was a woman who had power? Forget it. He could not handle it."

"Did Hugh hit you because you're pregnant?" I asked.

"No. He hit me because I was talking to another director about a project that didn't include him. No one knows I'm pregnant. I only just realized. I thought I was eating too much."

"What? Kitty?" How was that even possible?

"My period hasn't been regular my whole life, even when I've been on the pill. But I'd picked up a bacterial infection filming in Morocco last year and I was on a course of rifampin."

"Oh no," I breathed. Rifampin was an antibiotic that could lessen the effectiveness of the pill. Of course no one had warned her. "How far are you?"

"London was six months ago," she said with a shrug.

"Have you seen a doctor? At all?"

"I don't trust anyone not to get the news back to Hugh. I can't explain it, Betts, but he's all over my life. He was having lunch with my manager. He bribed my assistant. If he found out I was looking at a script he went and talked to the writer. If a director was attached he'd get that guy fired and take the job himself. I fought it as long as I could, but then I just gave up. I fired my assistant. My driver. My publicist. My manager. I have no one right now. No team. No help. No—"

"That's over," I told her. "You have me. You have Willis. Jenny will be up here in a hot second if we need her. We'll get you in to Greensboro. There's a good doctor there. He's young, modern, we can trust him—"

Kitty shook her head.

"Honey, you need to be examined and have an ultrasound."

If Kitty had her way, she would continue to pretend nothing was wrong and so I did what she'd done for me years ago. I made her face reality. She could hide her pregnancy but she couldn't hide from her pregnancy. Not anymore.

Willis and I got her in the next day to see Dr. Meadows, my ob-gyn. A young man with thick glasses and a cowlick that made him look like a cartoon character from the 1950s, he was discreet and kind. He agreed to come in late and we kept her appointment off the books.

Kitty asked me to stay with her and I held her hand while he did the ultrasound, turning the screen so she could see the fuzzy black-and-white picture of the baby-shaped object. I watched her, gauging her reaction, but she wasn't even looking at the screen.

"I'd like to do an internal exam," he said. "Is that all right?"

White-faced, she nodded and then winced and flinched throughout the exam.

"Well," Dr. Meadows said, taking off his gloves, which I couldn't help but notice were bloody. "The baby is fine. There is some bleeding, more than I like. And I don't like your weight."

"You sound like the producers of my last film." Kitty's joke only sounded sad.

"You need bed rest. You need sleep. You need calorie-rich food. I'm prescribing some iron pills and milkshakes."

He pulled out his prescription pad.

"Me," I said. "Prescribe the pills to me. I'll make sure she gets them."

Dr. Meadows stared at me and then back at Kitty's poor battered face and wrote out the prescription. This was illegal and he could get in trouble, but still he handed me that script.

He held on to the paper as I took it from him. "Keep an eye on her," he said.

"I won't let her out of my sight."

She slouched in the passenger seat wearing big sunglasses and chewing her fingernails down to the quick as Willis drove us home. Sitting between them on the bench seat, I could practically hear her mind spinning.

"You're staying here. With me and Willis. I'll take care of you. Don't worry," I told her, rubbing her shoulder.

She looked at me out the corner of her sunglasses. "Betts, there are three months between now and when this baby comes out of me."

"And the doctor wants you lying down for most of them," I said, as we turned up Elm to the house. "We have the room."

"Hugh knows about you, though. He knows we're friends. He knows I would come to you."

"If he shows up here you let me worry about Hugh," Willis said, sounding macho in a way he never did.

"Thank you. Both of you," Kitty whispered, and she wiped away the tears before they cleared the bottom of her glasses.

We pushed a new mattress up the stairs into the guest bedroom with the view of the park. We'd already painted the room a pretty yellow for our baby. I brought up the chair from the living room so I could sit beside Kitty when I was home from work. Willis made milkshakes of every flavor, and eggs and bacon because Kitty seemed to crave that most.

My own pregnancy seemed to accommodate Kitty's. Maybe it was adrenaline, but the nausea diminished and some of my energy returned.

I went back to work on Wednesday afternoon, and when I came home at eight, I found Willis in my chair by her bed, the two of them watching an old black-and-white TV he'd set up on the dresser, laughing at Jack Tripper.

"Hey, babe!" Willis said, flashing his dimples while I stood in the doorway.

"Come sit," Kitty said, patting the bed.

Willis made me a sandwich and we laughed our way through *Three's Company* and then *Taxi*.

"Danny DeVito is actually a really nice guy," Kitty said.

"Really?" Willis asked. "He's such a jerk on the show."

"Yeah, he's not like that at all. He's nice and funny."

"But he is really that short, right?"

"So short."

I ate my sandwich and Kitty told Willis all the Hollywood gossip she knew. *Oh, Kitty*, I thought, smiling despite the circumstances. *I missed you so much.*

When Kitty had been with us for two weeks, Jenny came up from Iowa City and brought us big grease-stained bags of Shakey's tenderloin sandwiches. It was one of those February days with a warm sun and no wind.

Jenny took one look at Kitty, scanned her up and down. "Come on," she finally said. "Let's get outside and blow that stink off you."

Kitty argued, but Jenny and I won, and we ate in our coats on plastic lawn chairs Willis dragged out of the garage. They were nothing like the chaise lounges at The Birdhouse, and the memory of those chairs and of Rex sat comfortably with me for the first time in a long time. Loving Willis had made me look at my whole life in a more forgiving way.

I wished someone could come along and do that for Kitty.

Jenny updated us on her boys and Jerome, who had retired from the air force and was working with a friend selling cars. "The man's a born salesman," she said.

As she chatted, I saw her sharp gaze taking in everything about Kitty. The bruising had faded to yellow and green, and she still chewed out one side of her mouth. I'd been trying to get her to the dentist but she told me she could only do one thing at a time. Her collarbones peeked out from the flannel shirt and fur coat she wore, and Jenny didn't miss that, either. I'd be getting a phone call when she got home.

"What about you, Jenny?" Kitty said.

"Well, I've been promoted to chief nurse." She'd been working at the VA Hospital in Iowa City since she got back from Vietnam. Chief nurse was exactly right for her.

"Jenny! Why didn't you tell me?" I cried, aware that I had my own news burning a hole in my mouth.

"I just did."

"Maybe I should have stayed at St. Luke's," Kitty said, pulling an onion out of its fried casing. She ate the onion and put the casing down on the pile of similar onion sarcophagi. "Been a nurse."

"Kitty," Jenny said. "You would have been a terrible nurse."

"That's not true. I mean… I could have figured it out."

"Okay, first rule of nursing is observation," Jenny said.

"It's kind of the first rule of acting, too," Kitty said, archly.

"All right, then tell me, how far along is Betts?"

"How far along is she with what?" Kitty asked, and Jenny howled. She laughed so hard she nearly tipped over in her chair. I couldn't help laughing, either. I hadn't told Jenny about the baby yet, but she must have taken one look at me and figured it out.

"What's so funny?" Kitty cried, her dark hair blowing in the wind.

"I'm pregnant, Kitty. Willis and I are having a baby."

"Why didn't you tell me?" Kitty asked later that night after Jenny was gone and she was getting back into her bed.

"You've only been here a few weeks," I said. "I was going to tell you at some point."

"How far are you?"

"Three months."

"You don't look any different."

"I'm not sure that's a compliment."

"They could be friends," she whispered. "If I was keeping my baby. We could raise them like cousins. Like sisters."

"We could," I said, staying as neutral as possible. "But that's not a good reason for keeping a baby you don't want."

She was silent but grabbed on to my hand.

"Kitty?" I crawled into bed with her, my head on my stacked hands.

"You're going to be such a good mom, Betts. You and Willis. You're going to raise good kids. You're going to let them eat dirt and bring home stray dogs."

I laughed. "Is that all it takes?"

"You know what I mean. You'll let them be kids. You'll make sure they're compassionate and brave. They have the courage of their convictions. They will be so loved."

"I hope so," I said quietly. This baby hadn't been planned, but it was dearly wanted by both of us.

"I wish…" She stopped, wiped her nose on the edge of my sheet, which was a little gross but not the time to bring it up.

"If you want to keep this baby we can figure it out, Kitty. We can put a legal wall between you and Hugh. We can tell the world it's not his. You can have this baby if you want it." I thumbed the tears on her cheeks. I'd never seen Kitty cry before, and here it was every day, part of the routine we'd all fallen into. I wondered sometimes if she was crying for more than this moment. It felt like she'd reached down into some forgotten, sealed-off well of grief.

"My mom died, did I ever tell you that?" she asked, and I shook my head. She had refused to talk about it when we were roommates in Iowa and California, and I stopped bringing it up after Jesse's visit.

"Jesse was like four and I was eight. She just took the car one day to go pick up groceries and got in a car accident on the highway. Died three days later."

"I'm so sorry."

"Before she died we lived in a little house in the suburbs. Mom did hair, Dad worked construction. She was so pretty, Betts. My mom, I mean. I know I was a kid and every kid thinks their mom is pretty, but she was an actual beauty queen. Miss Georgia Peach 1955. We went to church in our best clothes every Sunday and had picnics and learned how to ride bikes. I was in school and I had a new lunch box every year and my own room. We weren't rich, but I thought we were. We were happy." She shifted her body under the blankets, leaning in toward me.

I thought of that letter she got at school that she'd ripped up. The phone calls. Jesse showing up the way he did in LA.

"And then she was just gone, and Dad moved us back to live with his mom and committed to drinking himself to death. Meemaw lived on a chicken farm outside Atlanta and it was awful work. Dirty and smelly, and Meemaw was, God, Betts, she was so mean, and she treated us so bad. But we kept trying and trying to make her happy and to make her love us. We did all the work she asked of us, and we were quiet and clean, but none of it mattered. Until Jesse figured out that she liked it best when we were mean right back. Like she could only love us when we were just like her."

I wiped a tear off my own face.

"That's where I come from, Betts. That's what I know about family. I never loved anyone until I met you. Meeting you and Jenny made me want to be kind and decent."

I tucked the blanket up over her thin shoulder. "Meeting you made me want to be brave and strong. You taught me to stand up for myself. And you're not mean. You're the opposite of cruel."

"But what if this baby goes to someone like Meemaw?"

"That won't happen."

"What if this baby goes to someone like me? Someone who only understands love if it's mean. If it's..." She held up a shaking fist, her face contorted into a vicious scowl.

I put my hand over her fist and told her what I thought were the right things. That we would screen all the applicants. We'd be careful.

"We will find a family for your baby," I said quietly. "Someone who will love your child. Who will let them eat dirt and teach them compassion. We'll find the right person to be a mother to your child."

But we never called the adoption agencies. We never even tried.

The end of March, a storm blew in from the west. It started ordinary enough, a few thick flakes that melted the second they hit the grass. But then it got stronger, and then, in the way of spring snowstorms, it was a whiteout and school was canceled for two days. It was my day off and Kitty and I lay in bed reading *A Walk Across America* out loud to each other.

"This is boring," Kitty said, rolling onto her side and then onto her back. "Let's read *Shanna*."

"We read *Shanna* twice."

Kitty winced as she struggled to sit up. "You just don't like reading the dirty parts out loud."

"Are you all right?"

"No, I'm not fucking all right. This baby is—" She gasped and clutched at her stomach.

"Are you having contractions?" I asked. The baby wasn't due for another three weeks.

Her eyes popped wide. "Oh, Betts, I just wet the bed, I'm sorry. I'm so—"

I jumped out of bed and pulled the covers off Kitty's legs. The flowered yellow sheets were damp and so were the insides of her legs.

"Honey," I said. "Your water broke."

Willis bundled up to scrape the ice off the truck and shovel it out of the driveway while I got Kitty downstairs. She stopped every few steps to crouch and grip her stomach. "Come on," I said, a little nervous by how quickly this delivery was progressing. But it was a first baby and first babies always took a long time.

"Don't rush me, Betts," Kitty snapped. She was sweating, and her hair clung to her face. The neck of the flannel nightgown she was wearing was damp. "Fuck I want to push."

"You can't push! This is just starting. We don't know how far you're dilated."

"I said I wanted to. Not that I was going to." She sat down on a step.

"Kitty," I said with as much compassion and urgency as I could. "We need to get to the hospital."

Her groan turned into a scream and that sixth sense that nurses had finally kicked in. "Okay, let's just get down to the couch. Can we get down to the couch?"

The contraction passed and she nodded. I got her down the last of the steps hunched over and then onto the couch. She was panting through her teeth, holding her stomach, which was hard as a rock under her skin.

"Kitty? How long have you been feeling contractions?"

"I don't know," she said, and she was lying.

"Kitty."

"Middle of the night. I thought it was just cramps. Or the fake contractions. But they've kept on going." So, she'd been in labor for hours. "I'm sorry. I'm sorry, I just… I haven't made any plans. We never talked to the adoption agency. I'm not ready. I'm not ready for this." Panic made her voice climb up into the rafters.

"Hey," I said. "Shhh, shhh, everything is okay. The only plan we need now is getting you to the hospital."

"I don't… I want to push, Betts. Like it's hard not pushing."

"Okay. I'm going to check you. Is that okay?"

"Yes, it's fucking okay!" she screamed as another contraction bit down hard on her.

I lifted her nightgown and pulled down her soaked underwear.

"Oh Jesus," I breathed.

"What? What's wrong?"

"You're crowning," I said. "The baby is coming." Adrenaline electrocuted me and the whole world got crystal clear. There was no time to finish digging out the driveway. Getting dressed and getting across town on roads that might not be cleared. "We're having this baby, Kitty. You and me. Right now. Okay?" I looked into her face until she focused on me, and when I smiled, she smiled back as bravely as she could. "Don't be scared."

"You're the one who sounds scared."

I wasn't. My training kicked in. I ran to the front door and screamed into the driveway at Willis, nearly obscured by the snow. I washed my hands, grabbed as many clean towels as I could and sprinted back to Kitty.

"Lift your butt," I told her and slid towels under her as best as I could.

"I hate this couch," she said. "It's ugly and it sags in the middle and I don't... I don't want to have a baby on this ugly, saggy couch."

"You want to do this on the floor?"

"Yeah."

I got her down on the floor just as Willis came in. "It's really...holy shit."

"Yeah," I said to his wide-eyed, pink face. "I need you to wash your hands, boil water. Sterilize some string. Any string you can find. I also need you to get more towels. But wash your hands. And a knife. The sharpest knife we have."

"A knife?" Kitty asked.

"Just in case," I said.

"In case of *what*?"

Willis nodded, threw his winter coat in the corner and hustled to do as I'd instructed.

"Have I told you how much I like him?" Kitty said, panting on the floor. I positioned a pillow for her head. "You two are peas and carrots."

I nodded and got down between her legs. *Please God, see us through this.*

"Betts," Kitty said, panic and pain in her voice. "I want to push, I want to push."

"Push," I said.

"Don't leave me."

"I'm not going anywhere."

From that moment until a baby girl slipped into my hands, red-faced and screaming, it felt like the blink of an eye and a lifetime, all at once.

Sobbing, Kitty fell back against the floor and I found Willis looking at me, his face beautiful with love and awe.

"Help me," I whispered, and he was on his knees beside me. I tied off the cord, and cut it with a kitchen knife he'd sanitized, then handed him the baby to wrap in our best towels, our softest, most lovely towels.

"Hello, baby," he whispered, and tears stung my eyes.

I delivered the placenta and wrapped it in newspapers, cleaned Kitty up, marveling that she didn't tear. The baby stopped crying and I looked up to see Willis on his feet rocking her sweetly.

Our eyes met and held and we made a decision we didn't even have to say out loud.

"It's a girl," I told Kitty. A sunshine girl. "She's healthy and beautiful."

"Good," Kitty said, staring up at the ceiling. "That's good."

"We're going to keep her," I told her, and she lifted her head to look at me.

Katherine Simon and Kitty Devereaux. The woman in the hotel room and in The Birdhouse and on that stage in Vietnam. Holding me up, holding me together, taking pieces of me with her wherever she went. I could not give her child to a stranger. Her baby would be mine. As it should be.

"Me and Willis. We're going to keep her and raise her. She'll be a sister to our daughter. Just like you said. Just like you wanted."

"You'll keep her safe?" she whispered, bright tears on her flushed cheeks.

"Hugh will never know, and she'll eat a bunch of dirt. I promise."

"Will you name her after my mother?" she asked.

"Of course. What was her name?"

"Clara."

34

KITTY

Los Angeles, California
2019

KITTY HAD NO right to call the fierce, smart thirty-four-year-old woman in front of her *daughter*. Kitty hadn't raised her. Hadn't loved her. Hadn't seen her through any of the bad moments or any of the good.

Kitty understood all of that.

But selfishly, she granted herself this one moment to look at Clara with a mother's eyes and appreciate all the connections between them.

It was hard not to think of her own mother, the threadbare memories she had of her.

Kitty would like to think there was some of her in the way Clara held her head. The shape of her eyes. Perhaps, if Kitty could be so bold, the way her mind worked in the angles Abbie and BettyKay couldn't even see. The way she could be self-ish and cold and fierce. But that all that selfish cold fierceness hid a heart that beat in fear of being hurt. Loyalty, certainly. An eye for the finer things. A work ethic.

Clara, *my daughter.*

Clara stood up, her lean angular body so like Kitty's father's it was eerie. Abbie stood up, too, in solidarity, matching looks of confusion on their faces.

You did it, Betts. They are sisters. Thank you, dear friend, for giving them each other.

"My parents' names are on the birth certificate," Clara said quietly, her big brain sorting through what she'd always known and what she'd just been told.

"Dr. Meadows was extremely accommodating," Kitty said. He'd told them he'd been raised by a single mother, who would have and might have broken a lot of rules to keep him safe.

"I was born in June 1985. That's what it says on my birth certificate and Abbie was born in May 1986."

"Your parents lied. Clara, you were born in March and Abbie was actually born in August of 1985."

"I'm a year older than I thought?" Abbie asked.

"Hardly the point, Abbie." Clara closed her eyes, pinched the bridge of her nose.

"Well, it's *a* point."

"How did they get away with this?" Clara asked.

Of course, Clara would see it and frame it like a crime, when Kitty had always viewed it as a blessing. The singular blessing of her life.

"It was simple, really. They had a lot of help from Denise at the hospital and Dr. Meadows. Your mom went on leave after Clara was born, finally telling people she was pregnant, lying about her due date and claiming she needed to be on bed rest. She didn't go back to work until you were each two. She had you at home. Denise fudged the dates on Abbie's birth record at the hospital."

"You're telling me people didn't notice?" Clara asked.

"It was a different time. There were no pictures posted on social media. Your mom kept to herself. They told Denise the truth and they told Jenny, obviously. Willis, I think told a man he worked with and that man's wife helped spread the story that you two were eleven months apart."

"Mrs. Schutte?" Clara asked and Kitty nodded. For years Kitty sent the Schuttes a basket of fruit at Christmas because they never cashed the checks she sent.

"Your parents weren't married and that seemed to be the bigger conversation. And in the end, everyone loved your parents so much, they wanted to believe them."

"You're telling me our mother didn't leave the house for a year?" Abbie asked.

"She went down to stay with Jenny for a while when it was just Clara, and she was still pregnant. But yes, mostly, she stayed in that house for a year."

"What happened to you?" Clara asked, ignoring Abbie, her tone shifting toward anger. Which was inevitable, Kitty supposed.

"I stayed for a month and then left. I was worried that eventually Hugh would show up at the house on Elm."

"You left?" Clara asked. "Mom was pregnant, Dad was working, and you gave her your baby and just left?"

There was no *just* about it. *I fed you from my body for four weeks*, she wanted to tell her. *I sat with you in sunlight and moonlight and I held you to my body and told myself you were not mine. I sobbed alone in that yellow bedroom when I heard, through the wall, Willis and Betts whispering and laughing and cooing over some mir-*

acle you had performed. I stayed as long as I could until staying one extra moment would mean I could never leave.

"That must have been awful," Abbie said, and Kitty pressed her lips tight, moved by the sympathy.

"They tried to sell the house when money got tight. I bought it," Kitty said. "And tried to give it to them because they wouldn't accept any money."

"You tried to give them money for taking me?"

"Don't make it sound like that," Kitty said, because of all the things she felt bad about, this was not on the list. "Your father was a teacher, your mother was on leave for who knows how long, and two babies are expensive."

That was rather inarguable, yet Kitty could still see Clara yearning to argue.

"You had a baby, stayed for a month and then...never came back?" Abbie asked.

Kitty straightened her shoulders, used to being judged, but never about this.

Strange how much it hurt.

"I left, made sure there were lots of pictures of me out in the world looking like I'd never had a baby, and then when you were about three months old I had a conversation with Betts on the phone and I could tell she wasn't doing well. Hugely pregnant, struggling with a newborn, locked up in the house and the lie we'd concocted. I got on the next plane to see her. To see you," she said to Clara.

She'd rented a car out of O'Hare and driven through the night to arrive at 5 a.m., only to find Betts awake as if she'd known Kitty was coming. She and Willis were doing the best they could, but the house was a mess. Betts was a mess. But, despite the greasy hair and the dishes in the sink, Clara and Betts were a unit. Bonded mother and child. Clara lit up when she heard BettyKay's voice and would go calm and quiet in

BettyKay's arms. It had been the goal, of course, but to see it in action, well, it had been painful.

Betts held out the baby for Kitty and she'd taken her, awkwardly and nearly terrified, not of hurting the baby but perhaps of being hurt. Of feeling what she'd felt in the month of breastfeeding, her month in that yellow bedroom. The murky elemental connection that she would soon have to sever again. The sweet weight of Clara in her arms was pulling her down into something she could not get out of. It was like drowning in longing. In the ache and wonder of motherhood.

"Willis and I want the kids to call you Aunt Kitty," Betts had said, brushing out her hair after a much-needed shower.

"No," Kitty had said, the word bursting out of her with the self-preservation that had gotten her out of Georgia and away from her family.

"You don't like Aunt Kitty?" Betts had laughed. "Too pedestrian, I guess. How about—"

"They won't know me," Kitty told her, eyes closed so she didn't see the shock or the hurt or the anger on her friend's face. "We stay friends. I am yours and you are mine but these children." *My daughter.* "They belong to you and Willis."

Kitty had felt a sob that she shoved down. If Betts had known how hard this was she would say no. She would insist on *Aunt Kitty* and the pain would become so much, Kitty would stay away from Betts just to stay safe.

It was what Kitty had done to her brother. Leaving him behind on that chicken farm.

"Mom just accepted that?" Clara asked.

"No. Not at first. She tried to convince me it would get easier, and she was probably right, but in that moment." Kitty shook her head. "I thought it would be best for everyone."

"Cutting yourself out of my life?" Clara asked. "That's the best you're talking about?"

"At first it was about Hugh. I couldn't risk him even think-ing about you, Clara. He was a dangerous man. And Holly-wood is a small town. I asked that Betts and Willis never tell you about me, and I would never ask to see you. She didn't like it, but I made her agree."

"I mean...weren't you curious about me?" Clara said, rare hesitation in her voice.

Kitty pressed trembling fingers back to her stomach. *Touch your grief*, that yoga child told her. *Touch your grief, hold it, know it and then, once you know it, throw it away.*

She should know better than to trust children on the sub-ject of grief. They hadn't lived long enough or deep enough to know it.

"Of course," she whispered.

Abbie wrapped her arms around Clara, who squinted at the ground.

"I bet Jenny had something to say about all of this," Abbie said, quietly.

Kitty laughed without any humor. That argument with Jenny was not a good memory.

"While Hugh was alive, she agreed with me. It was bet-ter safe than sorry. But when he died when you were about eight, she pushed for me to be in your lives. But I said no. I liked things the way they were. She said I was holding on to the past. That picking and choosing how to be a part of some-one's life wasn't real friendship. Ultimately, when I made the decision to not be in your lives, I lost her, too."

Even though it hurt, Kitty's therapist had helped her under-stand it. As a new mother with babies of her own, Jenny could not accept Kitty's decision to remove herself completely from Clara's life but still choose to be in BettyKay's. There were no half measures for Jenny, and it was one of the things Kitty always liked best about her. Until she was on the outside of it.

Kitty accepted the loss of Jenny as part of the repercussions of her choices, but it had felt like she lost not just a dear friend, but part of her past, too. Part of who she was.

Losing Jenny still hurt.

"It didn't have to be that way!" Abbie cried while Clara stayed unusually silent.

"Perhaps," Kitty said. "But I am, at my heart, selfish. And I worried…" Her breath hitched. "That knowing you, even a little, even in some innocent, passing way, would be too hard. I didn't know how to go from mother to aunt and so it was easier to go from mother to nothing at all. And after a while, I think your mother ended up liking the idea that she had this relationship that was all hers. After giving so much of herself to you two and to Willis and to patients and the school…well, I was hers. And she was mine. And that ended up being just right."

"But why now?" Clara pressed. "I mean…why the hell now?"

"I lived without a mother for a long time," Kitty said. "And when Betts died—"

"You thought you'd step in. As a mother?" Clara asked, incredulous.

"No," Kitty said, though perhaps yes. "All of my reasons for doing this were…" Kitty struggled to find a word but there was only one, really. "Inadequate. But when your mother told you that Willis wasn't your father, she knew you wouldn't let this go and when she died before she could tell you the truth… well, I thought… I would do what she couldn't finish."

"You did it for me?" Clara asked, seeing through Kitty's bullshit right away. "BettyKay Beecher was my mom and Willis Beecher was my dad and you and Hugh Bonnet—" She looked up at the ceiling and Kitty realized she was blinking back tears and it felt awful. To make her cry. To break apart her life like this. *"Fucking Hugh Bonnet? Is my father?"*

"I'm sorry," she said because there was nothing else to say. No silver lining. He was a genius and he was a monster.

"He never knew?" Abbie asked.

"No."

"Were you with him again?" Clara asked.

Kitty shook her head. "After Clara was born I went back to Hollywood but he had me completely ostracized. I wouldn't have thought he had the power, but white men will always stand behind white men. He told me he would get me a job if we got back together, but I always said no. I had enough money to live on. I built this house. My garden. Your mom. It wasn't until he died in the '90s that I got that TV show."

In the end, those were all minor things, superficial. The real damage was the way he'd destroyed every relationship in her life, leaving her isolated and vulnerable and alone, suspicious of everyone around her.

Except Betts.

"He's not my father," Clara said. "He's not. He's—" Clara was out the sliding glass door of her office before Kitty could figure out what she'd been about to say. Before she could get her old and disobedient body to its feet.

Abbie stood and held out her hand in Kitty's direction. "I think..." she said and then stopped. There were a dozen ways she could finish that sentence.

You've done enough. Painfully true.

Kitty had robbed Abbie of something, too. Not a sister, no need to be melodramatic. But the story about her family that they all believed. The lore that created who she was.

"Go after her," Kitty said, and Abbie was out that door in a shot.

Kitty slumped down in her seat, staring at the places where the girls had just been, as if their shadows had been left standing.

The girls. That's what Betts always called Abbie and Clara. A unit like that. A force.

Kitty had always liked it.

Every actor Kitty knew had an office like hers. Scripts on shelves. Special cabinets made for trophies and prizes. Posters of favorite projects artfully framed. These offices were created to shore up their monstrous egos. Remind them when their raging self-doubt got the best of them that they'd done good work. That to someone, somewhere, they mattered.

BettyKay was dead. Jenny didn't speak to her. And the girls were undoubtedly packing their bags.

What did you think? she wondered. *You would tell them and after all these years of shunning family, they would gather around you and you wouldn't be alone?*

Sunlight poured into the room, illuminating all her Hollywood artifacts. Her beautiful, famous life.

All its glittering emptiness.

ABBIE

"Clara?" Abbie called. The rolling green lawn down to the garden was empty. The parking area, too. God. Would she go running? Down in those trails? That was a thing her sister did when she was upset. Abbie looked down at her sandals. Not the best for chasing after her sister but she'd go barefoot for Clara if she had to.

"Over here," Clara said.

Abbie blew out a nervous laugh of relief and walked around to the far side of the small cottage, where the eucalyptus bushes grew closer to the building. It was like Clara had to get as far away from Kitty as she could, without leaving the property.

Fiona did the same thing when she was mad, stretched the cord as far as she could without snapping it. Abbie suddenly missed her children with a knife-sharp pain.

"You all right?" Abbie asked.

"Peachy." Clara was standing, hands on her hips, but *vibrating* with emotion. Abbie knew this version of her sister. If Abbie touched her or offered sympathy, Clara would take all that emotion and start swinging it around at everyone around her.

"I really picked a weekend to quit drinking, huh?"

Thank God, Clara laughed at her bad joke and the tension cracked enough that Abbie could put her arm around her sister, and instead of bristling, Clara relaxed against her.

"What a waste," Abbie said.

"What do you mean?" Clara asked.

"A waste of all that time."

Clara stepped away, and Abbie got a look at her sister's face.

"I'm just saying," Abbie said weakly. "We could have all been—"

"Family?" Clara snapped.

"Yeah, maybe?"

The cabin's screen door rattled, and Clara shifted from the side of the house toward the garden. Abbie followed and they caught Vickie as she came out into the yard.

"Hey!" Vickie said with a smile that immediately dropped when she caught sight of Clara's face. "What happened?"

Clara turned to Vicki, arms outspread, her smile cutting. "Kitty's my birth mom. Who had me, dropped me in my mother's arms and walked away for thirty-four years, choosing Mom's funeral as an opportunity to just waltz back into my life."

Well, Abbie thought, *when you say it like that.*

"And that's not all," Clara continued. "The question that

started this whole thing is finally answered. Drumroll? Anyone?" Clara did not wait for a drumroll. "Hugh Bonnet, the raging violent narcissist film director, is my father."

"Wow," Vickie said. She looked at Abbie and then back at Clara. "Wow."

"But he's not," Abbie said. She wasn't going to let Clara's anger win the day. Anger and fear and pride had already won too many days.

"Excuse me? Were you not *listening*?"

"Mom is your mom and Dad is your dad. You know that. You just said it." Abbie turned back toward the glass house with its cold beauty. Its *Architectural Digest* photo spread rooms. And right next to it the cabin with its framed Polaroid pictures and slouchy couches. Its ancient kitchen.

That cold glass box was Kitty's life, but that cabin, it was full of BettyKay Beecher.

Abbie wondered if perhaps…*perhaps* BettyKay Beecher had known what she was doing that night of the fight with Clara. Not that she was going to die, or anything. But maybe Mom had realized that enough time had been wasted and she'd intentionally knocked over a domino hoping they would all end up here. Together. All the secrets out in the open.

The family they might have been.

The more she thought about it, the more Abbie was sure of it.

Oh, Mom.

"I have to get back to my kids," Abbie said. "I have to fix what's wrong at home and then… I want to come back here."

"What?" Clara asked.

"Yeah, I want to come back," Abbie said, holding her ground. "And I want you to come back."

"She lied to us, Abbie."

"Actually, she just told us the truth, and I get it if you want to be mad. I really do get it." Abbie was sorry to use this against her, but she had no choice right now. She tried to make her voice as gentle as possible. "You wasted those two weeks being mad at Mom. And what did it get you?"

Clara turned and faced the garden again. Vickie came up behind her, wrapping her arms around Clara's waist. Abbie pressed her luck and reached for her sister's hand.

To her surprise, Clara clung to her.

"I'd take this on for you if I could," Abbie said.

"You want to be the daughter of Kitty Devereaux?" Clara said, dubiously.

"No. I want to be BettyKay Beecher's daughter and I am. Just like you. But I'd like to get to know Kitty better. I'd like her to know me. My kids. My family."

"Why?" Clara asked.

"Because she loved our mom. And our mom loved her. Look at everything they did for each other. I want all those stories, Clara. I want all that love."

Clara made a sound in her throat and Abbie leaned her head against her sister's shoulder.

"I want to be mad for a few more minutes," Clara said.

"Go ahead," Abbie said. "We'll all be here when you're done."

This is your family, she thought but didn't say. They weren't there yet. Clara was still sore. Kitty was still brittle. They were all seeing how far they could bend. But they would... they would get there.

She hoped.

35

CLARA

THAT NIGHT, ABBIE went back into Kitty's house to say goodbye.

Clara and Vickie booked themselves on Abbie's flight and silently walked the trails until it was time to leave.

And then the three of them flew home.

Well, to Greensboro.

Clara could safely say being back in Greensboro for longer than a weekend was not as bad as she thought it would be, mostly because Vickie was there. That woman made everything better. Vickie and Clara were using up vacation days and working remotely for a few weeks while packing up Mom and Dad's house.

Vickie kept them moving when grief tied the Beecher sisters' feet to the ground.

Abbie went about the business of changing every damn thing about her life, and Clara could not have been more proud of her sister. She was embarrassed that she ever thought her sister's emotions made her weak. They were a superpower as she helped her kids weather the storm of Ben and her splitting up.

She drank the night they told the kids, but the next day she got herself into counseling.

Clara was also embarrassed that she even thought about not helping Abbie pack up this house. It was a monumental task. And one of the saddest things she'd ever done.

In the very back of Mom's closet they found—a silver go-go dress, a box of newspaper clippings all about Kitty. And—amazingly—one pink button.

The one that had gotten lost in the shag carpet.

They had no idea how Mom had it, or why she'd kept it of all the gag gifts that Kitty sent her after California. But it sat atop all those clippings in that box, a brighter pink than all the other buttons that got baked in bread and pickled.

"We should take it to Kitty," Abbie whispered, the two of them cross-legged on the floor of their parents' bedroom, surrounded by their old clothes.

"I'm just not ready yet," Clara said and went to help Vickie empty the garage.

It took a week to make a tough decision on BettyKay's diaries. They were private and not meant for other people to read, and so they burned them in Dad's firepit one night. Clara still wasn't sure if it was the right choice, but Abbie had pushed for it.

They're not for us, she'd said. *They were Mom's private thoughts and feelings and they deserve to stay private. Besides, we know where we can get a lot of these stories told to us.*

Clara knew what she was hinting at, but she wasn't ready yet.

After taking the last load of old bedsheets and furniture to the college resale shop, Abbie, Clara and Vickie stood in the kitchen, surrounded by memories.

So many memories.

"You think you can live here?" Clara asked her sister as Clara pulled cobwebs from Vickie's hair. The attic had been a real adventure.

Abbie nodded, blinking back tears. "I'm so happy to be living here, thank you, Clara, for giving me the house."

"Well, you should thank Kitty." Clara felt everyone's eyes on her. "Not ready yet," she said, holding up her hand to stop them.

They started to move Abbie's things into the house. So many toys. Clara made a decision not to give her niece and nephew any more toys. She'd give them trips. Experiences. Clara and Vickie could take them to plays in Chicago and ball games.

"Would you like that?" she asked them, shoving the last of the toys in Mom and Dad's old office, which was the new playroom.

"Yes!" they shouted and went running downstairs to find their mom.

Vickie walked over and wrapped Clara in her arms for a kiss.

And all at once and out of the blue Clara understood what her sister meant about wasting time. She felt every second she'd been too proud to bend. Too scared to open herself up. Lying to herself about being too busy. Or too rigid. And it had cost her precious time. Memories. Opportunities to love and be loved.

As uncomfortable as it was and as much as she'd rejected the idea, she understood Kitty. Because they were the same. Standing in the same moment. Clara was just going to make a different choice.

She was Clara Beecher, sister to Abbie. Daughter of Betty-Kay and Willis, and soon-to-be wife to Vickie. Hopefully parent to her own child one day. Time was finite.

Love was not. "We have a few more vacation days," Vickie said. "We could paint some rooms. Clara? What do you think?"

"I think we should go back to California," Clara said.

Clara called Sophia, and the next day they were on the jet back to California. All of them. Max and Fiona included.

And Jenny.

Clara had called her after making the decision to go back out to California and had a long talk with her about Kitty and these secrets.

"And you're going back out there?" Jenny had asked. "You're not mad?"

"I'm mad but I'm also...curious."

"I suppose I understand that. If nothing else Kitty was always interesting."

"And, Jenny, thank you for being there for us. For Mom when she needed you."

There was a pause so long Clara wondered if maybe the call had been dropped.

"Jenny?"

"I'm here, and you're not going back out there without me," she said.

Elroy had driven her up this morning. She hugged the kids, asked Max how soccer was going and how Fiona did on her history report, then buckled herself into her seat and made a quick sign of the cross with her eyes squeezed shut.

After a harrowing experience in a helicopter in Vietnam, she was not a fan of flying.

Clara reached over and put her hand over Jenny's as the plane took off.

Vickie was amazing with the kids. On those bench seats as they flew over the Rocky Mountains, she played endless thumb wars with Max while listening to Fiona talk fanatically about *Anne of Green Gables*.

"I loved that book, too," Vickie said. "Have you read *Emily of New Moon*?"

Clara caught Abbie's eye. "I feel like I should warn her," Abbie said. "Fiona will talk her ear off."

"She loves it," Clara said.

"Are you nervous?" Abbie asked.

"A little. You?"

"My kids are going to break something."

Clara laughed. "We all might."

ABBIE

They invaded the glass house. The kids. Vickie. Jenny. Clara had the button. Abbie carried the dress.

"Hello?" Kitty said, standing up from the white couch in the living room. She looked surprised.

"Didn't Sophia tell you we were coming?" Abbie asked, trying to squash her urge to take responsibility for Kitty's reaction. Her counselor told her it was not her job to be responsible for everyone's feelings and this had come as a real surprise to Abbie. But she was working on it.

She was working on a lot of things and none of it was easy. But all of it was good.

"Yes. But you're early."

Abbie realized that Kitty was nervous, too. The last three weeks must have been hard for her, shedding those secrets like a skin.

"Traffic was really light. Is that a problem?" Abbie asked. "We can—"

"Hello, Kitty," Jenny said, cutting through the crowd of Beechers stuck with indecision at the front door.

"Jenny," Kitty sighed. It was a sigh of relief. Of pleasure and surprise. And pain. She put her hand to her stomach and in a broken whisper said, "You're here."

"Yes, I am," Jenny said. "I hope that's all right."

"You going to yell at me some more?" Kitty asked with narrowed eyes, trying to make a joke. But no one was fooled. The confident movie star was gone, leaving a woman who'd made too many mistakes and was scared of making more.

"No. Betts always said I got my stubborn side from my father, and I've wasted too much time thinking I could change your mind, when I always knew better." Jenny blinked back tears. "I'm so sorry, Kitty. And I miss you."

"I'm sorry, too. You were right, I was a bull in a china shop, and I almost ruined everything Betts did for me," Kitty said. "And I missed you so much."

The two women crossed the room and all the years and their many mistakes to wrap their arms around each other.

Abbie saw how her mother must have fit between them, softening sharp edges and big personalities. She wished with a sudden ache that she could have known the three of them together. It would have been something to see. But those three women had made very different choices and lived with them their whole lives. And still were.

"Is this a museum?" Max asked in what was absolutely not an inside voice.

"Shhh, honey," Abbie hushed him.

"Come in, please come in," Kitty said, stepping back from Jenny, and wiping her eyes. She even cried pretty. It really was unfair.

"Is it?" Max asked again.

"Sort of," Vickie answered.

"I'm hungry," Fiona said and then grabbed Clara's hand and tugged on it. "Who is that?" she asked, pointing at Kitty.

Abbie hadn't thought about this. With Ben and the house and the move and then suddenly being out here, she hadn't thought about how to make all the years of friendship, of secrets and sacrifice something a little kid could understand.

"That's Gran's sister," Clara said.

"I didn't know Gran had a sister," Fiona said, eyeing Kitty in that way she had that always reminded Abbie of Clara.

"She had two of us," Jenny said, her arm around Kitty's waist.

"What do we call you?" Fiona asked Kitty.

"Aunt Kitty," Kitty said, claiming the name she'd rejected all those decades ago.

"Hi, Aunt Kitty," Max said in complete Max fashion. He ran over and barreled into Kitty's legs.

"Oof," she said, making a little show of being bowled over. "I'm gonna call you Cannonball. Cannonball Max."

"You are?" Max said.

"That all right?" Kitty asked, talking to him like he was an adult and not at all a kid. Max loved it.

"Yeah. I guess." He was practically vibrating with pent-up energy.

"I'm sorry," Abbie said. "I should really take him outside. Let him burn some of that off…"

"Let's all go," Kitty said, stretching an arm out toward the sliding glass doors. Jenny stayed back to put her feet up in one of the guest rooms.

The rest of them stepped out into the grass, the end-of-day sunlight the kind of gold it felt like Abbie could hold in her palm if she just tried hard enough.

Abbie, Vickie and the kids started a game of tag. Clara walked over to where Kitty stood by the green-and-yellow chaise lounges and pulled the pink button out of her pocket.

Kitty lifted a shaking hand to her mouth.

As Abbie strained to hear what they were saying, she was easily caught by Max. "You're it, Mom!" he yelled.

Kitty was crying now, and Clara pulled her into a hug.

"What's wrong?" Fiona asked, slipping her hand into Abbie's.

"Nothing's wrong," Abbie said, squeezing her daughter's hand. "A lot of things are really, really right. Hey, you want to hear a story?"

"Sure!" Fiona lit up at any mention of a story. "What's it about?"

"Best friends. Sisters, really. It's called 'The Sunshine Girls.'"

★ ★ ★ ★ ★

ACKNOWLEDGMENTS

WHILE WRITING A book is an incredibly solitary endeavor, getting that book published and into the hands of readers takes a real village. No disrespect to any other author—but I have the loveliest and best village. ☺

First, this book, the next book, the last book, my first book—all of it is thanks to Pam Hopkins, my agent. I couldn't do this without her, and I would not want to. She is wise and calm with an agent's knack for talking authors off all kinds of ledges. I am incredibly lucky to have her in my corner.

Melanie Fried, my editor, has made this book the best it could be and, in the process, has made me a better writer. I cannot thank her enough for all of her hard work and the absolute mountains of patience she has shown me over the last few years.

Gina Macedo's careful attention to detail as a copy editor is so appreciated and respected. Thank you for that fine-tooth comb.

This stunning, STUNNING cover is thanks to art director Alexandra Niit and cover designer Mary Luna—I gasped the first time I saw this cover and I'm still gasping. It's so beautiful and as Melanie Fried said it's like looking at BettyKay and Kitty.

The publicity team at Graydon House/Harlequin/HarperCollins—thank you for getting me in front of so many eyes and the sales team for getting me onto so many shelves.

To Crystal Patriarche, Hanna Lindsley and Taylor Brightwell at BookSparks—thank you for your hard work and imagination.

Amanda Skenandore, Kristy Woodson Harvey and Susie Orman Schnall—thank you for your support of this book and your kind words.

For the writers I am lucky enough to call friends—Maureen McGowan, Sinead Murphy, Zoe York, Brighton Walsh, Selena Blake, Ellis Leigh, Amelia Wilde and Skye Warren. You have kept me sane and productive. You've inspired me more than I can say.

Thank you to Annika Martin, whose critiques are always insightful. You are my favorite walking partner.

Stephanie Doyle and Simone St. James—there just aren't enough thank-yous. Steak dinners are on me forever. I don't know what I'd do without you.

Gayle Fader, thank you for letting me borrow your story. I love you. I'm so proud to be your daughter. Cherie Anthes, thank you for reading an early draft and cleaning up some of my nursing mistakes.

And finally for Adam, Mick and Lucy—forever.

AUTHOR'S NOTE

THE EXPERIENCE OF writing a novel varies each time I turn the page to start a new one. With *The Sunshine Girls*, I immediately envisioned that Midwestern funeral with its glamorous surprise guest. Kitty Devereaux showed up fully formed and ready to make trouble for Clara and Abbie. But where do you go from there? Surprisingly, in the Methodist church basement and the Singer sewing machines and Shakey's Tavern down by the river, I began to see parts of my own mother's life in the story.

For the whole of my life, my mother, Gayle Fader, has been trading five pink buttons with her friend Laura Peuse. Mom and Laura did not meet in nursing school, but were neighbors in Holstein, Iowa, where my parents moved when they were first married. However, the buttons were purchased in the exact same way as described in the novel—Laura was making a gray suit and Mom was heading over to her house and asked if she needed anything. Laura, joking, said buttons. Mom returned with the ugliest buttons she could find, and somehow, a fifty-year-old practical joke was born.

I remember the year they were sewn onto a nightgown. The year they were made into earrings. Pickled in a jar with cucumbers. Baked into a rum cake. When Mom and Laura get together, they laugh uncontrollably about the year Laura climbed through the window of my parents' trailer to hang the ornaments on their Christmas tree. The buttons survive to this day, traded in birthday cards and returned in pie pans borrowed over the years. They are faded, but just as ugly and strange as they were in 1965.

By the time I was born, Laura and my mom were no longer neighbors, but I was told stories of their friendship over the years. Those buttons coming and going in the mail felt like proof of a relationship I had never physically witnessed, talismans of an important time in my mom's life and a crucial, identity-forming friendship. I wanted the buttons in *The Sunshine Girls* to act as the same kind of proof for Abbie and Clara, even and especially when it seemed impossible that BettyKay and Kitty could have ever been friends.

It wasn't only the buttons and the friendship that inspired the novel. Many elements of BettyKay's life reflect my mother's own experiences as a nursing school student in the 1960s. Change was simmering all around the U.S. at the time, but nursing school in many ways remained fixed in old and sometimes sexist traditions. Ironically, at the same time, nursing was one of the few career paths, and opportunities for financial independence, easily accessible to women. This dichotomy was fascinating to me, and I thought it would be the right context against which BettyKay, Kitty and Jenny could each grow as individuals along with their friendship.

I was further intrigued by the idea that nursing school for many women was a crash course in physical intimacy that had nothing to do with sex. It also presented young women with life-or-death decisions that no amount of schooling could prepare them for. Years ago, my mom told me a story about a night she was working in a pediatric ward and a baby with catastrophic congenital disorders. It is the kind of tragedy that doesn't happen now, but in the 1960s, before ultrasounds and genetic screenings, it was horribly more commonplace.

The story, the kind that, upon hearing it, makes you wonder what you would do in the same situation, not only stayed with me but became a defining moment in BettyKay's life in the novel. If you are a nurse or are lucky enough to have a nurse in your life, you know they are deeply practical people, and while this event didn't send my mom into a crisis of confidence (like it would me), it stuck with her in perfect clarity for over 50 years.

My mother let me borrow that horrible night and the pink buttons and countless other details from her life ("dirty bottoms" is a direct quote from her) for *The Sunshine Girls*. This novel is written in honor of her and nurses everywhere.

THE
SUNSHINE
GIRLS

MOLLY FADER

Reader's Guide

GRAYDON
HOUSE

1. Discuss how society's expectations for women during the 1960s influenced Kitty, Jenny and BettyKay's choices and life paths.

2. How did the men in the three women's lives—Hugh, Dr. Fischer, Rex and Jenny's father, Roy—attempt to control them, and how were the women able to overcome such behavior?

3. Kitty, Jenny and BettyKay all have difficult relationships with their parents. How did those fractured relationships help form their friendship and guide each of their lives?

4. Discuss the difficult decisions each of the women make in the novel: BettyKay leaving Rex, Kitty's choice not to be in Clara's life, Jenny going to war to protect her brother. How did these decisions change each woman's life in positive or negative ways?

5. Abbie and Clara are estranged at the beginning of the book. If Kitty had not shown up at the funeral, do you

think they would have continued to grow apart? Why or why not?

6. How does Kitty's reveal about BettyKay's life and Clara's biological parents change how the two sisters view their mother? How did it shape their own feelings about motherhood and marriage?

7. Which character in the story was your favorite? Why?

8. Who are the "sunshine girls" in your life?